# BABY'S BREATH

## BD McDuff

D1716499

# CHAPTER 1 : THE CLIMB

Claire Dillon-McCormack had one foot on the first step of the stairway to Heaven and one foot on earth. She could feel the gravitational pull of her family, praying for her to come back. Her husband, Chet, daughter Jeannie, and son Jeff stood vigilant watch over her at St. Aloysius Hospital.

On July 3rd, Claire was prepping the yard for their annual Fourth of July celebration. She wanted to make sure her flowers looked as fresh as they could in the usual summer heat in their hometown of Hallowed, Ohio. Tomorrow, right before the party, she would pull the hose out for one last sprinkling. By the time family and friends arrived, dew drops would glisten on the pink and blue petals of the hydrangeas. The moist baby's breath and sweet pea vines would infuse the air with sweet fragrances.

Today, however, she would tackle the hard task of saturating the soil down to the roots. Claire had her own special method of plant watering. Neighbors had those fancy sprinklers twirling around all summer, but Claire preferred a hose with no nozzle. She'd move it to each garden area, screwing the hose into the ground, causing the soil to splash up and decorate her legs with mud. She loved the smell and feel of the dirt.

At 3:45 pm, Claire finished the yard work and planned to focus on shopping for the ingredients for her special holiday foods – burgers, the Dillon family macaroni salad, and her incredible apple pie. She turned the knob on the faucet to off and pulled the long hose toward the side of the yard. Something felt different in her head. There was a fast series of clicks--like a switch in her brain turning on and off repeatedly – then, excruciating pain. She fell face down to the ground.

Her son Jeff pulled into the driveway less than a minute after Claire's collapse and rushed to her side. "Mom, Mom, what happened. Oh, my God!" Jeff cradled his mother in his arms and gently turned her towards him, wiping the mud and sweat from her face with his shirt. He placed his head on her chest to listen for breathing, feeling a slight up and down movement, but her body was limp. Jeff had never seen his mother's complexion so drained of color, and even more frightening was a small bubble of spit that dribbled down her chin as if she were an infant.

After a few seconds, his adrenaline kicked in and prompted him to call 911, then his Dad, Chet, and his sister, Jeannie, who worked in a Chicago law firm.

"Hey, Jeff, what's up? Make it quick, bro; I've got an important meeting in five minutes."

"Jeannie, I just got home and found Mom unconscious. She looks really bad. I think maybe she's had a stroke or something."

"Did you call 911? And Dad?"

"Of course I did. They're on their way, but I wanted to let you know. Dad's going straight to St. Aloysius Hospital. He'll be there before the ambulance."

There were a few seconds of silence and then Jeff could hear Jeannie gasp, "I'll be there as soon as I can catch a flight."

"Okay, listen, I hear the sirens. I've gotta go."

"Jeff, tell Mom I love her?"

"I will."

Jeff could hear Jeannie telling her co-workers about their Mother. "Jackie, my Mom's on her way to the emergency room. Can you get me a flight as soon as…?"

Then he hit the off button on his cell phone as the ambulance pulled into the driveway. The paramedics carried their equipment to the yard. With little conversation they checked Claire's vital signs and verified that she had no broken bones from the fall.

As they carried the stretcher to the ambulance, one of them asked, "Are you a relative?"

"Yes, sir, that's my Mom."

"Are you twenty-one?"

"No, sir."

"Have you notified someone who can legally make decisions about her condition?"

"My Dad's on his way to the hospital."

Chapter 1 : The Climb

"Good.  Okay, you can ride in the back with us.  I have a few questions to ask you about what happened here and we need to notify your family doctor."

Jeff's Dad was waiting in the emergency room as the ambulance pulled up to the door of St. Aloysius Hospital in Cincinnati.  Jeff jumped from the ambulance as his father immediately went to Claire's side.

"Sir, are you Mr. McCormack?"

"Yes, I'm, Chet, her husband.  Is she breathing?  She doesn't look like she's breathing!"

"She is breathing, sir, but her vitals are marginal.  We notified your family doctor and he has called a neuro-surgeon."

"A neuro surgeon!  My God, what happened?  Did she hit her head?"  Chet touched his wife's cheek.  "Claire, I'm here, honey.  You'll be all right."

"She fell onto soft ground.  There appears to be little trauma due to the fall. The hospital staff is taking her to the operating room.  You need to go to the registration desk behind you to complete paperwork.  The woman over there will give you the forms.  Then, the ICU nurse will meet with you.  She'll have more information about your wife's condition. That's really all I can tell you right now.  I need your signature to confirm that we have safely transported your wife to the hospital."

Chet's thoughts were swirling like heavy debris caught in a tornado. "Okay, okay, sure."  He scribbled his signature on the paper.

"I'm sorry this happened to your wife, Mr. McCormack.  Good bye."

Chet sat down at the registration desk to complete the paperwork.  Jeff tapped him gently on the shoulder.  "Dad, I'm going to the bathroom to cleanup.  I've got mud all over me."

"Sure, okay, son.  I'll get this done and then we'll try to get some answers. Will this take much longer, miss?"

"There are only two more documents to complete and then I'll have a volunteer take you up to the surgery waiting room."

Chet and Jeff sat side by side on a brown couch in the surgery waiting room. Jeff nervously snacked on potato chips and stale cupcakes from the vending machine.

Periodically, they glanced at the clock. Claire had been in surgery three hours, but there was no indication if this was a good sign or a bad sign. Other than the crunch of Jeff eating, they waited in fearful silence.

Jeannie arrived at Greater Cincinnati Airport around 7:00 pm and took a taxi to St. Aloysius. As she entered the surgery waiting room, her father and Jeff wrapped their arms around her, but their embrace could not deter her litany of questions.

"Dad, the nurse told me she's in surgery. Did Mom have a stroke? Jeff, what happened today? I can't believe this. I talked to her this morning. She sounded fine."

"Jeannie, hon, take a deep breath. Sit down, we'll tell you everything we know."

Claire was in surgery for four and a half hours to repair a brain aneurysm. She survived, but doctors put her in a medically-induced coma for healing. Her breathing was steady, but her face was gaunt and pale. As her family surrounded her hospital bed, they could see Claire's brain was in a deep sleep.

---

Claire saw ethereal figures clothed in soft, pearl-colored garments going up and down the stairs. They did not seem to have feet or legs, yet each body moved from step to step in a purposeful manner. Every form was graceful, silent with a translucent face.

*I don't know. Can you call it a body?*

Claire studied the figures for a long time until one of them gently nudged her to join in the sequential movement. Now, she was moving up very far indeed. When she reached the top, Claire followed her gentle nudger, unsure of what was happening, but surprisingly unafraid.

The corridor was a bright cream-colored stretch that showed no signs of ending. In fact, Claire was not sure exactly when the hallway had begun. There was no beginning and no end. Then, all movement stopped.

She heard the sound of paper gently cutting through the air. And again, the same sound, like someone flicking through thin pages of a large phone book. She turned toward the sound and instantly knew what it was. The Book was displayed on a huge podium and a light shined on a particular chapter and verse. Claire stood alone in front of the Bible, not sure what to do. The light did not move from *Genesis*. She stared at the verse for several seconds, feeling compelled to read aloud.

> ***Then Jacob had a dream; a stairway rested on the ground; with its top reaching to the Heavens; and God's messengers were going up and down on it. (Genesis Ch.28:12).***

A very fragrant smell embraced the room. She remembered the wonderful aroma from when she was a child-- the sweet smell of baby's breath flowers.

*God's messengers?*

"Yes, Claire, we are God's messengers. I am your messenger."

Claire jumped in surprise, but recognized the nudger. "Oh, you're back and you talk."

The messenger laughed heartily. "We talk, we laugh, we cry. Mostly, we deliver His messages."

"So, that's why the Bible is opened to that verse? I'm supposed to climb into Heaven?"

"Well, not exactly, but God does have a message for you."

"Who are you? Do you have a name? And what is the message?"

"I am Zimelda." Embarrassed, she hesitated. "I don't know what He wants of you. He hasn't told me yet, but you wouldn't be here if He didn't have a message for you."

"And so, help me, Zimelda. What exactly is a messenger? Are you like an angel?"

"Yes, I am an angel. All angels are messengers, but there is a hierarchy of importance. There are nine classifications of angels...seraphim, cherubim, thrones, dominions, virtues, powers, principalities, archangels, and angels. Archangels, of course are assigned God's important tasks; hence, Michael, Gabriel, and Raphael. Angels have very specific messages to deliver to help humans in their struggle with faith. And then, there are the fallen angels whom Lucifer took with him to.." Zimelda noticed that Claire was dazed and worried. "I'm sorry, Claire. I tend to ramble on and on. I know it's a bit unsettling, but please be patient and have faith."

Claire remembered the Bible story of the woman who was hemorrhaging and believed that if she touched the cloak of Jesus, she would be cured.

*That poor, suffering woman had such faith.*

Again, she heard the sound of pages and saw the light shining on the Bible. Claire read once again.

> ***And there was a woman who for twelve years had had a hemorrhage, and had suffered much at the hands of many physicians, and had spent all she had, and found no benefit, but rather grew worse. Hearing about Jesus, she came up behind him in the crowd and touched his cloak. For she said, 'If I but touch his cloak, I shall be saved.' And at once the flow of her blood was dried up, and she felt in her body that she was healed of her affliction... But Jesus said to her,' Daughter, thy faith has saved thee. Go in peace, and be thou healed of thy affliction.' (Mark, Ch.5:25-34)***

The wonderful smell of baby's breath flowers filled the room again.

"Zimelda, I'm not sure I have that kind of faith. And I'm not sure I want to be here."

Zimelda raised one eyebrow with a look of disbelief.

Claire breathed a sigh of resignation. "I guess I don't have a choice, do I?"

Zimelda did not answer.

---

Claire remained in deep sleep in her room at St. Aloysius. She seemed to rest well that night, but Chet, Jeannie, and Jeff were still very worried. All three stayed in the anteroom of the Intensive Care Unit, but their sleep was intermittent and disturbed.

Memories of childhood ebbed in and out of Jeannie's mind. She remembered her eighth birthday. It was a sleepover party and her Mom had created a treasure hunt.

"Mom, I love that idea. Can you make the map look really old?

"Sure, pumpkin."

Chapter 1 : The Climb

Jeannie could see her Mom in the kitchen the night before her birthday party. Claire stood at the sink, soaking paper maps in tea, drying them in the oven, and then burning the edges to make them look authentically ancient. When her friends arrived, it was an exciting adventure searching for the hidden treasure of candy and toys.

Her friend, Lisa Redden, had jumped up and down in delight. "Oh, Jeannie, this is the best birthday party I've ever been to! Mrs. McCormack, thank you, thank you, thank you. I'll never forget you!"

Mom gave her a sweet little hug.

"I'll never forget you, either, Lisa darling."

Jeannie opened her eyes for a moment and gingerly moved to the doorway where she caught a glimpse of her Mom in ICU. She stared at her mother's motionless body. She had never seen her like this before.

*Mom is always moving, always talking, always involved in people and projects and my life. Always? Is it over now?*

Although Jeannie had a propensity for optimism, her anguish choked her with stark fear that her mother could die.

*I'll never forget you, Mom. Never. Oh, what am I thinking? I'm acting like she's already dead. She's going to be okay. She'd be furious with me if she knew I was giving in to dark thoughts.*

Jeannie fidgeted with the clear, jeweled ball at the end of her necklace. Claire had inherited it from her mother on her sixteenth birthday. In turn, Claire gave it to Jeannie on her sixteenth birthday. Of course, the necklace had a little history behind it. After the depression, Claire's parents were finally getting ahead, so Grandpa Dillon splurged on their tenth wedding anniversary by buying a fairly expensive piece of jewelry.

During those hard years of sparse jobs and hungry children, Grandma Dillon had bolstered Grandpa's confidence with words of encouragement. *'Carl, have faith the size of a mustard seed and nothing will be impossible for you!'*

When he saw that necklace at the jewelry store, he had to get it for Mary Margaret. Inside the clear marble sphere was a tiny mustard seed, looking as though it were floating in crystal clear water. Jeannie's Mom continued the tradition of the Dillon mustard seed jewel repeating the words of encouragement many times in Jeannie's life.

*Jeannie, have faith the size of a mustard seed and nothing will be impossible for you!*

Finding comfort in this tender moment of Grandpa and Grandma Dillon's faith and her mother's faith, Jeannie was finally able to fall asleep.

———————————————————

Jeff had been sleeping, but suddenly grabbed both arms of the chair to stop the falling sensation. He looked around the room.

*Wow, how can Jeannie sleep like that? She doesn't even look worried.*

Jeff tapped his Dad's arm. "Dad, you're snoring."

Chet yawned, "No, I'm not."

"Yes, you are. Mom talks about it all the time. Your snoring wakes her up every night."

"Okay if you say so. Can't sleep, huh?"

"Not really. Every time I close my eyes, I see Mom with mud on her face. Her neck was hanging over my arm like a new baby. I was scared, Dad. I thought she might die in my ar…"

Chet hugged him. Jeff sobbed into his Dad's shirt, and then wiped his hands back and forth across his eyes, embarrassed about crying.

"Hey, let's go down the hall and get something to drink. I saw a vending machine earlier. We can talk down there."

"Let's check on Mom first."

"I just talked to the nurse about an hour ago. There's no change, but she's hanging in there. Shhh, Jeannie's asleep. C'mon, let's go."

They tiptoed past Jeannie, envious that she was able to escape the anxiety for a while. Chet was six feet tall and had been told by many people that he looked like a young Jimmy Stewart. Jeff was still growing at six foot two. From the back, it was hard to tell who the son was and who the father was, except for Chet's thinning hair and Jeff's thick, dark wave of curls.

"Dad, it's been a rotten summer."

"Yeah, I know what you mean. Sometimes life tosses a surprise curve ball at us."

"Well, I always expect surprises to be fun. This is more like a bolt of lightning. Thanks, God, for the kick in the gut, really appreciate it."

"C'mon, you know Mom wouldn't want you to be talking like that. She'd rather you be saying a prayer for her."

"Okay, but I don't understand how someone like Mom can be taken down this early in life. She's never hurt anyone."

"She's not taken down yet, Jeff. She would consider this a little setback. I'm worried, too, but I think we should pray and focus on getting her back. Look, the good part is you saved your Mom. And she's in a great hospital with one of the best neurosurgeons taking care of her."

"I guess. It's weird with all that happened in the past few months. It's hard to believe that she's in ICU. Yesterday, she was joking with me about the macaroni salad. You know how she does that strict voice, but she can't keep from smiling. 'Jeffery McCormack, you are not going to devour the macaroni salad before the fourth of July. And you won't be spilling it on the floor like you did when you were twelve.' Then, of course, she pushed me against the wall like she's been doing since I was twelve. I know the only thing she can see when she looks up is my chin. Man, she loves to poke me in the chest five times. 'Listen, buster, you may be taller and bigger than me, but I'm tougher!' I told her, 'Okay, okay, I give. Not only will I not eat any of your macaroni salad before the party, I won't eat any at the party. I like Aunt Dee Dee's broccoli-cauliflower salad better anyway. Finally, she released her poking finger. 'Okay, smarty, I'm making it tomorrow afternoon. I'll have a special dish for you in the fridge.'"

Chet laughed. Jeff sighed, "Hmm, the Dillon macaroni salad. It's not even important, but …"

"It's one of those special things Mom does for us, right? Jeff, you know the story about when Mom and I separated three years after we got married. We told you and Jeannie some of it. We didn't want you to hear it from anyone else. If it hadn't been for your Mom, I'd still be in a hospital in Dallas, Texas or worse."

"It was a mess according to Mom. She said you were treated for an immature brain."

"Something like that. We haven't told you and Jeannie all the details, but it was scary for your Mom then, like it is for us now. There were many people saying prayers for us. It turned out to be a blessing in disguise because your Mom gave me a second chance. We finally mended our relationship. Then a few years later Jeannie was born and then my favorite son was born and we all lived happily ever after, somewhat. I guess my point is that bad things happen to everyone, but 'we know that all things work for good…'"

"Geez, I know. 'For those who love the Lord. Romans 8-28.'"

"Anyway, right now let's keep our attention on Mom. This may be happening for a reason. Jeff, I really do think she's going to pull through."

Jeff yawned. "Hmmm, okay, thanks. Let's go back to the room. I think I can sleep now. I'll say a prayer for Mom."

Chet reached up to put his arm around his son's shoulder and they returned to the anteroom.

Jeff fell asleep in a few minutes.

Chet dwelled on his own words, *'finally mended our relationship.' I wish it had happened that quickly. It took years and years and retreats and therapy before we finally healed our marriage. And now, when things are solid and happy, this happens to my Claire, my love. God, I pray that this aneurysm that has trapped Claire's brain has a good purpose. Please, God, you saved a wretch like me in Dallas. Please save my wife. All things work for those who love the Lord…*

———————————

At seven am, Dr. William McDaniel entered ICU.

Chapter 1 : The Climb

He was hopeful that Claire would fully recover from the aneurysm. She was a strong fifty-five year old woman, and by the grace of God, had gotten to the emergency room in time. The team of doctors had saved her life during the operation, but seeing her in a coma was unsettling for her family.

He talked pretty matter-of-factly to Chet and his children. "She's doing well. I know when you see her in a coma, it feels discouraging but it's necessary for her brain to heal."

Claire's complexion was pasty and her skin seemed to stretch across her facial bones like a thin scarf. Jeannie hung her head and then cupped her hands around her own face. Her Mom had to survive. She was her best friend – always cheering her on in activities through high school and college and now her job. Jeff tapped Jeannie on the shoulder in an attempt to stave off the sad thoughts he could read on her face. She clenched his hand as they had when they were frightened children.

Jeff fought back the tears. His memory fixated on May 10 when he and his Mom were returning from shopping for graduation clothes in Cincinnati.

# CHAPTER 2 BEGINNINGS

"Hey, Jeffy, it was a good day today, don't you think?"

"Yeah, it was great, Mom. Thanks for buying the clothes. Wow, I'm starved."

"Even after that huge breakfast at the Netherland?"

When they were shopping, Claire noticed Jeff's jeans hanging off him despite the entire apple pie he had eaten for dessert the night before.

"Never mind, of course you're starved. What are you in the mood to eat?"

"Cheese Coneys at Skyway Chili!"

"Gee, why am I not surprised? Okay, we'll stop at school to pick up your cap and gown. Then, it's you and me, kid, at Skyway Chili."

"Sounds good. My stomach's so hungry, it's slapping against my back."

Claire laughed out loud. "You know I'm really going to miss our drives in the car to Cincinnati."

As they approached the bridge leading into Hallowed, Jeff was thinking about the trip he and Kevin Combs, his best friend since kindergarten, were planning. This would be their last hurrah before work started. They decided that after graduation they would head to Moundview Campground for a few days of fishing, hiking, and campfire food. All of that had changed on the day Jeff heard Tarzan's jungle scream-- Kevin's ringtone. Jeff picked up his cell. "Hey, animal, what's swinging?"

Kevin choked out the words, "My dad died this morning. It was a heart attack. My Mom was going to call your Mom, but she's walking around in a daze. Can you guys come over?"

Claire could tell there was something wrong and tapped Jeff on the knee. "What's going on?"

Jeff waved his hand at her anxiously and ended the call with Kevin, "We're just getting back from Cincy, Kev. We'll be there in fifteen minutes."

"Jeff, what? Tell me."

"Mr. Combs died this morning."

"Oh, my God, what happened?"

"He had a heart attack. That's all I know. Let's get over there."

Chapter 2 Beginnings

As a knot of sadness gripped Claire's stomach, she imagined Anne's anguish. A deep pang of grief poured over her. She and Anne were best friends, but more than that, the Combs and McCormack families were intertwined with each other in a cohesive way, having shared both happy and unhappy memories. Claire called Chet to give him the terrible news.

"What the Hell? God, Claire, what happened?"

"He had a heart attack this morning. Don't know much other than that. Jeff and I will be at their house in about fifteen minutes. I know you have that big meeting today."

"Yeah, we're in the middle of it right now. I'll try to finish up as fast as I can, but I probably won't be able to leave until about 3 o'clock. How's Jeff?"

"He's staring out the window right now. Want to talk with him? Claire handed Jeff her phone."

"Hey, Dad."

"Hi, son, I know this is a blow for you. Kevin's got to be shaken up by all this, so hang in there with him. He's lucky to have you. I'll be home as soon as I can. Let me talk to your Mom again."

"Claire, are you going to be okay with Anne? I can find a way to leave now if you want."

"I'll be okay. It's probably good for me to see her first, anyway."

"I can't believe it. Drive carefully, hon. We can talk when I get home. Love you."

"Love you, too."

---

She drove through the little town of Hallowed, which was only a mile from her neighborhood. As she passed the water tower, she remembered the many times she had attended the Christmas Walk year after year since she was five years old.

Claire could see her five year old self, standing outside in the wintry cold, bundled in a fuzzy white coat and matching leggings, barely able to move with layers underneath, mittens, scarf, and hat covering her up so that all that was visible were her crimson cheeks and nose. She could smell hot chocolate from the bakery on the corner and jumped up and down like a snow bunny, hoping to catch a glimpse of the glazed donuts through the window.

One of the best Christmases Claire could recall was the year the Combs family moved to town. Jeannie, Jeff, and Kevin wore modern versions of the 1950's winter coat ensemble; puffy snowsuits with hooded ski jackets and matching snow pants. Their parents laughed as they watched Jeannie guide the boys to the horse and buggy carriage, looking like bulky aliens in space suits. Jeannie climbed into the back seat, pretending she was the holiday queen. Good old Santa put the boys on his lap and let them drive or at least think they were driving the wagon.

*Time has flown by. Only six months ago, we were at the Christmas lighting ceremony.*

Claire remembered Annie flailing her arms at Jack, shaking her head back and forth. As a not-so-welcomed surprise for the Moms, Chet and Jack had volunteered their sons to stream white lights from the top of the tower.

"Jack, are you crazy? I don't want Kevin climbing up there!"

"Oh, you're afraid your sweet little boy might get a boo boo, huh, ninny baby?"

Of course, Chet had to jump in. "I did this when I was their age. It's very safe. They'll be in harnesses and Jack and I will anchor everything at the bottom of the tower. The worse that could happen is they get a few scratches. Claire, how about a little reassurance for your friend?"

"Annie, nobody's ever gotten injured doing this since they first hung the lights in 1952. Anyway, give it up. Do you really think we can talk our stubborn husbands out of this?"

Claire's hands turned sweaty with fear as she pictured the boys climbing the tower and then rappelling down ever so slowly. Even Jack and Chet looked worried, concentrating intently on the tautness of the ropes. When their sons touched the ground safely, Claire and Anne breathed a sigh of relief. Fathers and sons hi-fived each other in testosterone revelry. Then the families walked to Skyway Chili for a celebration of the dangerous feat.

Chapter 2 Beginnings

If you moved your hand around the outside window of the restaurant, the watery circle would reveal two families sitting at a large table, coats hanging on the backs of chairs, mouths opened in conversation and laughter, sharing a yearly tradition. After the waitress served drinks, cheese coneys, and 5-way chili plates, she patted Jeff and Kevin on their shoulders in recognition of their entry into Hallowed history, joining the ranks of the triumphant tower climbers. The parents clanked beer mugs against their sons' mugs of root beer. Claire smiled at the memory of Jack and Chet making everyone laugh as Anne continued to freak out about the tower climb.

"Jack, you're going to make me have a nervous breakdown with stuff like this. My hands were shaking and sweaty the entire time they were up there."

Chet had to jump in again. "Annie, you were dancing around in a circle, like you had ants in your pants. Oops, I should keep my mouth shut."

Jack and Chet clanked their beer glasses. Chet teased even more. "Yeah, Annie, you're a good dancer. What's that called … the jitter bug?"

"No, Chet, it's the jitter-y bug. Only nervous ninny babies know how to do it."

Annie was miffed at everyone.

"Claire, you were scared, too. I know you were."

"Well, why do you think I wasn't even talking? I was saying the rosary the whole time they were up there!"

"Thank you, Claire. So, see Mr. smarty-pants Combs. I wasn't the only one jittery."

When the families were satiated with food, laughter, and all of the memorable trimmings of the Christmas Walk, they trudged up the hill to the neighborhood. In spite of cold sleet striking against their faces, all of them instinctively turned around at the entrance gazing back to see the exquisite tower – Hallowed's diamond ornament in the sky.

*Gosh, Jack, I can't believe you won't be at the lighting with us this year.*

―――――――――――

Chet sat in his office staring at the Cincinnati skyline. He wanted to be composed before he re-entered the meeting with Bartholomew Incorporated, a small firm that renovated historical buildings. This was a lucrative account for his company and he would be the Senior Architect.

*Jack's dead. Jack, Jack, why you, buddy? You were a good friend, the best.*

---

He remembered how much Jack had helped him when he lost his job in June 1998 Chet had known about it for two weeks, but still had not told Claire. Chet left work at 3 pm on his last day at Dawson, Meyer, & Romero Architectural Firm. He didn't want to go home. Instead he drove to Cincinnati.

On his way there, he called Jack.

"Hey, Chet. How's it going?"

"Fine. Sort of."

"To what do I owe this midafternoon call from the busiest man I know?"

"I lost my job. My last day was today. I've known about it for two weeks, but I haven't told Claire yet".

"Where are you now?"

"I'm about ten minutes from downtown. I was hoping to see you."

"Absolutely, I'll clear my schedule. When you get to the Federal Building, tell the guard I'm expecting you."

As Chet took the elevator to his friend's office, his stomach lurched more than it usually did zipping up twenty-five floors.

"Hey, Chet. Come in. Sorry about the job. That's a kick in the pants. What happened?"

"Remember, when I told you that my boss was traveling to Chicago a lot?"

"Yeah, he's one of the owners, isn't he?"

"Dawson is the majority partner. He's also the reason I lost my job. We were all excited when we got the contract for the new stage theatre in St. Louis, Missouri. I had never designed anything that big, but everyone from city council to the Arts Consortium loved the drawings. I knew I was on my way to the top."

"You and Claire were going to visit St. Louis in September, right?"

Chapter 2 Beginnings

"Not anymore. Seems, that Dawson has been caught with his hand in the till and he gave kickbacks to some vendors. Dawson's in big trouble and bottom line, DM&R is out of money and I'm out of a job. His partners, Jake Meyer and Phil Romero called all the employees into the conference room two weeks ago. They couldn't tell us the details, but they looked really worried. The most they could give us was two weeks notice. DM&R has no money."

"Any severance? Health insurance?"

"Zip. Starting from scratch once again."

"But, it's not your fault you were working for a crook."

"No, it's not my fault, but how can I tell Claire that our last paycheck gets deposited today and by the way, there's no severance package? I can't disappoint her again. She won't be able to handle another financial crisis. She might even leave me. It was pretty iffy in 1989 when we filed bankruptcy and closed our own company. Jack, I can't sleep. I'm drinking too much and my stomach feels like someone's throwing acid balls around and around."

"Okay, so you filed bankruptcy and closed a business. But then you got the job with DM&R and you'll get another one."

"Jack Combs, the invincible optimist."

"Well, it beats crying in your beer. Look, you're going to have to tell Claire. It'll be okay."

"Jack, you know a lot about Claire and me, but not everything. Fear of not having money is Claire's Achilles' heal. She grew up poor and no matter how much money we have, she still feels poor."

"Speaking of money, do you need some?"

"No, we'll be okay. We have money in a 401K we can borrow from."

"Well, if you need anything, you know where I am, Chet."

"Thanks for listening, Jack. I can always count on you." Chet grabbed Jack's forearm with his hand like an old Viking fellow warrior. "Wish me luck. I'm off to face the fire!"

Claire's reaction was exactly as Chet said it would be. She was panic-stricken. "They did what? And you didn't have any idea it was coming? Thanks for telling me on your last day. Here we go again."

———————————

As Claire approached the hill leading up to her neighborhood, she too recalled the summer of 1998 when Chet lost his job. One night at about 7:30 pm, Jack knocked on her door.

"Hi, Jack. Come in."

"Hi, Claire. Chet's at the St. Vincent de Paul meeting tonight, right?"

"Yeah, and the kids are at your house. What's going on?"

"Claire, it's not for me to say what you should or shouldn't do, but Chet's a good man. You know that, right?"

"I know that, but if you're talking about how I should be more supportive, I don't want to hear it."

"No, Claire, I think you try to be very supportive of Chet, but you both look so darn unhappy. Annie doesn't tell me everything you talk about, but she agrees that you both look unhappy."

"I am unhappy, Jack. Not only did he lose his job, he didn't even tell me until his last day at work."

"But, he did tell you."

"Yeah, he told me after the fact."

"He came to see me before he came home that day."

"I didn't know that. Why would he tell you before me?"

"Because he knows how you worry about money. And he has a lot of regret about the bankruptcy and closing the business, but c'mon, Claire, this wasn't his fault. Dawson's a criminal."

"If Chet had told me the truth from the get-go, maybe I could have accepted it more easily. Instead, he did what he's done many times. Not telling me the truth

18

makes it even worse. I guess I can't get beyond the fact that I can't trust him. I really haven't been able to trust him from our first day of marriage."

"He has a lot of regret about the first years of your marriage."

"Well, he might have regret, but he doesn't do anything to change. He still does things that chip away at my trust. I'm scared about our finances and the kids' college. I'm tired of worrying, Jack. And he refuses to go to a marriage counselor."

"Have you asked him recently?"

"No, not recently, but he won't go. I know he won't."

"Are you sure you want to go? Anne and I have had our issues too. We never told you, but the first year we moved here, we went to a therapist. Anne had trust issues with me. She kept waiting for the other shoe to drop, as she called it. I couldn't even talk to her about work because she was afraid I'd tell her we'd have to move again. It was money well-spent. Dave Marcovi, that's the therapist, helped us to go back and slowly examine what took place in each of our lives."

"Dave Marcovi?"

"Yeah, he's good at moving your marriage beyond guilt and regret. Believe me; I was tired of walking on eggshells with Anne. She had things from childhood that impacted her trust level. Annie's probably told you about it. And I had baggage, too. Anyway, after about a year, we were able to sort through some of the hurt and issues. It really helped our marriage."

"It would take more than a year for us, Jack."

"But wouldn't it be worth it, if it keeps your family together? And not just together, but happy. Jeannie's seventeen and Jeff is only eleven. Pretty impressionable ages. Here's his phone number. Make an appointment. Chet will go with you. I promise. And besides, Anne and I have selfish motives. We want you guys to be a part of our family for a long time."

*Dave Marcovi did work his magic with us. Thanks, Jack. You led us to him and saved our marriage.*

Claire turned the corner into Hallowed Haven. When the neighborhood was first built, she and a few other families who lived there created a beautiful entrance with lush green bushes, pink and blue hydrangeas, and amazing clusters of impatiens in the summer. White-marble fountains mirrored each other on both sides of the entryway. The fonts brandished a spiral of angels, arms outspread as if gently bringing the rain down from Heaven. One of the angels held a beautiful carved wood sign that read 'Hallowed Haven, Shelter from the Storm,' however this was not the original sign.

Claire experienced another bittersweet peek into a bygone year – spring 2002-- when Hallowed was hit by a powerful storm with wind gusts of 60 miles per hour. No one died, but six of the small homes in the surrounding streets were destroyed. In Hallowed Haven most of the damage was minor. From the hardware stores to the grocery stores, townspeople rallied to repair and rebuild their neighbor's houses. By the Fourth of July, Hallowed, Ohio was back to normal with a parade, celebration, and magnificent fireworks.

On Fourth of July morning, Jack had called Chet before leaving for the parade.

"Hey, Claire, Jack called. He wants you to walk down to the entryway. He has something to show you."

"Right now?"

"Yeah, right now. Let's go. We've got to get to the parade anyway. Jeannie and Jeff already left"

Claire had been upset that the etched glass signs in the entryway had been shattered into a thousand pieces during the storm. The marble fountains survived, but the Hallowed Planning Committee decided that they would not replace the signs. Claire was disappointed since she had painstaking designed the angel fountains and the etched glass signs that simply read Hallowed Haven.

When Chet and Claire reached the entryway, Anne, Jeannie, Jeff, Kevin and a group of neighbors were gathered with Jack at the head in his captain's uniform.

"Come up here, Claire McCormack. The Hallowed Planning Committee, under the adept direction of this 'carpenter,' has designed and built two new signs for the entryway which you conceived and created when this neighborhood was built."

20

Chapter 2 Beginnings

"Oh, my gosh, Jack, they're beautiful. I like these even better. You added a new line to it, didn't you?"

One of the neighbors shouted, "What's engraved on it, Claire? Hold it up."

Chet held it up high and Claire read, "'Hallowed Haven, Shelter from the Storm.' I love it, Jack. Beautiful carving and what you added is awesome. Thank you, Captain Combs. You're an officer and a gentleman. Thanks, everyone."

———————————

Once past the entryway, Claire jolted back to the cold reality of the present. *Hard to believe Jack's dead.*

Claire passed house after house in the neighborhood. Several quaint Cape Cods were nestled amid traditional and ranch houses. However, Hallowed Haven had only two contemporary homes with slanted roofs and vaulted ceilings. The McCormacks lived in one and the Combs in the other. Claire drove past her home and pulled into the Combs' driveway.

Kevin answered the door and led Claire and Jeff to the kitchen where Anne was sitting, staring out the window. As soon as she saw Claire, Anne practically jumped into her arms, crying in between wails of grief.

"Oh, Claire, I can't believe it. He's gone. What am I going to do?"

Claire held Anne even closer and rubbed her hand in soothing circles across her back whispering softly, "I can't believe it either..." Anne's long blonde hair was wet with tears and her eyes had a ghoulish cast to them. Claire guided her back to the kitchen chair and sat down beside her. "You want to tell me what happened?"

Kevin intervened. "Mom, you want me to tell her? I know this is hard on you."

"That's okay, Kevin. I can do it."

Not knowing how to help his friend, Jeff suggested Kevin and he shoot hoops in the driveway. Reluctantly, Kevin agreed. Anne waited until she heard the bounce of the basketball.

"It's going to be hard on Kevin. He and Jack were like two peas in a pod. They could finish each other's sentences." Anne stared at the clock on the wall for a few seconds, seemingly lost in another world. "Last night after dinner, Jack said he felt like he had acid reflux, so he took one of his pills. He stopped in Kevin's room to say good night and then we went to bed around 10 o'clock. The alarm went off at 6:30 a.m. I heard him hit the snooze. When it went off the second time, he got out of bed. And then, he, uh…"

Anne started to cry again and put her head on the table. Claire placed her hand on her back once more and pressed slightly for support. After several seconds, Anne forged ahead as if she had to tell it to Claire in order to believe it herself. "And then, he collapsed on the floor. Kevin heard me scream and came running into the bedroom. I told him to call 911, but I knew this was the end. I just knew it."

"But Jack was still breathing when you went to the hospital, wasn't he?"

"Yes, barely. I went in the ambulance with him. Kev drove the car. Poor kid. I should have called you and Chet to drive him, but I wasn't thinking straight. It happened so fast. Anyway, I'm glad Kevin didn't see what I saw in the ambulance."

Anne stopped again for a few seconds. Claire remained silent but continued to hold her hand on Anne's back.

"The paramedics kept doing things to him. They seemed to move in slow motion and I was frozen in place. They gave him a shot in his arm and he was breathing. Then, they put an oxygen mask on him to keep it going. After a few minutes, one of them placed two fingers in the side of Jack's neck to listen for his heartbeat. He stared at the other paramedic. Without one word, they began CPR. I could feel the paramedic's hot breath on my face as he pumped his hands into Jack's chest. I could hear the static sound of the driver on the radio saying 'possible DOA in two minutes.' It was a nightmare."

Anne glanced at the clock mentally putting the last moments of Jack's life on the dots between the numbers. "By the time we got to St. Aloysius, he was turning blue. I almost collapsed. Kev met us in the hall. They put Jack on life-support. I had a glimmer of hope, but then they told us to go in."

"To say good-bye?"

"Yeah."

Chapter 2 Beginnings

"I stood on one side of the bed and Kev on the other. Jack was still alive then. Kev and I held each other's hands across his body and I put my cheek…my cheek against his and said good-bye."

Claire closed her eyes envisioning their final moments with Jack and gently shook her head back and forth. "Poor Kevin."

"Kev, um, held up Jack's hand and pressed his against it. You know how they do the closed fist tap. Then the priest came. Kev came over to stand by me and Fr. Brown, I think that's his name, performed the Last Rites. Fr. Brown said something to us, but I can't remember what it was. Within a few minutes, the ICU doctor entered the room. We watched as he turned off the machines. I looked at the clock. It was 8:58 am. That's when he died. That's when my Jack died. I had to sign some papers. Then we left."

"Oh, Anne, I'm so sorry. How in the world did you get home? You both must have been devastated."

"Kevin drove us back to Hallowed. I don't remember much of that ride. Kev and I didn't even talk. We opened the windows and let the wind blow hard in our faces all the way back. We literally just got home."

Anne stood up and pointed to the clock.

"It's 11:58 on the dot. Only three hours since…" Once more, Anne turned to Claire and both of them wept. Through her hiccups and tears, Anne stammered, "I was going to call you, but Kevin insisted that he call Jeff. I guess he's thinks he needs to protect me."

"Aah, that's sweet, though. He's a really good son."

"Yes he is. Jack taught him well. Oh, now what, Claire? What am I going to do?"

"I know it's hard to accept, but we can pray. Do you want to pray now?" Anne bristled. Claire noticed and changed the subject. "Hey, what can I do to help? Do you want me to call anyone? I'll bring dinner over tonight. What else can I do?"

"Thanks, dinner would be nice, Claire. Kev and I are going to make the arrangements at Tippins Funeral Home and the church tomorrow. I know what readings and songs Jack would like. That's pretty much it for now. Well, there is one thing I need help with."

"Anything, Anne, name it."

"Could you plan the wake? We'll have it here, but I'm not up to dealing with planning it. You know, Jack always did the party arranging."

"Of course. Chet and I can handle all of that."

"Thanks, that will help. I'm sure all of Jack's friends will want to come and of course, his family will be flying in. God, I still have to call them." She exhaled a large sigh realizing she had to tell both the Combs and Madison family members.

Claire instinctively knew that Anne was dancing around the biggest worry. "Okay, Annie, do you want to talk about it?"

"About what?"

"How worried you are about the future, especially since…"

Anne held up her hand. "Stop! Jack died. Just like that. I went to bed with my husband and woke up a widow. And now, I have an unborn child and a dead husband. What do I do? What the hell am I going to do, Claire?"

She paced the floor of the kitchen, crying profusely. Claire winced in pain as she choked back her own tears. Anne continued in a rampage of anger, slamming the refrigerator door open and shut, blubbering tears into the sink, and finally stomping to the kitchen center island. She banged a pan that was hanging overhead. Then, she hugged the pillar sobbing. "God, this is a bunch of crap. I can't believe it. I can't believe it."

Claire got a dish cloth from the towel drawer and handed it to Anne. Anne wiped her eyes and nose and stood up tall. Claire tugged one end of the towel. "Can I have a piece of this? I'm crying too."

Anne started to laugh. "I guess I am a ninny baby, after all. Jack loved that story of when you called me that in grade school. You know how he teases me about it all the time. 'Okay, ninny baby. I'm going to tell your big sister, Claire, that you're worrying about something silly again.'"

Chapter 2 Beginnings

Their conversation continued with laughter and tears periodically interrupting their words.  After a few minutes, they both sat at the kitchen table drained of sentiments.

"Okay, little sister, you asked what you are going to do.  You keep on living.  That's what Jack would say.  He'd want you and Kevin and the baby to be happy, even though that seems impossible now.  Prayer helps, Anne, you know it does.  Our Faith is what keeps us going."

"I'm having a lapse of faith right now.  Jack's gone and I'm thirteen weeks pregnant.  I'm not depending too much on prayer at this point."

Claire was surprised at Anne's reaction to prayer.  She and Anne had shared many pieces of their lives with each other.  They felt comfortable praying spontaneously.  They belonged to the Bible Babes at church and even had their own one-on-one Bible discussions during the summer.  "Anne, when Chet and I were considering divorce, you and I prayed together.  I know this has a greater magnitude, but …"  She tried to channel Anne's mind into a happier time.

"I know Jack was excited about the baby.  He told Chet that Kevin would be a hard act to follow, but he was looking forward to being the father of a little one again."

"When I found out I was pregnant, my doctor suggested abortion as an option."

"Because you're forty-six?"

"Exactly.  I wanted to pick up anything in his office and throw it at him."

"I don't blame you.  You changed doctors, right?"

"Of course.  When I told Jack, he was furious.  He actually wanted to sue Dr. Blanco for suggesting 'the murder' of our baby because of my age.  I said, 'Jack, get serious.  Roe v. Wade has been in place for almost forty years.  Dr. Blanco has been deceived like many other doctors.  And then there's all the people, including other Catholics we know, who think abortion is a political issue.' Claire, I don't want to talk about it anymore.  I can't deal with this today.  It's too overwhelming."

"I don't know what to say except, 'I'm here for you.'"

"I know you are. I can't believe I'm even thinking about finances on the day Jack died, but I'm going to have to work full-time now. None of this part-time stuff. I'll get Jack's pension, but it's not even close to what he has been earning."

"Don't feel guilty. You'll be thinking about those kinds of things in the days ahead. It's the way it is."

"And, Kev's going to college. I'll probably have to sell the house and move. God, why Jack? Why now?" Anne stared out of the window twisting her hair into a taut coil. She pulled Claire to her side and whispered, "I'm ashamed to say this, but maybe Dr. Blanco was right."

Claire scanned the driveway to make sure Jeff and Kevin were still there.

"You mean you'd consider an abortion now?" Anne did not answer. Claire persuaded gently. "Don't do anything rash, please. Let's talk this out. Promise?" Anne nodded weak consent. Claire repeated, "Promise?"

Anne went to the sink and splashed water on her face. Her twisted hair strands loosened, unwinding slowly. She dried her face with a paper towel. "I promise I'll talk with you about it. That's all I can promise. Believe it or not, I'm starting to accept this and I know I can't afford to be a ninny baby anymore. I have to think of Kevin. I have to be stronger than I've been in the past."

Claire wanted to push a little harder to dissuade Anne from even considering an abortion, but Anne had already started twisting her hair again. "Okay, Anne, I understand. Listen, we'll stop by at around 5 p.m. to bring dinner. Chet's going to want to see you and Kevin."

Anne and Claire gave each other one final hug that day. Both sensed a slight divide between their hearts, slight but nevertheless significant.

"Jeff, let's go."

Claire held Kevin's arm. "Hey, hon, if you or your Mom need anything, you know we're here for you. We'll stop back around 5 o'clock to bring dinner."

"Thanks, Mrs. McCormack. I better go inside to be with her. See ya, Jeff." Jeff and Kevin did their buddy handshake and double tapped their fists slowly as if in honor of Kevin's Dad.

Chapter 2 Beginnings

Back in the car, Claire's stomach churned not only from the shock of Jack's death but also from Anne's dark impulse to abort her baby.  Operating on automatic, she passed their own home and drove to McNichols High School to pick-up Jeff's cap and gown.  As she turned left out of Hallowed Haven, she read the entryway sign, 'Hallowed Haven  -- Shelter from the Storm.'

*God, please help Anne to understand what a precious gift this baby is.  Help me to say the right words to keep her from having an abortion.  Help her to know that You are her shelter from this storm.*

"Mom, Mom turn in!  Are you okay?"

"Yeah.  No, I'm thinking about Anne and Kevin.  Sorry about that."

McNichols High School was a quarter mile from the city, nestled amid large pine trees.  As she parked the car in the school lot, she tried to comfort Jeff.

"We can still go to Skyway if you want, Jeff."

"I'm not very hungry anymore.  I'll get something at home later.  Mom, can you go in and get the cap and gown?  I don't want to see anyone from school."  His eyes were red and puffy from fighting back tears with his hands.

"I'll take care of it.  Be right back."

Claire opened the door to McNichols High.  She peeked into the cafeteria.  It's still there, the old snack bar.  Thirty-nine years ago, she had stood in line buying cheese crackers when Chet tapped her on the shoulder.  The fact that Jeannie had graduated from McNick and that Jeff would follow suit was singularly pleasing to Chet and Claire.

---

She remembered Jeff and Kevin's first day of high school.  On that day, Claire and Anne drove to McNichols to do a little spying.  The espionage duo hid behind one of the pines, excited to watch their sons enter the building.  As Jeff and Kev walked up the path to the school, a group of girls strolled behind them.  Then Jeff turned toward the girls.

"Well, hello ladies, welcome to the first day of high school."

"Very funny, like it's not your first day of high school. Or is that grade school?"

"Hey, Emily, are you coming to the football game this Friday? Reserves play at 6:30 pm."

"Of course, I am, silly. I'm on the cheerleading squad. Where have you and Kevin been all summer?"

"Football practice in 90 degree temps. That's where."

One of the girls softened her tone. "Are you guys going to the dance after the varsity game?"

"Absolutely. Jeff and I will meet you on the floor if you can handle it."

Emily added a gibe. "Okay, whatever. We saw your so-called dancing skills at the eighth grade graduation dance"

Jeff and Kevin ran ahead of the girls and began their routine, singing what they could remember of a Justin Timberlake song, *Rock Your Body*.

So you grab your girls
And you grab a couple more
And you all come meet me
In the middle of the floor

Claire and Anne laughed all the way home to Hallowed Haven, feeling very smug at having pulled off their snooping mission.

"So, you grab your girls? And you grab a couple more? Wow, Anne, and so it all begins."

Claire could see still picture the group of girls and Jeff and Kevin vanishing through the door to McNichols High School.

*Seems like it was yesterday. We'll all be at Jeff's and Kevin's graduation, but Jack won't be there. Jack won't be there.*

Claire opened the car door. "Okay, done. I picked up Kevin's cap and gown, too."

Chapter 2 Beginnings

Jeff murmured, "Yeah, that's good. I'll text him."

They drove home in silence, each absorbed in their own sadness. Claire broke the uncomfortable quiet.

"Uh-huh. I feel it, too." Jeff was never very talkative so Claire would often begin her conversations with him, as if he had just told her something. "I know it's scary when someone who's not an 'old' person dies. It hurts and it's unfair. And, people feel angry. Even angry at God."

"Mom, don't. I'm not in the mood for your script. If you want to talk, go ahead, but I'm not listening." Claire could hear the halting pain in Jeff's voice.

"Okay. Then, let's try this. Kevin's going to need your support this summer. In fact, you need each other to get through this."

Jeff opened the window and rested his head on the door edge, hoping the noise of the wind would drown out his mother's voice. Claire noticed the tell-tale redness of Jeff's left cheekbone. Since he was born, his cheekbone had turned red when he cried or was upset. At birth, the doctor had used forceps in delivery and the blood vessels were damaged. She was upset at the time especially when Chet said very bluntly, "Honey, our son is the ugliest baby in the nursery." But that minor injury at birth provided a valuable meter of Jeff's feelings. His red cheekbone told her volumes about his inner thoughts. Claire stopped chattering and drove home, thinking back to the first time they met the Combs family.

---

When Anne and Jack moved into the Hallowed Hills neighborhood in 1997, they immediately became close friends with Chet and Claire. Jeff and Kevin were five years old when they met. From the first day, they shared many things, including toys, sports, scrapes, and of course love of food, especially cheese coneys. They were inseparable friends from kindergarten through high school and planned to room together at St. Francis Bergio University in Cincinnati. Although Claire was several years older than Anne, they both shared similar backgrounds – large families growing up in modest middle-class neighborhoods, attending Catholic schools from first through twelfth. They also shared the experience of big family love, squabbles, and catastrophes that continued into adulthood.

In fact, Claire had actually known Anne briefly in grade school. Little Annie was six years old when Claire was in the eighth grade. Claire had approached Sister Maris Stella to ask about starting a mentoring program whereby the eighth grade students would be mentors for first graders.

"I think it's a great idea, Claire. Let's put a plan together."

Claire became Anne Madison's big sister mentor. Anne was tall for her age with long golden hair framing her beautiful face and eyes so blue they looked lavender. She was the youngest of seven, six of which were brothers. The Madisons lived in a small home on Gladden Avenue, four doors down from the Dillons. Claire enjoyed mentoring Anne, but at times referred to her protégé as 'ninny baby,' when she complained about the other girls not being fair to her. Still, at eighth grade graduation, Claire was touched that Anne had made a card and had picked a bouquet of dandelions for her.

After Claire's eighth- grade graduation that summer, Anne moved away. Her father was transferred – Fulton J. Madison was a Captain in the Army. When Anne started grade school, her dad had promised her mom he would take an office job in Cincinnati. That lasted one year because Captain Madison hated his office job and longed for an active Army life. Claire had not seen Anne since then.

Claire had driven by the day Anne was watching the movers unload the truck. She noticed a very tall, beautiful woman dramatically instructing them to be careful with her statue of the Blessed Mother for her back yard. Claire pulled to the curb. "I love the statue. I have one, too. Hi, I'm Claire. We live down the street."

Anne motioned for Claire to come over. "Hi, I'm Anne. Maybe you can help me decide where to put the Lady."

"Sure, I'd be glad to. Wait a minute. You look very familiar. Are you from Hallowed?"

"You could say that I'm from everywhere. My family lived here when I was six years old. After school was out, Dad moved us to Houston, Texas. Believe it or not, I attended ten different schools by the time I graduated from high school."

Chapter 2 Beginnings

Claire and Anne walked to the backyard. They exchanged names of children and Claire gave Anne some historical information about the neighborhood. As they talked, Claire realized that she had seen these incredibly beautiful eyes before.

"I'm sure I know you from somewhere. What street did you live on when you were in Hallowed as a kid?"

"Gosh, I was only six when we moved away. I'm not sure. Let's see, I went to first grade at Angel of God, but I can't remember the name of that darn street. I was an army brat. My family moved a lot. Ten schools – ten neighborhoods. Angel of God School was my favorite."

"Oh, I can't believe it! Now I know why you look familiar. Is your maiden name Madison?"

"Yeah, how did you know that?"

"My maiden name is Dillon. I'm Claire Dillon. When I was in the eighth grade at Angel of God, you were in the first. I was your big sister mentor. Do you remember me?"

Anne looked puzzled, but soon realized that this was her long-lost 'big sister.' She hugged Claire and laughed, "I remember you very well. You and I would do something fun every week. You taught me how to play croquet. Wow! My big sister mentor lives right down the street from me!"

"By the way, you lived on Gladden Avenue, 'ninny baby.'" Both ladies laughed and hugged.

"This is too funny. Would you and your husband and Kevin like to come to dinner tonight? We're grilling burgers and hot dogs. I know Jeffy would be excited to play with Kevin. And my ten-year old, Jeannie, loves to meet all the neighbors. Chet, that's my husband, is always up for a cookout. Anne, what's your husband's name?"

"Jack. Jack Edward Combs. He should be here any minute. He took Kevin to get lunch. Let me see what he wants to do, but he's a party animal. Definitely, a good chance we'll be there. Can I call you?"

"Sure, here's my number."

Cookouts with the McCormack and the Combs families became a weekly event after that.   The relationships were multi-faceted.  Chet and Jack became golf buddies, but also shared strong Catholic beliefs.  Jeff and Kevin played from morning till night. Jeannie liked visiting Mrs. Combs.  Even at age ten, she considered herself to be a sophisticated young lady and Mrs. Combs enjoyed the 'girl-talk.'

On the day Anne moved into the neighborhood, she and Claire embarked on a lasting relationship that had already been nurtured as little girls.  Once again, Claire assumed the role of big sister.   Anne was the youngest of seven siblings and was used to asking for help and assistance.  Claire was the fourth youngest child of nine siblings and was adept at toggling between being little sister and big sister.   Move-in day in 1995 was the second beginning of two friends who shared the usual ups and downs of life.

Fifteen years later in 2010, that friendship would become a matter of life and death.

# CHAPTER 3 : REFLECTIONS

For thirteen years the dynamics of their relationship had worked very well. Although Jack was Anne's number one anchor, Claire had been her confidant, advisor, and best friend.

*Hopefully, it will work now and Anne will listen to her 'big sister.' I can't believe she would even consider an abortion.*

The fifteen-minute drive from McNichols to home felt like ten seconds. It worried Claire a little that she really didn't remember how she got home. She pulled into the driveway and touched Jeff lightly on his shoulder.

"Hey, Jeff, we're here. Dad will be home as soon as he can. C'mon, bud, we both need some down time."

Claire had a staggering headache. She fixed a cup of tea, and grabbed her Bible, hoping to find comfort and wisdom regarding the issue of Anne and Jack's baby. During fall and winter months, Anne and Claire went to the Angel of God Church Bible study group each week. In the thirteen years they had attended, both had grown through the love of reading the Bible each and every day. Even during summer break, they continued their own Bible study. They would take turns picking a verse and then one of them would say, "Discuss, discuss."

Claire thumbed through the Bible searching for something that could jolt Anne out of this desperate plan. In short time she found a few verses about life and birth. Claire loved the sound and the feel of the thin pages of the Bible as she gently flicked through them. She found two readings that she really liked. The first one was:

*You formed my inmost being; you knit me in my mother's womb. I praise you, so wonderfully you made me; wonderful are your works! My very self you knew; my bones were not hidden from you, When I was being made in secret, fashioned as in the depths of the earth. (Psalm 139: 13-15).*

Claire loved the image of God knitting together the tiny heart, brain, skin, organs, and soul of a child inside the mother's womb. The second reading was also a beautiful mental picture:

*Now the word of the Lord came to me saying, 'Before I formed you in the womb, I knew you, and before you were born, I consecrated you; I have appointed you a prophet to the nations.' (Jeremiah 1: 4-5)*

That vision of God overseeing each and every conception and then blessing that life in the womb fortified her resolve to help Anne avoid a decision that she'd regret the rest of her life. She read each verse three or four times, imagining her conversation with Anne. At last the headache subsided and Claire fell asleep for a few hours.

She awoke at 4 pm and was preparing dinner when Chet arrived.

Chet entered the kitchen. "Hey, babe, how are you?" Claire turned around and immediately fell into his arms crying.

"I can't believe it, Chet, it's awful. Anne's a mess and I'm not any better."

"Wow, Jack's gone. Can't believe it, either. I was going to stop at their house on the way home, but I wanted to talk with you first. What happened?"

"I'll tell you as much as I can remember, but everything was in-between sobbing and a lot of what she said was incoherent. Both of us couldn't stop crying. Well, anyway, Jack had heartburn last night, but took some medicine and they went to bed. When he got up this morning at 6:30, he fell to the floor. He had a massive heart attack. Kevin called 911. The paramedics worked on him all the way to St. Al's, but he died at 8:58 a.m."

"How is Kev? What a rotten blow."

"Acting strong, same as your son, but they're both torn up. Kevin even drove to and from the hospital this morning."

"Why didn't she call us? I would've taken them."

"I asked her the same thing. She said it happened fast and there wasn't any time to really think."

"Okay, but damn, I wish she had called. Jack's like a brother to me. I should have been there with him."

"I know, but I think she was so upset, she couldn't think straight. Kevin called Jeff as soon as they got home."

"You mean Anne didn't call you? That's strange."

"Chet, she was in a panic and I think Kevin did what he thought he should do."

Chapter 3 : Reflections

"Be strong like his Dad?"

"Yep.  We went there as soon as we got back to Hallowed.  Anne was in the kitchen bawling.  She would cry and then get angry.  She must have opened and slammed the refrigerator door twenty-five times.  We were even laughing and crying together at one point."

"What about Jeff and Kevin…where were they?"

"They were playing basketball in the driveway.  I think Anne needed to break down and she didn't want to do it in front of Kevin.   She resented it when I mentioned prayer and she absolutely did not want to talk about the future."

"Well, maybe it's too soon."

"Maybe, but I've never seen her this angry.  At one point she held up her hand and said 'Stop!  Jack died.  Just like that.  I went to bed with my husband and woke up a wido*w*.  Now I have an unborn child and a dead husband.' "

"Does Kevin know she's pregnant?"

"I don't think so.  She barely shows.  You know how trim she is.  I haven't really asked her if she's told him, but my guess is they wanted to wait until after graduation."

"The whole thing makes me sick.  I mean it's scary to think we were all together last Sunday at the Sports Awards Banquet."

"Couldn't have been better seeing Jeff and Kevin win the McNichols' Spirit Award.  From K through 12, those two have been best buddies."

"Jack and I were laughing at them when they accepted and did their secret handshake."

"Well, you and Jack were pretty funny when you  mimicked them afterwards with your back to back version.  Even old Mr. stodgy Stodmann was laughing.  What a memory."

"Yeah, what a memory, another good one with Jack.  Now, he's gone."

Chet leaned against the kitchen island and hung his head.   Claire paused, rubbing her hand across the back of his neck.

"Hey, dinner's ready. Why don't you take it over? We'll eat when you get back. Anne needs a man's shoulder to cry on. She really does."

"Go with me, Claire."

"No, I think you should go. It would be good for her to talk to her husband's best friend. If I go, she'll just start crying again and so will I. Kevin needs some TLC too. Anyway, I'm going back over there in the morning."

"Okay, if you think it's a good idea, but I'm staying away from the pregnancy topic. Where's Jeff?"

"Hey, Dad. Bad day, huh?"

Chet hugged Jeff, patting him on the back.

"The worst, son, the absolute worst. How's Kev doing?"

"Okay. Not great."

"And how are you doing? You look groggy."

"Yeah, I had a really bad headache, so I took a nap. I still don't feel very good."

"Claire put a platter of meatballs and spaghetti on the table. Could be you're hungry too. Change of plans. Why don't we all eat now and then you guys can take dinner over to Anne and Kev?"

"Wow, I am hungry. I haven't eaten since this morning. Thanks, Mom."

After dinner, Chet and Jeff walked down the street to deliver the supper basket. At five o'clock, the sun was still shining brightly, and the pear trees that lined the street scattered soft white petals everywhere.

"Snow in May, huh?"

"Looks like it. Dad, why…?"

"Yeah, son?"

"What's the point?"

"You mean, what's the point of living?"

"Something like that. I mean why do things happen like this? Why spend your life working and going to school and whatever? Then one day you're gone, just gone."

Chapter 3 : Reflections

"Well…"

"And why does God let bad things happen? They never really covered that in religion class at McNick."

"I think it has a lot to do with free will and nature. God allows people to have free will and God allows nature to happen."

"So, it's nature's fault that Mr. Combs died."

"It's not nature's fault. It's nature's way."

"Sounds like a trap."

"What do you mean?"

"Well, I have free will to choose, but if I choose the wrong thing, I'm going to be punished. And even if I make a good choice, nature can zap me any time. Basically, I'm in a pickle. If nature's going to get us anyway, why not do anything you want?"

"Because it's not all about living on Earth and doing whatever you want and then dying. There's something more than this."

"Seems unfair. I know I'm going to make some bad choices. It's impossible not to."

"Hey, I know for a fact I have made many bad choices, but that's the beauty of free will. Even if I make a bad choice, I still have free will to ask Jesus for forgiveness. And, I can ask Jesus for forgiveness over and over, no matter how many times I fail. It's really more than fair, but I get your point. I felt the same when I was your age."

"So, what about Kev's Dad? What if he made bad choices? And what if he didn't ask God for forgiveness?"-

"I don't know every choice that Mr. Combs made, but you know he was a man of integrity and a great father and husband. He was religious, too. Mom said he received the last rites from a priest at the hospital. In that last millisecond of his life, he may have heard the priest reciting the Act of Contrition. I bet he was following along in his mind."

"Maybe. They say hearing is our last sense to leave us."

"Good point, but beyond that, you saw him at Mass every Sunday. He went to communion and received the body and blood of Christ. I think Jack was pretty solid in the eyes of God."

Jeff reacted sarcastically. "But he didn't choose to die, did he?"

"No, he didn't choose to die. Most people don't, but when he was alive, he made many good choices. Remember nature does not have free will. If it did, it would have chosen Jack Combs' body to live to be 100."

"That's what I mean, Dad. Why make all the good choices? What does it do for you?"

"It can make you and others happy on Earth, and an important part of free will is that your choices on Earth determine where you go after you die. Heaven or Hell. It's our choice. There is a life hereafter, Jeff."

"Oh, well, maybe it will make sense later, but I feel awful today. That's all."

"Hang in there. When someone dies suddenly, it gets our attention. It rattles our Faith. I feel pretty awful today, too, but we're alive and Mrs. Combs and Kevin are alive and we're here to help them. Let's go with that, okay."

"Sure, okay, Dad."

"Hey, ring the doorbell."

"Kevin answered the door. "Mom, they're here. She's on the phone with her oldest brother. Come in."

Chet grabbed Kevin in a bear hug. "Hey, Kev, I'm sorry about your Dad. He was one of the best." Jeff did the fist tap with Kevin."

"Mom will be out in a minute. She's been on the phone all day. We've got people coming in from all over the country. Wow, that smells great. Haven't had much to eat today."

"It's really good. I just ate a mound full, man. Mom makes the best meatballs."

"Why don't you guys take it to the kitchen? Mom said to put it in the oven on 250 for about twenty minutes."

Chapter 3 : Reflections

As Kevin and Jeff took the dinner basket into the kitchen, Anne sluggishly walked into the living room, looking frail and peaked.  She hugged Chet, placing her head on his shoulder.  "So, sorry, Annie.  So, sorry.  It's such a shock.  Claire told me what happened.  That must have been a nightmare for you and Kev."

Both sat down on the couch.  Anne crouched into a corner and Chet sat on the edge facing her.  She held a box of tissues dabbing her eyes and nose frequently.

"Can't believe it, Chet.  Just can't believe it.  One day I'm planning my son's graduation and the next day, I'm planning my husband's funeral. It's not fair."

"You're right, Anne.  It's not fair, but you and Kevin did everything you could to save him.  And, I know for a fact Jack was very happy to be married to you.  He told me many times that you were the best thing that ever happened to him."

"Thanks, Chet.  It helps to hear that.  I'm going to miss him."

"Me, too.  Jack and I were like brothers."

"The kitchen door swung open."

"Hey, Mom, is it okay if I eat?  I'm starving."

"Hi, Mrs. Combs.  I'm back again."

"Hi, Jeff.  Sure, you two go ahead and eat.  I'll have a bite later."

"Claire said to make sure you ate something.  I'll be in big trouble if you don't."

"I'll eat later.  Smells like meatballs.  I'll eat a little this evening.  By the way, where is Claire?"

"Jeff and I wanted to be the heroes bringing dinner.  She said to tell you she'll be over in the morning."

"She probably told you about our private wake in the kitchen today.  We were laughing and crying."

"Yeah, she mentioned it.  That must have been a sight."

"Claire's like a sister to me.  Moving to Hallowed Haven was one of the happiest days of my life.  That first day when I met Claire and realized she had actually been my big sister in grade school, I knew this was going to be our permanent home."

"I remember that day. You and Jack and Kev came to our house for dinner and the rest is history as they say."

"You know, as a child, all I did was travel from city to city, school to school. My six brothers seemed to adjust better than I could. I always felt out of place, except for that one year at Angel of God when I was six years old. Claire was the sister I never had. Of course we moved again and again and again. Then, I married an Air Force guy and we did the same thing for fifteen years. When Jack took the promotion in Cincinnati, I was really grateful. I didn't want Kevin moving around like I did as a child. Jack loved the Air Force life, but he knew I wanted roots. One night at dinner he said, 'Okay, Annie, terra firma. Do you know what terra firma is? C'mon you took Latin.' I answered, yes, smarty, it means firm ground. Then he smiled that devilish grin. 'You win the prize, Mrs. Combs. We are moving to terra firma or as it's actually called, Hallowed, Ohio.'"

"That's the kind of man he was, Anne. You and Kev always came first."

"It was a dream come true. The house was beautiful with a yard for Kevin. I was excited that he would be attending Angel of God School, the same school where I spent my first grade. And the icing on the cake was reuniting with Claire, who was married to a great guy who became friends with my husband. Those were the best years."

"They were fun. Jeannie pestering you every day, talking your head off."

"I loved it."

"Kevin and Jeff playing all summer and then starting kindergarten."

Anne took a deep breath. "I'm glad Kevin has Jeff as his friend. He's going to need a friend."

"Anne, listen, No one can replace Jack for you or Kevin, but we'll do anything we can to help both of you get through this."

"Thanks. I don't know what I'd do without you and Claire. Terra firma is feeling a little shaky now."

Chapter 3 : Reflections

"Claire told me about the wake. We'll take care of everything. Would you like me to have invitations at the back of Church?"

"Sure, that would be nice. Chet, there's something else, too. Would you be one of the pall bearers?"

Chet choked out the words, "Yes, I'd be honored."

"And one other thing. Fr. Hernandez said that one person could do a short eulogy at the end of Mass for Jack and I'd like that one person to be you. Can you do that?"

"Sure, Anne, sure." At that, Anne and Chet stood up and once again hugged. "This too shall pass, Annie, this too shall pass. We're here for you."

Anne shook her head up and down pursing her lips.

"Hey, remember what Claire said – eat something."

Anne slipped her arm through Chet's arm and led him to the kitchen.

"Okay, you guys, did you save any for me? I know what appetites you two have."

"It's great, Mom. Let me fix a plate for you."

"Okay, sounds good."

"Hey, Jeff, we better take off. Anne, call us if you need anything…anything at all."

"I will, Chet, I will. Tell Claire I'll have coffee ready in the morning."

Kevin gently moved his Mom to the table. He put spaghetti and meatballs on a plate in front of her. "It's good food, Mom. I'll get a knife and fork and water for you."

"Thanks, hon."

Kevin sat to the right of his mother staring at his Dad's chair that was empty now. Chet walked behind Kevin to place both hands firmly on his shoulders.

"Your Dad was quite a man, Kev. And you are a wonderful son. He was very proud of you."

41

As they walked out the kitchen door, Chet glanced backward.  He could see Kevin's reflection in the window wiping a tear with the back of his hand.

# CHAPTER 4 : ENDINGS

Claire called Anne the next day. "Anne, it's me. Did you get any sleep last night?"

"Not really, but I'm drinking coffee now. Kevin and I are meeting with Henrietta Cable at one p.m. today to select the music for the Mass and then we'll go to Tippin's Funeral Home to choose the casket." When Anne said the word "casket," she couldn't speak anymore. Claire heard the painful silence.

"Would you like me to come over now?"

"Yes, please."

When Claire arrived, Anne was sitting at the kitchen table staring at a picture of Jack, Kevin and her at the City of Hallowed's Fourth of July parade last year. Jack was in his Air Force uniform, standing behind them, strong hands on each of their shoulders. Anne gently tossed the picture onto the table. "I'm going to miss him so much. He was my rock. I know, that's a cliché, but I depended on him for everything. No matter what happened in our lives, he was able to help me get past the 'why me' attitude. Things will never be the same."

Claire could hear a palpable fear in Anne's voice. "No, things will never be the same, hon. They won't be the same for us either. Jeff and Kev are trying to be strong, but it makes me sad to see them fighting back the tears. Jack meant a lot to everybody. Chet didn't sleep much last night. He's sick about it."

Anne stared at the picture again. "We prayed together every morning. Our Father, Hail Mary, and Glory Be. When we had those two miscarriages before Kevin was born, I cried for days. Even though Jack was suffering too, he would hold me and comfort me. And every morning we would pray together. Little by little, the pain subsided. We still pray every morning. I mean we prayed yesterday morning."

Claire and Anne could not escape the flow of tears. Then Anne swallowed hard and tore two paper towels to pat their faces. "Yesterday morning is gone. No more praying with Jack in the morning. No more anything."

"Anne, for the first time in my life I'm really at a loss for words. Maybe God's words will help. Remember when Patti Waring's son died last year? Even though she realized that he wasn't going to survive cystic fibrosis, she still struggled with her grief, like any mother would. You selected the verse to discuss that week."

"I remember. It was something like don't worry or don't let your heart be something. I can't remember the whole verse."

"I think it was 'Do not let your heart be troubled.' It became Patti's mantra."

"Oh, yeah, that's it, 'Do not let your heart be troubled.' "

Claire stood in front of her friend and put a hand on each shoulder to give emphasis to her words. She stared intently into Anne's lavender eyes and gently swayed her back and forth.

"Anne, do not let your heart be troubled. God will get you through this. Do not let your heart be troubled."

Anne pulled away from Claire. Brimming over with anger, resentment, and grief, she slammed her fist on the counter top. "After the funeral, I'm not praying anymore. I'll do the visitation, the Mass, and we'll have the wake, but after that, I'm done praying. I'm just done. Why me? Well, Jack's not here now to get me through this 'why me.' I'll have to figure it out."

"You don't have to figure it out today. After the funeral, you'll be able to think more clearly. God will help you to deal with all of this. I know you-- you want this bab..."

Before Claire could finish her sentence, Anne blurted, "Don't start telling me to have this baby, Claire. You don't understand."

Claire was flustered, but continued, "Anne, you and I have always been pro-life. We planned to go to the March for Life in Washington in January, for God's sake. How can you even consider this?"

"Shut-up, Claire."

"I'm not going to shut-up. This is serious stuff. What about *'You knit me together in my mother's womb?'* What about *'Before I formed you in the womb, I knew you?'* What do you think that means? Please, please listen to me."

"You don't get it, Claire. You can't possibly understand what it feels like to lose a baby you want. And you certainly don't understand what it feels like to be expecting a baby you don't want!"

"I know you had it rough early in your marriage with three miscarriages, hon."

For a moment, Anne seemed to be calm and composed. "Claire, if Jack were here, I'd be able to handle this. It didn't matter to him that we were having a baby with Down's syndrome. He said our baby was one of God's perfect imperfections and that we should feel privileged to be the parents. That all changed yesterday and I do not feel privileged at all."

"But, you know it's a baby – Jack's and yours!"

Anne was agitated. She paced back and forth in the kitchen. "Those babies I lost twenty years ago were babies, too. Weren't they mine and Jack's? Didn't they have a right to live? But they died. Call it what you want – abortion, miscarriage – what difference does it make?"

Claire stared at her. Jack was gone and the look of sorrow covered Anne's face, but a different expression, one of anguish and torture put a gray pallor around her eyes. Finally, Anne sat down.

"And, don't you dare discuss this with anyone. Thank God, I'm thin and not showing yet. Kevin doesn't know I'm pregnant and he doesn't have to."

"Anne, you know I won't tell anyone about the pregnancy."

"Good and you don't have to tell anyone about the abortion, either. That's the only help I need. Please go, Claire. I've got a million things to do."

Claire choked back her tears. She knew Anne was in pain, but the icy sting of her words hurt deeply.

"I'm sorry if I sound harsh, but I really don't need any more pressure right now. Gotta pickup Kevin and then go to the church. I'll see you at the funeral home Thursday morning."

While Anne was locking-up the house, Claire bolted out the door and walked as fast as she could to her home, choking back her tears. Her mind was racing with confusion and guilt, *Why didn't I shut-up and listen?* She was thankful no one was home. She went to bed sobbing into the pillow.

Chapter 4 : Endings

Jeff was at graduation rehearsal when his Dad arrived home at 7 pm. The house was stone silent. "Claire, are you home?" As he walked into their bedroom, he was at first alarmed to see her in bed and rushed to her side. "Claire, are you okay?" She rolled over and sat up. Chet saw that her face was puffy and red. "You don't look good. What's wrong?"

"Nothing. I was crying. What time is it?"

"It's 7 pm. Something's going on."

"Can you get me a glass of water, please?" Claire gulped the water and sighed heavily.

"Chet, Anne said something yesterday that makes my skin crawl. I'm sorry, I should have told you last night."

"What? What did she tell you?"

"She mentioned something about getting an abortion. She's in this horrible mindset."

"Jack told me she's always been fragile. We both know she's not too good at handling a crisis."

"Especially with Jack gone. She's not thinking straight and we had a real blowout about the baby today. That's why I was crying. I mean she was yelling at me. Things like 'Don't you dare discuss this with anyone. Kevin doesn't know I'm pregnant and he doesn't have to.' "

"What did you say?"

"I said, 'Anne, you know I won't tell anyone about the pregnancy.' Then she screamed, 'Good and you don't have to tell anyone about the abortion, either.' I left and ran all the way home. I cried until I fell asleep. What a mess. Nothing I said to her sunk in, but I wished I hadn't talked with her about it so soon after Jack's death."

"I'm sure she'll calm down. You two will talk it through and Annie will have the baby. Of course, we'll help her any way we can."

"I hope you're right, Chet."

"Let it rest for a day or two. Let's get everyone through the funeral and the wake, okay?"

"You're right.  I'm going to take a shower.  Jeff will be home soon.  I really don't feel like cooking dinner tonight and it's late anyway.  There's chicken and potato salad in the fridge."

––––––––––––––––

On Friday, May 14th Angel of God Church was packed with high school students, friends, and the many relatives of Jack Edward Combs.   The Mass was solemn and sad, and tears flowed.

Anne's six brothers along with Chet and Jeff rolled the flag-covered casket up the long aisle of Angel of God Church, packed with friends, relatives, and many of the graduating class of McNichols High School.

Jeannie had arrived from Chicago the night before.  As she sat in the pew holding her Mother's hand, she felt a weird curiosity, an uncomfortable anticipation to see how grief had altered Anne's face.  When Jeannie first met Mrs. Combs, she thought she was the most beautiful woman she had ever seen.  Of course, she never revealed this to her own Mother.  Ten-year-old Jeannie secretly loved the fact that Mrs. Combs did not have a girl.  When she visited Mrs. Combs, she pretended she was her daughter.

The organ played an intro to the opening song.  The procession began.  Fr. Hernandez stood at the foot of the altar facing the pallbearers as they rolled Jack's casket down the aisle.  Anne and Kevin followed behind in solemn step. When they passed the fourth pew, Jeannie leaned into her Mom.  "Oh my gosh, Mom, Anne looks awful.   Is she sick?"

Claire whispered, "She just lost her husband, Jeannie. She's grieving."

"It's more than that, Mom.  She looks like she's possessed or something."

"Shhh.  She'll be okay.  She's been through a lot this week."

"Okay, but, I'm just saying this is more than a look of grief.  She looks like a vampire sucked out her blood."

"Jeannie, shhh!  Mass is starting." Claire could only attribute Jeannie's insight to woman's intuition.

Chapter 4 : Endings

*Anne does look horrible. There's no way Jeannie knows about her pregnancy, but she sees the same grotesque shadow that I see in Anne's face. And it is more than grief.*

The Mass was beautiful, rich with ritual and solemnity. Anne's oldest brother, Fulton, haltingly read Psalm 23:

***A psalm of David. The response is 'Though I walk in the valley of darkness, I fear no evil, for you are with me.' The LORD is my shepherd; there is nothing I lack. In green pastures he makes me lie down; to still waters he leads me; he restores my soul. He guides me along right paths for the sake of his name. Even though I walk through the valley of the shadow of death, I will fear no evil, for you are with me; your rod and your staff comfort me. You set a table before me in front of my enemies; You anoint my head with oil; my cup overflows. Indeed, goodness and mercy will pursue me all the days of my life; I will dwell in the house of the Lord for endless days.***

After the final response, Fulton returned to his seat, lovingly touching Anne's shoulder as he passed her pew.

Fr. Hernandez read the gospel that Anne had requested and then delivered an eloquent sermon:

"The Gospel according to John…

***Do not let your hearts be troubled. You have faith in God; have faith also in me. In my Father's house there are many dwelling places. If there were not, would I have told you that I am going to prepare a place for you? And if I go and prepare a place for you, I will come back again and take you to myself, so that where I am you also may be. Where (I) am going you know the way. Thomas said to him, Master, we do not know where you are going; how can we know the way? Jesus said to him, I am the way and the truth and the life. No one comes to the Father except through me. If you know me, then you will also know my Father. From now on you do know him and have seen him…If you ask the Father anything of me in my name, He will do it.'***

"When Jesus sat at the table eating his last supper, he gave his apostles a powerful message of Faith, 'And if I go and prepare a place for you, I will come back again and take you to myself, so that where I am you also may be.'"

"When we lose a loved one, when we lost Jack on Monday, we should cling to Jesus's words of faith, hope, and love. For in his promises we find comfort. In his profound assurance – 'I am the way, the truth and the life.'"

At the end of the sermon, Fr. Hernandez turned his eyes toward Anne. "As you remember the loving moments you had with Jack as a husband, father, son, and friend, you will also undoubtedly feel the pain of your loss. But do not forget what Jesus tells his apostles and he tells us, 'Do not let your hearts be troubled' for he has prepared a place for you, each of you. And though we leave here today with burdensome sorrow in our hearts, we have faith in Jesus's words, 'I will come back again and take you to myself, so that where I am you also may be.'"

At the Communion, the choir sang *'On Eagle's Wings.'* Tears trickled down the cheeks of women and the young high school girls. Many of the men looked down in somber sadness. Some swatted tears from their eyes, uncomfortable with their grief.

Before the final blessing, Fr. Hernandez nodded to Chet to begin the eulogy.

Chet walked in firm step to the pulpit, holding his speech in one hand and reading glasses in the other. He placed the one-page eulogy on the podium, held his fist to his mouth, coughed, put on his glasses, and took a deep breath.

"Jack Edward Combs –loving husband to Anne, devoted father to Kevin, caring son to Myrtle, and fine brother-in-law to Anne's six brothers. Jack was also a Captain in the United States Air Force, having served in the Gulf War, and since 1995 served as Director of Recruitment in Cincinnati. Our family is very close to each member of the Combs family. And now Jack is gone. So, our lives have changed. But, as Father said, 'Do not let your hearts be troubled.'

There isn't enough time to tell the entire story of Jack, but I have a few memories that will give you an insight into the kind of man he was. Jack coached football here at Angel of God when our sons were ten years old. They didn't win every game, but every kid got a chance to play. They learned how to play football and they learned how to be a team. Another example of how Jack lived -- in 2002, Hallowed was hit with a devastating storm. Jack was a really good carpenter and he didn't hesitate to bring his tools to repair the homes that were destroyed that year…no charge. He was generous with his time.

Chapter 4 : Endings

Jack and I were on the first Emmaus Retreat team. He could be very persuasive when it came to his Faith and he pretty much twisted my arm to attend that year. He helped me through some rough spots in my life – he knows what they are."

Chet looked up at the ceiling and choked a little, remembering Jack helping Claire and him stay together in 1998.

"I've known Jack for fifteen years and we had many good times together. I learned a lot from him, sometimes just from the way he treated people. He was a joyful guy and made every moment count, especially those moments with Anne and Kevin. They will miss him. I miss him. Jack thanks for being my friend."

As Fr. Hernandez swung the silver ball of incense around the casket, he solemnly blessed the body of Jack Edward Combs. The organ sounded opening notes of the final song. As the choir sang *Amazing Grace,* the pallbearers rolled the casket down the aisle in front of Fr. Hernandez. Anne and Kevin walked slowly behind the priest; Jeannie and Claire followed. Claire could see Anne's legs wobbling and motioned to Jeannie to assist. Most of the attendees were silent, but the high school students started chattering once outside.

Thirty-six cars with little purple flags, denoting they were part of the procession exited Angel of God Church to proceed to Angel of God cemetery one-half mile away. The participants walked briskly to the freshly-dug cemetery plot with a large mound of dirt next to it covered with a tarp. Spring trees were still not in full leaf yet, and the noon sun beat down strong beams of heat. Men in suits had sweat trickling down their temples. Women fanned themselves with tissues.

The ceremony was short, but felt like eternity for those in attendance. At the end, Anne kissed the casket saying private words of good by to Jack. She pulled one of the white roses from the bouquet and walked away with Claire and Chet on each side of her. Kevin also took one of the roses and then lightly punched the casket as though he and his Dad were sharing friendly fists. The funeral director said gently but firmly, "Ladies and gentlemen, this concludes our services." Then it was over. Jack would actually be buried a few hours later by the custodians. The wind whooshed underneath one edge of the tarp sending small twirls of soil onto the grass and sometimes the shoes of the mourners as they quietly walked away from the graveyard. All of the dots between the hours of Jack's life had been defined.

**Jack Edward Combs**
**Born September 10, 1954**
**Died, Monday, May 10, 2010**
**Buried, Friday, May 14, 2010.**

Afterward, the wake was held at the Combs' home with food, wine and beer provided by neighbors under Claire's direction.

Of course, there were tales of the Gulf War and Anne's brothers shared happy memories of Jack. Anne and Kevin graciously accepted condolences and praises of Jack throughout the wake.

By 5:00 p.m. all the guests were gone. After cleaning up the house, Chet, Jeannie, and Jeff also left. Claire told them she would walk home.

She hugged Anne. "Do you want me to stay for a little while?"

"I'm exhausted. I'll be okay, really."

Anne guided Claire out the front door, closing it so Kevin could not hear their conversation. They stood quietly on the porch absorbing the warm May sunset. The flowers along the sidewalk were beautiful and the smell of red roses hung in the evening air.

"Anne, you know I'll help you with anything, don't you?"

"I do, but I need a little space for a while. Let's get together after the boys graduate. I really want to focus on Kevin and make his graduation as meaningful as it can be. I'm sorry about my outburst this week."

"Well, I think you had a good reason to be upset. Anyway… not to worry. We were both pretty emotional. That's putting it mildly. We were over the top." Claire put her arm around Anne and pulled her close. "Anne, you were unfaltering this week for Kevin and for Jack's family too. I admire your courage. And, I know you have the courage to get through the…" Claire hesitated.

Anne finished the sentence, "the pregnancy? I don't want to go there right now."

Chapter 4 : Endings

"I understand. You're exhausted. Let's have coffee in the morning and talk then."

Anne bristled. She looked down at the flowers and sighed. Claire saw the toll of the last few days on her friend's face, tired and drained of emotion. "Please stop pushing," Anne cautioned gently.

"Okay, I don't want to hurt you or make you feel any worse. We can talk after graduation. This can wait."

They hugged and Claire walked home, second-guessing the conversation and then rationalizing her comment, 'This can wait.'

*Okay, maybe I should have pushed to see her sooner. But, waiting until after graduation gives me time to get information for her. I'll go online and find options, maybe even adoption. I'll talk with Laura Stedman at Pregnancy Center East. I know she'll have good ideas. Maybe giving Anne space is what's needed and it gives me time to get my ducks lined up. Then, hopefully, I can convince her to have this child. This can wait, this can wait.*

Claire arrived home exhausted and depleted, but she slept well that night. She had a liberating relief about Anne. She could put the conversation in abeyance and enjoy Jeff's graduation activities.

---

Kevin and Jeff graduated on Wednesday, May 19. They decided to take that camping trip after all and left the following day for Moundview Campground. It was exactly as they had remembered it when they had gone camping with their Dads on Memorial Day weekend 2009. Their campsite was positioned ten feet above the Little Miami River and at night the dark sky opened up wide with large clusters of stars splayed across the canvas. Jeff and Kevin cooked hot dogs and beans for dinner and settled down by the campfire.

Jeff had finagled enough beer to have three each per night.

After opening their third beer, Jeff said, "It's colder than it usually is this time of year. Remember, last year? It was really hot at night."

"Yeah, I remember."

"Sorry, Kev. I wasn't thinking."

"It's okay. I think about him all the time anyway."

"Yeah, I guess I would, too."

"Kev, do you ever think about why we're here? I mean like..."

"What's the point?"

"Yeah, what's the point of doing the right thing? My Dad was the best. My Mom needs him. I miss him. I don't think I even want to go to college now."

"Why?"

"Well, for one thing it's expensive and Mom only has a part time job. But mostly, I don't feel like there's any reason to go. I wish this knot in my stomach would go away. My Mom's a mess, too. She's walks around all day in a daze, saying 'Let not your heart be troubled.' I can't stand it."

"Well, you don't have to make a decision until late in the summer. Maybe you'll feel differently then."

"Maybe, but I doubt it. Like I said...what's the point?"

"My Dad said that our choices on Earth determine where we go when we die – Heaven or Hell."

"Well, if there is a Heaven, I think my Dad would get in. Hey, man, I'm really tired and I have to take a leak before we get in the tent.

As they walked toward the trees, Jeff pointed to the sky. "Kev, look at that star to the left of the moon. Man, it's bright."

"Maybe it's a planet."

"No, I think it's a star."

"And that means?"

"It's definitely a star and maybe it's a sign, you know like the Three Wise Men."

"There's only two of us, dope."

"Hey, we've come here a lot over the years, but I've never seen a star that bright. I was thinking it might be your Dad's way of being with us this year. "

Chapter 4 : Endings

They walked quietly back to the fire. Kevin didn't say a word for several minutes. Jeff fumbled for a stick to insert into his third empty beer can. Then he placed it on the last flicker of fire, watching it slowly melt into the embers.

Finally, Kevin responded. "Jeff, you don't have to makeup a dumb fantasy about a star in the sky followed by The Three Wise men to try to make me feel better. Nothing's going to bring my Dad back and pretending a star is his way of being with me is downright stupid."

"Okay, sorry. I know you were thinking about him and I wanted to …"

"Well, don't. It doesn't help."

"Okay."

"Thanks for trying. It's not you. It's me. I feel numb since Dad died. You know, like, someone sucked out who I am."

"I hear you, Kev. No more pie in the sky stories."

"Thanks. Wow, I'm tired. Let's get some sleep. The fish'll be biting in the morning."

Jeff entered the tent first.

Kevin watched the dying embers. He cried into his shirt sleeve. Then he stared at the brightest star and whispered, "Goodnight, Dad."

## CHAPTER 5 : ANNIE'S DARK IMPULSE

The day after Jack's funeral, after she had promised Claire to discuss her options for the baby; after crying for hours in bed and in the shower; after picking up the phone several times to call Claire, but not doing it; after vomiting every time she ate something; and after she had drained her heart and soul of joy, Anne made an appointment with Dr. Blanco to arrange the abortion. Anne chose May 22. Graduation would be over and Kevin would be camping with Jeff.

Dr. Blanco examined Anne on May 20. "You should be fine with this procedure and I'm in total agreement with you, Anne. Raising a Down syndrome child is a huge challenge. Sorry, to hear about your husband. He was a swell guy."

"Thank you."

"You still may want to consider sterilization in about six months. Of course, you should give yourself a little time to heal from the abortion. Then, we can take care of that problem."

Anne stared at him in disbelief, "My husband just died. I'm not really interested in that procedure."

"Well, you might be later. You're a very beautiful woman. In any event, I'm sending you to the Clifton Planned Parenthood facility in Cincinnati. Your appointment is 9 am on Saturday, May 22. Do you have someone who can drive you?"

"No, I'm driving myself there."

"Well, I don't anticipate any complications. Whole thing takes less than two hours, but if there is a problem, please call a friend or at least grab a taxi."

"I'll be okay. I want to get this over with."

"Well, then, good luck, Anne. Give me a call if you need anything. I'll order a pain prescription just in case. Remember what I said about that preventive procedure. Make an appointment with me around November and we can get that scheduled for you. Have a good day, Anne."

Anne almost ran out of Dr. Blanco's office. She felt defiled and angry, but was still determined to get the abortion. *After Saturday, I will be free of all of this. I'll bedone with the worry. I'll never have to see that creep again. This will finally put an end to the problem.*

Anne allowed an older female doctor to abort Jack's and her baby child on Saturday, May 22.

Claire called Anne on Sunday, May 23. "Hey, Anne, want to have lunch today? Chet's out for the day. I really want to see you before the guys come back from camping. It's been crazy the past week and I want to help you through this. Do you feel up to talking?"

Anne responded abruptly, "I don't feel well today."

"Do you want me to come over? The last time we talked, too much was happening. I still want to talk with you about the baby. There are other alternatives."

There was a momentary silence, and then Anne said in a whisper, "Claire, there is no baby."

"What do you mean 'there is no baby?'"

"I had the abortion yesterday."

Claire fumbled through "I'm sorry" and then said goodbye. As painful as it was remembering their volatile conversation the day after Jack died, this news placed a gripping knot in her stomach. *Why didn't I call sooner? Why didn't I say something?*

After that day, Anne and Claire no longer spent much time together. They would see each other at the library or the grocery store and were friendly, but uncomfortable.

Although ending their friendship was heartbreaking, what neither Claire nor Anne knew was that ending a baby's life would bring evil and terror to both of them.

# CHAPTER 6 ARIEL

Claire's oxygen tube provided her with deep and steady breathing. Chet noticed that beneath the eyelids, her eyes were moving quickly. *She must be dreaming.* The rapid eye movement gave him hope that at least her brain was functioning even if it was only in her dreams. Chet pulled a chair close to Claire's bed. He sat down putting his hands over his face praying, "Please, God, bring her out of this coma. Please bring her back to us."

Chet held Claire's hand in both of his. The medicinal and oppressive smells of the Intensive Care Unit took him back to 1975 when he was in a mental hospital in Dallas, Texas. In 1975 at the age of 23, Chet could attract any woman with his handsome physique, dreamy eyes, and long black hippie-style hair. Women were drawn to him, and he to them, even after he had married Claire. His downward spiral culminated in the Beverly Hills Hospital Psych Ward in Dallas, Texas far from the life he had with Claire. The fear, the paranoia, the distrust, the craziness – all self-induced with the help of LSD – brought Chet to his knees that year. He would not be alive today if Claire had not come to Dallas.

*Why did she come? Thank God she came. Thank God I finally realized I was running away from responsibility. We wouldn't have Jeannie or Jeff or the marriage we have right now if Claire had not commandeered my rescue in Dallas. God, she was only twenty-two years old when all that happened.*

Claire stirred slightly. Chet hoped to see more movement, but did not.

"Let her live, God. Please let her live."

---

Claire smelled baby's breath as Zimelda tapped her on the shoulder, "Come with me, Claire. I want you to meet someone."

Claire followed Zimelda down the hallway for what seemed an eternity. At last she stopped in front of an amazing green door. As the door opened, Claire stared in disbelief. The room was filled with beautiful angels. Angels with ivory wings floating in cool green mist. Some of the angels waited for their newborn assignment, excited, but anxious.

Chapter 6 Ariel

Some angels waited very quietly.  They had a solemn look of subdued expectation.  Their wings were outstretched, as if waiting for a fragile delivery.  Each guardian angel is given the task of guiding a person from the moment of conception to life's end.  However, those angels who are chosen to guide aborted babies have a much different task to fulfill.

Other angels were busy, either leaving or entering.  Even with the excited bustle of the angels, their activities seemed to have a quiet rhythm and definite purpose.  Zimelda gently nudged Claire to move her along.  She was perplexed when Zimelda said, "I will be leaving you for a while, but you are in the arms of someone who loves you almost as much as God loves you.  This is Ariel, your Guardian Angel."  With that Zimelda left the room.

Ariel surrounded Claire with her wings in a loving embrace.  Claire could feel her angel's strength and power.  And yet, her arms and legs were free to move with no hindrance from the embrace.  She experienced only comfort and security simply floating in and out of Ariel's encirclement.

"I've felt this way before, Ariel, especially when I was a little girl."

"Of course you did.  God sent me to be with you the moment you were conceived.  I've been at your side ever since.  The day you were conceived is also the day that I became an angel.  I only exist because you exist.  That's how God creates the bond of guardian angels with humans.  And that is what you see in The Angels' Room of Life.  Guardian Angels tending to the one soul God has entrusted to them.  You see, Claire, the scripture that humans read is the truth."

*In Psalm 91 God gives angels His mandate in one sentence:  'For to his angels he has given command that they guard you in all your ways.'*

"We have the privilege to guide one child on Earth and then return that child to the Father when it's time…hopefully."

In a very brief moment of time, Claire drifted back to her childhood in 1968.

*This is Hallowed, but it's the way it was when I grew up here-- exactly as I remember it.  There's the old library.*

Claire pressed her face against the library's side window.

*And there's Mrs. Winniback. Uh-oh, when she runs her hands through her thick red hair, someone's in trouble.*

Mrs. Winniback pursed her lips and brought an index finger to her mouth, chiding a young boy for talking in the library.

*That's so quaint. Everybody talks in the library now. This must be a dream, but I'm already in a dream. A dream within a dream? I don't care. This is fun. I'm going to Allen's Apothecary to get my usual treats.*

Patti and Susie sat at the fountain twirling around on the red plastic bar stools.

"Hi, Claire Bear. Where've you been? We already ordered. Hurry up. Tell Mr. Allen what you want."

Claire slowly slid onto the chair next to Patti. She could smell cough syrup and candy and soda pop. At the back of the store one of Mr. Allen's employees was opening boxes of magazines and cotton balls and all kinds of things sold in a drugstore. The dust from the mail boxes floated up to the fluorescent light bulbs.

"What can I get for you, Miss?"

"A root beer, two pretzels, and a French Chew, please."

"That'll be eleven cents."

Claire was amazed to find a dime and a penny in her pocket and handed it to Mr. Allen.

*Good old Mr. Allen. He was a pharmacist, but he still took time to wait on customers at the soda fountain, even the teenagers like us who spun around on his chairs talking nonsense.*

"What are you drinking, Patti?"

"I am deviating from the usual, Claire. I'm having a vanilla soda."

"Oh, I've never tried that. Can I have a sip of yours?"

"Sure."

Mr. Allen put a napkin on the counter, placing pretzels and the French Chew on it. Claire stared as he poured thick root beer syrup into a large glass mug, adding clear soda to give it the fizz.

Chapter 6 Ariel

"Patti, Susie…look at that! They use real syrup here for the drinks."

"They always do, Claire. How else is it done?"

"Mmmm. I haven't had my three favorite treats in such a long time. Ouch, why'd you throw ice at me, Patti?"

"Because you are acting like a crazy person. We were in here two days ago and you had pretzels, root beer, and a French Chew. You really think forty-eight hours ago is a long time?"

"Girls, behave. Don't throw the ice."

Each of the girls sipped the very last ounce of their drinks, trying to outdo each other with slurping sounds. Mr. Allen shook his head, but Claire caught his lips turning upward in a smile.

"Susie, are you going to the tower with us."

"No, I'm going home now. I have to babysit at 4 pm."

"Okay, see you tomorrow at practice. C'mon, Claire, let's go to the tower. Bring your French Chew with you."

"Eckert's Five & Dime, the old Kerger grocery store, Mr. Pepper's bike shop, Skyway Chili."

"What are you doing, Claire?"

"I'm reciting the names of the stores."

"Why?"

"So, I can remember them when I get older."

"Jeesh, you are weird today."

"Let's go to the side of the tower that faces Stanberry Park. The sun's shining there now. It'll be warmer."

"Did you see that? Over in the park. Jackie Hamilton and Tommy Matson are kissing. She acts like she's such a goodie two shoes, but look at that."

"Aah, Patti, give it up. We're not allowed to date yet anyway. Wow, 172 feet up. I wonder how many French Chews it would take to stretch them up the tower?"

"And her parents have lots of money, too. I hate her."

"Hey, look at this. I've got it stretched above my head, almost a foot. So, I'd only need 172 French Chews to reach the top if I stretched each of them to one foot."

"Claire Bear, you've been in the sun too long. Let's go home."

The two friends pumped their old bikes as fast as they could down the hill by the tower.

"Claire, your bike looks nice. I like the paint job."

"I am the fourth girl in my family to ride this bike. Dad painted it blue, my favorite color, but it's not shiny like normal bikes. Susie's bike is brand new."

"It's an English, right?"

"Yeah, and she thinks she's faster because she rides better than us, but it's only because she has a new bike."

"Well, at least you have a girl's bike. Tommy Matson told me I should change my name to Patrick because I got my brother's ugly red bike with rust all over it."

"Aah, he's nobody and he's not very smart either. All he does is listen to the Beatles. Well, here's Gladden. I go left and you go right. Hey, call me tonight. I'll tell you what Susie told me about Tommy Matson."

"Tell me now."

"No, I gotta get home. It's almost dinnertime."

Claire peddled as fast as she could on the inherited bike. She looked back once, but Patti was gone.

---

*Great, the forsythia bushes are in bloom. This is my home – 6417 Gladden Avenue. I love the graveled driveway. I love the sound it makes when I walk on the rocks. Four steps and I'm on the front porch. Hmm, Mom's got her sweet pea vines growing on the trellis already. They smell wonderful. She's got Baby's Breath growing, too. I love the smell of flowers and dirt.*

The front door was ajar inviting Claire to explore. As she carefully opened the screen door, she heard the familiar whine of the unoiled hinges.

Chapter 6 Ariel

*That old door still squeaks like a cat stuck in a tree. Daddy never did fix it. I think he wanted it to make noise. That way he knew when his daughters got home from a date.*

"Anybody home?"

*The living room looks the same. The green couch and the old black and white TV. Ugh, and those ugly pink lamps with black dots on them. Mom didn't want to hurt Dad's feelings when he bought them for her.*

As Claire entered the dining room, she could hear the hum of the aquarium.

"Ooh, Charley has eight fish. Tap, tap. Hello, fish. See you later. I'm going upstairs."

As Claire entered the hallway at the bottom of the stairs, she heard the phone ring. She instinctively grabbed the receiver and sat on the third step.

"Hello. Yeah, I just got home. What's up? No, I'm not mad at you. I was pretending about all that stuff. I wanted you to think I was crazy. It's a joke, Patti. Okay, here's the scoop. Susie said that Marilyn told her that Jackie's in big trouble with her parents, because they caught her and TM making out in the…"

"Get off the phone, Claire. I'm expecting a call from Grandma Dillon."

"Darn. I have to get off. When Mary Margaret says 'get off the phone,' she means now! I'll call you as soon as I can."

Claire hung up the phone and then leaped up the steps two at a time, anxious to see her bedroom. Well, it wasn't exactly her bedroom. She shared it with four of her sisters.

First she stopped in the hallway. Across from the hall window stood the v-shaped corner cabinet made of beautiful dark walnut. The surface was small but had large mirrors on each side. Claire loved those mirrors because she could admire herself in duplicate or she could lean in and see both her back and front simultaneously.

I think I'm pretty, not beautiful, but very pretty. I can't wait to start high school! Wow, Mom finished the bedspreads. They're beautiful -- purple and pink and green. Dad wallpapered the room, too. And lavender curtains.

Claire heard someone coming up the stairs. She knew it was her sister, Stephanie, from the bounce of both feet jumping up each of the steps.

"Stephie, hurry, come see our room. Isn't this beautiful. By the way, Mom changed the sleeping partners. I get to sleep with Tara and you get to sleep with Caroline. Mom said Dee Dee gets her own bed now."

Claire turned on the radio slowly moving the knob until she found WJLM, the station that played the top 40. She was excited to hear the harmony of The Beatles and began to sing along with them.

"I want to hold your haaaaand, I want to hold your hand." She held both of Stephie's hands in hers and began to twirl around and around. "I love the Beatles. I love this song. I love this bedroom. I'm home, Stephie. I'm home again!"

"Stop, Claire, I'm getting dizzy."

Stephie was only eleven years old and didn't really understand Claire's teenage-driven dramatics. She finally broke free, bolted down the steps and ran out the front door to play. Claire ended up on her back on the bed staring at the flowers on the wallpaper spinning out of control.

*6417 Gladden Avenue. Two bedrooms -- nine children. How did Mom keep it clean and tidy?*

As always, Claire was drawn to the smells of the kitchen -- breaded pork chops sizzling in the cast iron skillet, mashed potatoes with simmering melted butter on top, and of course the mandatory green vegetable and salad. But the best of all was the aroma of cinnamon sugar syrup bubbling over in the oven.

*Mmmm...apple pie for dessert.*

As Claire entered the kitchen, her mother, Mary Margaret, in a pink house dress with a flowered apron, was bent over checking the pies she was baking. She closed the door and turned around to see Claire.

"Well, hello, little miss sunshine. How was school today? Only two more weeks and you're out for the summer."

Claire pulled the lid off the skillet. "Be careful when you pull the lid off that cast iron skillet, hon. Breaded pork chops give off a lot of steam."

Chapter 6 Ariel

"Mmmm, Mom, you make the best pork chops. You've got mashed potatoes, right? You gotta have mashed potatoes with pork chops."

"Here's a spoonful with butter on it." Claire licked the spoon as she opened the oven door.

"Claire, how many times have I told you not to open the oven when I'm baking? It lets out the heat and lowers the temperature."

"Okay, Mom, but I absolutely have to smell your apple pies. Are they done, yet?"

"I think so. Let me get to them, missy. They need to cool."

"I love that dress on you and the flowered apron. You look very pretty."

"Okay, Claire, what's on your mind? You've got something up your sleeve. Are you flattering your mother because somebody's birthday is coming soon? I think it's in June, isn't it?"

"Mom, really, you know when I was born." Claire leaned against the kitchen doorway. "Mom?"

"Yes."

"Mom, can I have a party for my friends, just my friends, not Stephie's or Tara's? I'm going to be fourteen. I'm starting high school. I'll do all the work."

"Blow on it a minute. It's too hot. Let me think about the party, Claire. We might be able to have it outside. We'll see. Now go wakeup your father and tell him we're eating dinner in fifteen minutes."

*I know she'll let me have the party. I know it. Mmmm, Mom's apple pie. Heaven.*

Claire could see her father stretched out on the living room floor with a fan at his feet.

"Long work day, huh, Dad? I don't know why you sleep on the floor in the living room, but you sure make it look comfortable. I think I'll try it."

Claire lay beside her Dad. She could smell Old Spice cologne and then leaned over to place her cheek on his face. The whiskers scratched a little, but Claire didn't mind.

"Gosh, Dad, I remember. I remember how you worked for the city and had a second job wallpapering houses. How did you do it? How did you and Mom do any of it? Thank you, Dad."

Carl yawned, squinted his eyes, and held his head on his elbow.

"Hi, Claire. Oh, I must have been snoozing. Why are you laughing, kiddo? What's funny?"

"Snoozing. I loved when you said that word. Nobody says that anymore. "Mom said to wake you up. Dinner's ready in fifteen minutes."

"Okay, I'll be out. Smells like pork chops."

---

Without even a step, Claire realized she was sitting under the old oak tree in the front yard.

*I don't know how I'm seeing all of this, but I love being back on Gladden Avenue in the summer. Wow, that's where the Dannon boys lived. We'd play kick the can or whiffle ball almost every evening in the summer. Oh yeah, I loved sports -- tennis, kickball, and my favorite, baseball.*

"Hi, Bud. Why are you here? Oh, that's right. I'm somewhere out there."

"Hey, squirt, the Reds play the Pirates tonight. Want to listen on the radio in the garage? It's on at 8 pm."

"Sure. I'll pop some popcorn and make Kool-Aid. Bud?"

"Yeah,"

"Thanks for giving me your glove. I caught two pop-ups with it today."

"Way to go, Claire."

"When did Spike come back?"

"What do you mean 'when did Spike come back?' He's been here since I was six years old. You been sniffing airplane glue?"

"No, but I haven't seen him in a while."

Chapter 6 Ariel

"Your brain's been fried in the sun then. Claire, get that tennis ball over there."

"Here you go."

"Good throw for a girl. C'mon, Spike. Go get it, boy."

"Hey, wait for me, Bud."

Claire ran as fast as she could, following them to the back yard, but Bud and Spike were gone. She returned to the oak tree. As she leaned against the tree she heard someone giggling on the other side. Claire quietly tiptoed to where the little girl was hiding.

"Gotcha, Annie Madison!"

Annie shrieked and jumped into Claire's arms, wrapping her long legs around her back.

"You scared me, Claire."

"Oh, for gosh sakes, get down please. You're such a ninny baby!"

"Am not. Hey, Claire, look."

"Oooh, you lost a front tooth. Did the tooth fairy come?"

"This morning."

"How much?"

"A quarter."

"That's a lot of money."

Annie was a beautiful child with straight blonde hair that flowed to the middle of her back. Claire had been Annie's big sister mentor for the past nine months. Even though Claire loved her own five sisters, she had a special fondness for Annie and empathized with the little girl who had six brothers and no sisters. Annie was very quiet.

"Brother problems?"

Annie whispered, "No. "

"Tired of school?"

"No."

"So, what is it, Annie? You seem to be sad."

Annie started twisting strands of her hair around and around until it was one long, tight spiral. As she held the end of it to keep it from unwinding, she waved the tangled locks back and forth across her face.

"I'm not s'pose to tell."

"Then you better not."

Annie quickly unraveled her hair, fluffing it behind her ears. "Claire, will you put my hair in a real braid?"

"Sure, sit down in front of me."

"It's hard to braid your own hair, Annie. In fact, it's almost an impossibility. Tara used to braid mine for me."

"It must be nice to have sisters."

"Sometimes, but I think it might be nice to be the only girl in a family."

"You mean, like me?"

"Yeah, like you. You don't have to wear hand-me-downs. You have your own bed to sleep in. Everybody lets you go first."

"There, braiding is completed, but I don't have a rubber band to hold the bottom. It's only going to last a short time. Don't mess with it, okay?"

"Okay. Claire, I really do want to tell you."

"You mean the thing you're not suppose to tell me?"

Anne picked up a stick, pounding it against the ground. She shook her head back and forth in anger. Claire firmly grasped Anne's hands to stop the outburst. In the past nine months of mentoring Annie, Claire had never seen her so distraught. It wasn't ninny-baby stuff. Even at the young age of fourteen, Claire knew this was genuine heartache.

"Okay, Annie, you can tell me. I won't tell anyone else."

Annie turned slightly to look up at Claire. She had tears on each cheek and her lavender eyes glistened in the sun.

Chapter 6 Ariel

"We have to move far away. My Daddy's gotta go to another city cause he's a captain in the…oh, you know, the place where soldiers live."

"The United States Army."

"Yeah. And we have to go with him. Momma's crying. Oh, Claire, I don't want to move to Texas. I want you to be my real big sister."

"Now, Annie, you know that can't happen. Your Mom and Dad and brothers would all miss you. Turn around. Let me fix your braid. It's coming loose already."

Claire pushed her nose into the back of Annie's head and kissed her.

"Annie, it'll be okay. I'll miss you, too, but things happen for a reason. You may not understand it right now, but my Mom says that to me whenever things are not working out. And, most of the time she's right. Hey, I'll never forget you, Annie. You'll always be my little sister in my heart."

"Promise?"

"Promise."

Claire and Annie stood up. Claire wiped the tears from Annie's cheeks and hugged her.

"I hear your Momma calling you, Annie. See you at school on Monday. And, you're really not a ninny baby. You're getting to be a pretty big girl."

"Thanks, Claire. Bye."

"Stay in the yards. Remember count four houses and then you're home."

She watched her run through one yard after another. She could see the long golden braid unwinding as Annie disappeared down the hill of the fourth house.

*Poor kid. I'm going to miss her.*

Then Claire saw her oldest sister, Donna, get off the bus at the corner. Claire started waving to her. When Donna reached the driveway, her heels twisted into the gravel making her wobble slightly.

"Hey, Dee Dee. How was work? Dee Dee, wait till you see the girls' room. Mom finished the bedspreads. Dinner's almost ready. Come over to my tree."

"I'm really tired, Claire. The bus was hot and muggy today. See you at dinner."

While Dee Dee climbed the stairs to the porch, Charley, the oldest of nine pulled into the driveway. Dee Dee heard the loud muffler and turned around.

"Hey, Charley, you bought the car. That is wild. Give me a ride."

"Hop in, Dee, Dee."

"Charley, can I go?"

"Not this time, Claire. Tell Mom we'll be back in ten minutes"

*Okay. One of these days, Dee Dee and Charley are going to realize that I'm not a kid anymore. And Caroline and Tara will too. Charley thinks I'm a ninny baby because I cried at the end of **Old Yellar**.*

*Oh, gosh, there's Caroline and Tara coming home from McNichols High School.*

"Hi, Claire, what are you doing over there by the tree?"

"Just thinking."

"Thinking about what?"

"Well, I haven't started my period yet, Caroline. Seems like everybody else has."

"Not everybody."

"Tara, how old were you when you started?"

"Twelve."

"See what I mean. What if I don't start my period? I'm almost fourteen. I'll be a freak or something."

"You are not a freak. In fact, I heard from a very good source that Jimmy Jones thinks you are really cute. And, he's fifteen years old."

"Not to mention, the Dannon boys next door. Paul and Tommy drool over you."

"Thanks. Anyway, dinner's almost ready and wait till you see the girls' room."

Chapter 6 Ariel

"We already saw it, silly.  Flowered bedspreads, flowered wallpaper, and lavender curtains."

"When did you two see it?  I thought they just finished it today."

Tara and Caroline continued chatting with each other.  Claire heard the screen door open and watched them disappear into the house.  Then, she spotted her three youngest siblings.

"Steph, Karie, Jody.  Come over to the tree.  We'll play hide 'n seek."

"Steph, you're it.  Count to twenty."

"Shhh.  Come with me, Karie.  Jody, go stand behind the trellis on the porch."

"Nineteen, twenty.  Ready or not, here I come."

"Karie, let's make a run for it, okay?"

"Aaaaah.  Safe.  Home free!!!"

"Not fair.   Karie should have to hide on her own. She's seven years old, Claire."

"Too bad, so sad, too bad, so sad."

"Look, Jody fell off the porch."

"It's okay, Jody, don't cry.  Let me look at your knee."

"Does he need a band aid, Claire?"

"I think it's okay, Steph.  Our brave little brother will survive."

"Okay, let's do another round."

"Karie, Stephie's right.  You're seven years old.  You can hide on your own. I'll be it."  "Steph, you take Jody so he doesn't get hurt."

"One, two, three, four, five…….eighteen, nineteen, twenty.  Ready or not, here I come."

Claire waited several minutes, but no one ran to the tree for safety.

*I guess they're gone, too.*

The clouds turned dark and a foreboding fear crept into Claire's heart. As the wind began to chill, she started pulling bark from the oak tree until there were eight pieces on the ground.

"I hate you, oak tree. I'm going to pull off your bark. I want you to hurt, too. There, see, I've cut my leg with your bark. I want it to hurt. I want everyone and everything to hurt like me."

*Please, God, make me not exist. I'm afraid to die, but I don't want to live.*

From the time she was six years old, Claire periodically entered a dark corner of her mind that dragged her very being into a lonely place. There was no apparent reason for it, at least not that anyone knew back then, and she was adept at covering up her secret with a flair of confidence.

In this suspended moment in time, as she relived endearing memories of childhood, she also experienced her world in the graveyard. A cold fog crept in and out of the grave markers. Claire walked slowly touching the tombstones, caressing them as if they belonged to her and she to them. In spite of the sublime lack of joy or energy in this shadowy world, Claire felt that this was where she belonged.

"Claire, we're waiting for you. Dinner's on the table."

"I'm coming, Tara."

*God, do this now, please. If you erase me, I won't feel a thing. And Mom and Dad and everybody else will be okay because I would never have been born in the first place. I want the pain to go away. I hate you, oak tree. I hate me.*

Claire's left leg was scratched and bleeding. She knew she should go in, but she couldn't move.

"Claire, Mom's getting mad. You better come in. She's not going to let you listen to the Reds with me tonight if you don't get in here soon."

"Okay, Bud, I'll be there in one minute."

*Put me in a graveyard, God. Let me be in the cold fog. Let me pound on the gravestones. I don't want anyone around me. I want to disappear off the face of the Earth.*

*What is that? It must be the wind.*

Chapter 6 Ariel

Claire looked up at the trees. Neither limb nor leaf was moving. The eight pieces of bark were back in place on the tree.

"Who did that? My leg's not bleeding anymore. Who's doing this?"

*Thank you, God. I know you've sent my Guardian Angel to help me. 'Ever this day be at my side to light, to guard, to rule, to guide. Amen.'*

Claire, little fourteen-year old Claire, ran to the front porch, climbed the stairs, disappearing into her childhood home to eat dinner with her family.

Ariel was pleased that Claire understood the purpose of this visit to her past joys, hurt, and depression.

*So this is the real reason Ariel sent me back. To understand that she has watched over me and kept me from harm when I sunk into the graveyard. I think I've seen everything I need to see, but there's one more thing I want to hear.*

"Ariel, would it be possible for me to have a last peek into my home at bedtime tonight?"

------

Once again, Claire felt a light wind through her head as if someone were gently separating the strands and caressing each hair on her head.

She stood up and glanced at the upstairs window of the girls' room. She could see the lavender curtains blowing in the summer breeze. Four of the girls were doubled-up in two beds with Dee Dee in one bed. The boys each had a twin bed in the other room. Jody and Karie slept there as well on a trundle bed. Carl and Mary Margaret slept in the living room on a pull-out couch.

In the wind of the oak tree, the final memory of the smells and sounds of childhood beckoned Claire. She closed her eyes, taking in the lingering scent of apple pie, Old Spice cologne, line-dried sheets, and the Sweet Peas on the vines on the trellis. She choked when she heard the 'young' voices of her family saying a litany of good nights in her childhood home at 6417 Gladden Avenue in 1968. Dee Dee always started the good night ritual.

"Mooooooo, mooooo."

The girls giggled. The boys complained.

"Shut-up, Dee Dee."

"Shhh. They're knocking on the downstairs' door."

"Go to sleep, kids. Dee Dee, stop the moo-ing."

In this final suspended moment of childhood Claire listened to the rapid-fire patter of her own voice… "Night, Dad, Mom, Charlie, Dee Dee, Bud, Caroline, Tara, Stephanie, Karie, Jody, Spike."

"Night, Claire."

The light speed journey ceased and Claire was once again in the presence of Ariel. She had countless questions for her Guardian Angel.

"That was incredible, Ariel. I was able to see an entire day of my childhood. And, where am I now?"

"You're with me and I'm here with you."

"I don't know why I'm here, but I feel there must be a reason. And I feel safe and protected."

"That is why I exist, Claire, to be your protector on earth and to guide you to God when you die."

Suddenly, Claire realized that Ariel's lips did not move.

And she also realized she had not spoken any words to Ariel. Their conversations were merely thoughts bridging back and forth between them.

The scent of baby's breath flowers filled the air. Claire looked more closely at Ariel's wings. At first glance, she had determined that the wings were made of a beautiful ivory cloth. Up close, she discovered the wings were actually hundreds of baby's breath flowers woven together. Claire's very being was filled with love and happiness. In that moment, she experienced an overwhelming understanding of the precious gift of life. She breathed deeply to take in the full impact of the sweet scent.

---

Chet softly caressed Claire's arm. He smiled when the volunteer delivered a vase of baby's breath flowers, Claire's favorite. He put the vase on the bed table. The card simply read, *Love, Anne.*

## CHAPTER 7 : BELIEF

Claire and her Guardian Angel sat in the green-misted Angels' Room. Claire could sense a dark change in Ariel's demeanor. Then, Ariel conveyed the message.

"Claire, God has instructed me to take you to a very menacing area."

"Where? You mean there's a menacing place in Heaven?"

"The place we are to visit is not in Heaven, Ariel continued. In fact, you are not in Heaven."

"If I'm not in Heaven, then, where am I?"

"My sweet, Claire, remember, I told you I have been with you from conception and I've watched your body and soul on Earth. But, now, your body is asleep on Earth and your mind is deep in what you believe are dreams."

"So, this isn't real?"

"I didn't say that, Claire. I said your mind is deep in what you believe to be dreams. Your soul is here-- resting in God's light. As Zimelda told you, God has a message for you. Its significance will be revealed before you awake from the coma. First, it's His wish that you see the deep sorrow of the lost souls before you return to your life on Earth. Of course, you have free will to refuse and God will understand, but He sincerely wants you to witness the horror of the lost souls."

"But why, Ariel? Why am I supposed to see the horror? What does God want me to see?"

Ariel spread her wings as wide as they could go and wrapped them around Claire, locking the wing tips in the back. She whispered, "Claire, God wants you to visit Hell. "

Claire wanted to escape. She wanted out of the dream or whatever it was. She wanted to be back in her body. *Oh, God why me? Why me?* Claire still felt the protection of Ariel's wings, but fear gripped her in a way she had never experienced before.

"Okay, Ariel, Claire begged, What happens if I say no? Will God punish me?"

"Of course not. God loves you and knows He is asking much of you."

"Then, what?"

"Then, when you heal, you wake-up from the coma and go on with your life. And, I'll still be with you, though not as you have experienced here."

At that Claire was somewhat relieved, but still confused.

"What does He want me to do, Ariel?  And what is the message that Zimelda said God wants me to hear?  I feel like I'm going in circles."

"I don't know what the message is, Claire.  That's not for me to say.  I can tell you that God wants you to see a very specific view in Hell, one that holds the darkest of souls, a place where Satan snuffs out the essence of hope for those who aborted babies, but never asked for forgiveness.  For those who willingly smeared the blood of babies on their souls, but did not believe that this could lead to damnation in eternity. Most of these people did not believe in Hell.  Many people do not believe in Satan and that's the way he likes it.  God will reveal His message in His time, Claire, and I'll be with you every step of the way."

Claire heard the sound of pages turning.  The smell of baby's breath filled the corridor.  Her eyes immediately focused on a section where the light hovered

*No evil shall befall you, nor shall affliction come near your tent.   For to his angels he has given command that they guard you in all your ways.' Upon their hands they shall bear you up, lest you dash your foot against the stone. You shall tread upon the asp and the viper.  You shall trample down the lion and the dragon. (Psalm 91:10-13)*

Ariel and Claire sat in silence praying to the Holy Spirit for guidance.  There could only be one decision.

"I know I must obey God.  Ariel, please, ever this day be at my side."

"I will be at your side, Claire."

# CHAPTER 8 : THE DESCENT

Claire and Ariel exited the comfort of the Angels' Room and walked slowly to the opposite end of the corridor. The entrance door was dark and dreary and it seemed to breathe in and out.

Ariel wrapped her wings even tighter around Claire's entity, softly assuring her.

"I am with you always. You are only to witness the horrors of Hell. Michael guards the entrance and because he is most powerful, he will walk us through three chambers of suffering, but you will be safe."

Claire wondered, *Is Michael "the" Michael? Michael the Archangel?*

Ariel smiled and Claire knew he was "the" Michael.

Ariel did not wish to unduly alarm Claire, but she wanted her to understand the gravity of this visit. She transferred very important information to her.

"God has allowed your bodily senses to exist in this moment. You will see misery unlike any you have ever seen. You will smell the putrid stench of blood, sweat, urine, and rotted flesh on the walls of Hell. You will taste the food of despair that the condemned souls eat for eternity. And finally, you will hear tormented screams worse than anything you have ever heard on Earth."

"Ariel, I am scared."

"Remember I will protect you in all ways. Michael, the Archangel, will protect both of us through the power of God. However, when we descend, keep praying. Prayers will ease your fear."

Claire was already reciting prayers she had memorized in the second grade. Over and over, she repeated the Our Father, Hail Mary, and Glory Be.

Ariel opened the door. The descent was straight down into darkness. Claire remembered as a little girl feeling afraid at the top of the stairs late at night.

*The stairwell was blackened, and there seemed to be menacing shapes looming in the darkness, ready to take hold of my bare feet if I made a move. I called out, "Mommy, Mommy." Mommy would come to the bottom of the steps, "Come on down, honey." But I still did not want to go down those steps, so I willed myself to fly straight down into her arms. At least, that's what I thought I did.*

Even with Ariel's protection, Claire felt that human fear of falling as they plunged to the bottom. Then, they arrived safely into Michael's presence. His figure was powerful and his wing span could have cast a shadow on a large forest. He was not the comfort of her mother that she knew as a small child, but Claire felt secure and safe. Ariel explained to Claire that Michael would not be communicating with them.

"His job is to watch over Heaven, Hell, and Earth as God commands him. His strength and authority is more powerful than any angel created, and his adoration of the Father gives him power over Satan himself. Since the beginning, he has never faltered from his duties."

Claire wondered why Hell had to be guarded at all since it's eternal and no one leaves.

"No one can escape from Hell,Claire, but Michael knows that Satan is a liar and deceiver. He wants them to believe that they can escape. He particularly enjoys that part of their suffering. I tell you this now because the souls of the damned will beg you to pray for them. They cling to a false belief that "now" they can be saved by prayer. But Hell is forever. Lucifer spits at them and laughs."

"Should I say anything?"

"Do not say a word. You are here as an observer of God's plan. You will be safe, but you will witness pain and as I told you, your senses will be attuned to the sights, sounds, smells, and tastes of Hell. God's wall of protection is impenetrable. Michael the Archangel will watch your every move. He knows all things that transpire in Hell. I will be hovering above you, Claire, as I have done since you were conceived. There's one more thing I need to tell you."

Claire shuddered in fear. *What else could there be?*

"Once you enter the chambers, you and I will not communicate, but neither Michael nor I will leave your side. God will show you what He wants you to see. And you will understand. The first one is Chamber Dark. Are you ready?"

———————

Claire was about to answer Ariel, but suddenly felt pain in her head. She could hear people talking, really talking, not merely transferring thoughts. Wedged between two realities, she moaned and thrashed about her bed in ICU. Chet, Jeannie, and Jeff watched her in what appeared to be tormenting pain. Claire experienced her most troubling night at St. Aloysius. Her temperature was 101, her blood pressure fluctuated, and her heart rate was very rapid. Dr. McDaniel looked perplexed, only adding to their angst.

Jeff and his Dad went outside for a brief break from the unbearable vigil. Jeannie remained with her comatose Mom, holding her hand. The vase of baby's breath from Anne reminded Jeannie of her First Holy Communion prayer book—with a pearly white cover and gold edging on the pages.

*Mom bought a small strand of silk baby's breath flowers to be a place holder. On my First Communion Day, she picked some of the real baby's breath flowers from the yard and added them to the place holder. When I opened her book, I smelled a beautiful scent. I dreamed that one day when I get married, I will carry that book down the aisle with a strand of baby's breath tucked inside. My mom would love it.*

The painful possibility of not ever being with her Mom again stung like a hot needle in the pit of her stomach.

*Heck, I'm not even close to getting married. And when, and if I do, Mom may not be here.*

Jeannie sobbed into her Mom's nightgown. "Mom, please, come out of this. I need you. I love you so much." As she was crying, Jeannie heard someone praying. Her mother's mouth moved slowly in a weak whisper, and she was able to recognize the words she was mouthing.

"Angel of God, my guardian dear…" Jeannie joined in the prayer. "To whom God's love commits me here. Ever this day be at my side, to light, to guard, to rule, to guide. Amen." At that moment, Jeannie felt a calming sense of relief and the baby's breath smelled sweet.

---

"Claire, you went back for a moment, but it's not time yet. God still wants you to see the truth. Are you ready?"

"Yes, Ariel, I am ready."

# CHAPTER 9 : CHAMBER DARK

Suddenly, Claire no longer smelled baby's breath. The door to Chamber Dark opened and the hot smoke entered her throat. The stench of the chamber was much worse than Ariel's description. It reeked of blood, sweat, urine, and rotted flesh intermingled with a dank odor of animal fur. Beneath the smoke, Claire could see burning embers. Many human forms were positioned on the coals, their skin roasted hard and brittle; their bodies emitting red-blood steam into the chamber. Demons roamed through the mass of bodies. Though, they also were scorched and suffering, they seemed to be able to laugh at and scorn the residents of Chamber Dark.

Claire longed to hear Ariel's words of comfort but she knew that could not happen. She prayed and prayed. *God, please help me. Michael, please protect me. Ariel, please hear me and watch over me.* Claire looked up and saw the shadows of two sets of wings – Michael's large and looming; Ariel's much smaller, but comforting.

Then, a very young woman approached her. For a brief second, Claire could see the beauty this woman had when she was alive. Her eyes had been dark and dreamy. Her long black hair framed her flawless face. Her name was Angela.

She pleaded with Claire, "Please pray for me that I will be saved from this endless pit of suffering. I beg you, please pray for me. I didn't know it was a baby inside me. They told me it was a mass of cells."

A demon taunted. "That's what all of you say – I didn't know it was a baby – who are you kidding? You can't lie to yourself anymore. That's why you're here, Ms. Angela, hot shot movie star."

Angela bowed her head in admission of the truth. She turned toward Claire once more.

"Oh, please, please pray for me?"

At that, one of the demons pushed a sharp object into Angela's stomach and cast her further into the coals. Her cries bounced off the walls of the chamber, echoing hopeless desire, "Please let me die, let me die."

Her special demon sneered, "You are dead. And guess what, Angela, oh dear sweet Angela? You are in Hell forever. God doesn't exist here."

Chapter 9 : Chamber Dark

Claire's heart hurt for this poor woman, but she knew this was Hell and there was no exit. Why hadn't Angela asked God to forgive her when she had the chance? When she was alive? Claire did not fully understand how dead humans in Chamber Dark seemed to be so alive in the intensity of their pain and suffering. Horrific screams emanated from everywhere in the coals. Demons responded with taunts to the many prisoners of Chamber Dark. One after another, the prisoners begged for mercy. Similar to Angela, many of the residents believed they were still alive since their bodies experienced excruciating pain.

"Let me die."

"You are dead," her demon scoffed.

Someone screamed, "I'll do anything to get out of here. Anything."

The assigned demon smirked, "You're here forever."

A man said, "Dear God, dear God, I believe in you now."

"God does not hear you anymore," his demon laughed,

"I wouldn't have killed my baby if I'd known I'd end up here."

Several demons snarled, "Nobody thinks they'll end up here."

Another man said, "I didn't kill my baby. She killed it. I just paid for it."

"Yeah, you're paying for it now, aren't you?" his demon mocked.

"I couldn't have his baby. He was married."

"Oh, well take comfort. He's here, too," two demons smirked.

"I was only six weeks along. It was a blob of cells."

The evil spirits took great pleasure in the suffering of the residents.

"You see, that's your problem. Embryos aren't 'its.' They're human beings."

Finally, the last prisoner said, "They told us 'there is no Hell, there is no Hell.'"

In unison, the fiends of punishment screamed, "They were wrong, dead wrong. There is a Hell. You are in Hell."

When Claire felt that she could no longer tolerate the screams and the thrashing mass of human suffering, a tunnel of protection appeared within the chamber – all of Hell was outside of it. Claire entered the tunnel and saw the book and read aloud.

*What I say to you in the darkness, speak in the light; what you hear whispered, proclaim on the housetops. And do not be afraid of those who kill the body but cannot kill the soul; rather, be afraid of the one who can destroy both soul and body in Gehenna. Matthew, 10:27-28*

As if in a theater, a screen appeared. Claire was mesmerized by what she saw. Angela, a sweet twenty-year old laughing and flirting with a handsome young man named Jared. They were both in college somewhere in the Midwest and they were in love. He was studying to be an accountant. Angela wanted to be an actress.

Angela's story seemed so hopeful until the day she sobbed, telling Jared she was pregnant. Jared comforted her and half-heartedly said he was willing to get married.

Angela kept crying, "I love you, but this can't happen right now. I'm only twenty. I want to be an actress. It's my passion. You know that."

"So what are you saying, Angela? You want to abort our baby?"

"Oh, come on, I'm only seven weeks along. You don't believe that crap we learned in high school religion class, do you? This is not a baby yet, Jared. It's a group of cells, like a tumor. Nobody wants a tumor, do they?"

"Angela, you don't know what you're saying. And yes, I do believe that there's a baby growing inside you. Our baby."

Angela paused for a brief moment. Jared hoped that maybe he had gotten through to her. Instead, she said, "Jared, I love you and maybe one day, we'll have children, but now isn't a good time. I'm not ready for motherhood, yet."

"Listen, I'm not crazy about the pregnancy either, but we can get through this. You didn't get pregnant on your own, you know. Will you think about it tonight? We'll talk in the morning, okay?"

"Yes, yes, Jared, I'll think about it."

The next day Angela borrowed Jared's car and lied that she was visiting a pregnancy center to get an ultra sound.

"Let me go with you. I've been thinking about this all night and I want to be with you no matter what decision you make."

Chapter 9 : Chamber Dark

"Hey, it's a simple test. Besides, it's a little embarrassing to have you there."

Jared reluctantly agreed. "Okay, but call me as soon as you leave the center."

"Yeah, of course, Jared."

Instead of going to the pregnancy center, she drove to the Planned Parenthood Clinic. Angela signed the papers and consented to let them kill her baby. After that day, Jared and Angela moved on and away from each other.

The screen fast forwarded twenty years. Jared was married to Coni. Their happy life included four beautiful children. Jared asked God to forgive him for getting Angela pregnant and for not trying harder to stop the abortion of his first child. Coni and Jared prayed every day for that innocent baby.

Immediately after her abortion, Angela felt a trace of remorse, but was able to shove the guilt to the back of her mind. She remembered her mother telling her over and over, "With a man, honey, say yes, yes to his face. Then do whatever you want behind his back. No matter how good you might think he is, a man will inevitably put you under his thumb, like your daddy did with me." Angela's relationships with men from her father to Jared and other men in her life were steeped in rebellion.

She also surrounded herself with people who reinforced the "woman's choice" lie. Over time, the memory of the abortion faded to a hard kernel as tiny as a grape seed.

"No man, no how is going to make me do anything I don't want to do. I am going to take care of me. Yes, yes!" Angela had gotten her wish. She became a mainstream movie star. She never had any other children, although she married three times. Once in a while, she would think of Jared and feel scorched in her gut. Angela pushed that heartache far down in her heart and soul, convincing herself that her dark deed twenty years ago had been crucial to her success. Her rationalization was simple. "Jared is naïve about life and besides, it really can't be all that bad to have growing cells removed."

Angela was more than pleased with her choices in life. She had it all – money, glamour, parties, and adulation. She convinced herself that none of her success could have happened if she had not had the abortion. She detested those self-righteous people who condemned young girls for making their own choice. In fact, she had donated several thousand dollars to Senator McMann's campaign. At least he was a reasonable Catholic who believed in a woman's choice. Unfortunately, Angela was killed in a head-on collision of her Porsche and a semi-truck two days after her fortieth birthday.

Claire saw the dimly-lit Bible and re-read the words that Matthew had written centuries ago, words that came to past for the lost souls she had seen in Gehenna.

**Lose your soul on earth and you will suffer agony of both body and soul in Gehenna by the one who can destroy. Matthew, 10:28**

The final image Claire saw was Angela's most excruciating pain. It was not the burning coals or the perpetual taunting of the demons. For eternity, Angela would see a vision of Jared's and her baby being suctioned from her body. Each time, she would feel her baby's physical and mental pain. The most profound sadness was the total understanding of her destruction of this particular human being, one that came from her body, one that could never be born again. Angela faced eternal suffering in Hell, devoid of God's love and forgiveness.

She would ask over and over again, "Where is my baby, God?"

Satan would answer, "I don't know and I don't care." These words scorched her soul for eternity in Chamber Dark.

# CHAPTER 10 : CHAMBER DARKER

Shapes of men and women – all races, all sizes, all religions – roamed Chamber Darker, a much larger cavity of Hell than Chamber Dark. Each figure was covered in hot, melting tar. The demons poured the pitch black liquid over them perpetually, laughing as the condemned cringed and screamed.

A huge transparent sphere hung over Chamber Darker. Repulsive evidence of the misery that could have been avoided dangled inside the ball. Claire along with the residents of Chamber Darker saw a vision of humans suffering with cancer, AIDS, multiple sclerosis, starvation and even worse. Sometimes, they saw the outline of an innocent who would have found the cure for cancer, reaching out to the suffering humans. Sometimes an image appeared of one who would have discovered the remedy for famine, and at times they saw a simple outline of a person who would have provided a gentle touch to heal the suffering of one individual. Unfortunately, the aborted innocents had been denied an earthly existence. Their lives had been ended before they could make an impact on the human race. Residents of Chamber Darker were forced to look at the ominous globe that held images of innocent babies. Their journey to being born on Earth was viciously aborted.

As the sphere spun above Chamber Darker, it morphed into a portentous mixture of tiny arms, and legs, and toes, and organs of the millions of aborted babies. The blood from their torn-apart bodies dripped onto the residents of Chamber Darker. Each drop of blood that touched their forms caused them to writhe in physical and spiritual pain.

The sphere seemed to be made of transparent, pliable plastic. Heads of babies pressed outward into the plastic wall as though trapped in a universal womb. Residents had no choice but to stare at the faces, some only as big as a tiny grape seed. These were babies who would never live on Earth.

Then Chamber Darker started to churn, toppling this way and that, causing residents to tumble against each other. They felt the unbalanced evil they had perpetrated on the world. Not one of them had ever participated in an abortion directly; yet, they were doomed to spend eternity in Chamber Darker. Their pride and sins of omission condemned them to this level of Hell.

Claire was astonished at the types of people who comprised Chamber Darker – Bishops, Kings, Priests, Presidents, CEO's, people rich, people poor. They all had one thing in common. They were willing to omit devotion to the sanctity of life for their own purpose or pleasure on Earth. Politicians who voted for Roe v. Wade and other pro-abortion legislation. Pro-choice priests and ministers and nuns and rabbis and lay people. People who made up their own rules on Earth instead of following God's rules.

Over time, pro-abortion euphemized into pro-choice so as not to offend. Now, they saw and felt and breathed the fiery consequences of "not offending." Chamber Darker was the end result of their choices on Earth. Claire was once again approached by one of the members. As he was tossed about in the chaos of Hell, he wept bitter tears. He noticed Claire. He knew she was not a member and begged, "Please ask God why am I here? Please, please. I was a good priest. I did nothing to deserve this. Why, why?" His painful cries made Claire wince, but her compassion would be useless in the chamber. She knew it was too late for him.

---

The tunnel opened and the screen appeared again. Claire entered and read God's message in the Book:

***What does it profit man to gain the whole world and lose his immortal soul? (Matthew, 16: V.26)***

Together, Father Sean Mallory and Claire watched moments of his life. He was celebrating Mass. He was tall and lanky, not all that handsome, but certainly able to command his congregation's attention. This particular Sunday he was dressed in Irish green garments with gold trim. His beautiful tenor voice echoed off the walls of "his" church. On Sundays he sang as much of the Mass as he could. He loved it when parishioners, especially the ladies oohed and aahed over him after Sunday Mass. "Oh, Father Sean," one of them cooed, "I feel wonderful after hearing you sing." Father Sean feigned humility, but relished the adulation. His sermons made everyone feel good from the smallest child, to the teens, to the adults. His humorous tales of his childhood evoked laughter and a sense of well-being. On this particular Sunday, Father Sean Mallory was relaying one of those endearing stories from childhood. He said:

Chapter 10 : Chamber Darker

"I'd like to talk about what Jesus meant in the Gospel today when He said to his disciples, 'What does it profit man to gain the whole world and lose his soul.' But I digress for a moment to that Mallory household of old. You know, the one where Grandma Mallory had an answer and remedy for everything."

Smiles and nods of approval filled the church. Father Mallory continued.

"I was about twelve years old when Grandma and I went to the store to buy a new pair of school shoes for me. It was a yearly event that I looked forward to because after we bought the shoes, our next stop was Chili Dilly for hot fudge sundaes. Grandma was very particular about my shoes and would not be rushed.

She firmly believed that good shoes meant good feet. Good feet meant good walking. And good walking meant I could walk to school. Mr. Campbell owned the store and when he saw us enter, he knew he was in for about one hour of Grandma Mallory's' sermon about shoes. She would say, 'Oh that one's too stiff,' or 'the toes are too pointy. And why are these more expensive?'

That year, Mr. Campbell showed Grandma a pair of reasonably priced shoes that were held together with special glue instead of sewn thread. So, those were the choices…the expensive Glockens meticulously stitched together at a cost of $39.95 or the Jump-Ons made with glue at a lower cost of $19.95. I didn't really care which pair she bought. I wanted the ice cream.

But Grandma wasn't satisfied with merely making a choice. She had to teach a lesson, 'Mr. Campbell, you know the verse in the Bible about your soul?'

Mr. Campbell glumly replied, 'Which one, Mrs. Mallory?'

Grandma grandly delivered. "The one when Jesus tells His disciples, what does it profit a man to gain the whole world and lose his soul.'''

'Oh sure, Mrs. Mallory, I know that one, but with all due respect, what does that have to do with a pair of shoes?'

Grandma took a deep breath anxious to answer Mr. Campbell's question, 'It's the same with shoes. What good does it profit a man to buy a shiny pair of shoes and lose the soles in a bad rainstorm? We'll take the Glockens.'''

The congregation roared with laughter.

Father Mallory raised his condor arms and flapped them slowly to calm down the laughter. When the chuckling subsided, he continued his sermon.

"Brothers and sisters, my Grandma had a strange way of teaching things, but her logic still applies today. Are we going to be a pair of shoes glued together with a weak sole or are we going to be the Glockens, carefully stitched so we do not lose our souls? Carefully stitch your life together with love of neighbor and demonstration of this love through social justice. These charitable deeds will prevent you from suffering the loss of your soul. God Bless!"

Father Mallory was a good man. He did help people and he was loved. Claire watched him as he watched himself. His face was one of puzzlement. Then the bewildered look disappeared, replaced with cold fear.

His very soul witnessed the misery and agony of the souls that had been lost. Souls that he might have saved with the truth. Not once had he mentioned the evil of abortion in his forty years of sermons. Not once did he chide his friend, Senator Drake, for passing pro-choice legislation. Not once did he challenge his congregation to speak out against the politically correct world of pro-choice. Not once did he march in a pro-life demonstration. Now, Father Mallory understood. His pride and desire to be liked overshadowed the one thing that could have saved him. And that is, he could have saved others. His grave choice of omitting the true teachings of the Church, especially on the sanctity of life, cost him his soul.

# CHAPTER 11 : CHAMBER DARKEST

Claire's heart was racing. She did not question God's judgment, but the anguish she witnessed was overwhelming for her human mind. She cried for several minutes after leaving Chamber Darker, but she knew the darkest of the dark loomed ahead like an ominous intruder behind a door. There was no exit from this intruder. She entered Chamber Darkest with a heavy heart.

At first an Arctic blast of air hit her face, freezing her tears. Claire was confused. Hell was supposed to be fire. Through the crystal clear ice domes, she saw faces frozen in ghoulish frowns, eyes bulging with fear, skulls open with blood clinging to petrified faces. The horrific scene strangely reminded her of a Christmas globe she had owned as a child. In her five-year old innocence, she loved the beautiful scene of people floating inside the globe. Still, it made her sad that they were trapped in a circular prison with no way out.

When Claire heard an eerie hissing sound, she turned around abruptly. Snakes of all sizes slithered in the chamber. She looked up and gasped. Serpent tongues eagerly lashed at body parts frozen to the walls, floor and ceiling.

Then thousands, maybe millions of demons appeared. In unison they inhaled. Their nostrils opened wide to suck in the dark air. Snakes crawled into a deep hole to avoid what would happen next. In unison, the demons exhaled and a tsunami of fire roared through the chamber. Ice melted and then boiled. Figures in the globes stirred and body parts fell into place on each one of them like a mismatched puzzle. It didn't matter to the demons which resident got which arm or leg or head. Once each body was intact floating in boiling water, the screams of anguish began. Then the water was gone and there was only the inferno.

One of the demons had enough power to whisper in Claire's ear, "You came at the end of the show when Hell freezes over. The best part happens now." He laughed in a high, shrill voice full of evil sarcasm. Then, the demon spewed a long trail of the fire of Hell past Claire's cheek. It was a sliver, as light on her skin as a single strand of hair. Nevertheless she experienced a twinge of pain. At once Michael spread his powerful wings pushing the demon down into the deepest end of the snake hole. The power of Michael the Archangel filled Claire with awe.

She sensed Ariel's presence also. The angels' unfathomable dominion stoked her courage to forge ahead. She remembered Ariel's caution to ignore questions or comments from any creature in the chamber. She prayed the Our Father, Hail Mary, and Glory Be over and over.

Claire began to realize that each demon was assigned one resident. As soon as the ice melted, the flames steadily swept through the room. One demon stood watch over a particular individual. Satan made sure each of the condemned of Chamber Darkest had a personal punisher—his or her very own sentinel of destruction. The ruthless torture of the residents of Chamber Darkest persisted in a merciless cycle for eternity.

While the inhabitants were screaming and wailing for mercy, sentinels of destruction assembled their tools, sharp probes, suction tubes, knives, and chemicals. First, an egg-shaped balloon, filled with liquid, surrounded each resident. Their lopsided figures, assembled with assorted body parts, floated inside their womb of Hell. What happened next was almost too horrific for Claire to comprehend. Some of the sentinels of destruction jabbed razor sharp probes into the spines and necks of the residents. Some drove pointed spikes into the heads. Then, they suctioned the contents with their mouths, spewing it throughout the chamber. The only sounds were tools grinding, body parts smacking the walls, and the demon sentinels' taunts. The condemned inside the womb of Hell could not yell or speak or even cry. Their eyes bulged with fear and agony; their mouths were sealed in silent screams.

Claire watched in abject repulsion, but was finally relieved by the sight of the tunnel. She knew it was yet another sad story of a lost soul, but she was relieved to be away from the womb of Hell. The screen opened. This time it was more than one story of a person's journey to Hell. Several scenes evolved. And of course, the book awaited Claire.

> *Now the serpent was more cunning than any beast of the field which the Lord God had made. He said to the woman, Did God say, 'You shall not eat of any tree of the garden?'" The woman answered the serpent, 'Of the fruit of all the trees in the garden we may eat; but of the fruit of the tree in the middle of the garden,' God said, 'You shall not eat, neither shall you touch it, lest you die.'" But the serpent said to the woman, "No, you shall not die; for*

Chapter 11 : Chamber Darkest

***God knows that when you eat of it, your eyes will be opened and you will be like God, knowing good and evil.  Genesis, 3:1-5***

This was Satan's first lie to the human race.

The residents of Chamber Darkest had lived their lives as false gods on Earth. They embraced power over life and death, performing abortions with resolute determination.  These were the people who literally pulled babies apart inside a mother's womb.  These were the people who convinced themselves and others that it was a clump of cells, a useless tumor of sorts, a bug to squash.  Satan's lie allowed them to believe that they were 'like God.'  On Earth, they decided that abortion was good, not evil.  In Hell, the punishment paralleled the evil they had perpetrated on women and babies.

For some *"Satan's lie"* was the pride of their belief that they were helping women.  They believed they were pro-choice advocates for the world.  On Earth, they chose to condemn innocent babies to a painful death.  They had no remorse, no regrets.  Now, they had no more time to choose anything good and holy.  The eternal *"Satan's lie"* was the womb of Hell.

For some *"Satan's lie"* was their calling to save the Earth from over-population, especially over-population of females.  They banned a couple from having more than one child, preferably saving a male child.  Their misdirected fervor beckoned them to be trailblazing abortionists.  Now, they had reached their final destination – forever a prisoner in the womb of Hell – relentless agony evermore.

For some *"Satan's lie"* was to save the family and the world from the burden of the imperfect and the incomplete.  They could decide whose defect would not be tolerated.  They could eliminate anyone whom they deemed could not contribute much to the world.   They decided deficiencies should be suctioned out of the womb like raw sewage from a clogged toilet.  Now, for eternity, they would endure their own private womb of Hell with imperfect, mismatched body parts and a private demon to torment them.

For some *"Satan's lie"* was love of money, power, and the craving to obtain them at all costs.  Abortion was a lucrative business to them, nothing more, and nothing less.  Laws were passed; women were entitled to contraception, abortion, and sterilization. These residents served as competent providers for women. They had power, money, and very often, fame. Life on Earth was full of pleasure, adulation, and generous gifts. They had it all. In life, they had usurped the will of God. In death, they only had the womb of Hell.

Each person's story passed on the screen. One by one, they told their reasons, their motivations, their explanations, their excuses, but to no avail.

---

Dr. Leonard Sennett was fifty-eight years old when he died and went to Hell, after he had defiantly and deliberately aborted hundreds of babies. All for his own gain. Claire saw Dr. and Mrs. Sennett sitting at their kitchen table on a Saturday morning. Len had just returned from the Planned Parenthood Clinic where he had signed a lucrative contract to perform abortions. He was a partner in a successful group of surgeons, and was already well on his way to secure wealth, but for Len it was not enough.

Sylvia poured them both a cup of coffee and asked, "What happened at the clinic, Len. Did they ask you to work for them?"

Len cleared his throat with a raspy ca-ca, irritated that Sylvia would even doubt that they would want him. "Of course they want me to work for them. I signed the contract today."

Sylvia was used to Len doing whatever he wanted to do professionally without consulting her, but this decision disturbed her deeply. "Len," she cautioned, "do you really want to perform abortions? You were adamant in med school about '*first, do no harm.*' This is doing harm to a baby."

"Hey, I didn't make the laws. It's legal to perform an abortion. Remember *Roe v. Wade*, or have you been living in la-la land for the past forty years?" Len often chided Sylvia with snide comments like this one.

Sylvia remained calm. "It seems unnecessary for you to do this. We send our children to Sacred Heart Academy, so they can learn their faith. Having or performing an abortion is a serious sin. I can't believe this is happening. You've made decisions that I didn't like in the past, but this is unconscionable."

Chapter 11 : Chamber Darkest

Len screamed at Sylvia, "I didn't make the laws, and, we – you and me, Sylvia Dennison Sennet – practiced birth control. Isn't that a mortal sin, too? You had two miscarriages – what's the difference if you miscarry or abort. And you insisted I get a vasectomy. You think you're high and mighty?"

"No, I'm not high and mighty. I'm a sinner, too. "

Len was on a roll. "Besides, I haven't heard a fire and brimstone message from a priest in years, nothing about abortion, Sylvia. I guarantee nobody believes that archaic crap anymore. What's the big deal?"

Sylvia sighed, exhausted and sad.

Len tried to be a little comforting. "Look, calm down. It's a woman's right to choose when to have a child, and if she chooses to abort, somebody's got to do it. Why not me? The money's good."

Sylvia pleaded one more time, "Len, you're a good doctor. You don't have to make money this way. Are you leaving the group?"

Dr. Len Sennett became very excited at this point. "No. That's the beauty of this opportunity. I only have to go to the Planned Parenthood Clinic every Saturday for four hours. I'll earn several thousand dollars a month for performing about six abortions per Saturday…in one year; we'll have the down payment for that house on Cape Cod. Then, I can quit doing abortions or do them less often."

"Len, I don't need a summer home in Cape Cod. How could we live with ourselves? I don't think I can accept this."

Once again, Len became angry. "Accept what? More money to do things, to travel, to secure our future? Remember, I grew up poor with six red neck brothers and sisters. Dad knocked Mom up and they *had* to get married back then. First, they had me. Then, baby after baby after baby, one almost every two years. I hated it when Mom got pregnant. It meant more work for me and less money for all of us."

"Len, we have been blessed with two beautiful children. What if your mother had chosen not to have you?"

"Well, that would have been her choice. But she did choose to have me and then six more. Dad worked two jobs, but we still had nothing. Nothing, Sylvia."

"I know it was hard for you as a child."

"You don't know anything.  You lived in your pretty little home with one sister.  Daddy was a lawyer and Mommy belonged to the Women's Tea & Charity Club.  It was the Ozzie & Harriet show, wasn't it?"

"It wasn't perfect, Len, but my father was ethical."

"Oh, swell," Len shrieked, "so now I'm unethical.  I'm not good enough for you.  I'm not the perfect Daddy.  Go to Hell, Sylvia.  I'm doing this whether you like it or not."

Len began performing abortions the following Saturday.  Sylvia struggled with her decision to leave.  Her children were confused when she filed for divorce.  She did not tell them why.  Sylvia did not want them to know that their father was, in fact, a murderer of the worst kind.  To this day, they still do not know why their parents divorced.

Len was on his way to the Planned Parenthood Clinic on a Saturday four years after he became an abortionist.  His stomach was upset, his left arm was aching, and he felt exhausted.  Len had the classic heart attack in the doorway of the Planned Parenthood Clinic.  When the receptionist found him, his face was contorted in pain with a clownish upside down smile.  He died within minutes.

Claire read the final verse in the darkest of chambers.

***Depart from me, you accursed into the eternal fire prepared for the devil and his angels.  (Matt: 25:41)***

Len's body and soul were cast into the darkest chamber of Hell.

Once outside the chambers, Claire shuddered, drained and disturbed by all that she had witnessed.  As Ariel embraced her, a sense of relief swept over her.  Claire saw Michael out of the corner of her eye.  She wanted to thank him.  He did not flinch nor smile nor look away from his post. Michael the Archangel is and always has been the stalwart guard, vigilant forever.

"Claire, there's another aspect to the message that God has planned for you."

"That scares me."

"God wants you to return to Chamber Dark, Claire."

Chapter 11 : Chamber Darkest

Claire began to sob.

"Haven't I seen enough suffering? Is there something I missed in Chamber Dark? Ariel, I cannot; I will not go back in there. "

"You are being defiant."

Claire cringed. "Sorry, I know I must obey God's will, but why do I have to see all of that misery again."

Ariel patiently explained. "God had it planned this way from the first time you entered Chamber Dark. He wanted to wait for you to return. He knew that you would be more accustomed to the dreadful atmosphere of Hell."

"Ariel, I can't take the atmosphere of Hell. I don't ever want to visit that place again."

"This is the last time you will have to view any of the chambers, Claire. God wants you to see one more section of Chamber Dark--a place that has a personal impact for you."

Claire's mouth felt dry and parched with an abhorrence of what this visit might hold.

*Personal, personal...what does that mean?*

Her mind swirled with questions. Her stomach burned with fear as hot as the embers of Hell. Ariel tried to comfort her, but Claire sobbed uncontrollably. At that, Michael's wings enclosed both of them. The power and glory and love of God surrounded them. Michael, the Archangel, Mica-EL, which means *"Who is Like God."* Yes, Michael is like God, but he serves God. Unlike Lucifer, who would not serve God. Satan wishes to have his own kingdom. But, the power of Satan is not infinite – he cannot block the building up of the Kingdom of God. Michael gently urged Claire to pray to the Father.

Claire obediently said the Father's Prayer.

***Our Father, who art in Heaven. Hallowed be Thy name,Thy kingdom come, thy will be done, On earth as it is in Heaven, Give us this day, our daily bread And forgive us our trespasses, As we forgive those who trespass against us And lead us not into temptation, But deliver us from evil. Amen***

Her tears stopped.  She experienced an amazing surge of spiritual and physical well-being, wrapped in the protection of Mica-EL, who is like God.  After praying, Claire profoundly understood that God had chosen her to visit Hell and had delivered her from Hell.  She whispered, "Thy will be done, Father."

Claire entered Chamber Dark once again. It was no surprise to see the shapes entrenched in the burning embers. The demons still laughed with sinister glee as they delivered punishment. Claire briefly saw Angela again, looking sorrowful, lonely, totally devoid of hope.

Claire then noticed a very large grey steel door. It opened. She entered expecting to witness another level of anguish. She was taken aback to see nothing more than shapes carved out of what appeared to be transparent cardboard. The shapes sat silently two by two in a dimly-lit train car, traveling at a very slow speed. Claire somehow realized there were thousands of train cars behind this one, each filled with the eerie images. Some of the occupants had human resemblances. Features were vague, but she felt certain if she knew someone in life, she could recognize a person even in this indistinct shape.

Claire felt compelled to enter car after car after car. When she reached Car 522, she sensed a disturbing vulnerability. Someone or something evil was with her. She smelled and tasted sulfur. Then, she heard a deep guttural growl. The darkest figure she had ever seen slid itself across the train car. Claire felt as though her veins and arteries had been injected with liquid evil.

Then she saw the body of a serpent and the grotesque face of malevolence, oozing pus-filled wounds, overflowing with the current sins of the world. Satan, in his self-proclaimed glory. He suffered interminably from his fall, yet still populated his kingdom through human sin. Abortion was his favorite, because it destroyed and consumed completely. The conceived baby snatched from a mother's womb left in a basket, a toilet, a closet, or the garbage dumps at an abortion clinic. The mother, devoid of hope, trapped in regret the rest of her life. The father, either unaware or uncaring of the abortion, living in the shadows of his baby's lost life.

Satan's dark ruminations entered Claire's mind.

"Aah, yes, the death of a baby itself is delicious, but the depravity of the willing abortor and abortee is exquisite. The suffering they endure sometimes leads to suicide. And if they have one abortion, they'll probably have another and another. It becomes easy. And the abortors, well that's a no-brainer. They're doomed, unless they ask to be... Well, we won't say that word here."

Claire steeled against fear. She prayed and waited and prayed some more. Then, it happened very quickly. Claire realized the partners sitting two by two had distinct characteristics. One was grotesque and ominous. Next to it was an image that appeared to be a lifeless mock-up of a human being. Satan had placed the semblance of a particular human in each seat on his train. They were not quite his, but their souls were in mortal danger. Each of them was a potential lost soul in reserve for his chambers. The human likenesses served as a sinister reminder that Satan and his demons must roam the world seeking the ruin of souls.

Satan in his arrogant conceit decided to share some other world views with Claire. She listened as the demon bragged about his successful propaganda.

"I love those 'Save This Puppy' commercials, showing poor animals that have been mistreated, bleeding, limping, and almost dead. Sad music plays as a voice pleads for donations to rescue the helpless animals. It would really cut into my deep dark treasury of souls if instead of puppies they showed aborted babies with little arms and legs torn apart."

"Aah, but not to worry. I, Lucifer, have a bottomless pit of lies. I do take pleasure in the increase of humans who do not believe in me and therefore, do not believe in Hell. Why do humans think God gave the world The Ten Commandments?

I have done a magnificent job of creating the abortion masquerade era, if I do say so myself. Chambers Dark, Darker, and Darkest are the most lucrative side of the business. Oh, the excuses I hear. 'Stop judging me.' 'My body, my choice.' 'We have to control population.' 'We have to save the environment.' 'I don't want my daughters to be punished for being pregnant.' On and on and on ad naseum. Don't misunderstand me, I'm not complaining. Put up the mask, put up the mask, my rotting living souls and I shall have you soon. You've got a special ticket for my train. Don't cancel it by asking Him for___"

Satan paused and then blurted a malevolent taunt—"I DO NOT SAY THE 'F' WORD!"

Then, Claire saw the frightening image of a woman – a woman she knew. She studied her face carefully. There were dark circles under the woman's lavender eyes and her mouth turned down in an ominous frown. It didn't take Claire long to realize who she saw in the seat on Satan's train. *Oh, no, it's Anne.*

She tried to touch the image, but it was stiff and wouldn't budge. Still, she wanted to believe Anne could hear her pleas. She implored, "Anne, Anne, please don't let Satan take you. God loves you. He'll forgive you. Don't wait to ask. Do it before it's too late! Please, Anne, ask God for forgiveness."

They sat two by two in the seats, one a despairing sad figure; one a gruesome demon. Anne's demon caressed her ominously and glared at Claire with his yellow eyes. Then the devil's most horrifying secret was revealed to Claire. The disclosure was more frightening than what she had experienced in the chambers. She had smelled the putrid stench of blood, sweat, urine, and rotted flesh on the walls of Hell. She heard the tormented cries of the condemned souls. She had witnessed Angela falling deeper into the dark coals as a demon pushed a sharp object into her stomach. Claire's heart was flooded with Father Mallory's anguish and despair. She would never forget the vision of the sentinels of destruction gathering their tools, sharp probes, suction tubes, knives, and chemicals to torture Len and the other residents of Chamber Darkest.

Satan's most horrifying secret is that for each aborted baby, one demon is released into the world to wreak additional havoc on humanity. The fiend is allowed to remain on Earth as long as the mother of the aborted remains unwilling to ask God's forgiveness. And the most distressing images that Claire saw were not any of the visions she had seen thus far. She gasped in fear as she saw demons morphing into normal-looking humans. With prideful grandiosity, Satan waved his hand, releasing all the demons of Train Car 522 into the world.

Now, the number of the train made sense – 522 – May 22 – the date of Anne's abortion. Satan's long line of rail cars was in chronological order by date of abortion.

On the ceiling of each car his abortion counts were emboldened in bright red lights. Oh, what a macabre sense of humor the devil has, delighting in the limitlessness of his foul destruction. The numbers on the sign continually increased. Claire stared for a moment absorbed in the data of lost lives. Across the top of the sign were the words, 'Behelzelbub's Baby Blood Bath.' Underneath was Satan's arrogant boast, 'Billions in the World since the Beginning of My Reign on Earth.'

| | |
|---|---|
| 1,206,200 per year<br><br>3,307 per day<br>138 per hour<br>9 every 4 minutes<br><br>1 every 26 seconds | TOTAL ABORTIONS IN THE UNITED STATES 1973 - 2010<br>55,549,615 |

Sobbing once more, Claire ran through the train cars back to the first entrance. She kept repeating her plea to Anne-- *Please, Anne, ask God for forgiveness.* Satan's dark shadow loomed, his voice screeching obscenities and curses at Claire. Satan was fuming that Claire had the audacity to say the word "forgive" in his territory. The "F" word the "forgive" word enraged him beyond imagination.

As Claire scurried through the safe tunnel that God provided in Chamber Dark, she looked back one last time at the sinister evil one. He was cursing, dark pus covered his face, and his mustard yellow eyes spewed a vile discharge across the tunnel. Finally he laughed harsh, raspy bursts of fire and brimstone as he hung a sign on the entrance door, "NO BABIES ON BOARD!!!"

Claire ran as fast as she could, heart racing, out of breath. She remembered praying the prayer to St. Michael the Archangel as a little girl and instinctively mouthed the words.

> **Saint Michael the Archangel,**
> **defend us in battle.**
> **Be our protection against the wickedness and snares of the devil.**
> **May God rebuke him, we humbly pray;**
> **and do Thou, O Prince of the Heavenly Host,**
> **by the Divine Power of God,**
> **cast into Hell Satan and all the evil spirits**
> **who roam throughout the world seeking the ruin of souls.**

Claire could barely see a trace of light as she moved along the tunnel faster and faster. She continued to pray, this time the Prayer to her Guardian Angel.

Chapter 12 : Return to Chamber Dark

*Angel of God, my guardian dear*

At the moment Claire began to pray, she faintly heard someone praying with her – a sweet voice that she had known for a long time. The rhythm of their combined prayer comforted her.

*To whom God's love commits me here*

A hand touched her cheek; a wonderful caress. The smell of baby's breath spurred her onward. She felt safe, out of harm's way. *Jeannie, that's my Jeannie praying with me,*

*Ever this day be at my side*
*To light, to guard, to rule, to guide*
*Amen*

*I've got to get back to Jeannie and Jeff and Chet.*

"Oh, God, please let me go home to them. Please, God."

At last she jumped into the sweet baby's breath wings that Ariel held open wide for her. Michael stood strong against the doors of Hell, blocking the devil and his dominion of demons and lost souls. Ariel held her tightly. Claire felt secure in the same way she did as a little girl flying down the steps into her mother's arms, safe and sound. The ascent was straight up into the light.

# CHAPTER 13 : HOPEFULNESS

As Chet and Jeff re-entered the hospital room, they saw Jeannie stroking her mother's cheek.

"Talk to me again, Mom. C'mon, I'll keep praying with you. Dad, Jeff. I'm glad you're back. Mom talked to me."

"Praise the Lord," Chet whispered. "Well, what did she say, Jeannie?"

"Well, she didn't exactly talk to me."

Jeff snapped at Jeannie, "Then what are you getting us all excited about? It's hard enough waiting without you coming up with one of your fantasies."

Jeannie was too happy to be aggravated by Jeff's comments. "Dad. I'm not even sure she knew it was me, but she was praying. I prayed with her. It was the Prayer to Our Guardian Angel. When we finished, she seemed to be calm."

Chet and Jeff stood on either side of Claire's bed, trying to absorb what Jeannie had said.

"Her face is cool now. Feel it. I'm not kidding. One minute she was sweating and moaning and the next minute she started breathing calmly. It's like she was in a hot desert and then entered a cool rain forest."

Chet touched Claire's forehead. "She is cooler. Maybe this is the breakthrough."

While Jeff and Jeannie continued to bicker, Chet turned his full attention to Claire. He gazed at her intently hoping to see a flutter of an eyelid or her tongue move across her dry lips or her hand reach up to scratch her nose. Claire was as still as a fallen tree limb lying on the ground. Chet clung to the hope of Jeannie's words. After a few moments he was drawn back into the din of the squabbling.

"You always do stuff like this, Jeannie, making sure you're the center of attention."

"Stuff it in your ear, Jeff. I know what I heard."

Chet turned around abruptly. His face was red and he pointed to the door shushing in anger. "Get out right now!" He stepped into the hall with them, closing the door to Claire's room.

Chapter 13 : Hopefulness

"Stop it, Jeff and Jeannie. Your childish arguing doesn't help. What if your Mom hears you? Now get back in there and watch your Mother's every move. If you can't be civil to each other, don't talk at all. I'm going to get the doctor."

As they entered their mother's room, Jeff said, "I'm sorry for yelling at you."

"Not a problem. This has been tough for all of us. I know this sounds weird, but I think Mom knew I was praying with her. She reached for me and then she put her hand over her heart. Oh well, maybe it was one of my fantasies."

It seemed an eternity before their Dad and Dr. McDaniel returned to the room.

Dr. McDaniel examined Claire, checking all of her vitals. The smile on his face said it all. "Her temperature's back to normal as well as blood pressure. And she seems to be out of pain. I'm ordering an MRI. This will help us to determine if the swelling in her brain has been reduced. Then, we can decrease the meds and bring her back into consciousness."

Chet questioned, "Doctor, when will she come out of this coma?"

"I don't know. First things first. Let's get her to radiology. Why don't you folks grab something to eat in the cafeteria? She'll need to be prepped for the MRI and then moved to the fourth floor. She'll be back in the room in about two hours. They'll page me after the radiologist has looked at the results and we'll take it from there."

"Okay, Dr. McDaniel. C'mon, Jeff and Jeannie. Looks like we have more waiting to do. Let's get something to eat or at least get coffee. Thanks Dr. McDaniel."

As the three of them stepped into the empty elevator, Jeannie rubbed her Dad's back, "Sorry, Dad for the ruckus in there."

Jeff echoed. "Me, too, Dad. Sorry."

Chet put his arms around both of them and nudged their shoulders together.

"Mom's gonna be okay, guys. She's gonna be okay. Let's stop in the chapel and say a few prayers."

The quiet of the chapel flowed over each of them as they knelt by the cross. Chet led them in the Our Father, Hail Mary, and Glory Be, and in his own words a plea to God to bring Claire back home. In the hospital cafeteria, Chet and Jeannie sipped coffee, while Jeff ate three eggs, hash brown potatoes, bacon, toast, a donut, and orange juice.

"Nothing stops you from eating," Jeannie commented.

"Jeannie, don't start. You know Mom wouldn't mind one bit. She knows how hungry he gets. Everybody deals differently. Hold on, I'm getting a call. It's the doctor."

"Hello? I see. Yeah, good. What a relief." Chet winked at Jeff and Jeannie. "Okay, we'll be right up."

"What, what, Dad? What did he say?" Jeannie questioned.

"He said everything looks good and the radiologist did not see any apparent signs of brain damage. Dr. McDaniel is going to meet us in five minutes in the room."

Jeff gulped the last of his orange juice following Jeannie and his Dad to the elevator."

Chet, Jeff, and Jeannie entered Claire's hospital room. Dr. McDaniel waved them in.

"Doctor, that's good news that she doesn't have brain damage, isn't it? What happens next? I know I've asked you this a lot, but do you have a better idea when she'll come out of the coma?"

"I know you're all very anxious for her to wake up. It is good news, Chet, but these things take time. I've ordered a reduction of the meds. I would guess in the next 24 to 48 hours, we'll see Claire open her eyes and hopefully she'll acclimate to her surroundings. But, and this is an important but – while an MRI is extremely helpful, it doesn't always give us the full picture. The brain is complicated. An MRI shows us the physical condition of the brain, but the intricate workings of the mind sometimes contradict it."

Chet, Jeff, and Jeannie sighed in resignation. Dr. McDaniel responded to their angst. "Let's not go there just yet. Like I said, everything on the MRI looks normal. I'm encouraged, but I want you all to understand that this type of aneurysm may alter her personality and then again, it may not. We'll have a much better diagnosis once she is conscious."

Chapter 13 : Hopefulness

Chet pursued. "Can you tell us how we'll be able to tell if her personality is altered?"

"If she wakes up and she can talk and move and has some recollection of when she felt the pain on July 3rd, that's a good sign. If she recognizes all of you and passes a few psychological tests, she'll be good to go. Let's hope for that scenario. But sometimes there are permanent aberrations in memory. She may confuse reality with fantasy."

Chet shook the doctor's hand. Thanks, Dr. McDaniel for all that you've done."

"I played a small part. God did the heavy lifting." He walked out of the room, but stuck his head back in to encourage them, "Hey, I've heard a lot of praying in here. Keep it up. That's the best cure for all of you. I'll see you tomorrow. Good night."

Chet, Jeannie, and Jeff had been taking turns spending the nights with Claire over the past several days, but this night all three of them remained in the room. Each had a certain level of hopefulness emerging in their hearts, but they also remained cautious about Claire's recovery.

Claire breathed steadily. She no longer winced in pain and the frantic gasps had ended. Chet moved his chair close to the bed and gently held Claire's hand. Jeannie and Jeff sat in the two chairs by the window watching the moon rise in a summer sky. Exhausted from fifteen days of worry and fear, they all fell asleep. Claire opened her eyes briefly and saw her sleeping family. She tried to talk, but her mouth would not move.

Claire was beginning to have a better realization that she was between two worlds. As much as she loved the sweet comfort of what she now knew was Heaven, she longed to return to her life on Earth.

_____

"Come, Claire, come. They're all waiting for us." Claire closed her eyes and at once she and Ariel were back in the beautiful pearl hallway.

"Ariel, am I ever going back to Earth?"

Ariel cautiously responded, "Well, we still have one more place to visit. Claire bristled at this. No more visits to the nether world, Claire. God is pleased that you courageously endured the view of the chambers of Hell. I know you miss Chet, and Jeannie, and Jeff. Please trust that God is an omnipotent Father who will reveal His plan to you. You've seen the Angels' Room of Life. We're going back there now and in that room we'll pass through a magnificent archway. When we cross that threshold, I'm very sure that your soul will be enlivened with faith, hope, and love. God calls it Paradise Purest." Claire no longer felt fear, but her heart was aching for her family.

Ariel's voice was jubilant with anticipation: "We need to go now, Claire. This is the best part of Heaven."

At that, Ariel whisked Claire through pearl halls, one more beautiful than the other until they floated in the Angels' Room of Life. As they entered, Claire still marveled at the beauty and joy of the angels scurrying about, excited to be the guardian of a tiny human being. In the Angels' Room of Life, the conception of one person is heralded with glory and wonder. Even if there is a miscarriage, even if that human being lives ten seconds or ten days or one hundred years, that Guardian Angel rejoices in the miracle of conception.

Within the Angels' Room of Life, Claire and Ariel stood before a huge archway covered with baby's breath flowers and red roses. As they walked through the fragrant portal, Claire gazed in awe at the luminous streams of light that shone on rows and rows of angels, the caretakers of Paradise Purest.

Some angels held a single red rose and seemed to be in a waiting cue. Frequently, these angels floated to the arch, placed their rose in the blanket of baby's breath flowers and then joined another group of angels. These guardian angels held what had been a tortured, aborted baby. The horror was over. No more pain from suctioned arms and legs, no more sharp tools probing what should have been their protective womb, no more hopelessly hiding from the invaders of life, no more silent screams. Each baby now made whole and new, rested peacefully in the arms of their protector, their personal Guardian Angel.

Claire saw the book and a sense of joy and intrigue filled her spirit. The light shone on the verse she read:

> *Now the dwelling of God is with men, and he will live with them. They will be his people, and God himself will be with them and be their God. He will wipe every tear from their eyes. There will be no more death or mourning or*

*crying or pain, for the old order of things has passed away. He who was seated on the throne said, 'I am making everything new.' (Revelation 21:3-5)*

The ritual continued every moment of eternity. As soon as a child was aborted, his or her Guardian Angel held the red rose until Jesus placed that tiny soul in their loving wings. Claire noticed the angels who cuddled the babies seemed to sway gently back and forth as a unit. It was as though God, Himself, was tenderly rocking the cradle of little lost lives.

Ariel answered Claire's thoughts, "He is." Claire felt Ariel's loving embrace for the last time. Oh, Ariel would be with Claire to guide her as she had done for fifty-six years, but it would be a long time before she would feel the tangible presence of Ariel again. Claire's journey to Heaven and Hell was over.

She felt that familiar nudge. Zimelda moved her along the pearl corridors in lightning speed until they reached the stairway. Claire stopped at the top of the steps and asked, "Zimelda, don't get me wrong, I want to go back to my family, but you told me God was going to give me a message."

Zimelda responded, "He did give you a message."

"No, He didn't."

"Did you really think God was going to give you an instruction book? Claire, He showed you Heaven and Hell. Everything you need to know, you have seen."

"But what if I don't remember any of this?"

Zimelda raised one eyebrow with a look of disbelief, as she had done at the beginning of Claire's ascent. Only this time she offered encouragement. "Remember, Jesus told the woman who touched his cloak, *'Take heart, daughter, your faith has healed you.'* God has healed you, Claire, but not just the physical healing of your body. He has healed you of your procrastination. He has healed you of thinking you can wait to make a difference in the world. You cannot wait any longer now that you have seen the truth. You may not remember every moment that you have experienced, but God will reveal and clarify in His own time and in His own way. God will reveal and clarify through the Holy Spirit. Listen to the Holy Spirit. Claire saw the light on the book and read one final verse from the Bible:

*Finally, draw your strength from the Lord and from his mighty power. Put on the armor of God so that you may be able to stand firm against the tactics of the devil. For our struggle is not with flesh and blood, but with principalities, with the powers, with the world rulers of this present darkness, with the evil spirits in the Heavens. Therefore, put on the armor of God that you may be able to resist on the evil day and, having done everything, to hold your ground. So stand fast with your loins girded in truth, clothed with righteousness as a breastplate and your feet shod in readiness for the gospel of peace. In all circumstances hold faith as a shield, to quench all flaming arrows of the evil one. And take the helmet of salvation and the sword of the Spirit, which is the Word of God. (Ephesians 6:10-20)*

Claire felt the gravitational pull of her family's love. She became innately aware of the weight of her body as she descended the stairway. She squeezed Chet's hand and he woke-up. Claire opened her eyes and whispered, "Hi, hon."

# CHAPTER 14 : SHE'S BACK

It was 6:10 am on July 19.   As soon as Jeannie and Jeff heard her voice, they both jumped from their chairs and rushed to Claire's bedside.  Chet had tears in his eyes as he gently caressed his wife's cheek.  Jeff wiggled his Mom's big toe.  Jeannie held her mother's hand.   The waiting was over.

Claire tried to sit-up, but was very weak.  Chet propped two pillows behind her back for support.  Then, Claire spoke.  "Oh, my gosh, I missed you guys.  I didn't think I'd ever see you again, but I'm back, thank God."

Jeff laughed, "Well, Mom, you didn't really go anywhere."

"What happened to me?  How long have I been in the hospital?"

Chet responded, "You've been here sixteen days.  You came to the hospital on July 3rd."

"July 3rd?"  She tried to rewind the tape in her head.  She remembered mud splashing on her legs and hearing the sound of the hose. "Yeah, I was gardening.  I coiled the hose.  I had a horrible headache.  The pain was excruciating. Then, I must have passed out.   I don't remember much after that, but I do remember traveling somewhere.  There were these incredibly high stairs. Oh, well, I must have been dreaming.  I feel groggy.  Ouch, my head hurts.  Have I been asleep all this time?"

"Yes, you've been asleep all this time.  I'm going to the nurse's station and ask them to call Dr. McDaniel.  He'll explain everything to you, Claire.  The most important thing is that you're back.  Would you like something to drink or eat?"

"I guess I am a little hungry.  Juice and a piece of toast would be nice."

"Okay, then juice and toast it is.  Jeff, would you go to the cafeteria and get that for your Mom?"

"You betcha!  Mom, I love you."

"I love you too, Jeff."

Jeannie and Claire stared at each other for several seconds.

"Jeannie, you look tired, darling.  This has been hard on you, hasn't it?"

"The waiting was worth it, Mom.  I'm glad you're awake.  You know, Dad said you were asleep the entire time, but last night I heard you praying."

"What prayer?"

"The Prayer to Our Guardian Angel. I said it with you. Then you fell back into the coma…errr sleep again. Do you remember any of that, Mom?"

Claire sighed trying to recall that moment. Her recollection was veiled in vagueness, but she didn't want to disappoint Jeannie. "Things are a little foggy right now, hon, but I'm sure I'll remember it when I'm stronger."

"That's okay, Mom. I don't want to stress you out, but thank God for Guardian Angels."

"Yes, thank God for Guardian Angels and angels like you. Claire noticed the vase of baby's breath flowers with one red rose in the center. "Oh, I love the baby's breath. Who sent them?"

Before Jeannie could answer, Jeff returned with the food for his Mom. Chet and Dr. McDaniel soon followed.

Dr. McDaniel smiled broadly. "Well, Claire, welcome back. Are you enjoying breakfast? From what your husband told me, I believe you are 'out of the woods' as they say."

"Yes, I am enjoying my breakfast. But, I would like to know 'what woods' I was in."

Dr. McDaniel explained the gravity of the ruptured aneurysm, the operation, and the reasons behind the induced coma. After an hour of examining and questioning Claire, he pronounced, "Well, you can go home tomorrow, if you want. You'll be weak for a few days. I want you to take it slow; drink plenty of water. Stick with liquids for a day and then gradually increase your eating. Oh, and take naps."

Claire laughed, "I just woke-up and now you're telling me to take naps!"

Dr. McDaniel looked at Chet. "She's all yours now, Mr. McCormack. She's back!"

While Jeannie and Jeff were hovering over their mother, Dr. McDaniel motioned Chet into the hall.

"Mr. McCormack, she's back, but let me know if she seems to mix reality and fantasy. Sometimes there are permanent aberrations in memory. She may be confused at times as to what is real and what is imagined."

Chapter 14 : She's Back

Chet sighed, "Oh. What do you mean?"

"I'm telling you this because I don't want you to be alarmed if Claire tells a wild tale. Usually, over time, when the brain has finally settled down, the episodes become less and less. Call me if it happens too often, but be patient. Give her time to heal. She's been through a lot, but obviously she's a survivor."

As Dr. McDaniel walked down the hall, Chet took a deep breath and returned to Claire's room. Jeannie was combing what was left of her mother's hair. From the crown of her head down to her neck had been shaved for the operation. Jeff sat on the edge of the bed.

"Mom, everybody's been calling about you – Uncle Bud, Uncle Charley, Uncle Jody and all of your sisters. They were going nuts that they couldn't visit."

Chet interjected, "They were really worried about you, but I didn't want anything interfering with your treatment."

"I'll have plenty of time to talk with them when I'm home. I guess I missed the Fourth of July party this year. First time ever."

"They all got together, but Aunt Karie said it wasn't much fun, knowing you were in a coma. And I'm sure they missed your macaroni salad and apple pie."

"Ooh, you all had to eat Aunt Dee Dee's not-so-scrumptious broccoli salad."

Jeff acted out a choking victim, "Help, I'm gagging, it was the broccoli salad. Oh, Aunt Dee Dee, why'd you do it? Why do you make that awful broccoli mess every year?"

"Jeffery, don't make fun of my oldest sister. She tries her best."

Jeannie gathered her purse and overnight bag. "Mom, we're going home to cleanup the house. Key word being 'we,' Jeff."

"Hey, I pull my weight."

Chet smiled. "That's a good idea, Jeannie. I'm staying here for the night. I'll call you in the morning."

"Mom, you finally came back to us and I can't wait to get you home. I love you."

"Same here, Mom. See you tomorrow. Love you."

"See you tomorrow, darlings. Love you more."

The past few weeks had been a series of pizza, soda, sandwiches, and carryout burgers. Trash was everywhere. Jeff cranked up the music as he and Jeannie dusted furniture, did laundry, vacuumed, and cleaned the kitchen and bathrooms. It was a fun evening for both of them. Jeff teased Jeannie, "Hey, maybe now you'll find the right guy to marry, since you've demonstrated the ability to do what a woman should do – clean. Now, if you could only learn how to cook."

Jeannie threw a dish towel into Jeff's face. They laughed for a good two minutes at being able to stop worrying. Jeannie chided, "C'mon, bro, let's finish cleaning this mess."

After three hours of work, the house looked good. Jeannie took a shower and then went to the store to pick-up groceries and flowers. Jeff offered to go with her, but Jeannie declined the offer. "That's okay, Jeffy, I'm buying healthy food, not frozen pizza and potato chips. I'll be back in about an hour."

Jeff relaxed on the couch, surfing the TV channels for sports. It was the first time in almost three weeks that he even wanted to chill out. *What a summer, first Kevin's Dad, and then Mom. Wow!*

The doorbell rang. Jeff muted the TV and opened the door. Kevin stood on the porch holding a large crockpot. "Hey, Jeff, how's it going? We heard that your Mom is out of the coma. I'm glad she's better. Mom and I drove by a while ago. We saw your car in the driveway. I wanted to see how you're doing."

"Come in, Kev. Thanks, yeah. It's been weird, thinking that she might die." As soon as Jeff spoke, he wanted to suck the words back into his mouth. There was an awkward moment of not knowing what to do.

Then Kevin walked toward the kitchen. "Mom fixed chili tonight and asked me to bring some over. This is heavy. Do you mind if I put it in the kitchen?"

"No, no. Hold on, I'll get the door for you. Really good to see you, Kev. What's happening?"

"Been working at Tiggy's Landscaping. And you know how Tiggy is…a tobacco chewing redneck and proud of it."

"But a rich redneck!"

"Yeah, no wonder. That guy gets up with the sun and literally does not stop until the sun goes down."

"That's the truth, man. Did he hire someone to replace me?"

"Yeah, he hired Dylan Barry, but he's not as strong as you and me. I have to pick up the slack, which I hate. Tiggy would be glad to have you come back."

"I've got to see how things go with my Mom. Dad and Jeannie have to return to work. Looks like I'll be the designated caregiver."

"Totally understand. She woke up today, right?"

"Exactly and she's coming home tomorrow. Someone needs to be with her for awhile. How's your Mom doing?"

"Not great. Ups and downs. She cries a lot. I know she misses Dad, but she's sad all the time. It's like she's feeling guilty about his death. Now, she says this mantra over and over, 'Let not your heart be troubled, let not your heart be troubled.' I can't put my finger on it, but there's a creepy atmosphere in our house. Hey, I better go now. I'm kinda in the same place you are – designated caregiver."

"Especially when you're with Tiggy."

"You're jealous, cuz I'm making overtime pay. Hey, man, take care. Give me a call. Really glad to see you, Jeff."

Jeannie arrived home as Kevin was leaving. "Hi, Kevin. Tell your Mom thanks for the flowers she sent to the hospital."

"Will do. Good news about your Mom. Jeff says she's coming home tomorrow."

"Best news we've had in weeks, Kev."

"Oh, that reminds me. Would it be okay if my Mom stopped by in a few days? She told me to ask you."

Jeannie, as her Mom's self-assigned protector said, "I'm not sure if Mom will be strong enough for visitors. Maybe one day next week. Have your Mom call first, okay?"

"Will do. See ya, Jeannie."

Jeannie felt a twinge of guilt for delaying Anne's visit, but she realized her Mom and Anne had been on the outs since Mr. Combs died. She didn't know why, but she did know that her mother and Mrs. Combs had not visited nor talked to each other since mid-May. Even at Jeff's and Kevin's graduation, they spoke very little. Jeannie wondered what could have caused two women who had been friends for fifteen years to cool their friendship abruptly.

*Oh, well, the most important thing is that Mom's coming home tomorrow. She's back!*

As the summer moon once again glimmered through the window of Claire's hospital room, Chet dimmed the lights, fluffed the pillows, and filled her water glass. His mood was uplifted by the day's event, but he was drained physically and emotionally. He sunk into the chair by Claire's bed.

Claire smiled, patting his hand, "I'm going home tomorrow. What do you think of that, Mr. McCormack?"

"I think that's the best news I've heard in my entire life. Claire, we've been through so much, but nothing like this. I was really scared."

"Me, too."

"Do you remember anything from the coma?"

"Not really, but maybe I will over time. It took you a while to remember the stuff that happened in Dallas."

"Don't compare this to Dallas, hon. That was totally self-induced. You didn't do anything to deserve this. I have to admit the hospital smells reminded me of Parkland Memorial."

"You know, Chet, how you always say that verse from the Bible?"

"You mean 'All things work for good for those who love the Lord?'"

"That would be the one. I've reached the conclusion that all of those things that happened to us or that we did to ourselves have worked for the good. In spite of the turmoil when we first got married and then the bankruptcy and the job losses, we're still together."

Chapter 14 : She's Back

"And, we have some pretty good blessings too. Jeannie and Jeff."

"The house and my garden. Your job. Our health."

"Our Faith."

"And, each other. I know I was resentful for many years."

"Well, I wasn't exactly your knight in shining armor."

"But, you are the love of my life."

Chet put his arms around Claire and whispered, "Don't ever leave me, Claire. I need you. I love you."

"I love you, Chet. I am glad to be back, especially with you. I can't believe I'm saying this, but I am tired."

Shortly after that, Claire fell asleep breathing steadily. Her slumber was restful and uneventful. Chet stared at her for a long time to make sure she was okay. She turned on her left side with her knees curled slightly as she had done since they had first slept together. Then, he felt tears streaming down his face, tears of liberating joy and thankfulness.

# CHAPTER 15 : HOME AGAIN WITH FAMILY

Claire Dillon-McCormack was awake, alert, and more than ready to go home to Hallowed. After three hours of physical and mental testing, she was released from St. Aloysius Hospital. The McCormacks said goodbye to doctors, nurses, and staff. Then, Chet and Claire began their ride home, leaving behind nearly three weeks of nerve-wracking uncertainty. It was 95 degrees, but as soon as they approached the bridge leading into Hallowed, Claire opened the car window to smell the wonderful hot breeze of her hometown.

"Aaah, Chet, I am the most blessed woman in the world. There I was in a coma, sleeping through life for sixteen days and now I'm awake and going home."

"It was pretty scary the last few weeks. I don't know what I'd do if you were gone forever."

"Chet, you and I are both going to be 'gone forever' one day, but we believe in God, we believe that Jesus Christ is our Savior, and we believe in life everlasting."

Chet resounded with a loud "Amen!"

"Besides being with you and Jeannie and Jeff, guess what I'm really looking forward to."

"Hmmm, does it possibly have something to do with dirt and flowers?"

"I really want to get back to my garden. By the way, is everything dead in the yard?"

"No, it's not too bad. We, at least, kept up with the watering. And Tiggy's team stopped by once a week to mow the lawn. But your flowers need the Claire touch."

Claire closed her eyes envisioning the yard. She'd still have time to trim bushes, spread mulch, water the plants and enjoy the flowers for the remainder of the summer. She felt a wonderful sense of contentment knowing that she could soon be in her garden.

When Chet pulled the car into the driveway, Claire laughed as she saw a huge bunch of balloons tied to the mailbox with a super-sized one at the top that read, 'Welcome Home, Mom.' "Oh, for gosh sakes, those two are incredible."

Chapter 15 : Home Again with Family

Jeff and Jeannie bounded out the door anxious to bring their mother into the spotless home.

"Mom, wait till you see how many flowers have been sent to you. Aunt Dee Dee and Caroline sent a dozen roses and Uncle Bud sent a six-pack of beer with balloons attached. Hurry, Mom, come see all the stuff."

"Whoa, kids. Remember, this is your Mom's first day home. She needs to take it slow. Jeff, can you get the suitcase? I want to stay by Mom when she walks to the door."

"Sure, Dad."

"Chet, I feel pretty good. I'm not an invalid, you know."

"No, and let's keep it that way. Now hold on to my arm! The doctor said you'd be weak for a few days. I'm not taking any chances."

Jeff entered the house first, carrying the suitcase. Jeannie followed, holding the vase of Baby's Breath flowers that Anne had sent to the hospital. They faced their mother as she walked through the door, both of them as excited as the time they had made peanut butter on toast for Mother's Day breakfast years ago.

"Aaah, home at last. It smells great in here. Jeannie, did you bake something?"

"I did. I made brownies and there's Graeter's vanilla ice cream in the freezer."

Jeff chimed in, "And, the best of all, Mom. Aunt Stephie dropped off a double batch of her fudge. We can melt it and make hot fudge brownies."

"Mmmm, sounds wonderful."

"Mom, where do you want the vase of Baby's Breath flowers?"

"Let's put it in the sun room by the recliner. Speaking of which, you know I am a little tired. I thought Dr. McDaniel was kidding when he told me to take naps, but I think he's right."

"They put you through the paces this morning, hon. Tell the kids about it."

"Holy tomolli. They made me touch my toes five times, balance on one foot for thirty seconds, and perform a bunch of other silly exercises. Then I had to answer a hundred psychological questions that were all over the board like: 'In what city and hospital were you born?' 'Who is President of the United States?' and a very strange one 'How old were you when you realized you were alive?' "

"It's called the PBMRPCP -- Psychological Battery for Memory Recognition in Post Coma Patients. We studied it in Psych 101 freshmen year."

"You're right, Jeannie. I think that's what they called it. Little did you know when you took that course that your Mom would one day be scrutinized by the -PBM-whatever other letters- test."

"That's a cool question, Mom. When did you realize you were alive?"

"I think I was about four years old, Jeff. I was walking up a street with Aunt Dee Dee who must have been thirteen. We had moved that day from an apartment in uptown Hallowed to Gladden Avenue. Dee Dee and I were going to a local grocery store. I remember there was a cloud of smoke in the air and I was afraid it was a fire. Three or four men were working on the street with jackhammers and the noise scared me, too. Dee Dee assured me that the smoke was from their trucks and there was no fire. I suppose they were heating up tar to patch the street. Then, I was okay, because I knew my big sister wouldn't let me get hurt. I think that was the first time I remember being alive."

Chet stood behind Claire wrapping his arms around her from back to front. He kissed her cheek with a joyful smack. "And you're still alive and that's the best answer to our prayers. My question is do you want to sleep in the sun room, or go to our bedroom?"

"Well, I don't know if I really want to sleep. I think I want to take a little snooze on the recliner for a bit."

Jeff laughed, "Mom, what in the world is a little snooze? I mean I know what a snooze alarm is, but I've never heard anyone say they're going to take a snooze."

"Well, Jeffrey, Grandpa used to say different variations of that word, all of which referred to a special kind of nap whereby you sleep anywhere but in your own bed, so that you still hear things going on around you. When I was a little girl, I'd wake him up and he'd say, 'Oh, Claire, I must have been snoozing!' Wow, I haven't thought of that word in years."

"Snooze, I like it. I'll have to lay that one on Kev sometime."

"How is Kev?"

"He's hanging in there and he keeps busy working for Tiggy. Last night was the first time I've seen him in about three weeks."

"And, his Mom?"

"I asked him about her yesterday when he was here. He said that she's not great."

Jeannie added, "Last night, Kevin brought over a pot of chili that Mrs. Combs made. I told him to thank her for that and for the flowers she sent you. He mentioned that she wanted to visit you in the next few weeks."

"Yeah, I haven't really talked much with her since May. It'll be good to catch up."

"Anyway, I told Kevin to have her call you. I wasn't sure how you felt about her visiting."

Claire looked quizzically at Jeannie. "Okay, thanks Jeannie." She stared at the vase of Baby's Breath. Her eyelids felt heavy. *Annie, Annie, what went wrong?*

As Jeannie placed a pillow under her mother's head, Claire gently grabbed her hand pressing it against her cheek. Jeff positioned his strong hands on each of his mother's shoulders and kissed her forehead. Claire pulled both of his hands down and smelled the scent of chocolate brownies and fudge. She smiled and whispered, "You're secret's safe with me."

Chet closed the French glass doors to the sun room. He blew a kiss to Claire and she caught it in her right hand.

*Hmmm, thank you God for bringing me back to my wonderful family.*

Chet peeked in through one of the little square windows on the French doors to make sure Claire was resting comfortably.

*Thank you God for answering my prayers.*

Within days of Claire's homecoming, the Dillon clan began their whirlwind of visits or calls. Charley lived in Arizona, but called Claire every other day to see how she was doing. Her youngest brother, Jody, had started a new job in New York, but sent text messages to his sister daily. Bud visited for an entire afternoon, throwing one-liners at everyone.

"Jeff, I hear you're going to St. Francis Bergio in the fall, eh? What's your major?"

"Not sure yet, but I'm thinking of Civil Engineering."

"Oh, you'll be a courteous engineer as opposed to a rude engineer?"

"Groan, Uncle Bud. You can do better than that."

"Okay, Claire. Here's a question for you. What do you call a person who has a knee that can think?"

"I give, Bud. What?"

"Brainy." Bud spelled it out for emphasis. "B r a i n – k n e e."

Claire threw a pillow at her brother. "You never change, idiot!"

Chet laughed. "I like it, Bud. That's a good one."

"Dad, it's worse than courteous engineer. Groaner #2, Uncle Bud."

Jeannie wanted to ask her uncle the question of the day. "Uncle Bud, do you remember the first time you realized you were alive?"

Bud started walking like a zombie. "Thank you, Dr. Frankenstein for giving me a brain. I'm alive, I'm alive."

"Really, Bud, can't you be serious once in a while? Answer Jeannie's question. It was one of a hundred questions on my psychological test. What's it called, Jeannie – PBM?"

Jeannie looked at Uncle Bud. "PBMRPCP -- Psychological Battery for Memory Recognition in Post Coma Patients. C'mon, tell us."

"Hmm, let me think a minute. That's a strange question. Here goes. It was the day before Thanksgiving. I was four-, maybe five- years old. Dad took the boys in the backyard; not Jody of course. He wasn't born yet. In fact, Claire, you weren't born yet, either. At the time, it was me, Charley, Dee Dee, and Caroline. I remember being really excited because Dad was going to cut the head off of our turkey."

Claire cringed, "I've heard this story before. It gets gruesome now!"

Chapter 15 : Home Again with Family

Jeff urged, "I'm loving it!  Keep going, Uncle Bud."

"Dad sorta knew what he was doing, but I don't think he had actually killed any animal in his life.  A guy he worked with told him how fresh the turkey meat would be, supposedly.  He also told Dad that he would save a lot of money if he bought a turkey six weeks before Thanksgiving.  Problem was Charley, Dee Dee, Caroline and I had grown fond of our little pet.  I think we named him Tag-a-Long.  For six weeks, we fed him and petted him and Dee Dee even put a handmade leash on him to take him for walks.  She put one of her old Easter bonnets on the turkey's head."

"Uncle Bud, you're making this up and there's no one here to verify it," Jeannie admonished.

Chet corroborated Bud's version, "Jeannie, you haven't heard this story before, but I have.  Only, I heard it from Uncle Charley years ago.  So far, it's the same story that I was told."

"Thank you, Chet.  I appreciate the endorsement.  Anyway, Dad put the turkey on a chopping   block and with one whack of the ax old Tag's head fell to the ground, but the bonnet still hung on the stub of the neck.  Then, Tag started running around the yard like a chicken with his head cut off except he was a turkey with his head off."  Jeff was disappointed.  "Very funny, Uncle Bud.  Good joke.  I don't believe you either, Dad."

"Noooo, Jeffy, it's the truth.  Chickens, turkeys, even geese will run around after their head is chopped off, sometimes for as much as five minutes.  It has something to do with nerve endings.  What happened next is the real kicker.  Charley and I started chasing Tag around the yard.  We thought we could save him.  Dad went into the garage to get something to throw over him, but it was too late. Tag darted toward the house with blood gushing out his neck.  Lo and behold, Mom, Dee Dee, and Caroline were looking out the window.  I couldn't hear them, but I could see the girls screaming and crying.  Then, Charley puked and I ran into the house."

Claire grimaced, "Nice story, Bud.  No one's going to want to eat turkey for Thanksgiving anymore."

Jeff was enthralled.  "Did Grandma cook it?  What'd it taste like?"

"Grandma wouldn't touch it. I think we had hamburgers, corn, mashed potatoes, and cranberry sauce that year. And, of course pumpkin pie, but there was no turkey on our table that Thanksgiving."

"Why didn't Grandpa go to the store and get a cooked turkey?"

Bud and Claire roared as Chet explained. "Son, back then they did not cook chickens or turkeys in stores. In fact, there were absolutely no stores open on Thanksgiving. Sorry, Bud, go ahead."

Bud stared directly at Jeannie. "Shortly after dinner your Grandpa went out back and buried poor Tag. Before long, we all pretty much forgot about it, but I think that was the first time I remember being alive. Sorry, I guess that was a long way around of answering your question, Jeannie."

"Not a problem, Uncle Bud."

Chet concluded, "We would expect nothing less, Bud. Actually, it's a darn good story. We're ordering pizza tonight for dinner. Want to stick around?"

"Thanks, anyway, but Monica has something or other planned tonight. Time to take off."

The McCormack family stood to escort Bud to the door.

Claire hugged her brother. "Thanks for visiting today, Bud. When I came home from the hospital, I got a kick out of your six-pack with the balloons on it."

"You are very welcome, little sister. Seriously, Claire, glad you're out of the woods. Monica's going to call you this week. She wants all of you to come for dinner some time in late August."

"Sounds good, Bud. We'd like that. Thanks for the laughs, today. It was fun. Tell Monica I said hi."

"Well, see ya in August, squirt."

A few days later on Sunday afternoon, Claire's five sisters converged on the McCormack household.

"Jeannie, Jeannie, Jeannie," Dee Dee admonished, "Why don't you move back to Hallowed? Haven't you lived in Chicago long enough? Your Mom needs you now."

Chapter 15 : Home Again with Family

Claire jumped to Jeannie's defense. "No, I don't, Dee Dee. I am doing fine and Jeannie loves her job and friends in Chicago. She's twenty-five."

"Aunt Dee Dee, would you like a sandwich?" Jeannie offered hoping to keep Aunt Dee Dee's mouth full.

"Oh, thanks, Jeannie. I'll have the egg salad. Jeff, can you get me a glass of ice tea, please?"

"Sure, Aunt Dee Dee."

*I'm at your beck and call, oh Queen of the Dillon Clan!*

Jeff and Jeannie dutifully served the food and drink to their aunts and then went into hiding in the kitchen.

"Oh my gosh, Jeff, they all talk at the same time."

"I love how Aunt Dee Dee gives her unsolicited advice to you."

Jeannie rolled her eyes. "No kidding, but I noticed Aunt Tara nodding in agreement. Maybe I should move back."

"Mom's doing really well. I don't think she'd want you to become her permanent nurse maid."

"I know, but I'm worried about her being alone. When Dad gets home today, I'll talk to him about it."

"Let's shoot hoops. I need to get away from the cackling."

Back in the sun room, Claire held court with her sisters basking in the joy of being with each of them.

"Claire, you look good. I love the short hair. Are you feeling better now?"

"I'm feeling pretty strong, Karie. I had to get the front of my hair trimmed because they shaved the back of my head. Take a look at my peach fuzz skull."

The sisters moved around as a unit to look at the back of Claire's head.

"It doesn't look bad, Claire. It's growing in and the front looks great."

"Thanks, Jeannie cut and styled it. Anyway, it'll grow back. I'm glad to be alive."

Tara smiled, "We're glad, too, Claire.  Gosh, we weren't allowed to come to the hospital.  We waited and prayed and waited some more."

"Why didn't Chet want us to come to the hospital?  He's such a controller."

Stephie picked up the tray of sandwiches, "Dee Dee, why don't you have another egg salad sandwich that you like so much?"

Tara added, "And remember, don't talk with your mouth full."

Claire explained, "There really wasn't anything you all could have done.  I was out to the world for sixteen days.  Chet and the doctor agreed that they wanted to keep the stimulation to a minimum.  My brain needed to rest and heal."

Karie added, "Which it did, thank God.  And Jeannie was very good at calling one of us every day."

Stephie probed, "So now, what, Claire.  Let's see, it's been two and a half weeks since you got out of St. Al's.  Do you have to do physical therapy?"

"Not really.  The doctor told me I can do most of the things I've always done.  Mentally, I'm 'normal' as they say.  For the physical part, exercising and gardening should help.  I'm feeling stronger and better every day.  Hey, I don't want to be one of those people who gives a blow-by-blow description of their ailments.  Besides, I really don't remember much.  Karie, are those the pictures from your spring vacation?"

"Yes, I'll pass them around if you want."

"Myrtle Beach, huh?  Did you have good weather?"

"It was hot.  The girls all got burnt the first day."

"Did you put vinegar on them?" Tara inquired.  "You know it turns a burn into a suntan."

"Yes I did and Don said it made him hungry because they all smelled like salads.  He started chasing them around the beach house with a knife, fork, and salt and pepper."

Dee Dee asked, "Why'd he do that?"

"It's a joke, Dee Dee," Claire answered.  Everyone else was laughing, but Dee Dee didn't see much humor in things like that.

Chapter 15 : Home Again with Family

Karie continued, "The vinegar did help, though. Tara, how's Don feeling? Is he over the flu yet?"

"He's a lot better, but he was off work eight days."

Caroline complained, "I didn't know he was sick. Why doesn't somebody call me about this stuff?"

"I left a message for you, Caroline. I told you I didn't want to visit Claire until Don felt better. That was last week."

"Well, I didn't get the message."

Claire, Karie, and Stephanie said in unison, "You never get the message!"

"Caroline, I swear you're from another planet. I don't know how you can be as smart as you are, but still not remember what someone told you."

Dee Dee sat up very straight giving everyone her oldest sister 'pay attention' look. "Caroline, do you remember when I was in Mary Sue Evans' wedding and Mrs. Evans called to invite Mom to a bridesmaids' luncheon? Mom wasn't home, and you supposedly got the message."

Claire talked in a sing-songy voice, "Oh boy, do I remember that one. Caroline Jean, you forgot to give Mom the message that day."

Tara added, "Then, the next day Mom saw Mary Sue's Mom at Kerger's grocery store and Mrs. Evans asked her why she didn't make it to the luncheon the day before."

Stephie also in a sing-songy style asked, "And Mrs. Evans told Mom she had given the message to you, Caroline?"

"Oh, yeah. When Mom got home that day she started yelling and slamming down her purse and packages."

Tara, Stephie, and Karie stomped around the sun room picking up books and purses and anything non-breakable and slamming them on the table. Karie took a pillow and pretended to smother Caroline.

Tara did a dead-on imitation of their mother, "Hells bells, I don't get invited to that many events and this makes me sick. Why didn't you tell me, Caroline? And why did that stupid Mrs. Evans leave a message with a kid. Why didn't she tell Dee Dee? Maybe she did. I bet Dee Dee knew too! Wait till she gets home!"

When the hooting and the howling calmed down, Caroline looked a little sad.

"Mom, God rest her soul, finally got over it, but thanks, Dee Dee for reminding me. It took me thirty-five years to come to terms with my guilt for that mistake."

Claire spit out words through her laughter, "Now, Caroline, you have to admit it's a great memory."

"Yeah, it is, but I don't blame Mom for being mad. I guess I do forget things people tell me some times."

Caroline sat with her arms folded and started chuckling, "You probably don't know this, but when Dad found out, he tried to calm Mom down by sympathizing with her, but later that day he was in the garage building a table. I followed him out there to escape the wrath of Mary Margaret. He was sawing a piece of wood and without missing a beat said, 'Jeez, Caroline, you really did a humdinger this time. I haven't seen your Mom that boiling mad since 1938 when her sister borrowed her best dress and accidentally dropped it in the outhouse toilet.' Then, he snorted and laughed and snorted some more."

Her post-script to the story encouraged additional shrieking in amusement.

The Dillon sisters – Dee Dee, Caroline, Tara, Claire, Stephie, and Karie -- continued to laugh heartily for several hours as they chitchatted that Sunday afternoon in Claire's sun room. Their sequence of conversation always came full circle from what's new, to who's sick, to who's got problems, to children updates, usually winding up with recollections of childhood. Someone outside this unique sphere of sisters would find it difficult to follow their train of thought. The Dillon sisters, intertwined since childhood, intuitively embraced many conversations simultaneously.

"Let's cleanup," Tara suggested.

"Good idea."

"No, you don't have to cleanup. I'm not helpless and I'm feeling pretty darn good."

"Well, we're going to cleanup anyway, so there."

Chapter 15 : Home Again with Family

Claire's sisters performed the cleanup in less than thirty minutes. "Okay, Claire, everything's done. I don't know where this tray goes. I'll leave it on the counter."

"I guess Jeff and Jeannie went somewhere. Tell them we said good by. The sandwiches they fixed were great. You've got good kids."

Karie directed, "Time to get back in the bus, girls!"

"Oh, you guys, thanks for driving up here and thanks for the gifts." She walked to the end of the sidewalk, hugging each of them as they passed by.

As the sisters climbed into Karie's SUV, Claire experienced a strong yet brief memory of sitting by the oak tree in the front yard on Gladden Avenue.

"Be sure to use the gift I gave you, Claire."

"I will, Karie. I've been wanting to keep a journal. Thanks."

Claire stood on the front porch as the Dillon sisters drove down her street.

*When I see them, I can't help but remember the pretty girls' room on Gladden Avenue. I loved that wallpaper and the bedspreads, but mostly I loved my sisters.*

"Hey, Mom, how did it go with your sisters?"

"It was a lot of fun. Thanks, you two, for fixing lunch. They really enjoyed it. They said to thank you."

"We saw them as they were leaving. Aunt Karie stopped and we talked to them for a few minutes."

"When they drove away, Aunt Dee Dee yelled out the window to Jeannie, 'Move back home!'"

"Don't pay any attention to her, Jeannie. You love Chicago."

"But I love you more. Maybe I should move back to Hallowed to take care of you."

"Who's moving where?" Chet asked as he entered the sun room.

"Oh, hi, hon. You know how Dee Dee is. She told Jeannie she should move back here for me, but no one needs to be with me 24/7 anymore. I am feeling fine!"

"Well, maybe it's not a bad idea. Jeannie, could you take a leave of absence for a while?"

"I can ask. I've used most of my vacation already, but I'd probably qualify for FMLA."

Chet, Jeannie, and Jeff continued their planning as if Claire were still in a coma.

Chet pulled out his calendar. "I still have two weeks left on my FMLA. Jeannie, if you can take family leave starting the middle of August, we'd be covered through mid-September."

"Or, Dad, how about this? Why don't you take care of Mom for two more weeks, like you said? Then, Jeff could quit his summer job in two weeks and take care of her until he leaves for college in August. Then, I can be here from the beginning of September until around October 15. That way, I could go to Chicago now and come back to Hallowed in September."

"Great idea! That gives us about ten weeks of continuous care for your Mom."

"Jeff, how do you feel about that? Would you be willing to quit Tiggy's a little early?"

"Sure, Dad. I can let him know this week. He can get someone else."

As if watching a tennis match, Claire's eyes bounced from face to face as her family planned her in-home care schedule. Claire clapped her hands loudly. "Hello, Hello! Wait a minute; this is getting out of hand. What about what I want?"

"Claire, I think we have it figured out."

"Everybody! Stop talking! Please sit down. I'm going to say this calmly and rationally. I do not need a nurse maid. I do not need someone here 24/7. I have recovered quite nicely. Dr. McDaniel says I may resume most of the things I like to do."

"But, Claire, you were in a coma…"

"Chet, I am no longer in a coma. I am doing really well, but lately I feel that I'm being watched every moment of the day. Don't get me wrong, I love all that you've done for me. I am healing because of all of you."

Chapter 15 : Home Again with Family

"Okay, Claire, what do you want?"

"First, Jeannie, go back to your life in Chicago. Dee Dee's full of beans. I'll be fine."

"Jeffrey, you need to make spending money for college. I do not -- repeat do not -- want you to quit Tiggy's."

"And last, but not least, Chet, you have to get back to the D.C. project. It's not like you have to travel there very often, but I'm sure they need the Executive Project Manager in the office as soon as possible."

"Finally, I am over-the-top happy to be with you, but I am also anxious to get back to other things I want to do…like gardening – I am chomping at the bit to play in the dirt again. I want to take walks in the park, have lunch with my friends, and get back to volunteering at the pregnancy center."

"Are you sure you'll be okay, Mom?"

"I'm sure, Jeannie. Here's my plan: Chet, you go into the office tomorrow. Jeannie, get your laundry done tomorrow and drive back on Tuesday. Jeff, you continue to work for Tiggy and eat everything in sight when you come home. Agreed?"

Claire pointed her finger at each one of them in succession.

"Agreed? Agreed? Agreed?"

"Okay, Claire, I guess you've made your case, but you know I'm going to call you a lot. Keep your cell phone with you at all times."

"Will do. Now that we've got that settled, let's grill steaks tonight. Jeff, you and Dad can handle that, right? And, Jeannie, we haven't cooked together in a long time. Let's make the corn bread casserole."

"Yum, it goes great with steak. I can make a salad, too. And, let's make strawberry pie for dessert, Mom."

"Let's do it, family," Chet commanded, "the queen has spoken!"

# CHAPTER 16 : IN THE GARDEN

Everyone followed Claire's plan to the letter. By Wednesday, she was finally able to spend time in her garden. As she was about to go out the back door, the phone rang.

"Oh, Chet, come on, I'm okay."

She picked up the phone and heard Anne's voice.

"Hi, Claire."

"Anne, hi, I'm glad you called. Oh my gosh, the baby's breath flowers were wonderful. Believe it or not, I think I could smell them even when I was in the coma. And the chili was great. I really appreciate it."

"Jeff's been keeping me up-to-date on you, but I thought I should wait until you had spent time with Chet and the kids."

"Oh, believe me-- I've had plenty of time with Chet and the kids."

"Jeff said that Jeannie returned to Chicago and he's working for Tiggy again. Kev loves that. And, I hear Chet's been working since Monday. I assume you're feeling better?"

"I am, Anne. Chet and the kids have been great, but I am enjoying the solitude of my home. It's peaceful without anyone asking me if I need something every five minutes. Today, I was going to do a little gardening, but come over. We could have ice tea. It's a beautiful day, not as hot as usual."

"Well, I don't want to interfere with your gardening."

"You will not be interfering at all. I'm still taking it easy. The most I'll do today is water the flowers and pick a few weeds. Anne, I really want to see you. It's been too long since we talked."

"Okay, I'll be there in about a half hour."

"Great. Come out back when you get here."

Claire went outside and removed the nozzle from the hose, pulled it to the garden area, and pushed it into the ground. A cool spray of water and mud splashed onto her legs. She stared in awesome wonder at the beauty of the yard. Standing on the deck, she could only see trees and bushes and flowers. No other homes in the surrounding neighborhoods were visible in the summer.  Honeysuckle bushes full of sweet yellow flowers lined the fence here and there between the trees.  On two sides of the deck, sweet pea vines climbed wrought iron walls.  Beneath the vines, baby's breath grew amongst pink and red roses.  English Ivy vines twisted in and out of each other and covered the back side of the house.  In the fall they would be bright red, but in late July, they looked like a cool, green waterfall washing over the wall of the cedar home.  In addition to lush perennials that returned each year, Claire had chosen baskets of red, orange, purple, and pink impatiens.  On the edges of the baskets, lime- colored sweet potato plants had grown large and long, almost touching the ground.  And last but not least, Lady Di spiraled around the Blessed Mother, the statue she had bought Chet for Father's Day several years ago.

*Jeff was only thirteen then, but he was already taller than me.  He was proud that he was strong enough to carry the statue of the Blessed Mother from my car to where the lady stands now.*

Claire stood with her eyes closed, tilting her head to the sky to absorb the warmth of the sun.  She breathed deeply.  All of the flowers, but especially the baby's breath complied by wafting their sweet smell to her nostrils.  In that moment, she felt a heavenly peace and in that moment, she remembered a dream she had when she was in the coma.  She had walked through a beautiful archway covered with red roses and baby's breath.  There were rows and rows of beautiful, luminous figures.  She had a vague memory of one particular figure, who seemed to know her personally.  She had a name, but Claire could not recall anything very clearly.

*Anyway, I had an aneurysm; I was in a coma for sixteen days.  Maybe just maybe, I had some crazy dreams.*

Claire heard Anne's footsteps on the brick walkway leading to the backyard.  She dropped the hose and met Anne as she reached the far corner of the house.

"Anne, hi.  How are you, hon?"

Anne did not say a word.  She threw her arms around Claire and hugged her tightly.

"Annie, I missed you."

"I missed you too, Claire.  I haven't felt the same since May."

"Oh, gosh, Anne. Life is too short to lose the kind of friendship we have. Let's sit on the deck. I've made ice tea and little sandwiches. I have all afternoon to talk since I've finally shooed everyone out of the house."

"Claire, all the Bible babes keep calling me about you. Patti, especially, was very worried."

"I got cards from all of them. Last week, Patti put a beautiful candle by the front door with a sweet note. She wrote, 'put this candle by the Blessed Mother statue you have in your backyard. I've been praying night and day to Our Lady to ask Jesus to heal you.' Maybe, I'll have them over in a few weeks, but I'm glad it's only you and me today, Annie."

"Me, too."

Anne sipped her tea and intermittently nibbled on one of the sandwiches. She seemed to move in slow motion, as if mired down in invisible sludge.

"How are you feeling, Claire?"

"I'm A-Okay, Anne, but you're not, are you?"

"It's that obvious?"

Claire raised an eyebrow and nodded.

"I feel lost without Jack."

"I know you do, Anne. I should have stopped by to see you."

"Hmm, you had a good reason not to, Claire."

"Maybe, but it's not my place to judge. Anyway, it's time to put that behind us."

"I try to remember the good times with Jack and Kevin and I even feel a little joy for a moment or two. Then the days of May come tumbling down. I mean I don't go around all day crying. I try to be upbeat for Kev's sake. I'm pretty good at faking it, but then he leaves and the pain intensifies. Most of the time I choose to feel nothing, not sad, not happy, not anything. Numbness is my world."

"I understand that feeling, Anne. I really do."

Chapter 16 : In the Garden

"Sorry, yeah, I know you do. I guess I could take medication, but I don't think it's the same kind of depression that you have. It's not a chemical thing. I guess it's plain old grief."

"What about the Grieving Widows group at church? Did you go to any of the meetings?"

---

She found herself staring at Anne. Something looked different, yet familiar. There were dark circles under her eyes. Her mouth had deep downward creases on each side. Claire had not seen Anne up close for almost three months-- yet; she recognized this expression on Anne's face. She had seen this look recently, but where, when?

---

"I went two times, but I was the youngest one there and I couldn't relate to Alzheimer's and kidney failure and all those old people diseases."

"Why don't you tell me how you really feel?"

Anne smiled mischievously. "Well, they are old, some of them older than dirt. There was only one lady who I could even remotely identify with. Her husband died at age fifty-five."

"Well, thank you for not saying that fifty-five is old."

"He got drunk one night and killed himself in a car accident. It seemed his death was more or less self-induced and I think his wife was actually relieved."

"Annie Madison Combs, that's not nice!"

"Well, I don't feel too nice anymore."

"It was good to see you smile just now. That's when those lavender eyes of yours really light up."

"That's probably the first time I've genuinely smiled since May. You're working your magic on me, Claire."

"It's not magic, Anne. It's friendship. I'm here for you anytime you want to talk about anything."

"Thanks. Being able to talk with you again, Claire, gives me hope. Your flowers and bushes and everything in the yard are beautiful as usual. I'm glad you're back in the garden. But I've spent almost two hours talking about me--I haven't even asked you about your hospital stay or anything."

"Not necessary, Anne. I know you care."

"I better go now. I am glad you're getting better, Claire. I was afraid I'd never see you again and well, I hope we can get back to being as close as we were before." Anne teared up unable to finish the sentence.

"Oh, Annie, I don't think we ever really stopped being friends. I'll walk you to the front."

The two friends hugged, realizing that love and forgiveness transcend hurt. Claire stared at Anne as she walked down the street. She simply could not get over her intense recollection of Anne's dark eyes and creases around her mouth.

---

*Am I crazy? Is this a side effect of the coma? Or the medications? I swear I saw Anne while I was in the hospital, but Chet said he did not let anyone visit but Jeff and Jeannie. Maybe it was one of my many dreams, but it seems to be real. I remember seeing her in a bus or train. She was sitting next to someone. That's when I saw her sad eyes and downturned mouth. It had to be a dream.*

The nagging memory made Claire exhausted. She took a nap for the remainder of the afternoon.

In summer 2010 Hallowed was as hot as any old-timer could remember. Although August humidity hovered over the town for several weeks, there had been little rain. Claire watered her flowers everyday using her special technique of screwing the hose into the ground of each section of her garden.

She was overjoyed to nurture her flora children. "Okay, sweet peas, you're looking a little saggy today. How about perking up a bit and giving me a few more flowers? I want you to stay around as long as possible."

As Claire gazed lovingly at her yard, a pang of sadness penetrated her heart.

*I wish you could stay around longer too, Jeffy. Where did the time go? I can still see you as we sat on the front porch waiting for the kindergarten school bus. You wore khaki shorts and a blue shirt with those crazy red, white, and yellow suspenders. When the bus came, you announced, 'Mom, I want to get on the bus all by myself. I'm a big boy, now.' I watched as you climbed the bus stairs and began your disappearing act into adulthood. I waved. You waved back. Then I went inside laughing and crying at the same time. It was also bittersweet when Jeannie started her first day of school, but this time I was alone in the house when you got on the bus.*

"Mom, Mom! Where are the towels and sheets you bought for me? I want to pack them in my laundry bag."

"Just a minute, hon, I'll get them." Claire turned off the hose, happy to hear his voice and glad to be needed.

It was Friday, August 15, Jeff's last day at home before leaving for college. Jeff, his Dad, and Kevin had been packing their pickup truck all day. Jeff ran in and out of the house carrying one load after another of boxes and plastic cartons full of magazines, shoes, and sports equipment. Kevin drove to his home and back several times bringing much of the same.

On the last trip, Anne and Kevin drove to the McCormacks together and parked in front of the house. "Hey, here's the final load, Chet. Are you going to be able to fit everything in the truck?"

"Somehow, some way we'll do it! Dang, it's hot today."

"And that's why I'm going into your air conditioned home. Claire and I are reviewing the orientation schedule for the weekend."

"Okay, tell Claire we should be finished here in about an hour. Jeff, unlock Mom's van so Kevin can put his suitcases in with yours. Then, let's get the rest of this into the truck."

"Claire, hi, it's me. Are you in the kitchen?"

"I'm cooking dinner. Come in."

"Hi, Chet said they'd be finished in an hour. Yum, smells great. What's cooking?"

"Baby back ribs cooked in sauerkraut and of course, mashed potatoes – one of Jeff's favorite meals and apple pie, too. He loves my German food. You and Kev want to join us?"

"No, not tonight. I want to be with Kev alone this evening. We're going to eat at Skyway Chili. Then we're visiting Jack's grave." One tear slid slowly down Anne's cheek.

Claire stopped stirring the mashed potatoes and hugged Anne. "What a kid. Jack would be – no, Jack is –proud of him. And, he's proud of you, too, Mrs. Combs."

"I am getting better at handling things. I sold Jack's truck this week. You know how much he loved it, but…"

"Too many memories, huh?"

"No, it's not that. We need the money. I still haven't gotten the life insurance or even a check from Jack's pension, so I decided to sell the truck. I didn't want Kev going off to college without extra cash and of course, we have to pay for the books tomorrow."

"Anne, if you need money, you know we can help you."

"I know you would, but I want to start figuring things out for myself. We'll be fine. Our agent said I should receive the life insurance check by the end of the month. I call the Air Force Pension office at least twice a week. I try to compartmentalize things to keep my brain from exploding. Like today, I want to focus on college. Let's go over the orientation schedule?"

"Good idea."

"I want to make sure we're attending everything that we need to."

"I'll put the food on low heat. We can sit in the sun room."

Claire and Anne sat by each other on the loveseat reviewing the schedule for their sons.

"Chet said we should leave no later than 7:15, so we can get a good parking space. The first event is the welcome breakfast at 9 am."

Anne pointed to the schedule. "They have student orientation at 11 a.m. Oh, and we have parent orientation at the same time in another room. We're on our own for lunch and then there's a series of places to go-- bookstore, finance office, student union, and a tour of the individual colleges. I'm estimating we can get through all of that by two o'clock. That gives us plenty of time for moving in."

Claire sighed, "Sounds like a lot of standing in line. It's all coming back to me. When Jeannie started college, it took twice as long as we thought it would to get through everything. Be prepared for exhaustion."

"After we unload all of their stuff, that's it for the parents on Saturday. They have a social for the students at 9 pm." She pointed to the last line of the schedule in bold print and read, "Parents are to leave by 7 pm."

"Then, you and Chet and I can go to the hotel."

The back door slammed loudly as Jeff and Kevin entered the kitchen. Then, the Moms recognized a sound they had heard for many years – their boys rummaging through the refrigerator searching for food. Claire nodded to Anne. "Let's see what they're up to."

Claire noticed they were both sweaty like they used to get when they were little boys playing in the yard. Only now they were packing their belongings. Both had taken large bites out of two red apples.

"Are you guys finished loading the truck?"

Jeff mumbled, "Almost. We needed shomething shweet to keep up our energy."

"Yeah, it's hard work, Mrs. McShormack."

The Moms laughed heartily at the simple scene of their guys, not looking all that different from the day they started kindergarten.   Claire shooed them out the door. Anne waved her index finger at them.  "Well, you both better get back out there.  Mr. McShormack needs you."

After everything was loaded, Kevin said, "Oh, crap.  I forgot all the stuff we bought.  It's sitting in the driveway at my house.  I'll run down to get it now."

The dorms at St. Francis Bergio University would be sparsely furnished with bunk beds, two desks, two dressers, and one closet.  Since they were going to be roommates, Jeff and Kevin did a cost-effective purchase of several items that they could share:  small refrigerator, portable TV, DVD player, and a bookcase that they would have to put together in the dorm room.

Jeff and his Dad stood in the truck bed rearranging boxes and plastic containers.   As Jeff saw Kevin pulling an old red wagon down the street, he bellowed a jungle cry, "Hey, Tarzan, we could use a little muscle here."  Kevin was breathing hard and sweating profusely.  All he could muster was a wave.

"About time, my man.  I see you're bringing your little red wagon.  Is that gonna be your transportation on campus?"

"Very funny.  Man, it's hot.  Here's all the stuff we bought.  Let's take them out of the boxes when we get there."

"Good idea.  Hand them up."

Chet reached for one of the boxes, "Here, I'll get that one."

Kevin passed the boxes containing the small refrigerator, TV, and DVD player to Chet and Jeff.

"The bookcase is too heavy for one person to lift.  I'll need some help."

Chet surveyed the truck bed that was almost filled to capacity.  "Okay, Jeff, you hop down and help Kev."

As Jeff jumped off the truck he asked Kevin, "Why didn't you drive down here?

"Drive down in what?"

"What about your Dad's truck?"

Chapter 17 : Wagging Their Tails Behind Them

"She sold it. The guy picked it up yesterday."

"Why did she sell it?"

"We need the money."

"Okay, guys, turn the box on its side. We can slide it along the walls of the truck. Get it up on the flat bed first. Good, good, steady. Keep pushing. That's it. Now, both of you lift it up a little at the bottom and then start sliding it toward me. Got it. Good job, guys – we'll tie everything down with bungee cords and put a tarp over the top."

"Can we take a break, Dad?"

"Sure, son, let's get water. There's cold bottles in the garage fridge."

They each took two bottles of water-- one to drink and one to pour over their heads.

Chet handed them paper towels. "I think that's about it on loading. All that's left is to put the bungee cords and tarp over the truck bed and call it a day. It's five o'clock already. I'm getting hungry. How about you guys?"

"Kev, stay for dinner. Mom cooked sauerkraut and ribs. You know how good that is."

"Thanks, anyway. Mom and I are eating at Skyway, kind of a last pre-college dinner together."

"Okay, guys, let's git-her-done. Throw up the cords and tarp. Then we are done for the day."

While the men finished their work, Claire and Anne continued to discuss the schedule for the college orientation.

"Okay, Anne, let's look at Sunday's schedule."

"There's an outdoor Mass at 12:30 pm followed by a luncheon. Then, orientation is over."

Anne asked, "Should we call them Sunday morning to make sure they're up, so they don't miss Mass?"

"Let's play it by ear. Eventually, they're going to have to get themselves up on their own."

Anne looked concerned. "I hope they don't oversleep and miss a class."

"Annie, they have alarm clocks and cell phones. They should be able to figure it out. Time for them to grow up!"

"Sometimes I think Kevin's more mature than I am. He's a lot like Jack."

Claire noticed that Anne did not shed a tear when she said Jack's name this time. *Maybe she's finally moving on.*

The sound of men's voices filled the house.

"Aah, air conditioning. Feels wonderful," Jeff sighed.

Chet nodded in agreement. "It was hotter than blue blazes out there today."

Claire held her nose. "Whew, I can tell. You all need showers and maybe you should burn those clothes.

Anne sheepishly announced, "Guess what? Move-in time is tomorrow afternoon after 2 pm!"

Chet wiped his brow with his shirt sleeve. "Really? That's a joke. They schedule move-in at the hottest time of the day?"

"Claire, can I borrow a towel for Kev to sit on in the car? Yikes, you guys are disgusting! I don't know how you can stand to be around each other."

Jeff put his arm around Kevin's shoulder. "We have been sweating together since puberty. I think we can tolerate the odor!"

Chet added, "You two can tolerate each other, but I think your Moms are hinting about showers."

"Let's get home, Kev and cleanup."

"Okay, Mom. See you tomorrow, Mrs. McCormack. Thanks, Mr. McCormack for all you did for me today."

Chet put his hand on the back of Kevin's neck and shook his head slightly. "My pleasure, Kev, my pleasure."

Jeff walked Kevin out through the garage. "It's gonna be good, Kev. I heard there are some hot chicks in Cincy. See ya tomorrow."

Chapter 17 : Wagging Their Tails Behind Them

"See ya, Jeff. I'm hoping it'll be good. So long."

Claire handed Anne a towel and Chet walked her to the door. "Chet, thank you."

"For what?"

"It's hard on him, but what you did today really helps. Filling in for Jack."

"Like I told Kev, it's my pleasure. No one can really fill-in for Jack, but I'm glad I can narrow the gap a little."

"Thanks. Thanks for everything, Chet. I'd hug you, but you understand, right? Sweat is not my favorite perfume."

Chet laughed, "I understand. We'll pickup you and Kev at 7:15 am. It'll be fun."

———————————

When Claire heard the showers stop, she knew Chet and Jeff would be ready for dinner in less than ten minutes. She had set the dining room table with a white tablecloth and her best china and silverware. She scooped the sauerkraut and ribs into a silver serving dish with the lid tightly closed to keep them hot.

She pulled the silver double-sided serving bowl that Jeannie and Jeff had bought her for Christmas in 2002. It wasn't really silver, but they thought it was. Whenever she used it, she'd say, "The food looks wonderful in the silver dish you gave me. And I love that it has a warmer beneath it." She heaped the mashed potatoes into one dish and placed a half-stick of butter on top. It smelled exactly like her mother's mashed potatoes. On the other side, she put the mandatory vegetable-- broccoli, most of which would remain in the dish.

"There... looks nice. I'll light the candles."

Claire could smell Chet and Jeff before they even entered the room. They both wore the same cologne, a soft musk with a hint of pine and she loved the masculine fragrance.

"Wow, Mom, you've outdone yourself. This looks great!"

"Thank you."

Chet pulled out Claire's chair, "Here you are, Madame. The servants have prepared a most ostentatious meal this evening."

"No, darling, the servants are off today. I prepared the meal for my family all by myself."

"Okay, corny parents, let's pray. I'm starved."
*In the name of the Father and the Son and the Holy Spirit.*

*Bless us O Lord, and these thy gifts*
*Which we are about to receive from thy bounty*
*Through Christ, Our Lord.*
*And, God, thank you for our son, Jeffrey.*
*Please watch over him as he embarks on*
*this new adventure called college. Amen."*

Claire passed the sauerkraut and spareribs to Jeff. "Take as much as you want. I have more in the kitchen."

"Mom, this looks incredible."

"Chet, will you do the honors of opening the champagne?"

"I certainly will."

"Mom, can you please put a pile of the mashed potatoes on my plate?"

"Absolutely. Don't they look wonderful in the silver dish Jeannie and you gave me?"

"They'll look better in my stomach."

"How about broccoli?"

"One piece. There's not much room left on my plate."

Chet walked around the table to pour champagne in the flutes.

After he and Claire filled their plates, he lightly tapped his knife on the water glass.

"Ahem, I'd like to propose a toast to you, son. From the moment you stuck your ugly, little head out into the world."

"Chet, his head was not ugly. He was bruised from the forceps."

"It's okay, Mom. I know he thought I was the ugliest baby in the nursery, but I'm better looking than him now and I have hair!"

Chapter 17 : Wagging Their Tails Behind Them

"Touche! Excuse me, may I continue?" Claire and Jeff raised their glasses in silence.

"As I was saying, from the moment you were born, your mother and I have enjoyed every step you have taken from the day you first walked in your diaper, to that walk in your graduation gown down McNichols aisle and all the steps in-between. And now, we're looking forward to your big step into college. Congratulations, Jeff. Your mother and I are proud of you."

Claire blinked back a tear. "Cheers."

Jeff said, "Here's to you, Mom and Dad. You're the best!"

They did the proverbial soft clank of the flutes and then consumed dinner, Jeff's last meal at home before college.

"Mom, I am about to burst, but I think I'd like one more piece of apple pie. I know I won't get this kind of food on campus."

"Claire, Jeff and I can do the dishes."

"No way. I'll do them. You guys have been in the hot sun all day. Watch TV. Relax. You're going to have to unload all that stuff tomorrow."

Chet groaned as he rose from the dining chair. "Ouch, you're right. C'mon, Jeff, let's watch the tennis match."

Claire finished the dishes and put away what little was left of dinner. As she walked into the living room, she could hear Chet snoring and tapped him on the shoulder.

"Hmmm. What? Oh, I guess I fell asleep. I'm bushed."

"Chet, you need to go to bed."

"No kidding. See you upstairs, hon."

Jeff muted the TV and sat by his Mom on the couch.

"Mom, are you sure you're going to be okay? You know, I could start next semester."

"Don't even say that. I am fine and your Dad's here. I see Anne almost every day, Jeff. Do not worry about me."

"But you haven't been out of the hospital that long. I am worried. I don't want you to…"

"Die?"

Jeff answered softly, "Yes."

Claire tapped his hand. "Jeff, I am going to die. Everybody's going to die, but don't dwell on it. Live life to the fullest. If you were to stay here, that would make me unhappy. As much as I'm going to miss you, I want you try out your wings like Jeannie did.

"And still does."

"Yes, she's still trying out those wings. And now, it's your turn. This is your time."

"Kev worries about his Mom, too. He's not very excited about going to college. I think he'd rather have his Dad back."

"That's the toughest and the easiest part about death, Jeff. It's tough because we ache for the person we love, but it's also very easy because we are not in charge. God is."

Jeff sunk down on the couch and bounced his head backwards. "I'm still whacked about Mr. Combs dying."

"I feel the same way, but please don't blame God or abandon your Catholic faith. I know we've talked about this before, but going away to college is the crossroads to adult choices. Sometimes, young people lose their faith and stop going to Mass, even at Catholic colleges. I've heard about kids getting involved in all kinds of weird groups."

Jeff was annoyed. "You're right, Mom, we've talked about this before; Dad's talked to me about it before… many, many times."

Claire took a deep breath. She did not want the conversation to become confrontational on his last night at home.

"It's okay to be as you say, whacked, about Mr. Combs' death, but we have to accept that he is gone from this Earth. He's a great example of someone who lived life to the fullest and still remained a strong Catholic man with principles. All I'm saying, Jeff, is to be aware of secular influences. It's important to safeguard your principles."

# Chapter 17 : Wagging Their Tails Behind Them

"I will, Mom. I know all about weirdo groups and I'm not interested in them. I'll be fine, but I hope Kevin will be okay. He says his Mom tries to act strong, but he hears her crying at night when she's in bed. And sometimes she sleeps twelve hours when she takes sleeping pills."

"I'll talk to her about the pills. Assure Kevin that I'm going to be here for her."

"Did you know she sold his Dad's truck? Kev said they need the money."

"Anne told me that today, but she'll be getting Jack's pension soon. Look, we're getting off track here. You asked me if I want you to delay college and I said an emphatic no. I know what's wrong with you, Jeff." Claire sang out of tune.

"You've got that night before, not sure what I want to do in life, worried and concerned, excited and nervous, college blues."

"Mom, blues singer you are not."

"Well, it made you laugh."

"I laughed because you sounded awful."

"Thanks, I guess I better cancel my gig in Vegas! Look, your mind is swirling around, but the fact that you're worried about me is part of growing up. Experiencing the loss of your best friend's Dad and then the possibility of losing your Mom this summer makes you feel uneasy. And, I love that you care that much, but save it for when I'm ninety, okay?"

"Okay, Mom, but I'm going to call you a lot."

"In-between classes, right?"

"In-between classes."

"Keep focused on school, hon. I think you will be pleasantly surprised at what you learn in college -- not only in the classes, but in the day-to-day living. All of it leads to the rite of passage into adulthood. And, as far as Kevin goes, he'll be okay. His Mom is starting to heal and move forward and that will help him."

"I hope so. Thanks, Mom. I'm feeling better."

"By the time we pull away from the campus on Sunday, you and Kevin will probably be doing one of your comedy routines in front of some cute girls. But you look really tired.  Tomorrow's going to be fast-paced and crazy.  Go to bed, Jeff.  I'll wake all of us at 6:15."

"Okay, Mom.  I am sore.  Packing was worse than working for Tiggy."

"And, you have to unpack tomorrow.  You need a good night's sleep."

Jeff kissed his Mom on the cheek.  "Night, Mom.  Thanks for making the dinner special."

"You are very welcome.  Goodnight, Jeff.  Sleep tight."

"Love you, Mom."

"Love you more."

---

The house was quiet except for the hum of the dishwasher.  Claire sat in the sunroom watching a quarter moon above the woods.  She sipped her champagne and then opened the cabinet underneath the bookshelves. She pulled out the photo album dated 1991, smiling at Jeff's very first picture taken at the hospital complete with bruised cheekbone.

*He did not want to come out.  Or, I guess he was too big to get out.  Those darn forceps.*

Claire turned through the album page by page, recalling several milestones of Jeff's life.  She had written notes at the top of each page to remind her of the particular occasion.

**Jeannie holding her little brother for the first time**

*Gosh, look at Jeannie kissing him.  She was his second little mommy.*

**First Christmas – Grandma Dillon rocking Jeffery in the old rocker**

*Oh, gosh, Mom died shortly after Jeff's first Christmas.  And Dad was gone long before his birth.  I'm glad I took that picture.*

**First Communion**

*Does he look cute or what?  Little guy in his grown-up pale blue suit.*

**First football game**

*Chest bumping with Kev.  Jack and Chet imitating them.  They were crazy acting sometimes.*

Chapter 17 :  Wagging Their Tails Behind Them

### First Prom

*That was three years ago.  Jeff and his date look so young.*

Claire paged through the album until she came to the lighting of the Hallowed Tower last December.

### Jeff and Kev – First Climb up Hallowed Tower

*What a night and what a picture.  The entire McCormack and Combs families underneath the tower.  I think that was our last picture together.*

The final picture was one of Jeannie and Jeff on that day in July when Claire came home from the hospital.  They were standing on either side of the mailbox each giving a thumbs-up.

### Home from the Hospital

*I'm going to miss Jeff.  He's such a great kid to have around, but it's time, just like it was time for Jeannie a few years ago.  What did we expect?  We wanted them to do more and be more than us.  Give them wings and they fly away.*

Claire closed the photo album and stood up to return it to the cabinet.  As she was placing it on the shelf, an envelope fell onto the floor.  She picked it up immediately recognizing the handwriting – her Mom's flowing cursive letters.  The card inside showed Little Bo Beep and her sheep on the front.  Inside was the old English rhyme.

**Little Bo Beep has lost her sheep**
**And can't tell where to find them**
**Leave them alone and they'll come home**
**Wagging their tails behind them**

On the left side of the card Claire's Mom had written a note:

*Dearest Claire –*

*Little Jeffy is a doll baby, just like Jeannie.  I'm hoping to visit all of you in Hallowed around Christmas time.  I always loved this little nursery rhyme, but it has special meaning in regard to you. Not that you came home from California wagging your tail, but we had to let you fly away for a few years to spread your wings. Then, you finally came home. Remember this when Jeff and Jeannie go off on their own one day. You may have to stand back and leave them alone, but if you've been good parents - and I believe you and Chet are good parents - they'll return, maybe not wagging their tails behind them, but they'll return. Love always, Mom.*

*I thought I had lost that card. Hopefully, my little birds will fly around for a while and then settle down in Hallowed.*

Claire climbed the stairs still feeling sad that Jeff would no longer be a permanent resident in their home, but excited that he had this wonderful opportunity to attend college and explore a new world. She slowly got into bed and moved close to Chet. He rolled over and kissed her cheek, tasting a salty tear.

"Good night, Claire. Things will be okay." Chet's words reassured her. And, Claire felt a certain comfort from her mother's words on the card written eighteen years ago.

*Thanks, Mom. I needed that tonight. Hopefully, the Little Bo Beep rhyme is true. 'Leave them alone and they'll come home wagging their tails behind them.' Well, eventually. Right, Mom?*

Claire yelled up the stairs, "Jeff, it's 6:15. We're leaving in thirty minutes. Your alarm has gone off three times."

Jeff mumbled, "Okay, okay. I took a shower last night. Hold on, I'll be down in a minute."

Claire returned to the kitchen complaining. "I hope he makes it to his classes on time."

"Well, that's a big part of this. Mommy isn't going to be there to make sure her little boy gets up on time. He'll have to take care of himself."

"Thank you, all-knowing sage."

"Watch. This is how it's done." Chet poured another cup of coffee and stood at the bottom of the stairs.

"Jeff, I hate to tell you, buddy, but the wide screen TV fell off the truck last night and broke."

"What!" Jeff came out of his room and ran down the steps following his Dad into the kitchen.

"Are you kidding, Dad! Kev and I paid $400 for that TV."

"Yes, I am."

"Will your insurance cover it? Oh, you are kidding. Very funny, Dad, very funny."

Claire leaned into Chet, "Good job. Problem is 'the little boy who cried wolf' trick only works once. I used it years ago, but at least he's up."

"Jeff, you want something to eat?"

"No, I'm still full from last night. I'll just have coffee."

"That won't last long. We'll stop on the way down to Cincy and get a carryout breakfast. Mom and I are ready to go, so get dressed and we're out the door."

Anne and Kevin were coming out the door of their home when Chet and Claire pulled into the driveway. Anne put her suitcase in the back of Claire's van and then got into the passenger seat.

"Hi, Anne. Ready for this?"

"I guess."

Chet stuck his head out the window and yelled, "Follow me, Claire. I don't want you to get lost."

Claire stuck her head out the window and responded, "Okay, honey, you're the leader of the pack."

Then she closed the window. "At least when I get lost, I have enough sense to ask for directions. How was dinner at Skyway last night?"

"It was okay. It's like pulling teeth to get Kev to talk. When I mention his Dad, he clams up."

"Did you go to the cemetery?"

"We did. I put a bouquet of daisies in the vase on Jack's grave and Kev and I stood there for about five minutes. We didn't say a word. When we left, he had his hands in his pockets and shrugged. Then, he trudged up the hill to the car. I'm not sure it was a good idea to visit Jack's grave the night before he's leaving for college."

"Was it his idea?"

"Yes. He told me a few weeks ago he wanted to visit his Dad's grave before he left for college. I probably should have planned it earlier in the week."

"Hindsight's twenty-twenty, Anne. He seems to be fine today."

"Yeah, I'm really glad Jeff and he are roommates. Takes away some of his anxiety and mine, too. I hope he gets so involved and busy in college that he doesn't have time to think about anything else."

"Trust me, he'll be busy. Jeff and I talked last night before he went to bed. He actually proposed that he delay starting college until next semester."

"Really?"

"We got that straightened out. I told him he can take care of me when I'm ninety. Oh, Chet's turning in to McDonald's."

"Kevin's calling me."

"Hi, Kev."

"Okay, I'll tell her. She saw the turn signal though. Bye, Kev."

Claire glanced at Anne, "Bubba Feeding Stop?"

"Yep, drive thru. Chet doesn't want to eat inside."

They arrived early enough at St. Francis Bergio University to be able to park the truck by St. Ignatius Dorm, one of the oldest on campus. Then, all five of them drove in the car to the main auditorium.

It was a typical college orientation. The schedule of events unfolded without deviation. In the afternoon, Claire and Anne dropped off the moving crew at St. Iggy's dorm as the students called it. Then they drove to a restaurant to get carryout pizza.

"So far, so good, huh, Annie?"

"Yeah, it's going well, but don't you feel sad?"

"I do and I don't. Last night, after the guys had gone to bed, I looked through Jeff's picture album. You know – the typical ones – Jeannie holding him when he came home from the hospital, his first day of school, first of everything. Starting college is another first and I'm happy for him. Bittersweet."

"I went through Kev's album a few days ago. I do have sweet memories of Jack and Kev and me, but some days I can't seem to let go of the bitterness."

"I know. This year has been horrendous."

"I mean I'm trying to be upbeat with Kev. I don't want him to worry about me. He deserves to be happy."

"You deserve to be happy, too."

"I'm not sure about that."

Claire didn't know how to respond to the comment. Once in a while Anne would hint at the deep unrest in her heart because of the abortion.

"Okay, there's the pizza place. Can you run in?"

"Sure, back in a minute."

*She deserves to be happy, but she'll never be happy until she faces what she did. I'm the ninny baby for not getting through to her. I've got to get her back to Bible Babes this year.*

Anne put two large pizzas in the backseat. On their drive back to the dorm, the friends chatted absentmindedly about the orientation schedule. Neither of them had figured out how to cross the abyss that had divided them since May.

Chet and his crew made twelve trips from the truck to the dormitory, placing everything in the lobby until they could commandeer one of two elevators used by four hundred freshmen.

Needless to say, it took twice as long as they anticipated. In-between quick bites of pizza and sips of soda, everything had been unloaded in their eighth floor dorm by 6:45 pm. Once again, Chet, Jeff, and Kevin were as unappealing as they had been the day before.

In her fretful Mommy voice, Claire asked, "What are you guys going to do for dinner? We're supposed to leave here in fifteen minutes."

"That's okay, Mom. We'll figure it out."

Anne was concerned as well and proposed, "Kev, do you want me to pick up burgers for both of you?"

"No thanks, Mom."

Then, the scene played out in a similar manner to their first day of high school. A group of young ladies approached them.

One of the girls stood by Jeff, "Hi, I'm Darlene; I was sitting behind you today at the student seminar. I heard you say you live in Hallowed. My parents were born there."

"What's your last name?"

"Courtney."

"Doesn't sound familiar, but the town has grown over the years. Much larger population now. Where do you live?"

"I'm from Toledo. My parents wanted me to attend a Jesuit college. St. Francis Bergio it is."

Kevin was talking with the other girls. Anne smiled watching him charm them. A few minutes later, three young men joined the group.

Chapter 18 : Passages

"Hey, Kev, hi. We sat together at the Pre-Freshmen Luncheon back in April. Robby Jarvis. How's it going?

"Going okay, Rob," Kevin stammered. "Hey, good to see you." Rob introduced Kevin to his friends and the sports talk started.

Rob turned to Kev. "We're going to get cleaned up and then go to Wart Hole down the street. My older brother went to school here. He said Wart Hole is the best for burgers. You and your friend?"

"Jeff."

"Yeah, Jeff. You guys want to come with us?"

Darlene pulled Jeff over to the group of boys.

"Hey, Darlene, are you and your lovely friends coming to dinner with us tonight?"

"Sure, Robby. Want to go, Jeff."

"What do you think, Kev?"

"I've already committed, my man."

Jeff and Kevin walked about ten steps and then realized they had left their parents behind. Both turned around.

"See you tomorrow, Mom and Dad. Pick us up at noon."

"Bye, Mom."

"Bye, Kev."

Chet laughed, pointing his finger at Anne and Claire, "Well, I guess that answers your question – they're going to get burgers at Wart Hole with their college friends."

Claire sneered, "Okay, smarty, that's the second time today you've been the all-knowing sage. And for that, you get to take us to dinner."

"My pleasure, ladies."

"And I don't mean Wart Hole."

Anne and Claire both looked back to watch their sons. Kevin and Jeff were showing everyone their secret handshake frontwards and backwards. Darlene was laughing as she and her friends locked arms behind the boys. Then, the group turned the corner and disappeared into the elevator to go to their rooms.

"Should we do another spy mission, Claire?"

"Not this time, Annie. I don't think there are any pine trees to hide behind."

The next day when Chet pulled to the curb in front of St. Iggy's dorm, both Kevin and Jeff were wearing very nice shirts and ties and dress pants. Both of the young men sat in the back of the car with Anne.

"Good morning, Jeff. Good morning, Kevin"

"It is a fine morning, isn't it Kev?"

"Yes it is, Jeffer."

Claire questioned, "Jeffer? I've never heard you call him that before, Kevin."

"Well, Mrs. McCormack, that's his new nickname given to him by..."

Jeff nudged Kev. "Hey, man, off limits!"

"Okay, sorry."

Chet winked at Claire. "So, how was Wart Hole? What a name for a restaurant. Was the food any good?"

"Yeah, the burgers were fantastic. And they fry the potatoes in duck oil. Really different, but good."

"Kev, what time did you get back to the dorm last night? You look a little tired."

"Not too late, Mom. Jeff, did you look at the clock when we got back."

"I think it was a little past midnight."

Claire announced, "Okay, we'll stop asking questions. Looks like you two have already discovered the college law of the land."

Anne blurted out. "What happens on campus stays on campus!"

Kevin was impressed. "Hey, Mom, you're really with it!"

Claire turned around. She and Anne pointed at them and declared, "Busted!"

Chet completed the threat. "And don't think these two can't detect falsehoods over the phone. They know every fluctuation in each of your voices."

Chapter 18 : Passages

Surprisingly, the atmosphere in the car was light and playful as if all of the dark events from the past four months had stayed behind in Hallowed. Perhaps it was the fact that Jeff and Kevin got up on time and were ready to go to church. Or, it could have been the bantering about their Wart Hole adventure the night before. Or, Anne's campus comment. In any event, it was the first time in a long time that the Combs and McCormack families were together in high spirits.

---

There were white folding chairs set up on the lawn for the celebration of Mass. As Chet, Claire, Jeff, Anne and Kevin took their places, each was engrossed in quiet thought. Life was changing.

Anne twirled some of her hair strands gently. She felt a sense of pride and accomplishment. *Thank you, God. I didn't think I had the strength to do this without Jack. I'm going to be very lonely in that big house, but at least Kev is on his way.*

Kevin was relieved to be away from the constant reminders of his Dad. *I hope Mom will be okay. Dad, take care of her from up there. I miss you, but Dad, it feels really good to be moving forward. I didn't expect to feel this way.*

Jeff thought about his conversation with his Mom the night before. He realized that there had been very few, if any, times when his parents led him in the wrong direction. *Mom was right. Kev and I did our comedy routine in front of really cute girls. The dance was awesome. This is going to be better than I thought. Live life to the fullest. I'll do it, Mom and I'll keep my principles, I promise.*

Claire imagined her and Chet sitting in their very, very quiet house in Hallowed when they returned this evening. *It's going to be different in the house now. No more loud music or muddy clothes. Maybe Chet and I can do things together, just the two of us. I am grateful, Lord, to be alive to see our son begin his passage into adulthood.*

Chet thought about drinking a cold beer. *I am hotter than a hog at a pig roast. Please make this service move along. Thank God I don't have to pack or unpack any more boxes today.*

After Mass, parents and students enjoyed a picnic lunch on the lawn. Chet, Claire, and Anne were surprised at how anti-climatic their campus departure was.

They hugged and kissed and said goodbye to Jeff and Kevin. That was it. Most of their angst had dissipated on Saturday.

When they reached the parking lot, Chet raised his hands in the air and announced authoritatively, "Ladies, they have been launched on a new journey! Let's go home to Hallowed."

Anne nodded in agreement. "You took the words right out of my mouth, Chet."

Claire patted Chet on the back, "Good job, shepherd."

On that hot Sunday in August 2010 Kevin and Jeff finally began their long-awaited passage from growing up in Hallowed to commencing college life in the big city.

Claire and Anne were also about to enter a passage, as well--a passage into spiritual darkness and fear, challenging the sanity of both women.

# CHAPTER 19 : LISTENING FOR THE SOUNDS

Chet pulled into the driveway at 5:15 pm. Claire waved as she continued down the street to take Anne home.

"What a weekend, Anne. Mission accomplished!"

"You can say that again. I'm feeling pretty good about it. I miss Kev already, but I think he's in a good place. It feels right."

"Those two will be fine. Are you going to be okay tonight, Annie?"

"I'll get through it. I'll probably take a sleeping pill to make sure I can sleep."

"Really? I've never seen you take even an aspirin let alone a sleeping pill."

"It's okay, Claire. I take one sleeping pill once in a while."

"All right, but be careful. They can become addictive."

"I know that, but for now it's helping me. Hey, pop the trunk. I'll get my suitcase."

Anne walked to the driver's side, "You need to get home and take care of your aching husband. Tell him thanks again for all he did for us."

"Will do. See you tomorrow."

When Claire got home, Chet was in the shower. She fixed him a gin and tonic and carried it upstairs to the bedroom.

"Hey, nice. Thanks. I think I hurt muscles in my body that I didn't know existed. This tastes great!"

"You deserve it. Enjoy. I need a shower too. After I get dressed, I'll fix sandwiches and we can eat dinner on the deck."

"Sounds inviting. See you down there."

Chet put on a cool blue polo shirt and grey shorts, feeling a bit of a sting on his sunburned neck and arms. He pressed the gin and tonic ice-filled glass to his forehead breathing a huge sigh of relief.

*God, thank you for getting the guys settled in college.*

Then he toasted Jack out loud, "And, here's to you, Jack. I know you must have been with me this weekend, because I could not have done all of this on my own."

He was about to descend the stairs when he noticed the door to Jeff's room slightly ajar. He tapped it open further with his right hand. Chet sat on Jeff's bed, moving his eyes from wall to wall taking in the past eighteen years of Jeff's life and his own. Clothes that were too small for Jeff hung in the closet. Underneath were several pairs of shoes that no longer fit. The desk had been stripped of the computer and all of the attachments, leaving clean outlines in-between mounds of dust. A few of the chest drawers were open with socks and underwear hanging out. Chet could smell Jeff in the room. The aroma of young manhood and aftershave and potato chips melded together.

Chet walked across the room to a display case filled with dusty trophies. He held his drink in his right hand and fingered the trophies with his left taking in eighteen years of memories of his boy. Everything in Jeff's room brought back the past, including the sounds of Jeff as a baby, a little boy, and a teenager.

*Daddy, put me on your shoulders. I want to pick an apple off Grandpa's tree.*
*Daddy, I know how to read now.*
*Dad, want to toss football?*
*Bengals' tickets. Wow, thanks Dad.*

*Jeff McCormack scores his first touchdown of the season for the Rockets!*

*Dad, thanks for taking off work to come to the tennis match. Sorry, I didn't get to play today. Dad, can I borrow the car?"*

*And the 2010 McNichols' Spirit Award has two recipients this year -- Kevin Combs and Jeff McCormack – football co-captains.*

*But, that's what I mean, Dad. Why make all the good choices. What does it do for you?*

He sat down again on Jeff's bed, scanning the pictures on the walls: he and Jeff screaming in fear and delight at the top of The Beast roller coaster. Very young Jeff and Jeannie holding finger bunny ears behind each other. Friends and cousins playing tag football in 2002. One photo in particular caught Chet's attention-- sixteen year old Jeff standing beside a little boy named Ronnie who was born with Down's syndrome. Ronnie was holding up the medal for Jeff to see.

Chet murmured, "Son, I hope you know how proud I am of you."

Chapter 19 : Listening for the Sounds

"He knows, Chet."

"Hi, Claire. Busted. Caught in the act of reminiscing."

Claire sat down beside Chet on the bed. For a few seconds both held hands in silence listening for the sounds of Jeff.

"And he's proud of you, too, Chet."

Chet put his arm around Claire. "Thanks, hon. I guess it hit me all of sudden that he's gone. I mean he'll be back to visit once in a while, weekends and holidays, but this is the beginning of how it's going to be around here."

"I feel the same way, but now we can spend more time together. Do things we haven't had time for in the past."

"Hey, I'm all for that. I can think of one thing I'd like to do more often."

"Really and what might that be? Never mind, I know the track you're going down. I was thinking more in terms of exercising or going to the theater."

"Yeah, we can do some of that, but first things first."

Claire teased, "Well, the first thing we're going to do is eat dinner on the deck. How about a refill on the gin and tonic?"

The heat of the day finally dissipated as the sun began its slow decline behind the trees. A light breeze moved branches enough to cool Chet and Claire as they sat on the deck eating cold turkey sandwiches and chips.

"Think he's doing okay?"

"I think he's doing fine, Claire."

"When I said goodbye I almost asked him to call us tonight, but I stopped myself. I didn't want to make him feel obligated to call especially if he's in the middle of something."

"Hey, I had my moment upstairs in his room, but you're right about doing things together without worrying if Jeannie or Jeff will like it."

"So, what do you think about exercising?"

"It's not a bad idea, Claire. Why don't we look into Encompass Health Club?"

"I'd love to get back into swimming and they have a hot tub and steam room. I think they have tours of the facility on Tuesdays and Thursdays."

"Set it up."

"Okay, I will."

Even though they had been married thirty-six years, the silent moment was awkward. "Chet, do you keep waiting to hear him?"

"Sure"

"When I was fixing your drink, I kept listening for the sound of the back door slamming."

"How about the refrigerator opening and closing fifty times a day?"

"Chet, remember when he was twelve and he came home from baseball practice covered in mud?"

"You mean the time he spilled the entire bowl of macaroni salad down his muddy uniform and onto the floor?"

"But he didn't tell me. Instead he put all of it back in the bowl and poured a bunch of paprika on top. I thought it looked weird, but I assumed eggs had discolored the macaroni."

"Then, when we went to your sister's house for the Fourth of July party, Bud took a spoonful of your salad and put it in his mouth. And pulled out…and pulled out…"

Claire and Chet began to belly laugh until tears streamed down their face.

They both did a sort of wheezing to slow down their laughter. Then, Chet was finally able to complete his sentence. "Bud pulled out a twig with a bug on it."

"Oh my gosh, I had no idea what had happened to that macaroni salad, until I saw Jeff's face. He finally fessed up. I was hopping mad at him and embarrassed. When I looked closely I saw several bugs and twigs and a little pool of mud on the bottom. I had to throw the entire salad in the garbage and I never heard the end of it from my sisters. That's why I started hiding it every year."

"At least Bud was good natured about it."

Chapter 19 : Listening for the Sounds

"Yeah, after he chased Jeff around the yard swearing he was going to make him eat one of the bugs. You know, Chet, it's crazy how something that made you furious at your kids when they were little becomes one of the best memories."

"Uh-huh." Chet started winding down the table umbrella. "Sun's going down. Let's take in the dishes." He held the screen door open for Claire to enter. "Claire, remember what you said today about spending more time together? Want to spend some time together tonight?"

Claire turned around and winked. "With you? Absolutely."

———————————

Anne stood on her back porch drinking a glass of white wine. Only a few slim rays of light weakly glimmered through the trees. She strained longing to hear a hopeful sound; the sound of Kevin bouncing a basketball in the driveway; the sound of the TV blaring an odious teenage sitcom; the thud of the workout weights in the basement. Anne's pain of yearning for Jack was amplified by the quiet nothingness of the house. Still, she listened for the sounds of Jack. Still, she listened for the sounds of Kevin.

*I'm trying to be strong, Jack. I really am. I think you'd be proud that I got Kevin to college. Of course with the help of Chet and Claire, but I did it, Jack. Jack, I miss you the most at night when our home becomes silent. Don't get me wrong, my love, I know life moves on, but without you here and now without Kev, the silence is unbearable. It's hard to sleep. When I do sleep, Jack, the dreams are hideous. I hear a baby crying and women screaming and sometimes I'm traveling somewhere on a train and at first it feels comfortable like I'm going to escape the hurt. Then the train car starts filling up with people who have no expressions, but somehow I know they're sad. Then I wake up. Jack, are you sad with me? Do you hate me because I aborted our baby? Please understand, Jack, please. I couldn't face raising a baby that would require more than I could give. I'm sorry, Jack. I'm sorry for being weak.*

Anne sipped the last of the wine from the glass and went inside locking up for the night. She took the sleeping pill bottle from the window shelf, poured water in the wine glass, and swallowed two of the pills. She lay on the bed feeling tiny and vulnerable without Jack there.

*I hope I can sleep tonight.  I hope I sleep so sound that no dream can creep into my mind.  Goodnight, Jack.  I love you.*

––––––––––––––––––––

After a few minutes Anne fell into a deep sleep.  Sadly, the recurring dream of the past several months returned, and although it began as usual, there was a darker intensity than before.  A train whistle whined and she could see lights coming toward her.  It was an old, shiny black one with hot steam pouring out the top.  As it pulled into the station where she stood, she realized she had a ticket in her hand.  What appeared to be a kind man with a white mustache held onto the pole.  He leaned out reaching for her hand.

"Welcome aboard, young lady.  I'll take that ticket.  Sit wherever you want.  You're the first one on today, but we're expecting the train to fill up pretty quickly."

Anne took his hand and climbed into the empty train car.  She walked down the dusty aisle, noticing that the seats were covered with old-fashioned brittle red plastic.  She finally found a seat that didn't have its filling popping out and sat next to the window.  Even in her dream state, Anne knew what was coming next.  She braced herself for the weird characters that were supposed to board, but this time the dream deviated.  She heard someone climbing the steps and looked behind to see Jack entering the car.  In an instant he stood beside her.

"Jack, oh Jack, is it really you?  I've missed you night and day.  How did you get here?  Sit down by me, honey."

"I can't stay on the train, Anne, but I want you to see our baby."  Jack leaned into the seat and opened the pink blanket.  "This is our baby girl, Anne.  Isn't she beautiful?"

Anne was stunned.  "She's beautiful.  She's perfect.  How can she be perfect?"

"She's always been perfect in God's eyes, Annie."

"Can I hold her?"

Jack did not answer her question.  He simply wrapped the baby in the blanket and protectively held her close to his chest.

Chapter 19 : Listening for the Sounds

The gruff, annoying voice of the steward blared out, *"All aboard. All aboard."* His mustache was tinged with something red and his eyes had changed to a wicked yellow.

"Jack, don't leave me again. Please, Jack."

The strange characters began to board the train; stiff cardboard cutouts of human beings. They walked through and past Jack as if he weren't there. In between the procession of sad shapes, Jack whispered to Anne.

"I can't stay, Anne. You know that. And, our baby needs to be in the arms of her Guardian Angel."

Anne tried to get up, but she could not move. It was then she realized that she too was trapped in a one-dimensional flat form. Only her eyes could move. She strained to see Jack, but she only heard his whispered words.

"Annie, I forgive you and I'm praying for you, but I can't save you. You have to save your own soul."

Then, the train sounded its whistle and began to move slowly down the tracks. Anne moved her eyes towards the window, hoping to catch a glimpse of Jack and their baby, but she could only see the hot steam rising and falling.

───────────

She gasped and tried to raise her head off the pillow, but her body was heavy from the wine and sleeping pills and she fell back. The ceiling fan whirled softly above her, giving her a small sense of reassurance that it was a dream. With every ounce of strength she pulled herself out of bed, determined to evade the hellish nightmare.

*Coffee, I'm making coffee.*

At 4 am Anne stood in the kitchen watching the coffee pot drip its dark liquid slowly.

*Aah, at last.*

She opened the back door hearing the insect world warbling in the final hours of the night. Anne smiled, recalling how she and Kevin and Jack would listen to the sounds of frogs and crickets and other bugs on those wonderful family camping trips.

*Jack, you were so real in my dream tonight.  Then, it got scary, Jack.*

Anne closed and locked the kitchen door.

*Don't be a ninny baby.  It's a dream, only a dream.*

# CHAPTER 20 : VISITORS

On Monday, Claire handed Chet a piece of toast as he rushed out the door for the office.

"Have a good day, hon. Call me."

"Meetings all morning. I'll call after lunch."

Claire was inspired to take care of her own to-do list as the house had a too quiet hum she was still reluctant to embrace. As she was talking to a staff member at Encompass Health Club, Anne opened the screen door. She motioned for her friend to come in.

"Okay, sounds good. My husband and I will be there tomorrow evening at 7:30. Thanks. Bye.

Hi, what's up? Want a cup of coffee?"

"No, I got up at 4 am; I've already had four cups. I'll start shaking if I drink any more. Who was on the phone?"

"Belinda Deerfield from Encompass Health Club. Chet and I are thinking about joining."

"Sounds good."

"You look really tired. Of course you are. You got up at 4 am."

"Yeah, I didn't sleep very well."

"I thought you were going to take a sleeping pill?"

"I did, but they're not very strong. I still tossed and turned."

Claire changed the subject. "I guess the boys are in class right about now. Another first day of school."

Anne sat at Claire's kitchen table twirling her hair. "I'm going to go through Jack's stuff and give most of it away."

"That's probably not a bad idea as long as you keep what Kev wants."

"Of course, but I haven't been in the basement since May. I can't bring myself to go down there. The last thing Jack was building was a wooden flower box for the neighborhood entryway. I don't think he finished it."

"I can help you sort through the stuff, Anne. We can set aside the things for Kevin."

"Thanks. That would help, but I'm probably not going to start today."

"Okay, let me know when. By the way, I'm going to have a luncheon for Bible Babes. You are coming back to Bible Babes, aren't you?"

"I guess so. I miss everyone."

Claire scanned the calendar with her fingers. "Good. Labor Day is next Monday, a week from today. Let's look at the following week. I think Wednesday, September 15 would be a good day."

"What time?"

"Elevenish."

"Want me to make something?"

"Well, your peaches and cream cheese cake is fabulous."

Anne yawned, "I'll make two of them. It's only ten o'clock, but I need a nap."

Claire agreed. "It was a lot of work getting them off to college and you didn't sleep much last night."

Anne hugged Claire. "Okay, that's it. I'm heading out of here. Nap time."

"By, hon. Sleep well."

Anne walked down the street. Although it was still officially summer, several of the leaves had turned yellow. She could hear crickets chirping in the morning, a sure sign that fall was coming. *I'm tired all right from drinking too much and taking pills. Maybe the combination of wine and the pills is causing these strange dreams. Tonight, I'll just take sleeping pills.*

Anne struggled every night sometimes taking three or more pills; sometimes drinking her concoction of wine and pills with the hope that restful sleep would come. It did not. Instead, the dreams slithered into her mind, penetrating her innermost thoughts.

When Anne visited Claire during the day, she attempted to hide her secret with makeup and idle talk about politics or movies or anything but what she was feeling.

## Chapter 20 : Visitors

Claire knew something different was taking place in Anne's head, but was unable to put her finger on it.

"What's with the makeup, Annie?"

Anne retorted, "Well, thank you very much for the compliment."

"It looks good, but doesn't it take a lot of time?"

"That's why I do it every morning. It's kind of therapeutic."

Claire playfully pulled Anne's hair. "Okay, if you say so, but you've always been beautiful without makeup."

"Have you talked to Jeff this week?"

"He called last night. How about Kev?"

"Same. Gosh can you believe it's only been two weeks since we took them to St. Francis?"

"Feels a lot longer, doesn't it?"

On the Friday before Labor Day, Chet called Claire to talk about plans for the evening.

"What's cooking tonight?"

"I made lasagna. Why?"

"Well, why don't we invite Annie over for dinner? I know you two get together, but as a couple we haven't seen much of her."

"You know, you're right. She might enjoy sitting with us on the deck. Maybe we could play a little cards, keep it light."

"Good. Give her a call, okay. See you at 6:30. Bye."

As soon as the call ended, Jeff and Kevin exploded in laughter. In a burst of genius, Chet had arranged to pick up the sons for an unannounced visit. He was confident that Claire and Anne had not an inkling of his Friday night surprise.

"Dad, you are the sneaky one."

"Mr. McC., you know they're going to scream and hug us and then hug each other."

"I would expect nothing less. Glad you two could make it. I know you've only been in school two weeks, but it feels like two years to them."

"By the way, what's for dinner?"

"Lasagna."

"Heaven. I love Mom's lasagna. We call the garbage at school La-gags-me."

"Okay, guys, here we are. I'll pull into the garage and go in through the side door. They're probably in the kitchen. Wait about two minutes and then go to the kitchen door in the back."

"Okay, Dad. Sounds like a plan."

"Claire, I'm home."

"In the kitchen with Annie."

Chet kissed Claire and then hugged Anne. "Good to see you Anne. How about a glass of wine?"

Anne hesitated. "Okay, sure."

"One for me too, babe. Lasagna's about ready. Anne, could you pull the salad out and toss it with the Italian dressing?"

Claire pulled the oven door and bent over to check the lasagna. Anne opened the refrigerator, reaching for the salad bowl and dressing. At that moment, the screen door slammed. Claire banged the oven door shut, turned around, and screamed. Anne turned around and almost dropped the salad. Chet took the bowl and the dressing from her. And they did exactly as their sons had predicted -- a merry-go-round of hugs and kisses.

Claire stammered, "What, how? Chet, you planned this, didn't you?"

"Guilty."

"We were both in the car, Mom, when Dad called you."

Claire kissed Chet. "Thanks, this is great. What a surprise visit!"

Anne stood behind Kevin and hugged him around the waist. "I'm not letting you go, mister."

The smell of lasagna and garlic bread permeated the kitchen. Jeff and Kevin didn't talk much as they ravenously consumed dinner.

Chapter 20 : Visitors

Claire smiled. "I forgot how much they eat."

Anne raised her eyebrows. "Eating isn't a strong enough word for it. How about devour?"

Kev stopped for a moment. "Well, Mom, we haven't had real food in two weeks."

After eating, Anne and Claire cleared the table, putting away the leftovers. "I'll do the dishes tomorrow. Let's sit on the deck. It's going to be a beautiful evening."

"Good idea, Mom. I miss the backyard."

Although summer was waning, the fragrance of hydrangeas drifted through the air and the trees swayed waving in the sounds of the night. Chet removed the umbrella from the redwood table and Claire placed an apple-scented candle in its place. Instead of playing cards, the college visitors entertained their parents with stories of dorm life.

Jeff and Kevin stood up and began their show just as they had done as little boys.

"Okay, we have a great story to tell you," Jeff said. "Last weekend, it was raining really hard. A bunch of the guys on our floor decided to invite girls on the floor above us for a…what did you call it, Kev?"

"Stop-the-Rain-Dance-Party." Kevin looked up to the sky and waved his hands back and forth.

"It turned out to be very cool. The guys brought drinks and the girls brought all kinds of food. I love that part. Kev, tell them about Robbie Jarvis."

"Mom, you remember Robbie Jarvis. I sat with him at the luncheon in April and you saw him orientation weekend. Anyway, Robbie Jarvis' mouth starts moving long before his brain engages."

Jeff tapped Kevin on the shoulder. "Wait, Kev, give them the stuff leading up to it."

Anne smiled, "Yeah, Kev, give us the stuff leading up to it."

"Oh yeah, the night before Robbie had popped popcorn in his secret microwave."

Claire admonished, "I didn't think you were allowed to have a microwave in a dorm room."

"That's why I said it was secret, Mrs. McC."

"Will you ladies stop interrupting," Chet chided, "I can't keep up with the story."

Claire and Anne mimed locking their lips and throwing away the key.

"Thank you. Continue, guys."

"Robbie burned the popcorn and amazingly it did not set off the smoke alarm, but the burnt smell was everywhere on our floor. And it went up through a vent into Darlene's and Beth's room."

Jeff let out a snort. "Now, this is the kicker. Darlene and Beth did not realize that it was Robbie who had done it."

Kevin continued, "Robbie sat next to Darlene in Psych 101 the next day. Like I said, he can't keep his mouth shut. He says to Darlene, 'You smell like burnt popcorn.' Darlene says, 'Everything in our room smells like burnt popcorn, Robbie, thanks to some idiot on your floor.' Robbie agrees, 'We have quite a few jerks down there. I'll find out who did it and clean his clock.'"

Chet and Claire and Anne were swimming in details that only college students would believe to be important, but they still enjoyed watching their sons' drama as they prattled on about Robbie.

Jeff motioned, "Hold on, it's almost over and it's funnier than heck. Take it away, Kev."

"Saturday night, it's pouring down rain. Nobody wants to go out. Jeffer and I come up with the idea to have Stop-the-Rain-Dance-Party on our floor. Everyone was psyched about it. We're dancing in the halls and eating up all the goodies that the girls brought."

"Beth, Darlene's roommate, comes down about an hour into the party. She had made Skyway Chili dip, the kind you make Mom."

"Yeah, Mrs. McC., Beth made it exactly like yours – cream cheese on the bottom, Skyway Chili on top with onions and shredded cheddar. Problem was she didn't realize she wouldn't have any place to heat it up."

Chapter 20 : Visitors

"Well, Kev and I hear Beth say to Darlene, 'I guess we'll eat it cold.' Darlene says, 'Someone has a microwave down here because they burned popcorn last night. That's why everything in our room and our clothes smell like it.'"

Kev could barely contain himself. "Then, Robbie Jarvis, you know the guy that talks before he thinks, sees his favorite dip and says, 'Hello, beautiful ladies, I see you have made the traditional Skyway dip. Might I assist you in heating your delicious dish?' Darlene and Beth follow Robbie into his room."

Claire unlocked her lips, "Did they leave the door open?"

Both Chet and Anne yelled, "Claire!"

"Yes, Mrs. McC. They left the door open. So, Darlene and Beth heated the Skyway dish in the microwave. Of course then they knew that it was Robbie's fault for the popcorn smell."

"Is that it?" Chet asked.

"Mostly, I'll let Jeffer tell the final chapter."

"Darlene and Beth were steamed because of the burnt popcorn smell, but something else he did really irked them. Remember Robbie basically lied to them in Psych class. The girls wanted to get even and hatched a plot immediately. Beth asked Robbie to dance to divert him from their – together Jeff and Kevin sneered – 'evil plan.' Darlene went to Robbie's room. She took some of the Skyway dip and smeared it on the light bulb in the lamp by his bed. That night he thought it was a smell left over from heating up the dip in his microwave. But, the next night, he was reading in bed and the bulb started smoking. You can imagine day old cream cheese and chili and onions on a hot lamp. His room smelled like an animal had died in it."

Kevin and Jeff high-fived, laughing uproariously.

"Good story, guys. Funny," Chet said.

"Long, but entertaining," Anne added.

Claire chuckled, "That's a cute story."

Jeff noticed their less than enthusiastic responses, "I guess you had to be there."

"Claire and I have funny stories from college, too." Chet said.

171

Claire put her hand over Chet's mouth and warned, "Don't go there. Hey, we should put together a party for Labor Day. What do you think, guys?"

"Umm, sorry, Mom. Dad's driving us back tomorrow afternoon. There's a party Saturday night and then a bunch of us are going to the fireworks downtown on Sunday."

"Oh, no problem, Jeff. I'm glad you came even if it's only twenty-four hours."

"Same, here. Kev, want to head home? It's getting late."

"Sure, Mom. Thanks for dinner, Mrs. McC."

"Is that my new name, now – Mrs. McC?"

"Our psych prof says we could clear away a lot of space in our brain if we abbreviated words and names."

Anne refuted, "But you now call Jeff, Jeffer. That's longer."

"It doesn't always apply, Mom, but most names and words can usually be shortened. We call Professor Docker, Prof Doc. See, you can say it a lot faster. Prof Doc says it saves on oxygen, too."

Chet goaded, "Gee, I'm glad Prof Doc is sharing such valuable information with the next generation of workers. How much is tuition, Claire?"

Claire defended the boys, "When you were in college, Chet, one of your professors had the students stare at a lava lamp for an entire class."

"Touché! I guess things don't change all that much."

"Ready, Mom?"

"Ready, Kev. Thanks, Chet for getting them here for a visit. It's been a real pick-me-up."

"Mrs. McC, dinner was great."

"I'll pack some of it for you guys to take back tomorrow. Goodnight."

Anne turned around and waved as she and Kev walked down the street to their home.

"Fall's coming. I can feel it. It's still warm, but there's a chill in the breeze."

"Mom, how's it going for you? When I call, you sound good sometimes and other times you sound a little groggy."

Chapter 20 : Visitors

"I don't sleep well, Kev, but I'm okay."

"Are you sure?"

"Stop worrying about me."

"I'm not going to stop worrying about you."

"Listen, I keep busy and Mrs. McC, as you now call her, is there for me."

"When I called last week, you mentioned you wanted to give away some of Dad's clothes and most of the stuff in the basement."

"I do, but I want you to sort through it and take whatever you want."

"I'll go in the basement tomorrow and choose what I want. As far as Dad's clothes, I'd like his baseball cap, his Air Force uniform, and the necklace with the cross on it that you bought him when you got married."

Anne put her arm around Kevin and pulled him toward her. "You are growing up, my favorite son. I'm proud of you. You remind me of your father and that's a good thing."

As they entered their home, Kevin felt a bittersweet sensation. The rooms held powerful memories of birthdays and Halloween and Christmas and everyday occurrences. He and his Mom walked to the kitchen.

"Got milk, Mom?"

"I'll get it for you. Want a cookie?"

"No, just milk."

While Kevin drank the milk, Anne took the sleeping pill bottle and put it in her pants' pocket. I'm going to need these tonight. Let's see, I had three glasses of wine. Maybe, I should only take a half of a pill."

"Mom, it's really good to see you. Remember, the offer still holds about putting off college for a while."

"No way. You're having such a good time and I assume you are doing well in the core engineering courses."

"Absolutely. They're difficult, but Jeff and I study a lot. Tonight, it probably sounded like we party all the time, but I'm working hard, Mom. I'm not wasting your money."

"I know you're not. You look good, Kevin. More than good, you look happy. That makes me happy."

"Good night, Mom. How about pancakes in the morning?"

"You got it." Anne kissed the top of Kevin's head. "Good night, young man. Lock up, okay?"

"Sure, Mom. I'm right behind ya."

Anne put half of a sleeping pill in her mouth and sipped water. After two hours of restlessness, she took a whole sleeping pill plus the other half. Sleep came inviting wicked dreams.

---

This night was more subdued, but the shadowy visitors were never-the-less disturbing. Babies were crawling up the walls of her room trying to escape. Women with swollen bellies stood on tiptoe frantically stretching to pull their babies from the wall. Then, their bellies were flat and the wail of the women was gut-wrenching.

Anne winced in fear and disgust. For a while, she slept peacefully, but her dream was relentless continuing through the night at different intervals. At four in the morning Anne realized she was awake, but could not move. Once again she was immobilized from wine and pills. She stared at the ceiling fan attempting to move one body part at a time. After an hour, she was finally able to sit up. Her head throbbed with pounding pain, but she managed to walk to the kitchen.

---

*Kev, stay in bed, please. I need to get myself together. God, why did I drink that much wine?*

Anne took two aspirin, started the coffee pot, and then took a shower. Afterward, she felt somewhat better, but frowned at her image in the mirror. She grabbed her makeup bag and put beige concealer under and around her eyes. *Oh, great. I look like a raccoon."* Eventually, she was able to disguise most of the dark circles and red splotches. *There, that's a little better.*

Chapter 20 : Visitors

By the time she went back to the kitchen, Kevin was sitting at the table drinking coffee.

"Morning, Mom. Coffee's great."

"Good morning. Pancakes are on the way!"

"You look good, Mom."

"I am good, Kev. Did you sleep well?"

"I did. It was kinda weird being back here, but it was okay. I can tackle that stuff in the basement after breakfast."

"Thanks, Kev. Big help. I'll call St. Vincent de Paul this week to pickup the giveaway stuff. Put the necklace, the baseball cap, and your Dad's uniform with his captain's hat in your room before you leave today. You can go through his other things, too, if you want."

"I pretty much know what's in there. Those are the only three things I want."

"Here you go, Kev. Three on the plate."

Kev echoed, "Three on the plate and three on the griddle. Mmm, you make the best pancakes."

Saturday flew by in a whirlwind of Anne and Kevin confronting the basement. Kevin moved all of the tools and planks of wood to one wall for pickup. He put the workout weights and Jack's unfinished garden box under the stairs marked with his name. Then, he and his Mom took a look at the closet.

"This will be too much today, Kev. It's already 12:30. Claire will help me with the closet this week. I want to take you to lunch today. Mr. McC is taking you back at four o'clock, right?"

"Right."

"Let's just get the things you know you want."

"Here's your Dad's baseball hat. And here's the Air Force uniform. Can you reach his captain's hat on the shelf?"

Kevin took his Dad's hat off the top shelf and handed it to his Mom. She held the brim placing the inside against her face."

"I smell your Dad."

"You going to cry, Mom?"

"No, Kev, I'm all cried out. I guess you are, too."

"I think about him every day."

"So do I, but you know he wants both of us to keep on keeping on as he would say. There, put these in your room and then let's go to Skyway and have the real stuff. Oh, wait, the cross."

Anne stood at the dresser and carefully lifted Jack's gold cross that was hanging on a picture of Kevin. "Turn around; I'll put it on you. It looks good."

Kevin touched the cross. "Thanks, Mom."

Then, he carried his father's tangible memories to his room and put them in his closet. Anne closed the door to her bedroom.

Although brief, Kevin and Jeff's visit lifted everyone's spirits. The McCormacks spent their time with Jeff in ordinary ways. Jeff and his Dad tossed football in the backyard while Claire worked in her garden. Then, lunch on the deck with Jeff sharing more stories and assuring his parents he was on the right track academically.

Anne had finally mustered the courage to go into the basement to make decisions about Jack's stuff. They had jumped a large hurdle by opening the door to Jack's closet.

Chet pulled out of his driveway at 4 pm as planned. Jeff and Kevin waved to their Moms. The visit was over.

"How'd it go with Kev?"

"Good. He took care of almost everything in the basement and I actually went down there to decide what to keep and what to give away. It wasn't all that bad and we even opened the door to Jack's closet."

"That's real progress!"

"It was great to spend time with Kev."

"It was fun, wasn't it? I love my new name, Mrs. McC. What a loony professor. Sorry, I mean prof."

Chapter 20 : Visitors

They laughed lightheartedly, content to see their sons coming into their own. Both mothers knew that Jeff and Kevin were changing with every tick of the clock. Having them home for even one day softened the edge of missing their sons. The visit helped the Moms to realize that they could let go a little at a time. Hopefully, the goodbyes at the end of their visits would tug a little less at their hearts.

"Heading home, Claire. See you."

"Okay, call me."

Anne waved. *I am tired. I've got to sleep. Okay, tonight, no wine. I'll take three sleeping pills instead of two.*

Each day Anne made a promise to herself that she would skip the sleeping pills or drink only one glass of wine, but by dusk she had tossed aside her resolve. When the sun began to set, Anne would start twisting her hair until it hurt at the scalp. The loss of Jack still stung and when the memory of the abortion visited, she pressed it down further and further, repeating her mantra. "Let not your heart be troubled. Let not your heart be troubled."

Her heart was troubled by tormenting dreams of women screaming and babies dying and eerie rides on a train. At night, she was a vaporous shell forced to endure the attacks of the nightmares as they twisted around her, pouring more darkness and sadness into her heart. In the morning, she would take several hours to recover from the night before using makeup as her disguise. The two friends saw each other almost every day, but Claire noticed that Anne didn't talk about Jack as much. Anne's thick makeup, forced cheerfulness, and mindless chatter unnerved Claire.

━━━━━━━━━━━━━

On September 15, the entourage of the Bible Babes was to converge on Claire's home. Anne tapped on the screen door and chirped. "Hi, Claire. Thought I'd come down a little early in case you need help before the ladies arrive today.

"Great, I'm struggling to get this potato dish in the oven. Could you fill the glasses with water?"

"Sure. I'll put my pies in the fridge. Like my new eye shadow – Velvet Violet?"

"Looks nice." Claire stared at Anne's face. She was hoping that this makeup phase would be over by now, but instead Anne seemed to be doubling down on it.

*Thick makeup, thick eyelashes, thick lipstick, thick head. What is going on with her?*

A stream of pleasantries filled the air as the women arrived.

"Claire, your house is beautiful. I love the new wallpaper."

"Thanks, Roxanne, but it's not new."

"Guess it's been a while since I last visited."

"Oh, Annie, how are you? It must be difficult for you and Kevin."

"We're doing okay, Tekla. Kev's at college now."

Patti clapped her hands. "Ladies, ladies. Yoo-hoo. Did I tell you that a new woman is joining our Bible Babes? Her name is Maureen McFee. She and her family moved into the parish in July, just about the time you were going through that awful coma, hon. Anyway, I met her at church one morning and invited her to join our group. Did she rsvp for the luncheon, Claire?"

"She accepted the invitation. Maybe you should call her, though. She's never been here and she might be lost, Patti."

"Oh, here she is, now." Patti opened the door. "Hi, Maureen, come in. Welcome to Claire McCormack's home."

Patti and Claire had both attended Angel of God School from first through eighth grade. Because the Dillon family of nine children lived in a small home, Claire was reluctant to invite friends from school. She loved the house and yard and the fun times, but most of the girls at school lived in nicer, newer homes. It would have been embarrassing if her friends knew her Mom and Dad slept in the living room on a pull-out couch. Until she met Patti. Patti and Claire shared the shame of holes in shoes, hand-me down clothes, and the pervasive knowledge that their parents didn't have money for anything but necessities. Claire remained close to Patti, but not in the same way as her bond with Anne. Nonetheless, she and Patti shared several years of friendship from childhood to adulthood.

"Hello, Maureen, I'm Claire. We are thrilled you could make it. Lunch is ready, ladies. Let's go to the dining room."

Chapter 20 : Visitors

"Claire, the table looks elegant."

The pale yellow tablecloth was a perfect backdrop for the luncheon.  In front of each place setting was a small vase of flowers with a name card on the plate.  Claire had specifically selected a different bouquet for each woman.  The ladies found their places introducing themselves to Maureen and chattering about this and that.  Patti clapped her hands.

"Oh, we know what that means.  Patti's going to tell someone to do something," Tekla kidded.

"Well, not exactly, but Claire has her hands folded.  I think we're about to pray."

Claire said the simple prayer of grace before meals.  She moved her eyes around the table looking from woman to woman.

"I have something else to say.  I know I sent thank you notes, but I am overjoyed that all of you are here today.  I want to tell you how much it meant to receive your cards and flowers and food for my family.  And I know you were praying for me.  As part of our prayer, I want to thank God for all of you.  Amen.  Now, let's eat.  This tray is an ensemble of little sandwiches – egg salad, turkey with avocado, and ham with Swiss cheese.  I'll let you start, Maureen."

Roxanne said, "Claire, tinkled pink you recovered.  Fr. Hernandez talked about you on that first Sunday after it happened and everyone was in total shock."

"We each took turns going to Mass one day per week in-between our schedules," Dana added.

"Thank you.  All of your prayers truly helped.  It was almost a miracle.  Not many people survive a brain aneurysm like the one I had."

Claire continued to pass the dishes of food – fresh fruit salad, an assortment of vegetables with dill dipping sauce, and scalloped potatoes.  The ladies enjoyed each and every morsel.  There were group conversations and one-on-one discussions.  Phrases, fragments, and laughter filled the room as if balloon callouts protruded from each of the ladies' mouths.

"My daughter got a job at…"

"I'm excited the kids are back in school…"

"Did you read her second book?" Wasn't it awful?"

"Could you pass the potatoes, Roxanne?"

"Jeannie's in Europe for two months researching a tax case."

"Are you kidding me?"

"Our vacation was a blast. We stayed in a beautiful old colonial on Pawley Island, right on the ocean."

"Pass around the pictures…"

Since Anne was at the other end of the table, Patti felt safe to whisper to Claire, "When did Anne start using that much makeup? I've never seen her wear more than lipstick and a little blush on her cheekbones."

"I have no idea, Patti, none whatsoever."

Claire deliberately placed Anne next to Dana. She was pleased to see they were having a private conversation.

"Are you doing okay, Anne? I know it's hard."

"You understand better than anyone, Dana. How do you get through this?"

"One day at a time. Melissa was our only child. It was unbelievable that she got breast cancer at age thirty."

"That had to be rough."

"It's horrible seeing your child suffer. She had a really aggressive kind of cancer and died March 14, 2000. Fr. Hernandez came to visit us about a month after her death. He encouraged both of us to join Grieving Parents of Children. Phil went once. He couldn't get over losing his little girl. It played its toll on him."

"And, he died shortly after your daughter, didn't he?"

"Yep. December 9, 2000. He was 59. They said it was a heart attack, but I think he died of a broken heart."

Dana Dannon was sixty-two years old, as tall and slender as Anne. Dana was an only child and the mother of an only child. When the two people she loved the most died, she felt deserted and lonely.

Chapter 20 : Visitors

"How did you cope, Dana?"

"I didn't cope for a long time.  I stopped going to the grief meetings.  I felt there was no point.  I thought I could cope by taking medication.  I was on twelve prescriptions for two years.  I walked around in a daze.  Sometimes, people couldn't understand my speech."

Anne  twisted her hair.  "Obviously, you're not like that now.  What happened?"

"What happened is Claire.  I decided to go to Mass one morning and they had coffee and donuts afterward.  Claire sat by me.  I didn't know her very well, but I had seen her before.  She's really good at reading people and I guess she could see I was in trouble."

"She is good at that."

"Anyhow, she invited me to join Bible Babes.  I thought it would be a bunch of holier than thou church ladies, but it wasn't.  Well you know that.  After going to the meetings for a few months, I started feeling a little better.  It wasn't just about reading the Bible.  You ladies listened to me and consoled me.  I still take one medication for depression, but I flushed everything else down the toilet."

"Dana, I remember the meetings when you shared, but I didn't know the depth and details of all of that."

"You asked me how I cope.  If coping means that you put one foot in front of the other, I can do that, but it's still a daily challenge to move forward.  They've been gone ten years but sorrow visits me every day.  When I get really down, I pray the rosary and I keep busy doing things like our Bible group."

Anne let her hair unwind.  "I'm almost ashamed of how I feel.  I mean you not only lost your husband, but your child too."

"Don't feel ashamed, Anne.  Losing Jack suddenly was shocking and your nerves are still raw from the loss.  When you're ready, share your journey with us in the meetings.  It helps.  I'm a living witness to that."

"Okay, I'll think about it."

"Anne, I love listening to everyone and learning what in scripture changes their lives. I wouldn't miss it for the world now. Each week I feel a little stronger in my faith. Anytime you want to talk, give me a call. By the way, how is Kevin?"

Anne's eyes lit up. "He's going to college at St. Francis Bergio. As a matter of fact, he and Jeff surprised us by coming home to visit about a week ago."

"Okay, you two down there. You haven't eaten much. What are you whispering about?" Patti inquired.

"We're talking about our faith, Queen Patti."

Patti took the cue. "Speaking of which, we will have our first meeting on Wednesday, October 8th. As usual, I'll take care of the prayers and the readings for the first session, but I need a volunteer to bring a sweet snack and someone to bring a salty. Thanks. Okay, Tekla, sweet. Roxanne, salty."

Maureen sat back in her chair. "I am stuffed. Claire, everything was delicious. The scalloped potatoes were O-T-T."

Claire looked puzzled. Maureen explained, "Over the top – that's what O-T-T means. I have three teenagers. They taught me this crazy way of communicating with abbreviations. I had to learn it to know what they're talking about."

"Yeah, Annie and I have heard about the benefits of shortening words from our sons. Thanks, Maureen. I think you're going to like our group. We pray and talk and have a lot of fun."

Patti continued, "Okay, we start at the same time this year, 7:30. We will be in the room next to the library."

Claire asked, "That's the really nice one, isn't it?"

"Yes, I've been trying to schedule that room for two years and we finally made it to the top of the waiting list."

"Anything else, before I serve Anne's unbelievable peaches 'n cream cheese cake?"

"No, ma'am. Dessert comes first."

And so, on September 15, the Bible Babes shared stories, pictures, worries, and joys. The personality and experiences of each of the women infused the group with a mixture as diverse as the flowers Claire had chosen for them in the vases by their plates.

For Maureen McFee, daffodils indicative of rebirth, new beginnings, and eternal life.  For Roxanne Dietersheim a magnolia, belle of the south.  For Tekla Parker, pink roses suggesting gratitude, appreciation and admiration.  For Dana Dannon, a bouquet of daisies denoting the innocence of the Christ child and loyal love. For Patti Waring, fragrant sweet peas representing delicate and blissful pleasure.  For Bernie Deimler, a sunflower which signifies adoration and dedicated love. And for Anne Combs, a slender white lily symbolic of purity and refined beauty.

Claire felt grateful to be alive and looked forward to the first Bible Babes meeting.  The babes would continue to share sorrows, joys, difficulties, and victories, nurtured through scripture.  Each of the visitors that day held a special place in Claire's heart.

# CHAPTER 21 : AUTUMN

Each day the sun set earlier, nightfall came sooner, and Claire's garden was ready to rest for the winter. Late in September, Chet and Claire worked in the backyard. Claire raked leaves out of her garden beds, cut the dead flowers, and threw all of it into her compost container. Chet was almost finished blowing the leaves into several tall mounds around the yard. When he turned off the leaf blower, Claire could hear him complaining out loud.

"Next year, I'm going to hire Tiggy to do this crap. It's twice as hard without Jeff here."

"I hear grumbling. Someone doesn't like yard work."

Chet stomped toward Claire as she dumped her last load of compost material. He was red in the face, his forehead dripping with sweat. He threw the blower on the ground and yelled, "Well, dang it, Claire, it's taken me six hours to get the leaves in piles and if I don't put them in bags today, they'll be all over the damn yard again tomorrow."

"Don't yell at me, Chet. You get mad like this every year."

"I'm not mad. I'm tired of doing yard work."

"Why do you have to complain about it every year? You know the leaves are going to come off the trees and have to be raked. It starts off as a nice day in the yard and then you turn it into an argument."

"Yeah, right, Claire. You're always right. Go back to your smelly compost."

Claire was a strong person, but Chet could push her buttons at times. She didn't know how he did it. She usually didn't know when he'd get into one of his moods, but when he did, she'd cry as hurtful memories bubbled up. Claire half-heartedly raked the compost to spread it evenly, sniffling back the tears."

"Want me to help you, hon."

"No. I don't need your help."

"I'm sorry, Claire. I shouldn't have yelled at you."

"No, you shouldn't, but you do sometimes."

"I know."

Chapter 21 : Autumn

"It makes me feel small and worthless and hurt and then I start to remember all the things that happened."

Chet put his hand on Claire's rake. "I'm sorry, Claire. I really am. Forgive me? Here, hit me over the head with the rake. I deserve it."

Claire turned away placing the rake against the shed, "Grumpy old man."

"Did you call me a grumpy old man?"

"Maybe I did and maybe I didn't."

"Okay, that's it. You're going down." Chet grabbed Claire's arm and started running toward the tallest pile of leaves. I'm not letting you go. Get ready to jump."

As they landed in the red and gold and orange mound, Chet held Claire from behind and started rolling over and over until they landed on the ground beside the heap of leaves.

She sputtered an orange leaf out of her mouth, then picked up a handful and tossed it in his face.

"You're not a grumpy old man. You're a crazy old man."

Chet grabbed her again and was about to run to another pile when Claire heard her phone playing "Wide Open Spaces" by the Dixie Chicks. She pulled it from her pocket.

"Hi, Jeannie. It's good to hear your voice."

"Hi, Mom. Same here."

Claire put the phone on speaker.

Chet leaned in. "Hi, Jeannie, how's it going, baby girl?"

"Working hard, Dad, but enjoying the travel a lot."

"So, you were in Spain. Now, where?"

"I just landed at the Frankfurt airport. I leave for Rome in an hour. I wanted to let you know I'm doing fine. How are you guys?"

Chet winked at Claire. "We're having lots of fun. Your Mom and I were rolling around in the leaves in the backyard. We're sitting here on the ground now."

"Did you say rolling around in the leaves?"

"Jeannie, your Dad got a crazy notion that we should jump in a big pile of leaves."

"Really? Sounds juvenile."

"I got on top of your Mom and we rolled over and over until…"

Jeannie yelled, "Stop, okay? TMI."

"Oh, no, not you, too. Does everybody abbreviate everything now? And what is TMI?"

"Too Much Information."

"Oh, I see. Whatever. Anyhow, sounds like things are going well and you're enjoying it. That's what your Dad and I like to hear. We know our girl needs wide open spaces."

"Hey, I talked with Jeff today when I was at the Barcelona airport. He's seems to be doing great at school. Gosh, I can't believe my bratty little brother is in college now."

"Tempus fugit, non-combackibus."

"Huh?"

"It's Latin. Time flies and never comes back."

"If you say so, Dad. Mom, how are you feeling?"

"Feeling great. Doctor says I'm a miracle case. Dad and I joined Encompass Health Club. I've been swimming laps a few times a week. Dad works out and jogs. It's nice to have the time to exercise more."

"Okay, but don't overdo it. Dad, you still call her a couple of times a day, don't you?"

"I've got it covered, Jeannie."

"Good. Well, I'm going to grab something to eat before I board the plane. Mom, write me. I can stay in touch more often with e-mail."

"Will do, darling. I miss you."

"I'll be back in the states mid-November and then I'm coming home for Thanksgiving."

Chet cheered. "Great! All four of us together again."

"Gotta go. Bye Dad. Bye Mom. Love you guys. Ciao!"

"She sounds good, doesn't she?"

"She's a pip. We have good kids."

"Sometimes, I wish we had more of them."

"Now, Claire, we've talked about this over and over. Contraception was a sin, but we both confessed it."

"I know. It's not nearly as much about the guilt as it is about the regret. Those first years of our marriage were wild."

"Is this going to be about Dallas again?"

"No, I was the one that went to Planned Parenthood and got the pill. Before I married you, my Mom encouraged me to use contraception. She didn't want me to be, as she called it, straddled with nine children like her. I love her and she was a good mother, but I wish I had listened to my heart on this one."

Chet guided Claire to the bench by the Blessed Mother statue.

"Let's sit." He put his arm around her. "Maybe if I had been a better husband in the beginning, you would have felt more secure about having children."

"I don't blame you, Chet. Neither one of us was very strong in our faith back then. Even after the kids were born, we still had outside influences telling us to not have more than two babies. The world's over populated. College is going to be expensive even for two children. Women have the right to choose how many children they want. We both bought into the lie."

"But, hon, it's a moot point now."

"That's another thing, the vasectomy. Remember, when we were thinking about having a third baby?"

"I remember."

"We were all for it, until we started listening to other people. Remember that day I happened to run into Beth Vinson. I hadn't seen her since high school. We got to talking about our families. She had a son and daughter the same ages as ours. I mentioned that we were thinking about having our third."

"What did she say?"

"First, she looked at me like I had green horns growing out of my head. I remember exactly what she said to me. 'Are you serious, Claire? Jeannie's in the third grade, Jeff's in pre-school now. You'll finally have time for you! Go back to school – get your degree. It's your turn.'"

"Same with me. Good old Frank talked me out of having another one. He said I'd be crazy to have more children."

"Yeah, good old Frank, who had four children."

"He loved his kids, but he was trying to enlighten me, I suppose. He told me that he'd be sixty-four when his youngest got out of high school. Then, he looked at me and said one word…"

Claire finished his sentence, "Vasectomy. We made that decision together and that was the end of the birthing years."

"It seemed to be the right thing at the time."

"Yeah, it seemed to be the right thing, and I thought we were good Catholics, but were we? We chose to be in charge and ignore God's plan. And, early on, we dismissed Natural Family Planning as a myth. "

"It was strange how we were really set on having a baby and then within twenty-four hours two people put doubt in our minds."

"It was not a coincidence, Chet. It was the liar. The devil is an expert at placing people and doubts and opportunities at precisely the right moment. And both of us freely accepted Satan's plan without as much as a prayer to God."

"Wow, thank God for the sacrament of Confession."

"Agreed, but I think about what might have been and it makes me sad sometimes. And then, the mindboggling mess with Anne."

"It seems that things have smoothed over."

"Not entirely. I'm glad Anne and I are back to seeing each other, but I still find it hard to believe that she went ahead with the abortion."

"Does she talk about it?"

Chapter 21 : Autumn

"Never mentions it.  You know, you and I kind of did the same thing by using contraception."

"Claire, contraception is a far cry from abortion."

"I'm not so sure about that.  I regret not having more children, but it gives me a better understanding of how difficult it must be for Anne.  She doesn't even talk about how she feels but she must think about it all the time.  It's like an unspoken eleventh commandment between us – Thou shalt not talk about pregnancy or abortion ever again."

"Well, that was almost as much fun as our roll in the leaves – NOT."

"Sorry, I get moody when the kids call."

"C'mon, let's finish the yard.  It's going to be dark in about an hour.  Will you help me load the bags?"

"Sure, crazy old man."

Chet took a red leaf that had landed on Claire's head and tickled her nose with it.  "You're a lucky woman to have this crazy old man."

Eye shadow and thick makeup could not fully hide the unhappy droop of Anne's face.    Even so, Claire obeyed the unspoken eleventh commandment – Thou shalt not talk about pregnancy or abortion.    At times, she felt as though she were skating across a pond that was melting in spots. At any moment she might fall through the ice if she said something that offended Anne.

In October, Anne and Claire resumed their weekly Bible Babes sessions at Angel of God Church.  As Patti had promised, their group would have the use of the most comfortable room in the parish center which had been remodeled over the summer.  The scent of the room was that of newly purchased grey carpet and navy blue furniture.  The freshly painted pale blue walls had a calming effect.  When the ladies first entered the room, each of them took time to choose where they would sit this year.

Of course Patti Waring selected the chair farthest from the door, so she could see people coming and going.  It was a comfortable leather recliner nestled in the corner with a table lamp on the left side.  No one complained that Patti got the best chair since she did all of the organizing and planning.

Patti saw Maureen walk through the door.  "Hi, Maureen, glad you're with us this year."

"Me, too.   With three boys, it's almost impossible for me to get out of the house, but I told my husband I have to have time to myself, even though I know I'm with all of you and not really by myself."

Bernie moved from seat to seat in the room to decide what felt good to her. Bernie also had three children, but they were grown and raising their own families. "Maureen, what you really mean is you need time away from them.  It doesn't matter if you're around other people, as long as it's not them.  Them that wants something to eat.  Them that needs a poster for their project.  Them that leave empty potato chip bags on the couch.  And the one them that thinks you're sexy in his boxer shorts and a sweatshirt at eleven o'clock at night.   Been there, done that."

Roxanne loved to talk in her southern drawl.  "Lordy, Lordy, Bernadette.  You have the most creative way of saying things."  She had been born in Raleigh, North

Carolina, but moved to Cincinnati when she was nine years old.  No one questioned her accent, but once in a while, Roxanne would slip into Midwestern twang.

Patti led Maureen to a chair on the right side of the lamp.  "I want you to sit here, hon, since you're with child.  It's the second best seat in the house."

Bernie asked, "When are you due?"

"December 20th.  My babies come late.  I really hope this one is not a Christmas baby."

Anne pursed her lips when she heard the word baby and pretended to be looking for something in her purse.

Patti directed, "Ladies, pick a seat and get it over with, please!"  Within a few minutes each of them had chosen a place.  Although there were no rules for the group, it was understood by one and all that the chair you selected at the first meeting would be yours for the entire year.

Dana sat at one end of a loveseat near a window that overlooked the parking lot.  Anne sat at the other end by the door.  On the opposite side was a matching loveseat.  Tekla sat across from Dana and Claire sat across from Anne.  Roxanne ceremoniously smoothed her pink cotton dress in the back before sinking into a chair that was to the right of Claire.  There was only one chair remaining in the room.  Bernie sat down and patted Roxanne on the knee.

"I guess this is the one I like the best because it's the only one left."

Tekla scoffed, "You snooze, you lose."

Roxanne winked at Bernie in the simple understanding that this arrangement was exactly what they wanted. Although Roxanne and Bernie had very different backgrounds, they had developed a deep friendship over the years, partially bolstered by being married to strong German men.

Bernie married Ralph Deimler whose parents came to Cincinnati, Ohio in 1949, so his father could work in Woebensheim beer brewery that was owned by an uncle.  Ralph Deimler and Bernadette Schmidt were destined to meet and marry, since they lived on the same street in the most German populated area of Cincinnati.

Roxanne O'Bannon had grown up with all the amenities of a southern belle. While she had only lived in the south her first nine years, her mother sustained southern charm and traditions in Midwest Ohio. However, Roxanne's husband, Arthur Dietersheim had an unusual and sorrowful start in life during wartime Germany. Arthur Edward Dietersheim, was born on October 24, 1940 to a Catholic mother and a Jewish father. When he was eleven months old, Wilhelm and Katrina had to face the inevitable-- they would be sent to Dachau Concentration Camp. There was no place for them to hide from the Nazis, but they were able to save their son by placing him in the care of Katrina's sister. In the last days before she and her husband would be taken, Katrina Dietersheim asked her sister to make sure her baby boy was raised Catholic. Aunt CiCi left for America immediately with baby Arthur in her arms. Aunt CiCi loved her sister's little boy. His sky blue eyes, blonde hair, and quiet confidence reminded her of Katrina. She not only kept her promise to her sister, but CiCi made sure he attended Catholic grade school and high school. Arthur remained a very devout Catholic throughout his life. With the help of relatives in the United States, Aunt CiCi made sure Arthur went to college. He received a law degree from the University of Cincinnati and was fortunate enough to land a job with O'Bannon Law firm, owned by Roxanne's father. Mr. O'Bannon invited his protégé to dinner one night and the Arthur and Roxanne courtship commenced. They married the following June.

Bernie and Roxanne knew each other's life stories from beginning to end; hence, they were inseparable friends delighted to sit side by side at the Bible Babes meetings.

Tekla put a bag of store-bought chocolate chip cookies on the cocktail table in the middle of the room.

"Yum, can't wait to have one of those," Dana said.

Roxanne pointed to the tray of toasted small round bread covered with bruschetta and melted provolone. "I hope y'all like these. I made them right before I left. They should still be nice and warm."

Maureen smacked her lips. "Mmm, that's what I want. I love salty food. I know it's not good for me, but I'm hungry tonight."

Chapter 22 : Bible Babes – Week One

Patti tapped her pen on the glass lamp. "Let's get started, Bible Babes. After opening prayer, help yourself to the refreshments. Thanks, Tekla and Roxanne for bringing them. Also, we can get soda or water in the hall refrigerator. Just leave a dollar in the can on top."

Roxanne turned the rheostat to the left to dim the overhead lights. Patti lit the cinnamon apple candle that was in-between the refreshment trays on the cocktail table.

"Okay, let's relax. Take a deep breath and slowly release it. Good. Now, close your eyes and listen to our opening prayer."

*Dear Jesus,*

*Thank you for the gift of these women. For Dana, who brings the wisdom of truth. For Tekla, whose empathy and caring spirit lifts our hearts. For Roxanne, who gently shares her strong faith and life experiences. For Bernie, who unselfishly cares for the elderly, teaching us the value of charity. For Claire, thank you for bringing her back to us with her humor and passion. For Anne, who has endured the loss of her beloved husband this year with dignity and strength. For our newest member, Maureen, a devoted labor and delivery nurse who helps to bring infants into the world. Also, protect the baby in her womb. And for me, Patti. Lord, thank you for giving me the time and ability to bring all of these women together. Amen.*

"Let's get what we want to drink before we have the reading. Next week, grab a drink on your way in. That way we don't have to interrupt the meeting."

Maureen said, "I have a question. How come the church directory calls this group Bible Basics, but you call it Bible Babes?"

A titter of laughter filled the room. "It's our dirty little secret, Maureen," Patti explained. "When we started the group twelve years ago, our pastor, Fr. Albert, was a real fuddy dud and he wouldn't let us call it Bible Babes, so we changed our name to Bible Basics."

"Boring!" Tekla whined.

"We called ourselves Bible Babes anyway, but we list it as Bible Basics in the directory."

"I think Father Hernandez would let us change it now, Patti."

"Probably, Claire, but I like the idea that it's our dirty little secret. Gives us clandestine status like cloister nuns."

Tekla's eyes opened wide, "We're the underground!"

Patti laughed at Tek's comment. "In any event, that's the reason, Maureen."

"Thanks, I love it."

After the salty and sweet snacks had been passed around, Patti continued, "Well, as usual, I have the first Bible verse to offer for discussion. For Maureen, and to refresh everyone on how we do this. Basically, the presenter reveals her choice of scripture to the group. Then, each person shares her interpretation of the verse. Finally, the presenter reveals why she chose that verse.

Please turn to John, Chapter 14:1-14." Patti read aloud:

*Do not let your hearts be troubled. You have faith in God; have faith also in me. In my Father's house there are many dwelling places. If there were not, would I have told you that I am going to prepare a place for you? And if I go and prepare a place for you, I will come back again and take you to myself, so that where I am you also may be. Where (I) am going you know the way.' Thomas said to him, 'Master, we do not know where you are going; how can we know the way?' Jesus said to him, 'I am the way and the truth and the life. No one comes to the Father except through me. If you know me, then you will also know my Father. From now on you do know him and have seen him…If you ask the Father anything of me in my name, He will do it.'*

Okay, who wants to start?"

Roxanne volunteered, "Y'all know that I had one of my kidneys removed eight years ago. Patti, you sweet thing, you brought a gift to me in the hospital. It was a picture of a little girl. She had a scraped knee and a little tear running down her cheek. This verse was written on a plaque underneath; not the whole verse, just 'Let not your heart be troubled.' That really cheered me up. There's another verse that speaks to me tonight. 'I am the way and the truth and the life. No one comes to the Father except through me.'"

Roxanne cocked her head to the right, placing her index finger on her cheek and elbow on the arm of the chair. "I grew up believing in God and Jesus. Glory hallelujah, I lived in a southern Baptist home and went to Sunday school. We moved to Cincinnati when I was nine years old and I think my parents were surprised at how many German Catholics lived here.  My husband, Arthur Dietersheim, worked for my father in the O'Bannon Law Firm.  Mother and Father genuinely liked Arthur in spite of the fact that he was Catholic.  That is, until we got engaged.  Oh, my!  The day we told my parents that I was going to convert to Catholicism, they had a hissy-fit that was heard all the way to Charlotte.  In time, they got over it and after Daddy died, Mother converted to Catholicism too.  I like this verse because it spells it all out – we are only going to get to Heaven through our Savior, Jesus Christ.  No one comes to the Father except through Him.  I love being a Catholic especially receiving Jesus in the Eucharist."

Roxanne sat upright in her chair looking very prim and proper with her hands folded on top of her Bible.  She finished her rendition in the slowest drawl she could muster.  "I remember the day when I was a little girl and I proudly walked up the aisle to the altar in the Raleigh Baptist Church of God.  I announced to the world that Jesus is my Savior.  And I say, glory hallelujah once again!"

Tekla raised her arms in the air.  "Amen, sista.  Got a question, though.  How's your other kidney, Roxanne?"

"Well, it's fine.  Thanks for asking, Miss Tekla."  Claire rolled her eyes at Dana.  Dana smiled slightly, hoping Tekla had not seen Claire make the face.

Patti was somewhat stunned by Roxanne's revelation.  "Thanks, Roxanne, that is a precious story.  In all the years you've been with the group, I didn't know you converted to Catholicism."

"Well, I guess I felt moved by the spirit to share that tonight."

Dana added, "My mother was a Baptist before she married my Dad.  She was more devout than a lot of cradle-to-tomb Catholics.  I'm glad you told us, Roxanne.  I never knew that either."

"Thanks, Dana.  I've been wanting to tell that to y'all, but I've always been a little nervous about it."

Tekla probed, "What else do we not know about you, Roxanne?  Are you a spy?"

Dana stared at Tekla. "You need to learn when not to ask something." Tekla pretended she didn't hear her.

Patti moved things along. "Thanks, again, Roxanne. You want to go next, Dana?"

"Sure."

Dana wore soft blue slacks and a white blouse. Around her neck she had tied a coral sweater that had blue pearl buttons and delicate blue edging. No matter what meeting or event she was attending, everything was coordinated. Tonight was no exception. Her necklace, earrings, and bracelet matched the blue trim on the sweater. Even her coral shoes had a small blue flower at the tip. Dana had put yellow highlight on the lines of the reading she wanted to discuss.

"Patti, good choice of scripture. I love this Chapter in John. Building on what you said, Roxanne, verse 6 is a favorite of mine, too. *'No one comes to the Father except through me. If you know me, then you will also know my Father.'* Jesus was talking to His disciples at the Last Supper and they were terrified that He was leaving them. I think His words were probably very comforting. *'Let not your hearts be troubled'* has such a wonderful ring to it. And then, when He tells them, *'If you know me, then you will also know my Father,'* I feel hopeful that I will see my dear Melissa and my Philip one day."

Tekla looked at Maureen and blurted. "Maureen, since you're new, you may not know that Dana lost her daughter to cancer and then her husband died the same year. When was that, Dana?"

"In 2000, Tek," Dana flatly replied.

Although Tekla's comments were like unwelcomed robo calls at dinnertime, the ladies had come to accept and love her. She was a lonely forty-eight year old spinster who lived with her older sister, Georgia. Georgia had recently gone through a bitter divorce and sometimes waged her resentment against Tekla. For the most part, the ladies chose to overlook her insensitive comments.

Maureen teared up and reached for Dana's hand. "I'm really sorry for your losses, Dana. You've been through so much."

"Thanks, Maureen. Melissa was only thirty-four when she died. I haven't been the same since. I like the sound of 'Let not your heart be troubled.' I'm going to say that before I go to sleep tonight." As was her custom, Dana closed the Bible and nodded when she was finished.

Claire said, "I'll go next. I love this scripture too. Chet told me that Father Hernandez performed the sacrament of the Anointing of the Sick on me when I was in the coma. Bear in mind that I don't remember any of this, but my family told me what they heard and saw. Chet said that Fr. Hernandez suggested he read this chapter and to focus on the verse *'If you ask the Father anything of me in my name, I will do it.'* He and Jeannie and Jeff went to the chapel at St. Al's and prayed for me. They tell me I slept very well that night and a few days after I received the sacrament, I woke-up."

Patti comforted, "Our group wouldn't be the same without you. We're all happy you are back!"

Claire laughed, "Not as happy as I am! No need to go over the coma drama again. We talked all about that at my luncheon in September."

"By the way, Claire," Dana added, "the food was superb. I think we should do that every year at the end of summer, so we can catch up with everyone before the first meeting."

Bernie nodded. "That's a good idea, Dana. We usually get through very little scripture at our first get-together, but the luncheon this year helped us to get updates on everybody before tonight."

"We could take turns having it," Roxanne chimed in.

Patti guided them back to scripture, "Let's talk about that after our session, okay, or we'll be here until midnight. Did you want to share anything else, Claire?"

"Only that I really like Dana's idea of saying this at bedtime. It does have a comforting tone, doesn't it? Let not your heart be troubled."

Patti wanted to pull Maureen into the discussion. "Maureen, would you like to share? You don't have to, but now that you know the routine"

Maureen was not a shy person and immediately accepted the offer. "I guess I'm the new kid on the block, but here goes. I have a little bit different take on what

Jesus was saying to the apostles. Here He is the night before He was to die and instead of the apostles comforting Him, He's more or less holding their hands. My Mom used to say to me when I was worried about something, 'Today is the tomorrow that you worried about yesterday. Don't waste your time on worry, Maureen.' And I think Jesus was saying this in the same tone as my Mom. ***'Don't let your hearts be troubled***; stop worrying, my friends. All you need is faith in me.' He was getting a little testy with the guys. You know, exasperated that they still didn't get it."

Dana raised one eyebrow in disapproval.

"Oops, sorry. I hope this wasn't too irreverent saying Jesus was testy with His guys!"

Tekla couldn't resist a comment. "Testy, that's funny, Maureen. I bet no one else in the world has ever called Jesus testy."

"I know I'm a little off-kilter once in awhile, but that's who I am. It gives me a good dose of reassurance of Jesus' "tough" love for us."

Patti looked at Dana quizzically and then smiled at Maureen. "That's an interesting way to view it, Maureen. What you said is fine. We don't censor. Thanks for sharing. Let's keep going."

Bernie gave her review of the verse. "I think this verse is a little of what everyone's been saying. He very firmly tells them that He is going to His Father and they should not be worried because they know Him. Therefore, they, too, will go to the Father one day. It's kind of like when you have big problems going on and you don't want your kids pulled into the worry. You know you are the one who has to face it. I think Jesus is saying to the apostles and to us, 'I am the one who has to die on the cross. Therefore, let not your hearts be troubled.'"

Claire smiled at Bernie. "That is simple, yet insightful. We're supposed to become like little children and accept that Jesus died for us."

"I agree." Patti said. "Thanks, Bernie. That is very true about shielding our children from our problems when we can." She looked in Anne's direction and asked, "Are you okay, hon? Would you like to share?"

Anne choked back her tears. The only words she was able to share were "Jack used to say that to me all the time. Now, I say those words over and over every day,

*'**Do not let your heart be troubled**.'*" At that, she flung back her head to keep the tears from rolling down her cheeks. "I'm sorry, it's still hard for me, but I'm okay. Thanks for all that you ladies have done for Kevin and me. Really, I'm okay."

Roxanne handed Anne a tissue and then passed the box around.

Patti chuckled, "We certainly got right back into the swing of things. Maureen, we always have tissues on hand – we do this a lot."

A tear rolled down Maureen's cheek as she grabbed two tissues. "This is a wonderful group. I am in awe of all of your loving support. This is what I've been looking for."

Roxanne laid a tissue on Anne's lap. Claire stared at Anne as she dabbed her eyes with her left hand while twirling her hair with her right.

*Always the hair thing, Annie, when you're stressed or pressured or hiding something. You've had that nervous habit since you were a little girl. What is happening to you? I'm not sure I even know you anymore. How can I reach you?*

"You need some water, Anne? We can wait. You're more important than our discussion."

"No, Patti, I'm fine. I still have water in the bottle. Sorry, that's about all I can get out tonight. Let's keep going."

"Tekla, we haven't heard what you think about this scripture, yet." The room fell quiet as Tekla shared her unpretentious thoughts.

"I really like the verse, '*In my Father's house there are many dwelling places.*' I guess most of you know I live with my sister, Georgia. She's away a lot, travels all over the world. My sister is really good to me. I mean she lets me live with her even though I don't have any money to contribute. I'd like to work, but I don't blame people for not hiring me. When Georgia and I were young, we were close. We were about the same size back then and shared clothes and went to parties. Well look at me now. I've gone to hell in a hand basket wearing sweats and what not. Anyway, Georgia and I had a lot of fun together until I started acting weird when I was sixteen. When Mom and Dad found out I was bipolar, things were never the same. They spent all their time and money trying to make me well. My sister had to take a back seat.

They couldn't afford to send her to college with all the expenses I was costing them, so Georgia became an airline attendant. Within a few years, she met a handsome pilot and married him. He was a jerk. I won't go into that but let's just say, she's pretty bitter about him. Anyway, they divorced last year and she said I could live with her in her condo. I guess she felt sorry for me and she can be mean sometimes, but I am thankful for Georgia. I hope I can continue to live with her, but I know that if it doesn't work out, God has a big welcoming house where I really want to be."

Tekla folded her hands in prayer and looked at the ceiling, "One day, Lord, but don't make it too soon, okay?" A trickle of soft laughter filled the room.

Tek was right about how she looked. As far as the ladies could tell, she had only four sets of clothing – red sweatpants with a polka dot long-sleeved shirt, which she was wearing tonight – black sweatpants with matching top, baggy blue corduroy pants and a beige blouse, and one long dress with colorful psychedelic designs all over it. Her clothes were clean, but most of them had permanent stains here and there. When she first joined the group, Roxanne and Bernie offered to buy her clothes, but she declined saying her sister wouldn't like her to be taking things from other people. As with her inappropriate and blunt interruptions, everyone backed off and accepted the way Tekla dressed – stains and all.

Patti was moved by Tekla's talk. "That was eloquent, Tekla. You should become a writer. Thanks for letting us see a glimpse of your life."

"That takes a lot of courage to share," Maureen added. "I have a brother who's bi-polar. Maybe you and I can get together sometime. I'd like to talk more with you."

"Sure, if you want to. That would be nice."

Patti concluded, "Any other comments. Okay, I guess we're ready for why I chose this verse. The reason is very simple. When our boy, Tommy, died last year, I was a mess – I miss him every day. Oh, let's see, it will be the one-year anniversary on November 13."

"Patti, there were more than five-hundred people at his funeral Mass. Tommy was one special kid."

"No argument from me on that, Claire. He was special and funny. When I'd go out the door to come here he'd say, "Don't get too holy, Mom. Your crankiness keeps me going. Two weeks after he died I came back to this group."

"We all remember that night, Patti. Maureen, this will make you laugh and cry."

"We had about two inches of snow on the ground. As I was driving over here, I was having a pity party in the car. Oh, I knew from the beginning my son would not live to adulthood – not with cystic fibrosis. His Dad and I clung to the hope that he could be the exception. Then he got really sick last year in late October. He died ten days before what would have been his tenth birthday."

Patti stoically looked straight ahead at the picture of the Sacred Heart of Jesus. Neither she nor anyone in the room said a word. After what seemed an interminable length of time, Claire walked across the room and hugged her. "Hey, take a deep breath. We want to hear your story, my friend. It's inspiring."

Claire returned to her chair. She and Patti had been friends since the first grade and had helped each other through ups and downs many times over the years.

Patti forged on. "On a happier note, early in our marriage we adopted a boy and a girl. Then, lo and behold when Alex was twelve and Chelsea was ten, we got pregnant. I was thrilled from the top of my head to the bottom of my toes. Bill was overjoyed. Because I was forty-five, Dr. Runyon wanted to put me through special tests. I said no. Bill was adamant about it too. We wanted this baby no matter what. God chose us to be the parents of our precious Tommy."

Anne coughed and took a sip of water. Her hair was twisted tight enough to pull painfully on her scalp.

"Anyway, let me move this along. It's getting late. We refused to have any testing done. I knew what that was all about. If something was wrong with Tommy, they'd start talking about terminating my baby. There was no way we were going to let that happen. As you all know, he was born with cystic fibrosis and we didn't care one iota. He was the joy of our entire family."

Tekla was back in her zone again. "So, get to the part that happened last year with the snow and all that."

"Okay, Tekla. Thanks for keeping me in line."

"You're very welcome, Patti."

"Like I said, it had only been a month since the funeral. I wasn't sure I was ready to return to Bible Babes. Alex and Chelsea had to go back to their own lives. I cried every day sometimes for hours. Bill gently pushed me out the door that night. I pulled into the parking lot, still not sure if I wanted to go in. I was about ready to turn around and go home when I saw Anne get out of her car and slip on the ice. I turned off my car and rushed to her side."

Anne weakly smiled at the memory of that night.

"I asked old Annie if she was okay and she said, 'Yeah, I'm fine, but can you help me get up?' I gave her my hand and then I went down with her. We both started laughing as we crawled to the side of the car and pulled ourselves up. By then, all of you were looking at us from inside laughing your tushees off."

"You bet we were. There were five of us straining our necks to see you two slide around the parking lot."

"When we finally got into the room and settled down, Anne read the same verse that I chose to read tonight. And the message to me that night was one of hope. *'Do not let your heart be troubled. You have faith in God, have faith in me.'* I'm not saying that my grieving was over that night, but I realized that God is all-knowing and all-powerful. We come to Him through Jesus. He doesn't want us to worry about anything, even death because our faith in Him is all we need. I know I'll see Tommy again one day."

"I know you will, too, Patti. By the way, how are Alex and Chelsea doing?"

"They're doing fine. You know, they loved Tommy, but they're young and have their whole lives ahead of them. Bill and I don't expect them to live in Hallowed. Alex is stationed in Japan. Chelsea lives in New York and goes on tour soon with the dance company."

"I'm glad they're doing well, Patti."

"They call as often as they can and that helps Bill and me. They'll both be here for Christmas. I'm excited about that."

Patti was quiet for about ten seconds to gain composure and then concluded, "Tommy was my baby and I was with him 24/7. Now, there's a big hole in my heart 24/7. Still, I count myself to be blessed for having him in my life for ten years. *'Let not your heart be troubled'* still gets me through the day. Thanks, Anne, for bringing that verse the first time. I thought it was worth sharing again."

Anne was half-listening to Patti and half-rummaging through her conversation with Claire in May. She allowed her coiled hair to unwind and then started a new set of strands on the other side. Anne was bombarded with words -- Claire's words, her words, and even the babes' words tonight. In a matter of seconds, conversations blasted her from every which way, not always in the order they had happened.

*You know it's a baby. My babies come late. I really hope this one is not a Christmas baby. You know I won't tell anyone about the pregnancy. I knew what that was all about. You can't possibly understand what it feels like to lose a baby you want. We refused to have any testing done. Before I formed you in the womb, I knew you. Shut-up, Claire. Shut up, Claire. Do not let your heart be troubled.*

Dana touched Anne's arm. "Anne, Anne, Patti's finished. She was thanking you."

Anne was startled. "Oh, I'm sorry, Patti. Thanks for reminding me of that night and the verse. Thank you."

Patti felt a little put-out since it was obvious that Anne had not really been listening to her, but she did not want to add to Anne's embarrassment.

Anne sat very still staring at her water bottle. She could vaguely hear Patti talking.

"Thanks everyone for sharing tonight. I've set-up a rotation schedule for the rest of the year, but if you can't share a reading on your scheduled date, we can switch you around. Phone numbers are on the back. So, Bernie, you are the first official presenter next week. Tekla, can you bring the opening prayer and Dana, you have the closing prayer. Claire, you're salty. I'll bring the sweet. Well, that's about it, except for tonight's closing prayer, which I have brought. I say this prayer in the morning and at night."

Everyone relaxed once again as Patti prayed a familiar prayer.

*Angel of God, my guardian dear*
*To whom God's love commits me here.*

---

While everyone recited the Angel's Prayer, Claire experienced uneasiness. An indistinct memory slipped into her thoughts.

*Jeannie told me that she prayed this prayer with me in the hospital. I still can't quite remember that clearly. Why am I feeling that there was something going on that was not pleasant?*

*Ever this day be at my side*
*To light, to guard*

Claire squeezed her closed eyes tightly trying to remember.

*Remember, what? I was in a coma. What else could have been happening?*

Claire sensed she was moving at lightning speed. She could still see the women sitting on the furniture in the room, but the walls were spinning wildly around them like a carnival ride. She was terrified, imagining running through a tunnel. She heard an engine and the sound of wheels on a track.

*I can't breathe. I can't breathe. I've got to keep running.*

Then the dizzying spin of the walls slowed down and she could hear Patti ending the prayer.

*To rule, to guide, Amen.*

---

Everything was back in place. She looked around the room expecting a reaction, but, all eyes were closed during the final prayer. No one perceived anything unusual, not even Claire's quiet gasp at the end of her sojourn.

*That was strange. Good, no one noticed.*

Patti stood up and stretched. "What a first night for our Bible Babes."

Bernie and Maureen gathered up the trash. Roxanne blew out the candle and put what remained of her appetizer in the plastic container. "Tekla, there's half a bag of cookies. Do you want them?"

"No, give them to Maureen for her boys."

"Thanks, Tek, they'll wolf them down."

"Are you sure you want to talk with me about your brother?"

"Yes, he's not doing well and my Mom's really worried. I'd like to hear more of how you got through it."

Tekla smiled at Maureen. "So we could meet like normal friends do?"

"Absolutely. Thanks again for the cookies."

When the room had been tidied up, Patti locked the door. In the parking lot, laughter and goodnights permeated the crisp air of autumn. Anne and Claire drove home together.

"Well, what'd you think about the meeting tonight?"

"It was good to get back, but it's always draining with all the stories and Tekla constantly interrupting. I can't believe Maureen actually wants to be with her in private."

"Maureen sounded very sincere about meeting with her. I think it's nice."

"I guess."

"You didn't say much tonight. I haven't seen you tear-up like that in a while."

"I guess it was being around everybody again. I mean last year I was the one telling Patti 'let not your heart be troubled.' Now, those words are meant for me. It got to me. That's all."

Claire pulled into the Combs driveway.

"Looks like you have every light on in the house."

"I guess I forgot to turn them off. Hey, I'm getting a facial tomorrow. Want to come?"

"No. I've never had one, probably never will. Stop down afterwards. Night, Anne."

*A facial? She doesn't need a facial. She needs to face the truth.*

---

Anne sat at the kitchen table. After three glasses of wine, her mood sunk to a level of self-pity. She poured a fourth glass and took two sleeping pills. She put her head on the kitchen table and listened to blurred thoughts in her head. The same kinds of thoughts she had at Bible Babes tonight.

*Shut-up, Claire. Shut up, Claire. You know it's a baby. You know I won't tell anyone about the pregnancy. You can't possibly understand what it feels like to lose a baby you want. My babies come late. I really hope this one is not a Christmas baby. We refused to have any testing done. Do not let your heart be troubled. Before I formed you in the womb, I knew you.*

When she could bear it no longer, Anne pounded on the table screeching her pain out loud. "Jack you weren't here – what else could I do? I have to handle everything now for Kevin and me. I couldn't have that baby and not just any baby – a Down's syndrome baby. 'Before I formed you in the womb, I knew you.' Really, God, did you know that you were forming a Down's syndrome child in my womb, really? And, if that wasn't enough, you took my husband from me. Give me back my life."

Anne cried until she passed out on the kitchen table and slept there for the night.

On the following Wednesday, at exactly 7:35 all of the ladies were in their assigned permanent seats with water or soda in hand. Claire had baked sixteen individual pies in muffin pans stuffed with creamy spinach and cheese filling. Patti had made her luscious carrot cake. As they put the refreshments on the table, Dana lit the apple cinnamon candle.

"Tekla, you have opening prayer tonight. Ready?"

"Sort of. I didn't write a prayer, but I'd like to say the Our Father."

"Sounds perfect."

After the Our Father, Claire handed the plate of spinach pies to Dana to circulate. Maureen offered to cut and serve the carrot cake so Patti could do her duties as leader.

As the ladies were munching, Bernie asked. "Should I read my scripture, Patti?"

"Sure, let's get started. Do you realize we were here until 10:15 last week? Some of us have to get up early, so let's try to finish no later than 9:30."

"You're singing to the choir, Patti. I have to be at the nursing home at 7 am tomorrow," Bernie agreed. She put on her reading glasses and began. "This is a very short verse and of course, I'll share my reason for choosing it after all of you have talked. Okay, this is Genesis, Chapter 28, Verse 12:

*Then Jacob had a dream, a stairway rested on the ground; with its top reaching to the Heavens; and God's messengers were going up and down it."*

Tekla raised her hand. "I'll start. Wouldn't it be a hoot to climb up a ladder into the clouds? And then, maybe at the top, Jesus reaches down and pulls you into Heaven. I'm not sure there's anything here I can work with. It's an awfully short verse, Bernie, no offense intended."

"No offense taken, Tek. It's definitely short, but when I was looking at the Bible last night, this verse wouldn't let me go. Anyone else?"

Each of the women struggled with the reading, but attempted to express insight.

Roxanne went into a ten-minute dissertation about dreams in the Bible, ending with "Isn't it fascinating how many people in the Bible had dreams and saw angels appear?"

"I don't dream anymore," Tekla interrupted. "The meds keep my imagination below zero."

Patti guided it back to the specific verse that Bernie had chosen. "I think there's more to this than meets the eye. 'God's messengers were going up and down it.' Aren't messengers really angels? I think the main idea is that God sends messengers to us in the same way He sent them to Jacob. Even in the Old Testament God gives us hope. Notice, the messengers are going up and down. To me that implies that God sends angels or messengers to help us and perhaps they return to Heaven when their mission is accomplished."

"I guess that's possible," Claire said doubtfully. "I have difficulty understanding the symbolism in the Bible sometimes. I'll hear a priest talk about the Gospel and explain the symbolism or reasoning behind it. Then, I read it again and I still don't get it. I must not be a very imaginative person. Go ahead, Patti, sorry to interrupt."

"No problem; I'm finished. You can continue, Claire."

"Like I said, I have a hard time understanding symbolism in the Bible, but one thought I had was about the stairway. It's resting on the ground and its top is reaching to the Heavens. For me, that could mean we should be grounded on Earth in Jesus, always striving to get to Heaven."

"Bravo, Claire. Far out thinking!"

"Thanks, Tekla. I even surprised myself. Give me another piece of that carrot cake, Maureen. I'm ending on that happy note."

The women started chatting. Patti tapped her pen on the glass lamp to get their attention.

"Next. Dana?"

Dana waved her hand. "Pass and pray."

Patti put her hand to her mouth. "Oh, I completely forgot to remind everyone about pass and pray. I should have mentioned it last week. Maureen, you jumped right in there at the first session and I'm glad you felt comfortable. Sometimes, though, we draw a blank on what to say or we're not in the mood. If, on any particular night for any reason you don't want to share, that's perfectly okay."

"That's what I did tonight, Maureen. We've all had those times when the spirit did not move us or we wanted to relax and listen to others."

"Maureen, when you don't want to share, all you have to say is 'Pass and pray;' no questions asked. Thanks, Dana for reminding me."

Maureen replied, "I was wondering if we were obligated to say something every week."

"The first meeting was unusual because everyone shared. I guess that's why it ran late, but it was important to get that first night off the ground. I'd also like to remind us that we are here to serve the Lord and one another. Our format is simple and we are flexible. Sharing is encouraged, but not demanded. Sorry for the interruption. Okay, anyone else ready to share. Anne?"

"Pass and pray."

"That's fine.

"Maureen?"

"Pass and pray. Sorry, I don't have anything to say, but I'm anxious to hear Bernie tell us why she chose this piece of scripture."

"Take it away, Bernie."

"I chose this Old Testament reading because my good old German Dad painted houses as an extra job when I was growing up. If the house was vacant, he would take my sister and me with him once in a while. We were six and eight years old. Both of us were scared when he climbed the ladder to paint a ceiling and we'd say, 'Daddy, be careful up there.' He'd calm our fears by telling us he was on the stairway to Heaven. We giggled and asked excitedly, 'What do you see, Daddy. Tell us, what's up there.'"

---

Claire vaguely heard Bernie's words. Her body began to feel very light with an awareness of ascending as if going up an escalator. A cool green mist floated around her gently coaxing her up and up.

*Oh, no, not this again!*

---

"'Well, I see angels going up and down a golden ladder. After they reach the clouds, I can't see them anymore because they're going right into Heaven. And then, right behind them is another group of angels coming down to Earth to watch over my gold dust twins.'"

---

Claire's encounter intensified. The stairway moved faster and faster as she passed translucent shapes one by one. She tried to grab anything to hold onto. When she reached for the handrail, her hand passed through it. Her transparent body had no muscle or bone; yet, she felt someone touching her back, gently nudging.

*Why am I going up? Where am I going? Babes, can't you see that something's happening to me! Help me, Patti. Somebody help me, please.*

---

Maureen giggled, "Wait a minute, Bernie. Why did your Dad call you the gold dust twins? I know it's not the main point, but that's cute."

"I never did understand why he called us the gold dust twins, because we weren't twins at all, but it was a sweet nickname."

"Better than being called the saw dust twins." Tekla loved to play with words.

Patti pleaded, "Tek, come on. Go ahead, Bernie."

"I love the memory of that image of angels going up into Heaven, but also coming down to Earth to be with us."

---

As quickly as Claire had risen up the green-misted steps, she descended. She seized the chair on both sides, rubbing her arms up and down with her hands to make sure they were flesh and bone.

*Thank God, I'm back.*

---

"I don't usually read the Old Testament, but last night as I was preparing, I decided to start at the beginning of the Bible. I read a few pages of Genesis and found this verse."

Maureen clapped her hands. "I love that story, Bernie. Sounds like you had a loving Dad. A real kidder, too."

"You wouldn't believe some of the silly things he did with us. I'll tell you sometime, but that's all I have for tonight."

"Bernie, that was very uplifting. I think we're ready for closing prayer. Claire, are you cold? You keep rubbing your arms and hands."

"It's a little chilly in here. The air conditioning is a bit much for me."

"I like the room to be cold. I get hot flashes."

"Same here, the colder the better."

"I'll bring a sweater next week. Not a big deal."

Dana coughed. "Ready for the prayer?"

All eyes closed as the women bowed in prayer. Claire braced herself for another out-of-body moment, but it did not happened. She was relieved to hear Dana's sweet prayer.

*"Dear Jesus, when I am quiet, I know You lay Your hand upon my head. When I ask for Your guidance, You take my hand to point the way. When my mental, physical, or spiritual weakness is in harm's way, Your touch brings me strength and healing. When my human weakness makes me stumble and fall, You lift me upon Your Cross with you, giving me the power to climb and strive. Because your touch still has its ancient power, I can go forward into the future bravely and unafraid."*

"Beautiful, Dana."

"I found it in a book called Prayers to the Savior. I have copies of this prayer for everyone."

"Wonderful."

Maureen said, "I have to give that prayer to my mother. She'll love it."

"Anne, can you bring the reading next week?"

There was a slight reluctance in her voice when she answered Patti. "Umm, sure. I can do that."

"Thanks, hon. Claire, opening prayer, Roxanne, closing prayer, Maureen, sweet; Bernie, salty. Let's clean-up and go home. We did good this week. It's only 9:25."

Claire and Anne drove home separately. For Anne, the remaining hours of the evening were pretty much the same as every other night-- watch TV. Drink wine. Maybe read. Take sleeping pills. Cry a little, sometimes a lot; and hopefully end up sleeping in bed.

When Claire arrived home, Chet was watching football. He heard Claire hanging up her keys in the kitchen. "Hi, hon. How was it tonight?"

Claire lied, "It was fine."

*Except for the fact that something bizarre has happened two weeks in a row.*

"Chet, did you get something to eat?"

"Yeah, I finished off the pork chops. Go, go, go! Strip the ball, you moron!"

Claire peeked into the TV room. "Hope you don't mind if I skip the game tonight."

"That's okay. Oh, for crying out loud, these guys do this every game."

"I'm going upstairs to read. Goodnight. See you when I see you."

"Yeah, goodnight, honey. That's it! You got blocking! Dive! Touchdown! All right, now kick it between those two beautiful goal posts!"

Claire washed her face and put on pajamas. In bed, she propped two pillows behind her head and unfolded the prayer that Dana had given to her. She read the entire prayer, but was drawn to one sentence, '*When my mental, physical, or spiritual weakness is in harm's way, Your touch brings me strength and healing.*' *Lord, when I was in the coma, you pulled me out of harms' way. Am I in harms' way, again?*

It was still warm enough at night for open windows. Claire walked to the window and pulled the frame open. She breathed in the autumn air, staring pensively at a full harvest moon tucked neatly into the black sky.

*Okay, what is it? Do I have another aneurysm? Has my brain been damaged from all that happened? Is it the medication? Chet leaves for D.C. on Friday. He'll cancel the trip if I tell him what's been happening.*

Claire returned to bed still contemplating whether to tell Chet about the occurrences the last two Wednesdays.

*Nothing hurts. I feel good most of the time. Maybe it's the medication. I'll make an appointment with Dr. McCormack some time next week. I'll tell Chet when he gets back from his trip. That's it. Done. Decision made.*

She picked-up the prayer again and read the last line. 'Because your touch still has its ancient power, I can go forward into the future bravely and unafraid.'

Chet's noises downstairs began to filter up the steps. Claire wanted to avoid talking with him for fear of revealing the truth. She turned off the light and pretended to be sleeping.

*Lord, help me to go forward in the future bravely and unafraid.*

Chet peeked into the bedroom and noticed that Claire was asleep, so he performed his nightly rituals as quietly as possible. He walked softly to her side and kissed her on the forehead. The night breeze was beginning to chill. Chet closed the window, and stared at the full harvest moon nestled in the dark sky. "Thank you, God. You brought her back 100 percent."

By the third meeting, the routine of Bible Babes was solidly established. Patti kept the meeting moving along, assigned who did what and when, and made sure whoever wanted to share felt comfortable. Opening and closing prayers were either ones that everyone knew or were inspiring like Dana's from the Book of Prayers to the Savior. Once in a while they were poorly prepared. In regard to the sweet and salty appetizers, the assigned participants never ever forgot to bring them. At the beginning of the evening someone lit the apple cinnamon candle. At the end of the evening, closing prayer and then everyone cleaned up the trash. Roxanne brought her own air freshener and pumped three sprays of it into the room before Patti locked the door each week. Bible Babes functioned with smooth consistency.

Each of the ladies carried a drink and a plate of appetizers to their seats. Bible Babes were ready to be inspired.

"Bernie, I want this recipe. What's it called?"

"Hankie Pankies. Easy to make. One pound of sausage, one…"

Patti cleared her throat.

Bernie whispered to Roxanne, "I'll e-mail it to you tomorrow."

"Claire, opening prayer? Let's bow our heads."

*Father in Heaven, bless the Bible Babes this evening. Help us to listen to your holy word with intensity. Fill our spirits with your wisdom. When we speak let it be with tongues of fire to celebrate our faith. May this evening bring us closer to each other, closer to Jesus and closer to Heaven. In all things, may we honor the Father, Son, and Holy Spirit. Amen.*

Patti said softly, "Nice. Anne, ready?"

"I have to admit that since Jack died, I really have lapses of faith, but I'm trying to work through it. This story of a woman's faith is one of my favorites, so here goes. Turn to Mark, Ch.5:25-34

*And there was a woman who for twelve years had had a hemorrhage, and had suffered much at the hands of many physicians, and had spent all she had, and found no benefit, but rather grew worse. Hearing about Jesus, she came up behind him in the crowd and touched his cloak. For she said, 'If I but touch his cloak, I shall be saved.' And at once the flow of her blood was dried up, and she felt in her body that she was healed of her affliction. … He said to her, Daughter, thy faith has saved thee. Go in peace, and be thou healed of thy affliction."*

Maureen was biting at the bit to share her story. "Is it okay if I go first?"

Patti waved her hand in approval.

"I have to tell you that in my twenty years of working in Labor and Delivery, I have witnessed several miracles, but none as moving as the one I'm about to tell you. It happened in another city several years ago."

"What city?" Tekla's first interruption.

"I can't really say, Tek. It's confidential, but without using names, I think I can talk about what applies to this reading. Anyhow, a young couple came in to deliver their first child. She was definitely ready to have this baby. I prepped her. After a few hours of contractions, I rolled her to the delivery room. The young father was also in the room and I noticed he tried to appear calm to his young wife even though he was obviously anxious. The doctor delivered their beautiful, healthy baby boy. I was touched that he and his wife said a prayer of thanks to Jesus immediately after the birth.

"Was it a regular prayer or one they made-up?" Tekla's second interruption.

"They used their own words. All was well until about two hours later. I discovered she was bleeding heavily and called her doctor. As quickly and as forcefully as I could, I told her husband he had to leave. One of the nurses took the baby to the nursery. We rushed the mother to the operating room. At that point, we could not get her blood pressure to register. We called the lab to deliver several units of blood to OR. After receiving four units of blood, she remained non-responsive. No one spoke a word. We kept trying to stop the bleeding of this young, sweet mother."

Tekla was about to say something, but Dana stared at her and mouthed "shhhh." Tekla wrinkled her nose, but Dana had already returned her focus to Maureen.

"We continued giving blood, but it poured out as fast as we put it in. Even after we gave her eleven units of blood, she was still bleeding out. We watched this poor woman's face turn to a pallid shadow of death. The doctor was ready to let her go. He reluctantly nodded in defeat and we ended all life-saving activity. I was going to get her husband to come in to hold her in her last breath, but suddenly the bleeding stopped and color returned to her cheeks."

Maureen took a deep breath and closed her eyes. Everyone in the parish room sighed.

Tekla saw an opening. "Did you get a lot of blood on you?" Maureen heard Tekla but ignored the comment.

Patti said, "That's an incredible story. It's inspiring that you played a big role in saving her. Thanks for sharing that with us."

Maureen opened her eyes. "No, that's not the end. I get all choked up at what happened next. The mother's blood pressure returned to normal and she lived. The doctor and I went to the waiting room to talk with the young father. We expected him to be sad and distressed. Instead, he was smiling as he stood by a painting of Jesus. He asked us, no, he told us confidently, 'She's okay, isn't she?' We both looked at him in amazement, not understanding how he knew.

Then, I saw that he had his hand on the cloak of Jesus in the painting and he explained, 'I came out here and I was scared, but I remembered my Grandma reading the Bible to me. She told me this story about a woman who was bleeding for twelve years, but she believed that if she touched Jesus's cloak she would be healed. Grandma said Jesus healed her because she had faith. And that's what I did. I touched Jesus' cloak, well at least the one in the painting. And I knew He would heal my beautiful wife.' And yes, Tekla darling, I had blood all over me."

"Gross."

After that, there wasn't a day that went by that I didn't look at that painting of Jesus and think of that verse. There was still a little smudge from the father's thumb on the picture."

For the first time ever, the Bible Babes applauded a presenter. Maureen's story made the room buzz with intense excitement. Similar to the conversations at Claire's luncheon, the chattering and comments darted around the room in rapid fire.

"How do you do it, Maureen?"

"What a stressful job."

"I admire nurses. They are the backbone of hospitals."

"When I had my middle one, it was touch and go. My nurse saved my baby's life."

"How long have you been a nurse?"

"Tell me how you get the blood? Do they bring a big bucket of it?"

"What a beautiful story, Maureen. I was on the edge of my seat."

When everyone settled down, Claire spoke. "Do you think miracles like this one take place very often? We hear about miracles like the ones at Medjugorje, but how often do we see one? Either we've tuned God out or we're so busy we can't see miracles that are right before our eyes."

"You don't have to be in the medical field to know needing eleven units of blood is incredible and surviving what she went through is a miracle," Dana added. "That's the obvious one, but the phenomenal faith of that father is the not-so-obvious miracle."

"I see what you mean, Dana. We have no way of proving that the mother survived because her husband touched Jesus' cloak in the picture. We can only guess."

In a moment of clarity, Tekla offered, "We hear about the miracles in the Bible, like the one in the reading tonight, correct? None of us was there when the woman touched Jesus's cloak, right?"

"Of course we weren't, Tek."

"Who was there when Jesus said to that woman, 'Daughter, thy faith has saved thee. Go in peace, and be thou healed of thy affliction'?"

"The people in town?"

"The Apostles?"

"Bingo, Claire. We weren't there, but the Apostles gave us the account of witnessing Jesus' miracle. And who was working in the hospital where this modern miracle happened?"

"Okay, now I get it, Tekla," Dana responded. "We weren't there, but Maureen was and she told us about the story of the miracle tonight. Excellent lesson."

"Thank you, Dana. I appreciate your compliment."

"Oh, my, it's 9:20, but I don't want to shut down the discussion. Any more observations, questions?"

Maureen shared one last comment. "Claire, you asked if we thought miracles take place like this very often. I don't think any of us can say for sure whether this or any happening is a miracle, but in my heart I do believe that miracles happen each and every day. A miracle may not be documented, maybe only one person witnesses it, but I believe Jesus walks the Earth with us just as he did with the Apostles. He doesn't ask us to understand his teachings perfectly. He asks us to have faith."

Patti concluded, "Totally awesome evening. Since we're running over, I'll e-mail whose doing what next week. Roxanne, would you please say our closing prayer?"

*God, thank you for the holy insight of these women. We have been blessed this evening with Maureen's beautiful story of a father and mother. Please watch over them and bless them as you did when their first child was born. Our prayer to you, Jesus, is to help us to have the kind of faith that this father held in his heart. Amen.*

Claire bristled anticipating another strange episode.

*I'm not sure I have that kind of faith. And I'm not sure I want to be here.*

There were no extraneous noises or visions, but she was disturbed.

*Where in the world did that come from? I love these women. I want to be here.*

"Claire, you coming? We're leaving now."

"Okay, sure, sorry. I was thinking about something else."

Anne had barely spoken after she read the scripture verse. She was increasingly tired from the wine and the pills. Even the daily application of makeup was draining her strength. She waved goodbye and drove home thinking of Jack, always thinking of Jack and the baby.

*Why do they always talk about babies? Now we have pregnant Maureen. And I never dreamed this scripture reading would lead to more talk about babies. Of course, she works in labor and delivery and that means I'm going to have to listen to this crap every week. I don't think I can stand it. I don't want to hear about babies and I don't believe in anything anymore.*

---

When Anne got home, she opened the chardonnay and sat in the living room looking at their family portrait on the fireplace mantel. As soon as the memory of her abortion invaded her thoughts, she tried to force it out of her mind with alcohol. That night, along with a broken wine glass, Anne's faith lay shattered on the floor in bitter pieces.

As Claire drove home, she was entangled in worry about what was happening to her in the weekly meetings.

*Patti says the Angel of God prayer at the first meeting. Then the walls start spinning and I'm running through a tunnel. It feels like someone is chasing me. I'm terrified but I don't know why and I'm out of breath. Then, last week, Bernie talks about Jacob's stairway to Heaven and before I know it, I'm climbing stairs with figures made of air floating up with me. Okay, this week wasn't as bad, but it was odd what I said to myself.*

The words kept echoing in her head.

*I'm not sure I want to be here. I'm not sure I want to be here. I've got to tell Chet tonight.*

---

Chet arrived home from his business trip at 11:30 pm. As he stepped into the kitchen, he could hear the TV.

"Claire, Claire?"

"Oh, you're home. I'll be right out."

They kissed. "Good to be home. I'm exhausted. Why are you up late?"

"Waiting for you."

"That's nice, but you usually can't make it past ten o'clock most nights. Anything I should know? Jeff and Jeannie are okay, aren't they?"

"Yeah, they're fine. I talked with both of them yesterday."

"C'mon, Claire, come clean.  What's on your mind?"

"Let's sit in the living room.  Want a glass of Jamison's?"

"Sure.  Will I need one?"

"That depends."

Chet looked directly into Claire's eyes.  "Now, I'm worried."

Claire handed him the whiskey and then sat on the couch opposite him.

"Don't make fun of me and don't give me any advice, but I've had a couple of weird episodes during the last two Bible meetings."

"You mean like an argument with Annie or someone?"

"No, it's nothing like that.  Let me tell you what happened and then you can ask questions, okay?  The first meeting was the craziest.  We always say a closing prayer.  Patti chose Angel of God, the same prayer that Jeannie said she prayed with me when I was in the coma.  When Patti said the Angel of God prayer, I got a really bad feeling and I remember thinking to myself – 'why am I sensing evil when this is the prayer that Jeannie said we prayed together in the hospital?'  The room started to spin around me and I was terrified, but I didn't understand why.  All I was aware of was that I was breathing so hard I could hear my heart pounding and someone or something was chasing me through a dark tunnel."

"Can I ask a question now?"

"Yeah, go ahead."

"Didn't one of the babes notice?"

"We always keep our eyes closed when we say the final prayer.  No one mentioned a thing."

Chet sipped the whiskey.  "Then what?"

"That was it for that night, but last Wednesday, Bernie brought a verse about Jacob's stairs reaching into Heaven.  She was the last one to talk about what the verse meant to her and when she did, I had another occurrence.  Only this one didn't feel evil, but, I was still scared because it was like I was traveling up an escalator going in and out of figures that had no form.  There was a green mist all over and I couldn't see where it ended.  I was afraid of falling.  I grabbed the railing, but then I realized I was exactly like the shapes.  My arm went straight through it.  You're looking at me like I'm nuts."

"I didn't say a word and I know you're not nuts, but I'm sitting here wondering why you didn't tell me about this last week."

"I didn't want you to cancel your business trip."

Chet raised his voice to an angry volume.  "That makes me really mad, Claire.  You're more important than a damn business trip.  Don't ever do that again!"

"Okay, I won't, but don't yell at me."

Chet's voice softened.  "Sorry, but I don't want to lose you, honey."

"I know.  You're right.  I should have told you.  Anyway, tonight wasn't too bad, but I heard words that I know I had said before.  I don't want to go into our entire discussion, but Maureen talked about a woman who was bleeding to death after her delivery.  Her husband had complete faith that she would survive, even though the doctors did not.  She survived.  Enough said.  Towards the end I was thinking 'I'm not sure I have the kind of faith that young father had.'  That was okay, but then this popped into my head, 'And I'm not sure I want to be here.'  I love going to Bible Babes, you know that."

"That doesn't sound that bad."

"Except for the fact that I distinctly remembered being somewhere when I was in the coma saying those very words to ... gosh, I don't know who I said them to."

"Claire, that's not like you to have fantasy trips saying things you don't mean, even if you're saying them to yourself."

"That's irritating.  What does that mean, 'even if you're saying them to yourself?'  Do you think I'm crazy?"

Chet knew he had to back peddle.  "You know I don't think that.  Sorry, I could have worded that better.  But I am concerned that you might have repercussions from the drugs or…"  And then he hesitated.

Claire completed the sentence, "…or that I have another aneurysm working on me?"

Chet sighed in deep concern. "Claire, I love you and I want you to be around for a long time. You need to see Dr. McDaniel."

"I have an appointment with him tomorrow afternoon. It's probably a side-effect of some sort, but I'm worried, too. I'm really glad you're home."

"Me, too. Let's get some sleep. I'm glad you told me. 'Let not your heart be troubled.' Other than those weird experiences, you're in really good health."

The next morning Chet sat on the edge of the bed staring at Claire.

*God, I love her. Please let all of this be okay.*

As she moved slightly, he ran his fingers through her hair. She opened her eyes.

"Hey, how long have you been staring at me?"

"Hours. Okay, minutes. I love your hair. I always have."

"Don't get sappy on me, stalker. I'm going to be okay."

"Call me as soon as you get out of the doctor's office."

"I will. Chet, I really think I'm fine. As soon as I'm in the car, I'll call. Now off to work you go."

———

Claire saw Dr. McDaniel late that afternoon.

"Claire, your tests show no signs of another aneurysm. There's something I'd like to recommend that might help you to relax. For one hour per day meditate, nothing complicated or strange. Sit or lie down. Do deep breathing and relax. It will clear your mind and give your brain a rest."

"Give my brain a rest?"

"Seriously, there have been studies on this. They may not describe it as resting your brain, but isn't that what we do at night when we sleep? Why not give yourself a break during the day. You don't take naps anymore, do you?"

"No, I stopped that in early September."

"Good. A nap would probably keep you from sleeping at night, but meditation is a way to simply relax."

"Okay, I'll give it a shot."

"I doubt seriously, Claire, after four months that you would have any reaction to the medications you received in the hospital.  The meds you take now should not cause hallucinations or dreams."

"Will I have to take them the rest of my life?"

"I don't think so.  Probably just a few more months.  Come, see me in January and I'll reassess where we need to go with your recovery."

"Okay, sounds good.  Thanks for listening to my crazy stories and not laughing."

"Claire, sometimes after patients have been through something as traumatic as an aneurysm, their sensibilities become sharper.  There's a case of a man who had a brain tumor.  After surgery, he became an incredible artist.  Maybe you're experiencing an upsurge in creative imagination.  Sometimes fantasies and realities merge.  It takes time for our brains to heal."

"Wow, you think I could become an artist or even a composer?"

"Of course, miracles happen.  You know that!"

"Well, that's interesting because in art class, I was told to stay away from paint unless it was for a wall and I certainly can't read music."

"Thanks for the laugh.  I might not even charge you for this visit."

"I'll pay you right after I sell my first song."

"Claire, you're basically healthy.   Keep up the exercise and the good attitude.  You're too hard on yourself.  Don't think you have to justify every thought that comes into your head."

"Okay, that's a good way to look at it.  I'm glad I made the appointment."

"I am, too."  Dr. McDaniel had sincere affection for Claire and Chet.

"I know you're a praying woman.  Take time each day to pray, meditate, and clear your mind.  Use a mantra of some sort, like the word 'Heaven' or any word.  Repeat it over and over as you breathe and relax.  Don't hesitate to call me, if you have anxiety about anything, Claire.  But, give it time.  Say hi to Chet for me."

As Claire exited the parking lot, she called Chet to give him the good news. She felt giddy and light now that the heavy stone of worry had been lifted.

"Hi, on my way home."

"What did he say, Claire?"

"He said nothing's wrong. I'm basically healthy."

"Praise the Lord."

"Oh, yeah, he wants me to start meditating every day."

"That sounds a little out of your realm."

"That's what I thought at first, but he talked about a recent study that concluded it's a good idea to rest your brain during the day."

"Well, anyway, that's good news, honey. You hungry?"

"I'm starved. Want to meet at Skyway for a five-way?"

"When?"

"It'll take about twenty minutes."

"See you there. Claire, sorry for raising my voice last night."

"That's over and done with. Your feelings get the best of you when you're worried."

"Especially when it concerns you. Drive carefully. Love you, babe."

---

After the visit to Dr. McDaniel, Chet and Claire had a fresh sense of hope having shed their anxiety. They resumed their routine with the addition of Claire's meditation sessions.

On most days around 3 pm, Claire would light a scented candle and lie down on the recliner in the sunroom. Sometimes, she would say a prayer; sometimes she would read a verse from the Bible. Then, she would close her eyes and gently breathe in and out, repeating her mantra – *Holy Spirit, Holy Spirit, Holy Spirit.* The rhythm of the words Holy Spirit seemed to match her breathing pattern and before she knew it, she would feel relaxed and replenished.

And at last, the visions at Bible Babes had ceased.

# CHAPTER 25 : MEDITATION

The next day, Claire re-read the verse from Bible Babes' meeting and then began her slow deliberate breathing. She repeated the mantra a few times – *Holy Spirit, Holy Spirit, Holy Spirit.* Claire was relaxed, her mind tottering one notch away from sleep. She remembered a series of events which made her feel serene and protected.

She saw what appeared to be angels, beautiful angels, happily floating above her.

*That's right. They're here to guide and protect.*

No one spoke, but Claire seemed to hear their thoughts.

*Come with me, gentle, tired old soul. God will give you rest.*

*Praise to you, God the Father for giving me this child, this one soul that is mine to protect on Earth.*

Claire breathed in and out very slowly. In the quiet stillness, she was peaceful.

*This is not a dream. This is a memory. A memory of something that really happened. A beautiful moment that God allowed me to see.*

Another group of angels hovered overhead. They seemed to be waiting for something.

---

"Claire, wake-up. Chet kissed her on her forehead and she jumped in surprise."

"Oh, hi. You're home already? What time is it?"

"It's four o'clock. How was the meditation today?"

"It was nice. I can't believe I was lying here for an hour having lovely thoughts. I feel great. Hey, let's eat out tonight. Italian?"

Chet cheered, "Sounds good to me. Yeah, no dishes!!!"

Chet and Claire sat in the corner table of Kitchen Italian. As Chet drank a martini, Claire sipped red burgundy wine.

"Jeannie called me at work today to check on you. She does that once a week, you know."

"No, I didn't know, but that's sweet of her. I talk to her every other day and tell her how I'm feeling. You didn't say anything to her about the weird things that happened at Bible Babes, did you?"

"Are you kidding? She'd be calling Dr. McDaniel to find out what to do. Your secret's safe with me."

"Well done." Claire lifted her glass, "Cheers."

"Tell me about the meditation today. What do you do?"

In-between bites of salad, garlic bread, and lasagna, Claire tried to explain her hour of relaxation.

"I lie down on the recliner in the sunroom and close my eyes. My mantra is Holy Spirit. I say it several times and breathe in and out slowly. I don't fall asleep, but I'm in that kind of vague zone in between."

"Twilight sleep?"

"I guess you could call it that. Today, I felt very relaxed. It was pleasant. Pass the salt and pepper, please?"

"Here."

"This tastes really good. Want a bite of my lasagna?"

"No, I'm good. Is that it?"

"What? You mean the meditation? Pretty much."

"No visions, no spinning?"

Claire hesitated. "No weird sensations, but I was thinking about angels when you woke me up today. I don't recall much."

"Sorry, I disturbed your session. It's hard to remember what you were dreaming or thinking when someone wakes you from a deep sleep."

"Oh, that's okay, hon. Hey, you've just given me a good idea!"

"I have?"

"Yes. You're right about the interruption. I felt relaxed today, but I was not in a deep sleep when you kissed me. I was half asleep with random thoughts and images and half awake with sounds and smells of reality like the tick of a clock or kids yelling outside. The Dillon word for semi-sleep is snoozing."

Chapter 25 :  Meditation

Chet looked worried.  "Whether it's deep sleep or semi-consciousness or snoozing, Dr. McDaniel cautioned us about issues of fantasy versus reality.  That makes me nervous."

"He also told me that I do not have to justify every thought that comes into my mind.  And by the way, you don't have to justify every time you worry about me.  It's nice that you do, but please, don't dwell on what might happen."  Claire took a sip of wine and smiled.  "First of all, I'm in good health.  Secondly, I can tell the difference between fantasy and reality.  And finally, after meditation I feel relaxed and that brings me to the idea that you inspired."

"Which is?"

"You said 'It's hard to remember what you were dreaming or thinking when someone wakes you from a deep sleep.'  When I first opened my eyes this afternoon, I remembered everything that I had seen, but within seconds much had disappeared.  Within minutes, the only thing I could remember were the angels."

"And the idea that I inspired is….?"

"Writing down what I experience immediately after meditation while the thoughts are still floating in and out of my mind."

"That is a good idea, Claire.  They say if you want to remember your dreams, write them down right after you wake up.  Most people don't because they're too darn tired and then they forget."

"It's different, though, during meditation because when the hour is up I feel rested, not like in the morning when I have to drink a cup of coffee to get going.  When you said 'it's hard to remember,' the light bulb turned on.  If I write immediately, I think I can capture most of what I'm experiencing in that hour."

"So, you want to keep a diary?"

"Yes.  When my sisters visited in August, Karie gave me a blue leather journal.  Tomorrow, I will write my first meditation happening."

"Sounds like Woodstock.  It's a happening!"

"Okay, my first meditation entry.  Seriously, I love to write and this is a good way to track my semi-sleep snooze news."

"Snooze news.  Groovy."

"Oh, hi.  Thanks, but no dessert for me.  Chet?"

"Just the check, please."

As they walked hand in hand to the car, Chet was laughing as Claire repeated another one of Jeff's college capers that he had e-mailed to her that day.  Life was good.

———————————

The next afternoon at three pm, Claire again began her meditation routine.  The first few meditations had been very relaxing.  She was emboldened by Dr. McDaniel's non-judgmental view of her Bible meeting experiences.  She trusted his advice to meditate every day and up to this point, the time spent in the sunroom alleviated anxiety.  However, lately, she had begun to question the why of what she envisioned during meditation.

Never sure whether these were dreams or memories or both, Claire had a nagging suspicion that these were not random thoughts.  She lit the white linen scented candle and began the rhythmic breathing saying *Holy Spirit, Holy Spirit, Holy Spirit*.  As soon as Claire ended her meditation session, she quickly filled the page in her journal.

*Today, I was able to catch a glimpse of the waiting angels.  I felt a twinge of sadness for them as they stood wingtip to wingtip patiently waiting for something or someone to hold.  It was a very real and strange sensation for me because I wasn't just observing. I was in the middle of all of this.  And there seemed to be someone moving me along and explaining things, although no one spoke.  Right before I stopped meditating, the grasp of what they were waiting for hit me as if someone had thrown a hard icy snowball in my face.  These particular angels were waiting to hold a beautiful baby, who only moments before had suffered an excruciating death at the hands of an abortionist. Each angel who was assigned a tiny infant would never experience the joy of watching over a life from birth to childhood, to adulthood, middle age, old age and then death. However, God gave these angels the gift of being the first to tenderly hold the newborns of Heaven.*

She stared at what she had written.

*Where did all that come from?*

Claire rushed to hide the journal in the drawer.

Bible Babes gathered in the church room for their fourth week. Anne set a box of mixed chocolates on the table alongside Dana's plate of salty soft pretzels and warm cheddar cheese dip.

After Bernie read a short opening prayer, Roxanne said, "I have no introduction. Turn to   Psalm 91:3-13.

> *No evil shall befall you, nor shall affliction come near your tent.   For to his angels he has given command that they guard you in all your ways.'  Upon their hands they shall bear you up, lest you dash your foot against the stone. You shall tread upon the asp and the viper.  You shall trample down the lion and the dragon. (Psalm 91:10-13)*

Maureen pointed to an angel pin on her blazer. "I love anything to do with angels. It seems that God created them to watch over us – 'they shall bear you up, lest you dash your foot against the stone.' I don't know why, but there seems to be lots of scripture about our Father in Heaven protecting us; Jesus walking with us; the Holy Spirit guiding and inspiring us; our Blessed Mother watching over us; and angels keeping us out of harms' way. It's a very comforting verse, Roxanne."

Tekla reached for a piece of chocolate candy and then mumbled some words in between chomps of caramel and nuts.

Rather than shout out a cross response, most of the time Dana opted to ignore what Tekla said.  She held up her left hand to stave off additional comments from Tek, as she was searching her Bible. "Hold on, I lost my place. Here it is. 'For to his angels he has given command...' God doesn't request His angels to watch over us; He commands it. I've had an epiphany with the second half of this sentence – 'about that they guard you in all your ways.' I've read this verse several times, but tonight I have a new understanding. It seems obvious that He tells them to 'guard you in all your ways,' because what else would an angel be guarding, but you as you are. Think about the fact that we have free will. That is simply our nature as human beings. God knows it's a difficult task to guide us, because often we use 'our ways,' our free will that damages our souls."

There was silence for about one minute as the other ladies contemplated what Dana had said. Sometimes, it took a few moments to understand Dana's line of thinking, but very often her concepts were profound.

"Wow, Dana. That makes a lot of sense. I grew up thinking angels were like a six-inch cartoon character standing on one shoulder and the other kind of angel was a red devil complete with horns and pitchfork standing on the opposite shoulder."

"I did too, Patti. Or, that angels would magically turn us in the right direction."

Tekla said, "Yeah, the cute little guy would be whispering in one ear – 'Don't do it, girl. You'll be sorry.' And, then the old devil would say, 'What's wrong with taking a small amount of money? He doesn't need all that, anyway.'"

"Exactly, Tek. That would certainly make choices easier if a heavenly figure forced us to make the decision they knew was best for us. Based on this reading, I think Dana has touched on a basic truth. Our Guardian Angels are commanded by God to protect us, but they will not override our free will. Anyone else ready to share? Anne?"

"Sorry, pass and pray."

Claire raised her hand. "I have something to share, Patti. It's easy to believe in the good angels. Who wouldn't want an angel watching over you twenty-four-seven? This is going to sound like an editorial, but here goes. How many people really believe in the other kind of angels, the fallen ones? How many people believe in Hell? Read this verse carefully -- *'you shall tread upon the asp and the viper. You shall trample down the lion and the dragon.'* He's talking to us. We shall tread upon the asp and the viper. We shall trample down the lion and the dragon. We have to fight evil. And, how do we fight evil? Prayer is important, but we also have to speak out against evil and when we do, He's given us angels to protect us."

Tekla took another piece of candy from the box. This time she talked before she popped it into her mouth. "Man alive, Claire, you've got the passion! You're scaring the heck out of me."

"I didn't mean to scare anyone, but I think we all need to face the reality that evil exists in this world."

Roxanne shuffled in her seat and said softly. "Patti, if it's okay, this would be a good time for me to explain my scripture choice."

"Let's see. I think everyone has had a chance to share. Tek, did you have anything else to say?"

Holding three pieces of candy in each hand, she declined, "No, I'm good."

Bernie grabbed Roxanne's hand holding it tightly for a brief moment. Then Roxanne said, "You are correct, Claire. There is evil in the world. Hell is a real place and my husband's parents died in a Hell called Nazi Germany during the winter of 1941. Arthur's father, Wilhelm was murdered at Dachau because he was Jewish and Arthur's mother, Katrina, was murdered because she had the audacity to marry a Jew. It was very dangerous for Aunt CiCi and baby Arthur to get out of Germany, but they did escape the horror. And because of that, Arthur and I have been blessed with forty-two years of marriage and a wonderful son. I chose this scripture tonight for my husband who turns sixty-eight in two days. I am thankful that the Holy Spirit has guided you to the same conclusion that I have. Each of your comments rings true. Dana, what you said about free will is insightful. The talk about angels and demons whispering in our ears on each side is not as trite you might think. Claire, you said it perfectly. He most certainly is talking to us in regard to trampling down the evil one. Those people who killed Arthur's parents surely had doubts as they carried out the evil deeds, but the great liar gave them reasons not to listen to their good angels. Daily prayer is one of our best defenses against sin in the world. Sometimes, though, it requires more than prayer. It requires speaking out. God does not override our free will; the devil cannot force us to do anything against our free will. We choose. If only more people had listened to the cries of anguish and had voiced their outrage against the Holocaust, Arthur's parents may not have died. I think the most compelling lesson in this scripture is that God wants us to speak out against evil, but we are never alone for He has given His angels to protect us."

The two wives of the German men stood up and hugged.

Then, Bernie whispered, "Nimnermehr" (Never again).

Roxanne held her friend tighter and repeated, "Nimmnermehr. Immer gedenken. Danke, liebster freund." (Never again. Always remember. Thank you, dearest friend.)

Chapter 26 : Bible Babes – Week Four

Week Four of Bible Babes had ended on a very solemn yet truthful note. After closing prayer, the ladies moved about the room quietly to perform weekly chores. Bernie sprayed her air freshener three times, Dana blew out the candle, and Patti locked the door.

The Bible Babes walked out into a chilly fall evening with the wind howling a haunting cry.

During meditation the next day, Claire's recollections were unsettling, but she realized a new meaning and clarification of the verse. She wrote rapidly, her handwriting getting larger and larger, sometimes unreadable. Finally, she underlined the last sentence for emphasis.

*You shall tread upon the asp and the viper. You shall trample down the lion and the dragon. These are the words that were vivid to me today. Oh boy, Roxanne, you are right. I had a clear awareness that Hell is a real place and that Satan and his fallen angels roam the world, ardently pursuing the ruin of souls. Yet, God is more powerful. He empowers our guardian angels to bear us up lest we dash our foot against a stone. <u>We - no I - could march into Hell if God wanted me to and be unscathed by the asp, the viper, the lion, the dragon - and any other of Satan's disguises.</u> Wow!*

The mystery of the meditations continued; Claire was at times confused. She reminded herself what Fr. Hernandez said quite often during his sermons. *"God works in mysterious ways"*

*So maybe this is his way of working with me.*

The phone rang at 4:15 pm immediately after Claire had completed her journal entry.

"Hi, Chet. What's up?"

"Want to meet me at Encompass Health Plex?"

Claire hesitated, "I don't know. I just finished writing in my journal. I'm not in the mood for swimming tonight."

"Oh, yeah, how did that go today? I mean writing in your journal?"

"Good. Even before I started the journal, Thursday seems to be the most intense day of the week for meditating."

"How so?"

"I guess because it's the day after Bible Babes. I have what everyone said spinning around in my head. Writing it down is great because once I've put the words on paper, the blitz of thoughts disappears."

"Speaking of disappearing. We could make a few inches disappear from our waistlines if we hit Encompass tonight. How about the treadmill?"

"How about the couch?"

"Claire, we haven't exercised since last Saturday. C'mon, you won't regret it."

"Okay, okay. You're guilting me into it. See you in twenty minutes."

There would be no going back to the life they had before. No matter how many times Jeff and Jeannie visited or called or needed them, their parents had entered that unmarked map of empty nesters. It was a passage that had its moments of sadness and regret, but most days it was a chance at renewing their relationship. They were able to spend more time together, exercising, eating out, reading, and doing things they did before having Jeannie and Jeff.

Claire's newest undertaking of journaling became an important occurrence on Thursday, the day after Bible Babes meeting. Those meditations provided the richest and most compelling entries. After she wrote each time, Claire would put her journal in the middle drawer of the table by the recliner.

Some evenings after dinner Claire would pull her journal from the drawer, quietly turning the pages to review her reflections. Chet sat in the rocker by the window pretending to read *Sports Illustrated*, hoping that Claire would offer to let him read her journal. She did not.

---

On the following Wednesday, when Claire was at Bible Babes, Chet opened the middle draw and stared at the pale blue leather book, debating whether he should open it or not.

*I'll only look at the first page.*

He opened it gingerly. On the inside left cover was a line on which Claire had written her full name – *Claire Marie Dillon-McCormack* Above her signature in gold threaded lettering were the words, 'For My Eyes Only.' Chet closed the book quickly, realizing that the publisher had designed this with purpose.   This was a warning to anyone who might venture into the owner's intimate thoughts that they would be in violation of 'For My Eyes Only.'

A few mintues later, he opened it again.  Beneath the cautionary threat was a note from her sister, Karie.

> *Dear Claire,*
>
> *I thank God you are back with us.  The Dillon girls would not be the same without you.  From what you told me about the coma, you must have experienced an intense journey.  Perhaps, one day, you will be able to remember everything that happened and write your story in this journal, even if it is for your eyes only.*
>
> *Love always, Karie*

Chet held Claire's pale blue leather journal in his hand staring at the inside cover, unsure of what to do.  The grandfather clock in the hallway chimed nine times.

*She'll be home in a half hour.  Why does it have 'For My Eyes Only?'  Claire and I don't hide anything from each other anymore.  Maybe, I should ask her if I can read it.  No, that would stifle her writing and she'd hold back.  What good would that be?*

Chet opened and closed the book in a frenzy of guilt.

*The meditation does seem to help her, but how am I going to know if she's mixing reality with fantasy? That's what Dr. McDaniel told me to watch for.  I have to be on guard in case she starts confusing what is real and what is imagined.  What better way than to read her journal.  She'll kill me if she finds out.  On the other hand, she hasn't told me not to read it.*

He opened the drawer of the table by her recliner and placed the book inside.  He closed it quickly.  After staring at the drawer for several seconds, he justified his overwhelming compunction

*Darn, it's no use, Claire.  I can't take a chance on losing you again.*

Chet picked up the journal and read Claire's first entry.

*Today, I was able to catch a glimpse of the waiting angels...*

Roxanne entered the school meeting room in a whirlwind.  She was breathing heavily and started ranting.  "Oh, jumping junipers!  What is going on at this school tonight?  I had to park a mile away."

Bernie tried to calm her.  "They're having confession for the little second graders who will make their First Communion in May."

"So, couldn't they have left a few spaces for us aging ladies?"

"You mean old hags, don't you, Roxanne?" Tekla poked.

Southern drawl exaggerated, Roxanne replied, "Oh, hush, Tekla or I'll make you eat pickled pigs feet.  I swear I will."

"I like pickled pigs feet."

At that, Roxanne smoothed the back of her knitted grey dress and plopped into her chair.

One by one the Babes entered the room.  Claire rushed through the door, thinking she was late.

"I thought I'd be the last one here tonight.  Wow, the parking lot is jammed full."

"First confession, Claire."

"So, that's it.  I remember when Jeannie made her first confession.  Fr. Albert met with the parents ten at a time to tell us that as Catholics, we also had to go to confession the same night our children did.  He checked off your name as you went into the little room on the side of the church.  The only adults who got a pass were non-Catholics, but man oh man. he gave the Catholic parents a talking to."

"Do they still do that, now?  Dana asked.

"I think so, but Fr. Hernandez handles it a bit differently.  I hear he meets with the parents, too, but is a lot more tactful and understanding than Fr. Albert was."

Anne was the last member to arrive.  Before she could say anything, Tekla yelled, "Overflow parking lot.  First confession for the little tykes."

As they heard the tap of Patti's pen on the lamp, each of the ladies sat down quietly.  Roxanne had finally recovered from her tantrum.  She opened a small, very old prayer book, gently turning the pages as if she were holding the hand of a loved one.

"This is my husband's prayer book. The night before Aunt CiCi and Arthur were to sail to America, his mother had tucked it inside his kindzudecken (baby blanket). The prayers are in German, but when we were first married, Arthur wrote the English in neat tiny letters underneath. This one is called 'Give Me Your Burden.'

> *Jesus knows your innermost needs and he will say to you: Give Me your burden of thoughts pounding with worry. And I will touch one strand of your head and you will be calm. Give Me your burden of anger seething on your lips. And I will drain the resentment from your heart and fill it with my love. Give Me your burden of loneliness having no one to be your friend. And I will walk alongside you so your aloneness is no more. Especially, precious child, bring Me your dark despair, when you are tired and weary from what tortures you. And I will give you rest. And in time I will give you eternal rest. Amen."*

Together, everyone repeated "Amen."

Claire interjected, "Roxanne, I have to say that after last week's emotional account of how your husband came to America, and then, your incredible interpretation of the reading, I didn't think you could outdo that. Your prayer tonight was breathtaking. Thank you."

"Oh my, thank you, Claire. You and some others weren't here when I arrived tonight. I was spittin' and sputterin' about not having a closer parking space. When I read 'Give Me your burden of anger seething on your lips,' I felt ashamed that I had complained about something that trivial especially since those precious little children are going to their first confession tonight. I apologize for being such a spoiled, southern belle."

"Not to worry. You're only human. Let's get refreshments and then ,Maureen, you're on tonight. Your first time to present a reading to Bible Babies. Maureen, are you ready for your premiere?"

As the ladies settled down with a drink and snack, Maureen prefaced her scripture reading with a warning.

"This is probably not going to be one of your favorites. Halloween is Saturday and you see all of the ghoulish decorations in the stores. It amazes me that people let their children wear costumes of murderers and devils and all that evil stuff.  With three kids and one on the way, it worries me that there is such casual acceptance of evil in the world.  Bear with me, I promise I'll get to the reading.  When I was driving home, I heard about the death of Jocelyn Pellino– what a beautiful talent at twenty-four and gone to waste on booze and drugs by forty-four.  At ten o'clock, I finally get to sit down with my Bible.  I read a verse from Matthew *'What does it profit man to gain the whole world and lose his soul.'*  I'm trying to concentrate on what to present, but I can't get Jocelyn's death out of my head.  ''

Tekla rubbed her hands together in delight.  "Yackity Chat!  Yackity Chat!"

Patti was annoyed but relented.  When the ladies drifted into what they called Yackity Chat, she had decided long ago that they may as well take a short hiatus from the meeting to get the gossip out of their system.

"I loved her first song.  She had a powerful voice."

"Did she overdose at home?"

"I think she was on tour."

"Sad, sad.  She has two teenage children, too."

Maureen noticed that Patti was about to tap her pen on the lamp, so she concluded the yackity chat interlude.  "I don't know if Jocelyn is in Heaven or Hell, but I do believe we can lose our souls and if we don't ask for forgiveness before we die, there's a good chance we're going to Hell.

Then, I read more of Matthew and decided on the verse I'm going to read now.  It seems to be a continuation of what we discussed last week – having that good angel on our shoulder whispering to us versus the other kind of angel; namely, Hell's angels.  Well, not the motorcycle gang."

Tekla put both hands on an imaginary motorcycle and revved up the engines.  "Brummm, brummm.  You crack me up, Maureen."  Patti gave her the 'look.'

Maureen nervously cleared her throat.  "Here goes.  My scripture this week is Matthew Chapter 10:28.

*What I say to you in the darkness, speak in the light; what you hear whispered, proclaim on the housetops. And do not be afraid of those who kill*

***the body but cannot kill the soul; rather, be afraid of the one who can destroy both soul and body in Gehenna."***

Dana started the discussion, "No offense, Maureen, but I really cringe at the fire and brimstone scriptures. It creeps me out. That's all I've got tonight."

Roxanne came to Maureen's defense. "Well, it is not pleasant to talk or think about Hell, but maybe we all need a little more of the fire and brimstone language. Although what happened in Nazi Germany was horrific, I don't have to look any further than right here in modern day America to find evil. We have kids using drugs, adults molesting little girls and little boys, women having multiple children by different men, and the worst of scourges – abortion. I believe in Hell and I believe in Satan. He does destroy both souls and bodies."

Claire glanced furtively at her friend across from her. Anne had begun her nervous hair twirling during opening prayer even before Maureen had read the sobering verse. When Roxanne said 'worst of scourges – abortion,' she could almost feel the heat radiating from Anne's face.

Claire talked quickly, hoping no one had noticed Anne igniting into rage. "Roxanne, you and I are on the same page as we discovered last week. I also believe in Satan and Gehenna – Hell. They've gotten away from even mentioning it on Sundays. I think a lot of priests and ministers want to avoid the topic. But, a bright side to this is what we discussed last Wednesday. We know that our guardian angels protect us against Lucifer and his evil minions. God is more powerful than Satan and He endows our guardian angels with the authority to light, to guard, to rule, and to guide us."

Patti noticed that Anne looked feverish. "Are you sick, Anne? Your face is flushed."

Dana placed her left hand on Anne's forehead. "You have a fever. Probably a cold's coming on. You should go home to bed."

Anne started coughing. "Yeah, I think I will. Hope I'm not contagious. I'll throw my trash away so no one has to touch it."

"You sound a little nasal, too, hon. Take something for that when you get home."

"I will, Bernie. Good night. See you all next week."

Claire closed her eyes and sighed.  She knew Anne was facing her own private demon.

*Anne, you don't have a cold.  You don't have a fever and you're certainly not contagious.  It's time to take off the makeup, Annie.*

———————————

Anne arrived home at 8:15 pm.  Once inside, she leaned against the door relieved that she had avoided a meltdown in front of the Babes tonight.  Barely.  She stared at her face in the hallway mirror.  Resentment churned her stomach as she mimicked Maureen.

*With three kids and one on the way, it worries me that there is such casual acceptance of evil in the world.'  Yackity, yackity, yack!  You wouldn't recognize evil if Satan himself was braiding your shiny red hair.*

Anne threw her purse and jacket onto a dining room chair and then went upstairs to her bedroom. After putting on lavender sweats, she was eager to begin her escaping ritual a little earlier than usual.  As she started down the stairs, she realized that the lights were on in almost every room of the house.

*I know Claire's going to stop by after the meeting. I don't want to talk to her. Not tonight, anyway.*

Anne went from room to room upstairs and downstairs, turning off the lights. The only light she wanted was the dim florescent bulb above the sink which provided enough glow so she could see the glass to pour her wine.

———————————

Bible Babes continued, but Anne's 'fever' slowed down the pace and passion of the discussion.  Maureen stumbled through a brief summary of why she had selected the scripture.

"Like I said in the beginning, I guess because of the talk of angels and demons, I thought it might be a good idea to use this reading.  Dana, I didn't mean to creep you out.  Maybe, it wasn't such a good idea, after all.  Do you think Anne left because she was offended?"

"She's not offended," Claire said.  "Don't worry about it."

Maureen looked at Dana. "I guess I didn't do too well my first time presenting. I'll choose something a little less dark next time."

Tekla stood up indignantly. "Now, just a heart-stopping minute. Back up the truck. It's not up to us to make you feel that you have to bring an all hearts and flowers reading from the Bible."

"Tek's right," Patti agreed. "We don't censor any reading from the Bible. And we don't censor what anyone wants to say."

Tekla glared at Dana, who turned away looking at the flash of headlights through the window.

Claire again talked in an unequivocal manner. "Maureen, we all bring something of value to Bible Babes. I firmly believe that people enter our lives for a reason. Please hang in here with us. We've been doing this a long time and believe me; every one of us has felt at one point or another that what we said was a mistake."

Bernie felt bad for their newest Babe. "Gosh, one time Roxanne and I got into a big debate when the priest scandal first exploded in the news. We were flipping through pages of our Bible trying to find certain verses in regard to hurting children."

"I actually tore one of the pages out of my Bible," Roxanne laughed. "We were saying the same thing, basically, but we weren't listening to each other. Patti finally got everyone calmed down."

"I had closing prayer that night and I was upset. I couldn't even remember the words to the Our Father. Afterwards, Roxanne and I talked in the parking lot and realized how silly we were."

Only Claire understood the impact of tonight's reading on Anne. Just as a surgeon removes the diseased organ to preserve a patient's life, Claire knew that the decayed secret inside Anne's heart was destroying her. She could not reveal to anyone the reason behind Anne's departure, but she wanted Maureen to understand that Bible Babes was more than prayers and readings and sharing and refreshments. Once again, Claire underscored her words.

"Maureen, sometimes in our weekly gatherings, you see someone smile and you realize that you've touched them in a certain way. At other times, you may hear a negative reaction or worse, no reaction to what you say, but that doesn't mean your words had no impact.  Bottom line, we don't run Bible Babes.  The Holy Spirit does.  We have to trust that He gives us the wisdom to say what is true."

Patti was somewhat bewildered by what had transpired in the meeting.  "Who has closing prayer?  Oh, yeah, Anne.  Anyone want to volunteer?"

"Why don't we sing "Come Holy Ghost?"  Claire suggested.  "We could use a good dose of His spirit."

Patti was relieved.  "Let's stand in a circle and hold hands."

Tekla motioned to Maureen to move in between Patti and her, so she wouldn't have to hold Dana's hand.  Maureen smiled as she took Tek's hand.  Dana had no reaction.  Claire prefaced the closing song.  "Holy Spirit, fill our hearts with understanding.  Jesus, we offer this song especially for those who have a heavy heart tonight.  Please place their burden in your hands to give to the Father.  Holy Spirit, fill our hearts with peace."  Their singing voices were soft and tentative.

*Come Holy Ghost, Creator blest*
*And, in our hearts take up thy rest*
*Come with thy grace and heavenly aid*
*To fill our hearts which thou has made*
*To fill our hearts which thou has made*

After the song, Claire immediately moved toward the door.  "I'm taking off, Patti.  I want to stop at Anne's on the way home to make sure she's okay."

"Go, Claire, go.  Of course."

The remaining ladies cleaned up the room very quickly, feeling a sort of disconnectedness from each other.

---

Claire pulled into Anne's driveway.  The house was dark except for the chimney lamp on the wall by the front door.  Claire knocked several times.  No answer.  Then, she rang the doorbell.  Still, no answer.  She knocked again, louder, looking upstairs to see if Anne's bedroom light was on.

"Annie, it's Claire, are you okay?"  No movement, not a sound.

On the tail of a night wind, Anne could hear her friend's voice through the open window above the sink.

*Please go away, Claire. Please. Oh no, she'll come to the back door!*

In a panic, Anne pulled her cell phone off the table and dialed. Claire had reached the stone sidewalk leading to the back yard when her phone rang.

"Hi, Claire. I was almost asleep when I heard your voice."

"Are you okay, Anne? I was getting scared when you didn't answer."

"I took a dose of cold medicine," she lied, "and I guess it knocked me out."

"You really sound groggy. Do you need anything?"

"I'll be all right. I've got one of those pre-winter colds, that's all."

"Are you sure it's just a cold?"

"Yes… I'm really tired. Let's talk tomorrow. I'm exhausted and I'll probably sleep till noon."

Claire walked slowly to her car. "Okay, I won't call in the morning then."

"I'll call you in the afternoon, Claire. Goodnight."

Annie had always been an enigma and tonight was no exception. Claire pulled out of the driveway and away from her friend's blackened house. As she rounded the cul de sac toward her home, she glanced in her rearview mirror. There was a single dim light in the kitchen. Anne was sitting at the table.

There's only so much I can do for her. I can't make her accept the truth, but at least she heard the truth tonight.

The next day Claire read all of the verses in Chapter 10 of Matthew. Although Matthew's scripture offered hope of seeing the Father in Heaven for those who acknowledge Jesus, the only verse that seemed to be wedged inside her head was '***And do not be afraid of those who kill the body but cannot kill the soul; rather, be afraid of the one who can destroy both soul and body in Gehenna.***' Her breathing became deep and long. Memories were elusive, yet vivid in sensory awareness. When she emerged from an hour-long meditation, Claire was anxious to write in her journal.

*Sometimes I think I'm either crazy or I am the most outlandishly creative dreamer ever born. Last week the images of angels were absolutely exquisite. In sharp contrast, this week I had some truly disturbing glimpses of misery. About fifteen minutes into meditation, I sense dreadful surroundings; growls and screams of pain and all sorts of unearthly images. Then, I enter a room - no, it was a tunnel. Everything quieted down and out of nowhere a podium materializes with a beam of light shining on the Book. No one tells me, but I feel compelled to read a verse from the Bible. The verse is, 'What I say to you in the darkness, speak in the light; what you hear whispered, proclaim on the housetops. And do not be afraid of those who kill the body but cannot kill the soul; rather, be afraid of the one who can destroy both soul and body in Gehenna.' I remember that I read this very scripture when I was in the coma. That is strange enough, but to make matters more confusing, it's the same verse that Maureen read last night.*

*The rest of what I see is a vague memory, but the experience is very powerful. The only way I can describe it is to say that it's as though I'm sitting in a theater watching a movie, only it's not a movie. It's someone's life story. There's a beautiful young woman talking to her college boyfriend. They are not married, but they are sharing intimate details that make me blush in embarrassment. Why do I know that* she's pregnant with his child? Why do I know he's lying when he says he's willing to marry her? And why do I know she will abort their baby at a clinic the next day? I have no idea why I know these things; yet, it seems natural that I do. In what feels like a mere thirty seconds, I see her again, many years later into her future. She is, maybe thirty-five, thirty-six years old, but is still beautiful with long black hair and eyes that are effervescent blue. Then, another quick thirty seconds passes. When I turn to leave, I see a hollowed-out version of this woman, this Angela. That's her name, Angela. Oh my gosh, Now, I remember her name – Angela. It's a horrific scene as I stare at her body filled with burning coals. I can't make out the individual faces of demons who surround her and others in this dark pit. Somehow, above the sorrowful whine and mocking condemnations, I hear the words meant specifically for Angela, 'You chose to kill your baby and you chose to deny the severity of that choice and that means, Angela, you have chosen Hell for eternity.' As swift as the snuffing out of a candle, the images were gone for the day.

All of this is unsettling whether it's a dream or a result of the aneurysm, or a true memory. Thank you, Karie, for the journal. I believe the Holy Spirit prompted you to give me this gift. I am quietly compelled to accept that God has a reason that I have experienced this and I cling to Dr. McDaniel's comforting words, 'Don't think you have to justify every thought that comes into your mind.' God works in mysterious ways. Who's to say this isn't one of them?

---

On the following Wednesday, Claire left for her 7:30 pm Bible Babes meeting. Chet was anxious to read Claire's entry and seized the opportunity as soon as her car pulled out of the driveway. He went to the sunroom and lifted the journal from the drawer. As he read intently, his heart beat faster and he became increasingly disturbed at Claire's writings.

*She sees 'unearthly images?' She's walking through a tunnel? And the Bible verse is the same one Maureen read last night – last week. Oh, she's probably mixing up everything from that day including Bible Babes. That's what she means by semi-sleep or snoozing.*

Chet read on, but found no solace in the next part.

*Okay, what's this? She's in a movie theater watching something that happened to another person. That's straight out of fantasy. Oh, for God's sake, she thinks she's visiting Hell. This is getting way too weird. Who is Angela? And she's in hell because she had an abortion? Claire, you've been reading too much about abortion.*

Chet slammed the journal shut without having read the last paragraph. He walked to the kitchen and poured Jamison whiskey into a glass.

*Claire and I have to talk. Maybe, I need to call Dr. McDaniel. Maybe you need to take a deep breath, idiot. You have no right to be reading her journal in the first place. Confronting her will result in a big argument. Mission accomplished – NOT.*

Chet returned to the sunroom. He re-opened the journal and read Claire's final paragraph out loud.

*"I am quietly compelled to accept that God has a reason that I have experienced this and I cling to Dr. McDaniel's comforting words, 'Don't think you have to justify every thought that comes into your mind.' God works in mysterious ways. Who's to say this isn't one of them?"*

Claire's final paragraph gave him little comfort, but her written word was all he had for now.

Last week's meeting had the drama of Anne's leaving early with her feigned cold, as well as the added chaos of Dana's snappish remark to Maureen about her choice of scripture.

Roxanne, Bernie, Patti, Claire, and Tekla were skittish as they waited for Anne, Dana, and Maureen to arrive at the sixth Bible Babes meeting. The women clustered around the window with a view of the parking lot to guarantee they could see the three approaching.

"Claire, how's Anne. Is she feeling any better?" Patti asked.

"I saw her Sunday. She went to breakfast with Chet and me. She said she thought maybe it was an allergy when she left last week."

"She did not look good. She hasn't looked good in months, even though she wears all that makeup now."

Roxanne shook her head sadly. "I agree, Bernie. My mother used to tell me, 'you can hide your facial scars with makeup, but there will never be enough to hide the scars of your heart. Poor, dear Annie. She's plum brokenhearted."

"Claire, don't you two ride together each week?"

"It's fifty-fifty, depending on what's going on. She told me she had a pedicure appointment at six this evening. I assume she's coming here after that."

"What time is it?"

"7:35. We'll give them a few minutes before we start. Oh, there's Anne, now. Good."

Everyone scattered to their seats before Anne entered the meeting room. Bernie and Roxanne rushed to the doorway to greet her. Roxanne put her arm around Anne and walked her to the loveseat.

"Hi, hon, how are you feeling? You still look tired. Claire told us you think it's an allergy that acted up last Wednesday."

"Well, I had an allergic reaction to something, but I'm okay now."

Patti asked, "Has anyone talked with Maureen or Dana this week? I wonder why they're late."

Chapter 30 : Bible Babes - Week Six

There was a series of heads shaking no back and forth. The ladies wriggled in their seats, not wanting to rehash last week's fire and brimstone fiasco. Tekla had no compunction about adding a cup of gasoline to the fire. "After you left, Anne, it was hot pandemonium with Dana and Maureen."

Anne muttered, "Why? What happened?"

"Now, Tek,' Patti rebuked, "That's an exaggeration. We had a good discussion and by the end of the night, we were holding hands and singing."

"Yeah, a real Kumbaya. Annie, some of us moved so we didn't have to hold certain people's hands," Tekla laughed.

"Quiet down," Bernie said. "I hear someone coming through the outer door."

Dana and Maureen were in a friendly conversation as they entered. "Hi, sorry, we're late. I got lost trying to find Dana's house tonight." The other Bible Babes were wide-eyed with grins of surprise.

"I, for one," said Patti, "am very happy that you're here, even if you are late. I was beginning to worry that we'd have to cancel since you're the presenter, Dana."

"It was my fault, Patti. I have no sense of direction. I could get lost in a wind tunnel," Maureen confessed.

"All's well that ends well. If you don't have a drink yet, go ahead and get one. Fix a plate of food, too, and then we'll get down to business."

With water or soda in hand, each of the ladies put a stack of Patti's appetizer, a gherkin pickle and cream cheese rolled inside a slice of salami. Bernie had baked eight extra large snicker doodle cookies."

Bernie, you're going to make us fat with those snicker doodles."

"Don't worry. You're only allowed to have one."

"Clever, Bernie, very clever. Anne, are you ready?"

"Yes. This is a prayer that my hair stylist gave me a few weeks ago. I think it makes more sense than some of the Catholic or even Christian prayers we say. Anyway, here goes.

***Prayer to Cleanse My Soul***
***I cleanse my soul of all bitterness, anger, and fear.***

*I cleanse my soul of blame, self-doubt, and misinterpretation of my life experiences.*
*I immerse myself in the cleansing waters of this life on Mother Earth.*
*May the clarity of who I am refocus my beliefs and lead me to the all knowing one.*
*Let the wind of confidence elevate my being so that I may elevate others to a greater understanding of self.*
*I will accept what is good in everyone and overlook offenses. I will accept myself as I am and overlook my flaws.*
*Finally, I will cleanse myself of past regret, so that I may have an illuminated understanding of my life experiences today and return my life-force to the cosmos tomorrow. Amen."*

Tekla put a napkin to her mouth to hide her cackle. Patti scanned the faces around the room. The look of stunned disbelief was unanimous. Anne bit into her snicker doodle cookie, seemingly unaffected by the silence of the Bible Babes.

After swallowing, Anne stared at Patti. "I said Amen, Patti. The prayer's over."

Claire was seething to an internal boiling point at Anne's mockery of the group.

*Okay, Annie, I'm not going to embarrass you here, but I am going to talk to you about your new age self-centered, so-called prayer.*

Patti was flustered, but answered, "Okay, yeah, thanks Anne. Let's see, Dana are you ready?"

"I am ready, Patti. First, I want to apologize to Maureen for not being receptive to the reading last week. I didn't mean to be rude."

Maureen said, "Gosh, Dana, that's okay. Other people say a lot worse to me than that. Remember, I work in a hospital. Besides, I really enjoyed our talk on the phone today."

Dana sat upright and declared, "Well, I also enjoyed our conversation, but I wanted to publicly apologize to you at the meeting tonight."

"Apology accepted."

Dana patted Maureen's arm in a friendly gesture and continued. "Well, I realized I was being close-minded about the Hell and Satan discussion. It does scare me, but what Claire said last week, took away some of my uneasiness.  God is more powerful than Satan and if we hear His Word and abide by His Word, He will protect us.  And Maureen, I'm glad you had the courage to bring us that reading."

"Thanks, Dana, I appreciate that."

Patti looked around the room.  "Anyone else want to comment?"  No sound came from anyone; once again; there were only quick back and forth nods of no.

Dana took a deep breath and presented her scripture choice.  "Actually, I have two readings this week.  They are about Satan and Hell; yes, I think we should have more discussion on this topic.  I'll read them and then each of you can choose one or both of them to discuss.   Please turn to Genesis 3:1-5:

> *Now the serpent was more cunning than any beast of the field which the Lord God had made.  He said to the woman, "Did God say, 'You shall not eat of any tree of the trees in the garden?'"  The woman answered the serpent, 'Of the fruit of all the trees in the garden we may eat; but of the fruit of the tree in the middle of the garden,' God said, 'You shall not eat, neither shall you touch it, lest you die.'"  But the serpent said to the woman, "No, you shall not die; for God knows that when you eat of it, your eyes will be opened and you will be like God, knowing good and evil.*

The next one is Matthew: 25, 41.

> *Depart from me, you accursed into the eternal fire prepared for the devil and his angels.*

Patti began, "Wow, we are really tackling weighty readings this year.  Whatever happened to the undemanding verses like *'Suffer the little children to come unto me?'*  Actually, I enjoy this kind of discussion and I love the juxtaposition of the Old Testament verse with the New Testament verse.  I remember hearing the story of creation from Sister Veronica in the second grade.  First she would read the actual Bible scripture and then she sparked our imaginations as she told the story in her words."

"That sounds like she made learning about God fun.  Tell us how she did it," Maureen asked.

"Sister Veronica described the Garden of Eden in a most glorious way.  She talked of lush flower gardens, beautiful flowing brooks, and sun dripping through the trees like honey. As we rested our heads on our desks, we could almost taste and smell the magnificence of the Garden of Eden. Her description of Adam and Eve made me want to be just like them. Well, at least before they ate the apple. Sister Veronica gave us little ones a true understanding of God's generosity. I loved when she told us the Bible stories."

"I loved Sister Veronica, too," Claire added. "She also taught us about the existence of Satan without giving second graders nightmares. Remember, Patti, you sat across from me and we'd pass candy back and forth during Bible story time? We knew she'd be too busy to notice when she was acting out the Bible."

"We were bad little girls sometimes, Claire-Bear. As I think back on it, I know that her lessons were deeper than I realized at the time. She gave us both sides of the coin."

Tekla questioned, "Pray tell, how do you teach a seven year old about Hell without making her scared to death?"

"First of all, Sister Veronica emphasized how much God loves us, but she also informed us that we have free will and therefore, responsibility for our actions."

"Patti, tell them how she acted out her little play. You were the volunteer that day. I remember you took a piece of candy out of your mouth and handed the sticky mess to me when she called you to the front of the room."

"I'll never forget it. Sister Veronica gently put her hands on my shoulder. She had a way of making you feel that you were special. She said, 'God loves you, my little one, but He will not chain you to Him. He waits patiently behind you to catch you if you fall backward.'"

Claire started acting like a seven year old. "Let me tell this part, Patti, please, please. I'll be your best friend!"

Everyone except Anne laughed heartily. Patti said, "Go ahead. You look like you're about to bust open, little girl."

"Thank you, Patti. Okay, Patti's standing in front of Sister Veronica. Then, Sister spreads her arms out as wide as she could. The nuns wore about seven layers of clothing back then. When she opened her arms she looked like a huge bird. She asks Patti, 'Do you trust me?' Patti nods her head yes and then, Sister says, 'Patti, turn around with your back to me. On the count of three, I want you to fall back. I will catch you.'

You can imagine a classroom of seven-year olds jumping and screaming in fear for Patti. Sister waves her arms to quiet the room. Then she begins the count: one, two, three. Patti falls back and, voila, Sister Veronica catches her. As she gently pushes Patti back on her feet, she looks at us and says, 'Remember, children, that God is always with you, but you have free will to choose. Sometimes you may choose something that is not good, but God loves you so much that when you fall, He will catch you if you have Faith in Him.' It's all yours now, Patti. I just wanted to tell that part about you."

"Okay. The next scene was a little scary, but Sister Veronica made her point. This time Sister did not ask for a volunteer. She says, 'Now, remember, we read today about a serpent tempting Adam and Eve. The serpent in one of his many disguises stands behind you with his arms outstretched also, but he's always leaning in toward you in case you fall, trying to get you to do what he wants you to do. He only likes your free will when you choose him and he spends a lot of time tempting people. Satan wants humans to turn away from God and will tell them lies like *'Go ahead, you can steal that cookie-- no one will know.'* Then, he snatches you like this. Sister started grabbing different children in the class to make her point. At the end of the lesson, she asked, 'Who would you like to catch you when you fall? God the Father who gently holds you and then returns you to your feet; or the serpent who lies to you, so he can clench his arms around you, just as he did to Adam and Eve?"

Patti and Claire stood up and did a double-hip bump. Bernie and Roxanne laughed until they started choking.

In her childlike way, Tekla shared, "As a little girl, I was confused that Adam and Eve would go against God and do something they were told not to do. It still makes me feel sad for them."

"Me too, Tek, but all of that original sin was washed away at Baptism and we have been redeemed by His son."

Maureen said, "That was such a good story, Patti and Claire. I've got to tell my kids that one. Even at a young age, a child can be taught about Satan's lies and temptations."

Then, Claire brought the discussion into the adult version of sinning. "When I was a child, I understood this in very simple terms like the stories Sister Veronica told us. As an adult, I understand this verse in a more serious context. Unfortunately, as we get older the choices become blurred and Satan's lies continually feed into our pride. We tell ourselves, 'I know better than God. I'll figure this out. I'll decide what's good and what's evil.' One of the biggest lies Satan told my generation was to use birth control. The slippery slope started in the sixties."

Roxanne added, "Actually probably way before that."

Maureen said, "You are right, Claire. Nothing, I mean nothing is more important than being alive in God's plan. And God's plan includes having babies in His time, not our time."

"It's pointless to dwell on it too much, but Chet and I regret not having more children. With a little coaxing from the devil, we freely chose contraception."

Bernie was very interested in Claire's connection of contraception to the temptation in the garden. "So, are you saying that the serpent continues to blatantly tempt us?"

"No. His temptations are not obvious. They're quite subtle, really. I'll read the last verse again, 'But the serpent said to the woman:

***No, you shall not die; for God knows that when you eat of it, your eyes will be opened and you will be like God, knowing good and evil.'***

The serpent doesn't actually tell her to eat the apple. He lies to her that she will be like God if she eats the apple. Then, she makes the choice, not Satan."

"Good point. Satan is as cunning as ever. He points out the pleasure of the sin, but not the consequence. I could have had more children, too, Claire. The problem is we get advice from people who mean well; sometimes people who love us. My mother had eleven children, so when I got married, she strongly advised me to limit my family to three."

"Exactly, Bernie.  Satan gets ordinary people to do some of his dirty work.  He loves chaos and confusion, manipulating choices that aren't entirely clear.  I feel I was really duped into thinking I should only have two children."

"Let's face it.  Satan's been working overtime in the reproductive area for many years now."

"It took guts to talk about something that personal tonight, Claire," Maureen added.  "Maybe I should think twice about the contraception thing.  Don and I have been discussing vasectomy lately, since our fourth is coming and it's going to be a stretch financially."

"That's the dilemma.  Now, I understand even better that discussing temptation and sin and the devil can truly lead us to make holier decisions and to influence others to do that too," Dana said.

"Hey," Claire continued.  "I'm not saying this to make anyone feel guilty, but the fact is the Catholic Church teaches that artificial contraception is wrong.  I turned a blind eye to the teachings and followed what is basically a man-made or in this case a woman-made rule, 'Thou shalt have complete control over your body and any other body in your body.'  Maureen, you might want to talk to Karen Upholtz.  She teaches couples how natural family planning works.  Call the parish office tomorrow.  They have her number."

"I will, Claire.  I love this group.  Bible Babes keeps getting better week after week."

Anne glared at Claire.  She was simmering in the belief that Claire's words were aimed at her.  Because the other ladies were enthralled with the discussion, no one noticed her agitation.

"I had several miscarriages," Roxanne quietly said, "and then finally, Arthur, Jr. was born.  I could not get pregnant again.   I'm not sure I agree about the contraception thing being a mortal sin."

"Well, I can't speak for anyone else.  It was years before Chet and I really understood that it was a mortal sin and that we absolutely had to go to confession.  We both experienced great relief when we did.  My Mom used to say to me, 'Pride goeth before the fall.'  My pride made me think that I could decide, not God, how many children I should have. I went to confession and was forgiven with an Our Father, Hail Mary, and Glory Be as penance. All of us sin, but our faith teaches us to fall back into Jesus' arms and we will be forgiven because He died on the cross for all of our sins."

"Well, no matter what the sin is," Maureen said, "confession gives us the grace to avoid sin in the future and the ability to forgive ourselves."

Roxanne continued, "Maureen, your account of the father touching Jesus' cloak – in the picture at the hospital – says it all about faith. That young man chose to believe in the power of God. That's a miracle. Unfortunately, there's the dark side of people choosing evil – evil that runs the spectrum of the less offensive sin of gossiping to the very grievous sin of abortion. What a sad tale we have woven about the destruction of babies. I think it's the New Age Holocaust."

"In total agreement, Roxanne," Dana offered. "When I first chose these verses, I didn't think there was much correlation, but after hearing all of you tonight, it's apparent that they complement each other. Satan has been in our presence for a long time. He tempts a child with cookies. You either steal it or you don't. As adults, his temptations can be very grave, like choosing artificial contraception over having more children. They can become deadly serious for souls who choose abortion instead of life."

"Regrettably," Bernie said sadly, "there are people who never ask for God's forgiveness. Instead they bury their guilt and pain in the dark recesses of their heart. I pray that no one I love dies in a state of grievous sin only to hear the ultimate condemnation '...*Depart from me, you accursed into the eternal fire prepared for the devil and his angels.*'"

Patti motioned to Anne. "Any thoughts on this tonight, Anne? You're awfully quiet over there."

Feeling awkward at the very topic that haunted her sleep each night, Anne responded, "You know, I sometimes think that we all read too much into this stuff. Maybe the story of Adam and Eve is just that – an interesting tale that Saint Sister Veronica and all the nuns and priests used to help little boys and little girls feel guilty about everything they ever do in life."

The room was silent. Even Tekla held her tongue.

Patti stammered, "Closing thoughts on your verse, Dana?"

"Only one. Satan's lies may ensnare us, but forgiveness is ours for the asking."

Shocked by Anne's remarks, the ladies swiftly accomplished their ending ritual of prayer and cleaning.

Anne was the first one out the door. "Good night."

Patti was stunned, "What in the world is going on with Annie, Claire? First, she says that ridiculous 'me-me-me' new age prayer and now this."

"I don't know, Patti, but let's pray for her before we leave here tonight."

Claire, Patti, Tekla, Dana, Maureen, Roxanne, and Bernie stood around the cocktail table. The candle was still lit. As they bowed their heads and held hands, their powerful faith connected them, coursing through the Bible Babes with spiritual authority.

Claire prayed, "Dear God, watch over our sister Anne this evening. Help her to feel your loving presence and to ask for your help, falling back into your caring arms. We ask this in Jesus' name. Amen."

Bible Babes, week 6, ended with whispered good nights in the parking lot.

As Claire drove past Anne's home, she was barraged with examples of Anne's downward spiral. First there was the exaggerated makeup. Soon after came manicures, pedicures, hair appointments, and other fruitless activities; a series of pointless pursuits to muffle her cries of pain. Claire physically cringed as she relived Anne's awful prayer and her juvenile outburst at the end of the meeting.

*Anne's not ready to face it, but she's getting close to rock bottom. Right now, the only thing that I really can do for her is pray.*

As Anne drove home, she was stunned at how often the weekly meetings seemed to pick at the scab of her wounded soul. This week was no exception. She even questioned whether Claire had perhaps revealed to them that she aborted her baby and this was a way to get her to confession.

*Stop that crazy thinking. Claire would not do that to me. Oh, Jack, I miss you so much! Now what?*

Tears streamed down her face.  She screamed out loud.  "I've really made a mess of my life.  I'm lost and I've done the unforgiveable.  My heart is broken, Jack."

At 2:30 am, Anne turned off the late night drivel of the radio and closed her third Hollywood trash magazine. In the course of about five hours, she drank two bottles of wine, used twenty-five tissues, and broke one wine glass. She turned out the sink light and in total darkness crawled up the steps to her bedroom. As she fell into bed, the walls began to spin, so she put her foot on the floor for stability. Then, Anne passed out.

At 4:30 am, Anne awakened with a painful stomach ache. She could taste bitter acidic liquid in her throat and within seconds, stumbled to the bathroom. She knelt on the floor, head in toilet, spewing pieces of salami, gherkin pickles, and snicker doodle cookies until she could only dry-heave. After resting on the bathroom rug for a few minutes, she pulled herself up and looked in the mirror.

"Oh, crap, it's on my sweats. Damn, I didn't even put on pajamas?"

As she placed a cool washcloth on the back of her neck, dizziness subsided. After a quick shower, she dressed in a clean blue nightshirt and gently positioned her body on the bed.

*I'll clean that mess up tomorrow. I've got to stop drinking.* Anne checked the clock. It was 5:15 am. *Oh, this bed feels good. I'm exhausted.* She tossed and turned until 6:35 am. *Why can't I get to sleep?* She checked the clock again and again and again until 7:45 am. *Okay, that's it. I'm taking a sleeping pill. Everything's cleaned out, so that should be fine.*

Anne took one sleeping pill and waited fifteen minutes for results. When nothing happened, she took another. Again, no sleep. After four pills, she finally sank into a deep slumber, but not a pleasant slumber. Daytime or not, dark hauntings imprisoned her dreams.

The dream sequence began as usual, but it lasted longer, flooded with a mishmash of details, some ordinary and some shocking.

A train whistle whined and Anne could see the lights of the old black steam train coming toward her. As the steward helped her onto the train, she noticed that it was full of all kinds of people chattering away. Some she knew; some she didn't.

Then she saw Bernie and Roxanne sitting in the third seat. As Anne approached them, they turned away, staring out the window. Roxanne opened it and a cloud of dusty air filled the car. It didn't stop Roxanne from screaming, "There they are, there they are. Stop the train. Den zug anhalten."

Anne stood on tiptoe, straining to look over her friends' heads. She could barely see a young couple clinging to each other as they waited on the train platform. She heard yelling and gunfire as they began to run down the sidewalk stumbling at times with soldiers behind them prodding them along. The woman was crying and kept looking back at another woman holding a baby. In an instant, Bernie and Roxanne pushed Anne out of the way and ran down the train steps. Anne scooted into the seat just in time to see soldiers forcing the couple into one of about twenty-five cattle cars. As the train of prisoners moved slowly down the tracks, Anne could see Bernie and Roxanne running as fast as they could, screaming at the soldiers, 'Nimmnermehr, Nimmnermehr, Nimmnermehr.' Eventually their cries floated into the night air on puffs of steam until there was silence. Anne noticed that the chatter in her train car had stopped. Startled, she stood up. Everyone was gone.

---

Although agitated, Anne did not toss and turn in her bed. During her drug-induced sleep, she would not be able to move so much as a toe, but she would be the hub inside the wheel of her subconscious dreams.

---

"Patti, what are you doing here in my kitchen?"

"Oh, Tommy doesn't feel well. I thought I'd stop at your place and let him rest a while. He's on your couch in the living room. That's okay, isn't it?"

"Sure, but, I thought Tommy…"

"Died when he was ten? Tommy didn't die last year, Anne. I lied to all you Bible Babes. And I'm lying to you right now, hon." Patti's eyes lit up like a little Irish pixie. She laughed and laughed as she danced around the room.

"Bill and I told the doctor we would not accept anything, but a perfect baby. You know what I did, Annie? When the test showed that Tommy might be born with cystic fibrosis, I had him removed. Just like that – snip, snip – he was gone. And we lived happily ever after."

Then Patti was gone.

---

Anne opened her eyes and saw the ceiling fan circling slowly. She still could not move any of her body parts as the pills pulled her back into sleep.

---

Anne was lying on a bed in labor and delivery at St. Aloysius Hospital. She could see snow falling outside and heard other patients talking about going home for Christmas. A nurse entered the room.

"I think I know you. Is your name Maureen?"

"Yes."

"Are you here to deliver my baby?"

"Yes."

Then blood started flowing into the delivery room from every crevice. Anne could see people mopping and filling buckets with the red liquid. Maureen opened the door calling out orders.

"Call the lab. Tell them to send eleven units of blood to OR. We've got to deliver this baby before Christmas."

Suddenly Anne was alone and sat upright in bed with a beautiful baby girl in her arms. She felt content as she gazed at her sweet daughter. Within seconds, the door opened and Maureen re-entered snatching the baby from Anne's arms.

"My babies come late, so I'll be taking yours home with me today. I'm glad she's not a Christmas baby. Thanks, Annie."

"No, it's my baby. She's mine."

"No, she's mine. You wanted to get rid of her. I told the authorities I'd take her home with me. And that's just what I'm doing, whether you like it or not."

Tekla and Dana entered the room and walked to Anne's bed.

"Oh, thank God you're here. This is awful. Tell Maureen to give my baby back to me."

Dana said, "Anne, you had time to change your mind, but you insisted you did not want this baby. I have no sympathy for you. Stop crying like a ninny baby."

As they escorted Maureen from the room, Tekla turned around and admonished, "You should take a shower. You have blood all over you."

─────────────

A tear slid down Anne's cheek and onto her pillow. She tried to stay awake, but even opening her eyes was an impossible task. She had no choice but to endure the nightmares, like a tortured animal caught in a trap, freezing to death in winter. Finally, the last of the tortuous images appeared.

─────────────

Anne smelled the summer night air, sweet with honeysuckle and mint and basil scents. She was dressed in a stylish navy blue dress as the steward led her up the steps to the train.

"You're the first on board, young lady, but I believe there will be many others joining you today."

She looked out the window of the third seat, relieved that there were no soldiers or gunfire. Then she sat in the same place that she always did in her dream – a seat that was whole without the filling popping out. Her secret hope came true as she heard someone climbing the steps.

"Jack, you came again. Can you sit with me this time?"

"I can't, Annie."

"Where's our baby? She's okay, isn't she, Jack?"

"She's okay, Annie."

"Jack, you know why, don't you? What else could I do? I had to handle everything for Kevin and me, but I couldn't have that baby. And not just any baby – a Down's syndrome baby. Please forgive me, Jack."

"It was hard on you, I know that, but …"

"…but you can't forgive me?"

Chapter 31 : Hauntings

"I do forgive you, my love, but my forgiveness is not the one you need. You have to ask God's forgiveness, not mine. I'm getting off the train, Annie. I love you."

Before Anne could respond, Jack was gone.

The steward yelled "All Aboard, All Aboard."

Once again stiff cardboard cutouts of human beings took their window seats. Instantly, Anne also became trapped in the one-dimensional form.

At the next railroad station, another group boarded. Each of the new passengers was twisted into a uniquely gnarled shape. Hundreds of irregular bumps on the shapes were covered with pus and scales emanating a pungent odor as they strolled down the aisle. One by one they took their places as the custodian of one human cutout.

Anne's body was frozen in place. She could only move her eyes left or right. Her heart was pounding against her chest as she tried to escape the evil caress of her demon. He licked her face. She smelled hot putrid breath. The train began to pull away and her sentinel moved a little closer. Then, he caressed her strands of golden hair and whispered, "Going my way?"

At that, Anne had reached her threshold of fear and pushed the demon away. Somehow, she was able to run down the aisle and screamed at the steward.

"Stop this train. I don't belong here!"

The steward emitted a long line of fire from his nostrils and laughed, "You belong here, Annie Madison Combs. I'd like to get her in here, too."

At first Anne did not understand, until she saw the yellow-eyed steward point to the door at the end of the aisle. She saw Claire moving toward the door, and started running as fast as she could to catch her.

"Claire, Claire, stop! It's me, Anne."

Anne was sweating and crying and screaming. She thought she was running fast, but Claire seemed to get farther and farther away.

The demons jeered her. "C'mon, ninny baby, you can catch her."

The steward bellowed, "You're not going anywhere, not after what you did with your baby. This is where you'll stay until I finally get your soul."

Anne kept running anyway and started praying.

"God, please forgive me.  Claire, wait, please, Claire, I need your help."

———————————————

Anne thrashed about on her bed pulling the covers every which way until her legs were free.  She stumbled down the stairs to the kitchen and splashed water on her face.  Her body was shaking from weeks of wine and sleeping pills and hellish nightmares.  Weak and scared, she tried to decipher her emotions. It was 3:45 pm.  The hauntings of her dreams lingered from the past several hours.

*Am I dead?  No, I'm alive.  I can feel the pain.  My soul is dead, though.  Will I ever be forgiven?  Will I ever have restful sleep again?  Will I be haunted by demons night after night after night?  I'm at the end, Lord.  I know I can't be forgiven for what I did.  I am at my darkest hour.  I don't want to live, but I know I have to for Kevin. I'm afraid.*

Although she felt wobbly and broken, she grabbed a jacket and her keys and drove to Claire's home.

At 3:45 pm, Claire had finished her day-after-Bible-Babes meditation session. She opened the journal to a blank page and began to write the entry for Thursday.

*Patti and I had a good laugh about Sister Veronica's Bible stories, especially the one about Adam and Eve, but once again the topic of Satan and sin rears its ugly head.*

*I wish I could get away from these dark verses. Hopefully, we will read something more uplifting at Bible Babes next week. Today was particularly frightening. All I could think about was the verse '...Depart from me, you accursed into the eternal fire prepared for the devil and his angels.'*

Claire's journal-writing was interrupted by the doorbell. The non-stop ringing alarmed her, so she walked briskly to the front door. As she carefully pulled back the lace curtain of the side window, she saw Anne barefoot wearing only a blue nightshirt and a jacket. Her slumped body was leaning against the doorbell. As soon as Claire opened the door, Anne burst into the hallway. She was shaking and crying, trying to explain what had happened, but her words were incoherent blubbering.

"They took my baby. Maureen did. Jack was on the train. But he left. Then Roxanne and Bernie were there. I don't know. I don't know. It was horrible."

Claire put her arm over Anne's shoulders moving her toward the kitchen. "Come, sit down. I'll fix tea and then you can tell me what happened."

Anne took a seat at the table, staring straight ahead as if hypnotized. Claire filled the kettle and pulled two cups and saucers from the cabinet, all the while watching her terrified friend. Anne's face told a story of fear, anguish, and regret. She still had a thick layer of foundation makeup smothering her skin. Streaks of eye shadow, mascara, and tears rippled down her face creating several dark rivers winding from her eyes to her chin.

"Tea's ready. You want sugar or honey?"

"No." As Anne sipped the tea, she gradually stopped shaking. "I always feel safe in your kitchen, Claire."

"Safe and secure, Annie. I'm here for you. Want to tell me what happened after you left the meeting last night?"

"Oh, God, the meeting. That stupid prayer."

"That doesn't matter now. Please talk to me."

"I'm not good. I can't stop crying. Just when I think I'm going to be okay, something happens or someone says something that makes me fall apart."

"What do you mean?"

"It seems that no matter what Bible verse we discuss each week, the conversation turns to abortion or contraception or having babies or about Maureen having her fourth baby."

"That does seem to be true."

"Like when Roxanne said abortion is the worst scourge of our time, and then another night she called abortion 'The New Age Holocaust.'"

"I know."

"Why are we reading all of the dark verses this year? It's like I'm in a play and everyone else knows their lines except me."

"No one really decided this would be the theme this year. You know we've always believed that the Holy Spirit guides us to bring a reading that is needed. I agree that we've been discussing serious topics, but that's not what's on your mind, Annie. Something happened to you last night or today. What?"

"It's what I said. Someone says something and it gets in my gut and then once in a while I have a horrific dream. I think it's because of all of this fire and brimstone talk."

"Did you dream last night?"

"No, not really."

"So, the Bible Babes' comments made you drive over here at 3:45 pm wearing no shoes and a wet nightshirt and a thin jacket in forty degree weather, bawling so much you have streams of makeup running down your face? And guess what? I can smell the alcohol. You were drinking last night, weren't you?"

"I had wine."

"How much wine, Annie?"

"Why all the questions?   Maybe five glasses."

"Did you get sick?"

"Yeah, I got sick.  I threw up salami, pickles, and snicker doodles.  Happy?"

"Anne, you're at the bottom, aren't you?"

Anne flailed her arms around crying, "I can't take this anymore.  I can't pretend I'm okay because I am not okay."

"Let's take the tea into the sunroom.  Chet goes to his St. Vincent de Paul group tonight right after work.  He'll be home late."  Anne's body shivered from fear and cold.  Claire covered her with the afghan her mother had crocheted.

"There's a lot going on, Claire.  All I can think about is what I've done to my baby.  Remember when I had the test right before Jack died, um, the CVS – chorionic villus sampling?  I was worried that something was wrong with the baby.  And there was."

"That was a rough day for both of you."

"Our child would be born with Down's Syndrome.  Isn't it great what science can do now?  They took a little piece of my placenta, sent it to the lab, and in a few days Jack and I were sitting in front of my doctor getting the news."

"I remember the next evening, when we all went out to dinner.  You and Jack were fearless in your decision to have the baby."

"As usual, Jack looked at all obstacles as stepping stones to Heaven.  He convinced me that there was no other choice, but to have the baby.  'It'll be all right, Annie.  God chose us because we can do this.'  Yes, 'we' could have taken care of our baby – our little imperfect Down's Syndrome baby – but, I couldn't do it alone."

"When we got home that night, Chet and I talked about how determined and joyful you were."

"Yep, for a few days anyway.  As long as Jack was there for me, I could come to grips with the decision.  And then, Jack was gone.  The day he died was pretty much the day I decided I couldn't have our baby."

Claire resisted the urge to say anything, trying to absorb what the suffering must have been like for Anne-- pain so intense and powerful that it thrust her into the awful choice of abortion.

"Well, you know the rest. Jack died and there I was, weak and grieving. I saw no way out except abortion. I can't believe you and Chet even want to be around me anymore."

Anne choked back tears. "This is the part you don't know. I haven't told another living soul. I went back to Dr. Blanco and he arranged for me to have the abortion on May 22 in Cincinnati."

"You mean the idiot that you had first gone to?"

"That's the one. He even suggested that I get sterilized as soon as possible. I felt that I had been defiled, but I was still determined to get the abortion."

As Claire listened intently, the sunroom seemed to swell with the somber breath of Anne's voice.

"There would be no complications, at least according to him, but now I have serious complications. Guilt, fear, anguish and nightmares from Hell. I had a horrible one today."

"I thought you said you didn't dream last night."

"That wasn't exactly the truth. I didn't go to bed until 2:30 this morning. A few hours later, I got sick and threw up. I couldn't get back to sleep, so I took four sleeping pills. I didn't have the dreams last night. I really had the dreams today."

"Of course, I should have known that. Keep going, Annie." Claire sighed in frustration. Anne began to twist her hair.

"That's when the nightmares came on full force. I couldn't even move."

"Of course, you couldn't move, Anne. You're playing with fire, drinking and taking pills. What are you doing to yourself?" In a softer voice, Claire consoled her, "Annie, Annie, you've had a very painful year and I don't have any right to judge you. But I want to help you. Tell me what happens in the dreams."

"The nightmares are horrific, always about babies dying and sometimes Jack is there and sometimes other people. In the first dream this morning Patti is standing in my kitchen telling me that Tommy is sleeping on my couch. Then, she starts telling me that she lied to all of us about him. That she got rid of him because he wasn't perfect. Then, I was in St. Al's Hospital having a baby. All of a sudden, Maureen came in and took my baby from me. Dana and Tekla were there, also. They all taunted me and I was screaming, but I still couldn't move. Then, I slept a while before the next onslaught. This one was the worse."

"The ones you told me about are bad enough."

"The last nightmare before I woke up had images in it that were bizarre. I saw what seemed like people in the train car, but they were flat forms."

Claire gulped in surprise. "You mean like a piece of cardboard?"

"Yeah, kind of."

"Was everyone like that?"

"No. Jack was there and he looked good, but he said he had to get off the train. And then, I saw Roxanne and Bernie. It seems they got off the train in Nazi Germany and were running after a couple they knew."

Claire didn't want to show too much interest, but was compelled to ask, "So, the only people on the train were the cardboard people and you and some of the Bible Babes?"

"Oh, no. There were these grotesque figures. One even sat down by me. That's when I started running down the aisle." Anne paused for a moment, rewinding the tape of what she could remember.

It was difficult for Claire to hide her anxiety. "Then, what happened?"

"Then, I saw you at the other end, Claire. I tried to run toward you, but the aisle kept moving backward. I remember crying and asking for God's help. There was this awful steward who spit fire at me. I guess that's when I woke up. I ran downstairs, got my keys, and came here."

Claire stammered, "That must have been awful for you."

"You're probably going to think I'm insane for saying this, but I know I'm going to Hell. Ever since the abortion, I've been dreaming about it every night. What kind of a person am I?"

"The same kind that we all are, Anne…sinners. But, you can be forgiven."

"I'm not so sure about that. Remember when you called me and I told you 'There is no baby. I've ended it?'"

"Of course, I remember. It was heartbreaking, but I could have been a better friend than I was."

"You don't have anything to feel guilty about, Claire. You tried to help me. I couldn't see myself taking care of a baby who would require more than I could give. Don't misunderstand me; I am not condoning what I did. I murdered my baby and I know I'm going to have to pay for that in Hell."

"Anne, come on, you can be forgiven even for an abortion. That's why Jesus died on the cross, for everyone's sins – the venial sins and the mortal sins."

"All that remains is for me to die. Oh God, I killed my baby."

"Anne, you're scaring me."

"Don't worry; I'm not going to kill myself. I wouldn't do that to Kevin, but in my dream I'm on a train and there's something evil sitting next to me. He keeps telling me I'm never getting off that train. I'm sure that when I die, I'm going to Hell. When you have a dream like this almost every night, you believe it."

Anne's description of the train and the evil figure terrified Claire. *How does Anne know anything about this? These horrible images were in my dreams, in my head, not hers. What is going on?* Claire put aside her own fears. She knew Anne needed more help than she could provide. *Holy Spirit, please inspire me to say the right words. I'm at a loss here. Please guide me.*

As the afternoon wore on, Claire finally mustered the courage to say to Anne the most significant words that would put her on the path of healing. "Have you considered talking to a priest? Fr. Hernandez is kind and I'm sure he's more capable than I am to help you through this."

"I don't see how God can forgive me. This is the worst thing I've ever done in my whole life. I'm such a phony, going to Bible Babes, sharing scripture, after what I've done."

"Anne, go to confession. That's what our faith teaches. Jesus knows what's in our hearts, but he told the apostles, 'Whose sins you forgive are forgiven them, and whose sins you retain are retained.' When we confess our sins to a priest, — even mortal sins – Christ is present. After you confess your sins and you receive absolution, you'll have a fighting chance to forgive yourself."

"I don't know if I can forgive myself."

Anne started sobbing again, but Claire was determined to push. She wasn't going to repeat the mistake she did in May, regretting that she had not done more to protect Anne and her baby from the evil of abortion.

"Okay, that's enough. Stop crying. Stop suffocating yourself with despair."

"I'll be okay, Claire. I have to be stronger. I can get through this on my own."

"Oh, really? And how is that working for you? How are the wine and pills working for you? You can't do this on your own. You need help. It's true that you have committed an awful sin, by your own admission, but there is forgiveness. There is hope. Please, let me call Fr. Hernandez. I know he'll see you, maybe even tonight."

Anne stopped crying and looked in the mirror, "Wow, what a mess. I don't want to feel this way anymore." She sighed in resignation. "Okay, give him a call."

Much to Claire's relief, Fr. Hernandez was available at seven pm. Anne went home to take a shower and dress. Claire insisted on driving her to the parish rectory.

"Anne, it's up to you now. I'll say a prayer for you while I'm waiting. Remember, I'm not in any hurry. Take as much time as you need."

"Won't you be cold out here?"

"I'm fine. I'll turn the heat on periodically. Besides, I'm dressed in a winter coat unlike someone I saw this afternoon."

"I guess I better go. This is it."

"This is it, Anne. You'll be fine. Now, go."

Anne rang the doorbell and was greeted by Fr. Hernandez. She had known him a long time, but this was going to be difficult.

"Hi, Anne. Please, come in. Let's go to my office. It's quiet and private."

Fr. Hernandez was of slight build with deep-set brown eyes that matched his deep voice. He looked much younger than his forty-five years. His wisdom and understanding of life issues were grounded in faith, nurtured long ago by his parents. He guided Anne to his office by gently placing his hand on her elbow.

His office was small but welcoming. He had a modest desk with a laptop on it and various papers and books. There was a table by the window with comfortable chairs on each side.

"Let's sit here."

Anne sat down cautiously. She gazed through the sheer white curtains and could see Claire waiting in the car. She thought of running out the door right then, but the guilt and fear and dreadful nightmares had drained her of all resistance.

"Would you like some water? A coke?"

"No, Father, thanks anyway."

"I'm really glad to see you. I thought maybe you had moved."

Anne was embarrassed that she had not attended Mass since Jack's funeral.

"No, we're still in the same house. Kevin started college at St. Francis Bergio University in Cincinnati."

"Impressive. Good for him. Okay, let's talk about you. Claire said you wanted to talk with me about concerns you have."

"Thanks, Father, for seeing me. Yes, I've been having disturbing dreams since Jack died. They're frightening and I can't seem to get beyond them. Is it possible to see your future fate in a dream?"

Chapter 33 : Forgiveness and Healing

"Anne, there are many people in the Bible who had vivid dreams, but the Church teaches that we should not depend on dreams for guidance. We need to be careful when we start listening to our subconscious, since it has no reasoning ability."

"But, these dreams are very specific and extremely dark."

"I know there are times that our subconscious mind gives us a glimpse of our conscious state. When we sleep, it's possible to have disturbing dreams because of anger or guilt or any other emotions. Tell me about the dreams."

"Well, there's several and there are babies dying, and one time a dead child visited me, and the most terrifying is the one where I am on a train. It's moving very slowly. Something or someone is sitting next to me, but it's not a person. It's evil, maybe a demon. And he keeps telling me I'm going to Hell. He touches my hair and whispers in my ear, 'I'm waiting for you. You are going to Hell.' There are different variations of the dream every night, but the message is always the same. God is going to send me to Hell."

Fr. Hernandez firmly held both of Anne's hands. "First of all, God does not send anyone to Hell. It is the choice of self over God that is the essence of Hell." Father Hernandez could see the agony emanating from Anne's lavender eyes. "Anne, tell me what's in your heart. I can see that you are burdened. Do you want me to hear your confession?"

Anne stared at Fr. Hernandez for a moment, terrified of admitting her sin to him, but more terrified of what could happen if she did not.

"Bless me Father for I have sinned. It has been two years since my last confession." Anne hesitated and then said almost in a whisper, "I had an abortion last May right after Jack died. The baby…our baby had Down's syndrome. I killed our baby." She expected Fr. Hernandez to be stunned by her confession.

Fr. Hernandez spoke softly. "The abortion of a baby is a grievous sin that separates God from all the people involved, but the guilt of the mother is particularly painful. You have found the courage to admit your sin and express your regret. Please say an Act of Contrition?"

Somehow, Anne remembered the words and in almost a whisper recited the prayer.

*O, my God, I am heartily sorry for having offended you. I detest all my sins because of your just punishment, but most of all because they offend you, my God, who are all-good and deserving of all my love. I firmly resolve, with the help of Your grace, to sin no more and to avoid the near occasion of sin. Amen.*

Then, Fr. Hernandez extended his hands over Anne's head, and recited the prayer of absolution.

*God, the Father of mercies, through the death and resurrection of His Son has reconciled the world to Himself and sent the Holy Spirit among us for the forgiveness of sins; through the ministry of the Church may God give you pardon and peace, and I absolve you from your sins in the name of the Father, and of the Son, and of the Holy Spirit. Amen.*

Anne, for your penance, I'd like you to say an Our Father, Hail Mary, and Glory Be." Fr. Hernandez handed her a card. "Also, after you say these prayers, I'd like you to read this verse from the Bible." Once again Fr. Hernandez placed his hand above Anne's head as he said a final prayer of forgiveness.

*It's all right. You are forgiven. God loves you and desires to be reconciled with you. Let it go because God now lets it go. Amen.*

Whether it was static electricity or the miracle of a holy hand blessing her, Anne was sure she felt a wisp of her hair gently touching Fr. Hernandez' palms as if her grave sin had been lifted up and out of her.

"Thank you, Father. Is that it?"

"Yes, that's it. I have a pamphlet I'd like you to read about abortion and forgiveness. There's a retreat coming up for women who have gone through an abortion and are struggling with forgiveness of themselves. Think about going to it, okay? I'll leave you alone now to pray." Fr. Hernandez held Anne's hands gently. "God bless you."

Anne knelt on the floor of Fr. Hernandez' office and prayed. Then, she read the card he had given her and for the first time in months she wept tears of joy and peace.

*Matthew 26: 26-28. Now as they were eating, Jesus took bread, and when he had said the blessing he broke it and gave it to the disciples. Take it and eat," he said, "this is my body." Then he took a cup, and when he had given thanks he handed it to them saying, "Drink from this, all of you, for this is my blood, the blood of the covenant, poured out for many for the forgiveness of sins."*

———————————————

While Anne was with Fr. Hernandez, Claire waited in the car. She could vaguely see their outlines through the curtains in the dimly lit room. She drifted in and out of snoozing. Once again, Claire was in a train car, the one that she had visited in the coma, only this time something had changed. Anne was no longer in the seat. At first, Claire was alarmed, not understanding why Anne was not in her seat on the train, until she realized a wonderful truth. Anne was no longer shackled to her demon of guilt and shame. Nevertheless, Claire wanted to get out of there. An awful creature was howling foul words and screaming in pain. She could hear herself saying, "Depart from me, you accursed into the eternal fire prepared for the devil and his angels." Claire suddenly awoke startled by the pounding on her car.

———————————————

"Claire, are you okay?"

It took Claire a moment to realize that she had awakened from the dream, but she felt relieved to see that it was Anne knocking on her car window.

"I'm fine. I fell asleep and was dreaming. More importantly, how are you?"

"I'm good, Claire. Really good. I feel like a cinder block has been lifted off my chest. Thanks for getting me here."

"I'm happy for you. Now, you can start to heal. I can be your sounding board if you want."

"You know, there's still a part of me that can't let go, but at least I feel forgiven by God. Now, I have to learn to forgive myself. Fr. Hernandez gave me information about a retreat for women who have had abortions. I might go to it. What do you think?"

"I think it's a great idea. You don't have to go through this alone. Hey, let's celebrate. How about a root beer float at Allen's?"

"Sounds great."

Anne slept restfully that night. Her demon companion was gone forever.

Claire reviewed the dream she had in the car that night, feeling relieved that Anne's soul had been restored.  Claire believed she had witnessed Hell tonight, the same Hell she had endured during her coma.  Still, doubt obscured the boundary between her reality and fantasy.

An unfamiliar silence pervaded the room as Claire and Anne entered together for Bible Babes, Week Seven.  The other six ladies were in their seats perusing their Bibles or eating snacks.  Roxanne had made miniature apple dumplings and Maureen had prepared bite-sized corn dogs.

"Okay, everyone's here," Patti began.  "Dana, opening prayer."

*Lord, we humbly pray*
*Give us a foundation of Faith that plants our feet firmly in your care*
*Instill in us the hope of our salvation far from the lion's lair*
*As your Sacred Heart fills our hearts with your divine blood*
*Let us be thankful for the greatest of all your gifts, your sacrificial love."*

After the opening prayer, Tekla, was about to read when Anne stood up.  "If it's okay with everyone, I'd like to say something."

"Sure, Anne, go ahead," Patti answered.

"I want to apologize for how I behaved last week.  I am very sorry for reading that stupid new age poem and for ridiculing Sister Veronica.  You have all been very patient with me.  You don't deserve to be treated the way I treated you."

Patti consoled, "Oh, Annie, you've been through a lot this year.  We understand hon."

"I know you do, but I still want to apologize for the way I've behaved starting with our first meeting this year.  All I've done for the most part is 'pass and pray,' only I didn't really say a prayer.  I am truly sorry."

Roxanne and Bernie hugged her.  Maureen dabbed a tissue to her nose.

"Glad you're back, Annie," Tekla said.  "Hey, I have a question.  I'm counting nine apple dumplings.  Who gets the extra one?"

Roxanne chuckled, "Of course, you do, Tekla."

Bible Babes laughed in relief.  They were back in business and the room returned to its cheerful ambience.

"Okay, now that we're one big happy family again, let's have the reading," Patti directed.  "Tekla?"

"Turn to Revelations 12:7-9

*And there was a great battle in Heaven, Michael and his angels fought with the dragon, and the dragon back with his angels; and they prevailed not, neither was their place found any more in Heaven, and that great dragon was cast out, that old serpent, who is called the devil and Satan, who seduceth the whole world; and he was cast unto the earth, and his angels were thrown down with him."*

"What a perfect way to frame our recent discussion of Satan," Bernie volunteered. She then winked at Tekla in acknowledgement of Tekla's unique ability to bring a topic to full conclusion. Not understanding Bernie's friendly gesture, Tek winked back anyway.

Maureen opened the discussion. "I bet Sister Veronica had a great description of St. Michael. I went to a Catholic school in Milwaukee, but I never had a nun as a teacher. It was a good school, but back in the seventies they didn't talk much about any of the saints. My Grandma was a big supporter of St. Michael. She told me the story. I think the prayer to St. Michael is one of the deepest prayers ever written."

Bernie added, "It's almost a warning to the devil, don't you think?"

"I agree and I'm glad my Grandma taught me that prayer. That's all for this week."

"Bernie, why don't you go next," Patti suggested. "I'm interested in why you think that it's a warning to the devil."

"Okay. My Grandma taught me this prayer, also, Maureen. Of course, we learned prayers in school, but Grandma told me that the devil is always listening trying to find a way into our lives. And, not only that, he absolutely has his own legion of evil spirits who roam about the world seeking the ruin of souls. How else can you explain why a doctor would snip the spine of a baby who survived an abortion?"

Anne bristled, but listened intently.

Tekla interjected, "Is this going to be yackity, chat about Dr. Damon?"

"No, I don't want to waste another ounce of my breath talking about that monster. I only bring it up because it proves the existence of Satan's evil influence in the world. Now, back to St. Michael and his warning. As I said, the devil and his evil legion are in pursuit of our souls. When we say the prayer to St. Michael, those evil angels hear us and they are reminded that St. Michael defeated them. The warning is that through the power of God, St. Michael will cast them into Hell.”

"Wow, who’s going to top that? I’m passing and praying,” Claire said.

Dana stated, “Me too.”

"I think I’ve talked enough about evil in the world in the past few weeks. I’ll pass and pray also,” Roxanne said.

"I have one small thing to add,” Pattie said. “Bernie, you said it eloquently, but I have to admit it’s the first time I realize that this one prayer defines both the battle against Satan and the power of St. Michael to defeat him. Such a short prayer, but powerful. Anne, any thoughts?”

"Well, I think St. Michael the Archangel has been watching over me especially in the last few months. I should have been doing more praying than crying when Jack died. I must admit I feel St. Michael’s presence in this room with all of you tonight. I feel protected and safe.”

Claire sent a slight smile across the room to Anne.

"I think that’s it, except for you, Tek.”

Tekla took a deep breath and stated, “I am bi-polar. I have trouble admitting that sometimes, but the fact is I have a chemical imbalance. I take medication for it, but there was a time in my twenties when I refused to take the pills. It was dark and scary for me. I lived on my own in New York. The only reason I survived the painful horror of my thoughts was my little holy card of St. Michael the Archangel.” Tekla pulled the holy card from the back of her Bible. It was laminated, but the card itself was yellowed and tattered. She handed it to Patti. “You can pass it around. It’s such a comfort to know that St. Michael serves God and protects us. Even though Satan and his demons roam through the world seeking the ruin of souls, St. Michael the Archangel is more powerful. I recently picked up a little pamphlet in the back of church and the author wrote that St. Michael is the guardian angel and the protector of the Catholic Church.

Now, that part sounded familiar to me, but he also wrote that the magnificent job of guarding Jesus during his thirty-three years on Earth fell to God’s zealous believer – St. Michael. And, he protects the reigning Pope. It makes perfect sense. I remember being in that Hell hole of ugly delusions when I'd wakeup sweating and screaming. I kept that holy card on my night table and I'd say the prayer to St. Michael over and over and over until the fear passed. I figured if St. Michael was chosen to protect Jesus when He was on Earth and if he protects the reigning Pope, I was darn lucky that I had him in my darkest hour."

Tekla seldom cried; instead, she diverted attention. This night she took a bite of the apple dumpling, so her mouth was full.

Roxanne rescued her from speaking. "Tek, I think maybe you and I should get together and write a book some day."

Tek ate the miniature dumpling in two bites, swallowed and sipped her water. "That would be interesting. We could call it 'St. Michael the Archangel KO's the Devil's Advocate, Adolph Hitler and Other Demons Post World War II.'"

"Sure, Tek," Roxanne laughed.

"Anyway, there was one other thing I read that was very interesting. Let me see if I remember this correctly because I didn't take Latin." Tek spoke slowly, "Quis ut Deus, Who is like unto God. That's the inscription on his shield and that's what the name, Michael, means. That's why I chose this reading which is the basis for the prayer to St. Michael the Archangel. When the evil spirits see that shield, you bet your bippy they know it's a warning. Wild, huh? Done, Patti."

"Tekla, that was inspiring. And, Roxanne is right, you should become an author. Well, it's 9:15. Shall we say closing prayer-- Anne?"

"I had brought a beautiful prayer written by Mother Teresa, but I think I'll save that for another night. Why don't we close with the Prayer to St. Michael? Tek, may I borrow your holy card?"

"I'd be honored."

Claire noticed that the lines in Anne's face had softened. She wore very little makeup, just a sweet blush of pink on her cheeks. Her eyes were clear lavender pools again. Forgiveness had made a difference.

With the influence of the Holy Spirit, week number seven brought the Babes together in a special way. Tekla shared just enough of her life story to make each of the ladies realize that darkness exists, sometimes merely in the confines of our mind. Tek's witness heightened their regard for St. Michael the Archangel, who through the power of God protects us from the wickedness and snares of the devil.

"Okay, then, let's begin," Anne said softly. Take a deep breath, close your eyes, and feel the presence and power of God through St. Michael the Archangel.

> *St. Michael, the Archangel, Defend us in battle*
> *Be our protection against the wickedness and snares of the devil."*

---

Claire winced as a glimpse of a yellow-eyed demon penetrated her closed eyes.

---

> *May God rebuke him, we humbly pray;*
> *And do thou, O Prince of the Heavenly host,*
> *By the Divine Power of God*
> *Cast into Hell Satan and all the evil spirits."*

---

Claire envisioned a room filled with snakes, evil figures, and screams of pain. An angel with a wingspan wider than the Golden Gate Bridge stood watch. A stream of sweat trickled down her back.

---

> *Who roam through the world seeking the ruin of souls. Amen.*

The last words were from Patti as she locked the door. "Remember, no meeting next week. Gobble, gobble. Have a great Thanksgiving everyone."

On the way home, Claire nodded occasionally while half-listening to Anne talking joyfully about the evening.

"Claire, stop. You passed my driveway. Are you okay?"

"Yeah, I've got too much on my mind. Sorry. Come over tomorrow and we can rehash Bible Babes. It was a good meeting. Goodnight."

"Goodnight."

Claire drove home and parked her car in the garage.

*Why is this happening again? I can't let Chet know. Put on your game face, Claire.*

On Thursday Claire began the meditation session as usual, pondering what she had experienced the night before. This time meditation offered little comfort. As much as she wanted to avoid the image of the yellow-eyed demon, she could not ignore what had happened at Bible Babes.

*I've got to get this written in the journal before I forget it.*

Claire began the Prayer to St. Michael the Archangel. Reluctantly, she pushed herself to evoke memories of the visions from the meeting.

**St. Michael, the Archangel, Defend us in battle
Be our protection against the wickedness and snares of the devil.**

*My eyes were closed like everyone else, but I saw something staring back at me. Something evil with yellow eyes.*

*I could hear Anne leading the prayer and I mouthed the words, but I was not in the moment. There was something else going on. I saw movement and heard voices, sometimes even a scream of pain. It reminded me of the old reel to-reel film. I watched a movie humming quietly through the reels, beaming a story across a screen - a sad, sad story.*

**May God rebuke him, we humbly pray; And do thou, O Prince of the Heavenly host,
By the Divine Power of God
Cast into Hell Satan and all the evil spirits.**

*And then all of a sudden there's this sensation of overwhelming strength and power. I only saw the shadow of his wings, but I intuitively knew it was St. Michael the Archangel. And I had an awareness of perfect safety and protection. I remembered that St. Michael the Archangel could stretch his wings as far as he wanted, perhaps from one end of the Earth to the other. Anne must have felt it, too. She even said - 'I feel St. Michael's presence in this room with all of you tonight.' When these visions happen, I seem to be pulled into something I've already experienced, but did I? And why does my memory seem far away and long ago?*

**Who roam through the world seeking the ruin of souls. Amen**

*Finally, everyone said 'Amen' and I opened my eyes. As much as I dreaded meditation today, I know I have to face the fact that for whatever reason, I am remembering things that happened. More than ever, there is a nagging sense that I have seen a demon, somewhere in time in the coma and that St. Michael was there also. There's more to this than simple memories of dreams in the coma.*

*God, please help me to understand. I could be wrong, but I feel that something is being asked of me, something I'm suppose to do, but it's not clear. God, I'm afraid of the things I think and see, but I put my trust in You. Please reveal and clarify Your plan for me. Thy will be done, Father. There it is again – the memory of saying these exact words before. I'm exhausted. No more writing today.*

Although it was November, the weather had sporadically spiked to 70°. Since freezing temperatures were predicted for the next day, Claire delighted in the idea of spending one more afternoon in her garden. There wasn't much left to do before winter, but she cut the remaining dead leaves from the bushes and organized clay pots for next year.

Wonder how Jeannie's doing? She hasn't called yet this week. Jeff said he'd call today. Maybe I should call them.

Just then her phone rang.

"Hi, Mom."

"Jeff, hi hon. Good to hear your voice. Are your ears burning? I was thinking of you."

"Mom, you really need to get new material. That's something Grandma would have said."

"Whateva. How's that word? That's more contemporary, isn't it?"

"Sure, Mom. Hey, just checking. What are the plans for Thanksgiving?"

284

"Turkey, mashed potatoes, dressing, cranberry sauce..."

"That's not what I mean. Are you inviting any family?"

"Actually, I was thinking about inviting Anne and Kevin. You know, they used to go to New York City for Thanksgiving. It's going to be strange for them this year."

"Yeah, that's why I called. I wanted to make sure we were on the same page."

"Now, who's talking in clichés? Anyway, I mentioned it casually to Anne and she seemed to be receptive, but I'll confirm with her. Gosh Thanksgiving is one week from today. Dad will swing by campus next Wednesday afternoon to bring you guys home."

"I can taste the turkey already. Better make a double batch of scalloped oysters. I'm sure Kevin will eat a lot of it."

"Have you talked with Jeannie lately?"

"Haven't talked, but we text each other a couple of times a week. She's back in Chicago."

"I know. I talked to her last Tuesday when her plane arrived, but haven't heard from her since then."

"Listen, Mom, I've got to go or I'll be late for class. Can't wait to be home again."

"Love you, Jeff."

"Love you too, Mom. Bye"

Claire sat on the steps of the deck reviewing her conversation with Jeff, laughing at their bantering when her phone rang again.

"Helloooo."

"Jeannie, hi hon. Good to hear your voice. Everything okay?"

"Things are fine. Whatcha doing today?"

"Right now I'm sitting on the deck talking to you. I just finished talking to Jeff. I swear this happens all the time. I'll be thinking of you two and then you both call one right after the other."

"Yes, mommie dearest, you are the Psychic of Hallowed Haven, for sure."

"Okay, smarty.  What's going on in Chi town?"

"Nothing special this weekend.  I'm thinking of coming home next Tuesday evening.  That way you and I can get started on the Thanksgiving meal the night before."

"I love it.  By the way, I've invited Anne and Kevin for Thanksgiving."

"Oh, I figured you would.  Jeffy said he and Kevin are having a blast at school, but the courses are hard."

"Well he better tone down having a blast and hit the books.  Dad and I aren't paying for Blast 101."

"Mom, you have some of the corniest sayings.  He told me he studies a lot and he's getting decent grades.  How is Mrs. Combs doing?  Is she looking any better?"

"She's doing okay.  Looking and acting more like her old self now."

"And, the most important question of all, how are you?"

"I'm fine."

"Really?  Your voice tells me something else."

"Jeannie, I'm fine.  I still take naps once in a while and I meditate a few days a week, but I'm fine."

"Okay, I'll take your word for it.  However, when I get there next week, I will do an in-depth examination.   I want to see the reaction on your face."

"Whatever, missy.  You and your Dad can have an executive meeting about my health if you want to, but I am A-ok."

"Looking forward to being home.  It's been three months since I've seen you guys."

"Feels like three years.  I miss you."

"I miss you, too, Mom.  Sorry, gotta go.  Have a meeting in five minutes.  I'll call you next Tuesday when I'm on the road.  And, I've got a surprise for you and Dad – a gift from France."

"I'm excited, but I'm more excited to be seeing you.  Love you, darling."

"Love you too, Mom.  Bye."

Claire jumped and turned toward the back door as Chet walked outside.

"Hey, there you are."

"Hi, babe.  Is it that late already?"

"It's almost 6.  What are you doing out here?  Summer's over, you know."

Chet sat on the step next to Claire.  He kissed her and she explained, "Well, it was like spring today.  I did a few things in the yard, but for the last half hour, I've been talking to our children.  First, Jeff called.  Then, Jeannie."

"Great.  Did you tell Jeff I'll pick them up next Wednesday?"

"I did.  Oooh, it's getting chilly out here.  No more seventy degree weather after tonight.  Sorry, I didn't fix dinner.  How about ordering pizza?"

"Pizza sounds fine.  Can you call it in?  I want to get out of this suit.  The meetings were grueling today."

"Sure, I'll call Italian Kitchen Carryout.  Meat eater's pizza?"

"Absolutely.  Do we have any beer?"

Claire opened the refrigerator.  "There's four."

"Sounds good.  I'll be down in about twenty minutes.  Getting a shower."

Dusk settled in.   Though there was only a half-moon, it was bright enough to illuminate bare limbs on the windows of the sunroom.  Chet entered wearing his comfortable black sweats.

"Hey, this is nice.  Exactly what I need after this day."

"Gourmet pizza in a box and a bucket full of beers.  Just for us."

"And even a romantic candle.  Thanks.  Seriously, this is great, Claire."

"Tell me about today.  What was the grueling part?"

"Well, nothing unusual, but when we have to negotiate with the political types, it's always stressful.  First of all, they don't have a clue about architecture, so we have to spend a lot of time educating them.  They nod their heads back and forth as if they understand."

"Kind of like children?"

"Pretty much.  We finally got the contracts approved.  Looks like we'll be able to start remodeling the Archer building in D.C. within weeks.   Of course, the weather is going to play a part now."

"I heard DC doesn't get that much snow."

"That would be nice, but even without snow, cold weather is another matter. Anyway, nothing really out of the ordinary today.   After the meeting, I took Senator Davis and his assistant to the airport.   That's about it.  How about another beer?"

Claire opened a beer for each of them.  "Hey, you need to get working on this pizza, mister.  You've only eaten two pieces."

"Don't worry.  I'll get to it.  I'm starved.  How about your day?  Did you meditate?"

"I did," Claire answered hesitantly.  "Then I worked in the garden."

"Doing what?  We finished that up weeks ago."

"Well, there were still a few dead branches to cut and I organized the clay pots. Jeff called and then Jeannie called right after him."

"What's going on with them?"

"Let's see, Jeff is having a blast at school.  He didn't tell me that.  Jeannie did."

"Oh, great.  $32,000 a year for having a blast."

"That's what I said.  Jeannie quickly came to his defense.  She told me he studies a lot and is getting good grades, but you might want to have a little talk with him next week."

"He's a good kid, but we need to keep on top of things.  You know how I was in college."

"La-la-la-la-la, don't want to go there.  Anyway, Jeannie sounds good.  We haven't seen her in three months."

"Really, that long?  I guess I'm used to her being gone.  Time gets away from me.  It's going to be great to have all of us together next week."

"You can say that again.  Oh, Jeannie is a female version of you – analytical. She even scrunches her eyebrows together like you do.  I could almost see them creasing through the phone."

"I love that girl. She's a pip."

"She asked me how I was feeling. All I said was 'I feel fine' and she says 'your voice doesn't sound like it.' Then your pip tells me she's going to conduct an in-depth examination next week. She wants to see my face when I react to her questions."

"I do that all the time with you."

"I'll give you that. You can push my buttons sometimes for an expected reaction. However, I've learned over the years to give you the reaction you anticipate. What do you think of that?"

"I think you're feeling the beer."

"Anyway, Jeannie's coming next Tuesday evening. We can get started on the two-day cooking marathon on Wednesday."

"But you have Bible Babes on Wednesdays, don't you?"

"Not the Wednesday before Thanksgiving. We're all cooking that night."

Chet was disappointed, knowing he would not be able to read her journal next Wednesday.

"Speaking of Bible Babes, how's your journal coming along? Did you write today?"

Claire knew she had to divert Chet's attention to avoid discussion of her journal.

"A little bit. Then, I went outside since it was warm. Oh, that reminds me. I want to tell you about last night. Bible Babes was unbelievable. After opening prayer, Anne stood up and apologized to everyone for her childish behavior in the meetings over the last several weeks. Of course, the babes don't know the half of it and probably never will."

"Maybe she's finally turned the corner. I still can't believe you got her to confession."

"It wasn't me. It was the Holy Spirit. Wait till you see her next week at Thanksgiving. Her appearance is entirely different; no more heavy makeup and her eyes are bright. There's a softer look to her now."

289

"Is that what you wrote about in your journal?  About Anne?"

"No, actually Tekla presented a verse about St. Michael the Archangel."

"Have I met her?"

"Yes, last year at the summer festival.  She called you a buffoon right before she pitched a baseball at the dunking target.  You dropped like a rock into the water tank."

"Now, I remember her."

"When she tells stories about her childhood, everyone listens intently.  She's had a difficult life, but she's very intelligent.  When she puts her mind to it, she can be inspirational. At the end, Anne said the Prayer to St. Michael.  It was one of those moments that happens once in a while.  It started with Anne's apology and ended with all of us feeling the presence and protection of St. Michael the Archangel.  Kind of special."

"Sounds like it, Claire.  Is that what you wrote in your journal?"

"Somewhat."

Claire blew out the candle.  "I'll put the leftovers in the fridge and then let's get to bed.  I'll clean this up in the morning."

"Do you mean bed choice #1-making love or bed choice #2-going to sleep?"

"The choice you like the most.  Number one."

Claire had other ways to divert Chet's attention.

# CHAPTER 36 : THANKSGIVING

Jeannie arrived home to Hallowed Haven on Tuesday evening at 8 pm. Chet and Claire had been staring out the front window for thirty minutes in anticipation. As soon as she pulled to the curb, they bounded out the door to greet her.

"Get out of that car right now, girl. I haven't hugged you in over three months."

Jeannie jumped out of her SUV into the cold moist air of Hallowed and hugged her Mom.

"OMG, it's great to see you, Mom."

"OMG? Talk English to me, darling."

"Hey, what am I, baby girl, chopped liver?"

Jeannie hugged her Dad and whispered, "It's good to see you too, Dee-Da." Since Jeannie was two years old, Dee-Da was her pet name for him.

"You ladies go inside. I'll get your luggage, Jeannie."

"Okay, thanks, Dad. Wait, there's something I want to bring in myself." Jeannie entered the house and placed the large square box by the basement door.

"Mom, when do you want to start the cooking marathon?"

"I've got everything in the fridge already. We'll have plenty of time to cook. Dad's picking up Jeff and Kevin around 5 pm tomorrow. What's in the box?"

"You'll see. Be patient. It's going to be good to see Jeffy. I need to sharpen my wit."

"Well, be prepared to listen to his crazy college stories. Sometimes, Kevin and Jeff go on forever. Anyway, it's going to be fun, fun, fun."

"Cheese and crackers, Jeannie. Are you staying a few months?"

"Dad, you ask me that every time. Sorry, I know the bag weighs a lot. When I fly, I travel light. When I drive, I bring several clothing choices."

"Oh, no, it's fine," Chet groaned as he dragged Jeannie's belongings up the stairs.

Claire opened the refrigerator. "Did you have dinner, honey?"

"Yeah, I got a roast beef sandwich and fries about an hour ago. Wouldn't mind a beer, though."

Chet returned in time to hear Jeannie's request. With slumped shoulders, he limped to the refrigerator like a wounded football player. "Coming right up, if I can make it there. Don't worry about me. I'll heal one day. Maybe a beer will help."

"Mom, you wonder why Jeff comes up with his silly antics?"

"No, I don't wonder. I know where he gets it. Okay, Chet, the gig is up. How about a glass of wine for me?"

Chet, Claire, and Jeannie settled into their favorite room in the house – the sunroom. From the day they moved into Hallowed Haven, the McCormack family was fond of the view of the back yard from the sunroom. Even in November, the swaying limbs of trees added special comfort, like a protective cave surrounding their home.

Jeannie regaled them with stories of her business and personal adventures in England, Germany, Spain, and France. She had several pictures from various cities, organized in photo albums with the flag of the designated country on each of them.

"That is clever, Jeannie. Let me see England, please."

"Mom, look at the room I had for two weeks. I stayed at Park Plaza Westminster Bridge. It's a gorgeous hotel. I could see Big Ben and Westminster Abbey from my window. Absolutely fabulous trip, but the weather was awful, almost like it is today in Hallowed. Only I was in London in August."

"You are living the dream, Jeannie. Let me see the pictures from France."

"Dad, Paris is the most exciting city I have ever visited. Oh, that reminds me. That's where I bought something for you two. Well, it's not exactly from Paris, but it's from a small town near Paris." Jeannie walked to the kitchen to get the mysterious box. "Now, mommie dearest, you and papa may open the gift. Here's a knife, Dad, to cut the tape, but be very careful. Open the top and you'll be able to pull it out."

"Okay, it's open. Claire, you want to help me?" Chet and Claire carefully lifted the item from the box. The gift was inside a beautiful blue cloth sack. Then, they gently pushed the sides of the sack downward, revealing a painting.

Claire gasped. "It's a Monet."

Chapter 36 : Thanksgiving

"Well, it's a replica, Mom, but let me tell you the story. One weekend I rented a car and drove to Argenteuil which is northwest of Paris."

"That's where Monet lived."

"I knew you'd know that, Mom. It is the most incredible town. I met this charming elderly couple, Jules and Isabel Partone. They both speak English. The Partones had actually known Monet's oldest son, Jean."

Chet mimicked Jeannie's pronunciation, "Jaaannn."

"Dad, please. It's spelled J-e-a-n, but it's pronounced softly – Jan.

"Is that why you bought it? Their son had the same name as you – Jean or Jaannie."

"Dad, that's absolutely too corny to consider. I bought it because it was one of fifteen duplications made in 1936. Jules and Isabel knew Phillipe, the art dealer who still owned three of them."

"I thought that was illegal."

"It was then. Now you can buy replicas online."

"How did they do it back then?"

"This painting is special. It was one of the first attempts to take a photo of a work of art and than transfer it to canvas. They also used oil paint to make it look like the real thing. It's not as perfect as the copies you can buy now, but that's what gives it charm. " Jeannie coached her father into a more refined demeanor. "Dad, read the bronze plaque, please."

"It says 'From Monet's Garden at Argenteuil to your Garden at Hallowed Haven.' Nice, really nice."

"This is a special gift, Jeannie. Thank you, darling. Where do you think we should hang it?"

"Well, there are too many windows in this room. The sunlight might cause it to fade. How about the living room? The wall by the fireplace has nothing on it. Then, when you enter the sunroom, you'd be able to glance at it."

Chet and Jeannie held the painting against the wall by the fireplace. "What do you think, Claire?"

She paused for a moment taking in the simple beauty of Monet's painting – the view of the back of a modest home that looked sturdy yet welcoming. In contrast multi-colored flowers grew wild in the yard. Claire loved Monet's work because his art allowed the imagination to wander in and out of his impressions, never really knowing exactly how they appeared on the day he painted them.

Chet and Jeannie carefully leaned the painting against the wall behind the chair.

Claire held her hands to her mouth. "It looks absolutely perfect there."

"When I saw it at Phillipe's little shop in Argenteuil, it reminded me of growing up here. It's like we're standing in our back yard looking at our house. The trees and bushes are beautiful, thanks to you, Dad. And of course, the flowers remind me of your garden, Mom."

"You better stop, Jeannie. Dad's going to cry."

Chet hugged his daughter. "Thank you, sweetheart. It will be hung on the wall by Thanksgiving."

"Wow, two beers and I'm fading. It's good to be home, but now, I am going up to my little girl bedroom and sleep until noon. That's early enough to start cooking, isn't it, Mom?"

"Noon is fine. Good night, Jeannie."

"Night, Mom."

"Pleasant dreams, XOXOXO."

"Night, Dad."

"It's eleven o'clock. We better get to bed, too. You have to work tomorrow."

They paused for a moment at the top of the stairs. Claire pointed to the light under Jeannie's bedroom door.

"It's nice to know she's in there. I'm happy she's home."

"Me, too, Claire." As they lay in bed, Chet held Claire's hand tightly. "I'm happy you're home, Claire. We are very blessed. Good night, hon.

Chapter 36 : Thanksgiving

Claire and Jeannie commenced the cooking marathon at high noon on Wednesday. By five o'clock most of the recipes had been prepared – dressing, scalloped oysters, green bean casserole, homemade cranberry sauce, and pecan and pumpkin pies. The turkey, mashed potatoes and gravy would be cooked on Thanksgiving.

While Jeannie and her Mom were cleaning the kitchen, the door burst open.

"Let the party begin. Jeffer is here! Hey, sista, great to see you F2F."

"Same here, little brother."

"Speak English, please."

Jeff snickered. "F2F, Mom. Face to face."

"Thank you. I hate text talk."

"Hey, bro, it's great to see you, too, but what's with the Jeffer?"

Chet patted Jeff's head. "Because, one pretty young tootsie gave him that name on his first day of college."

"Okay, Dad. We're not dating or anything. We all get together and have fun."

Claire intervened, "So, everybody's still friends. Darlene and Robbie, etc."

"Yep. Mom, I smell the pies. I'm starved. Can I have some tonight?"

"Absolutely, but how about limiting it to one piece of each?"

"Will do."

"Hey, where's Kevin, Jeff?"

"He wanted to get home. He and his Mom are going to dinner and a movie tonight. They'll be here all day tomorrow. Hey, Jeannie, how was Europe? Thanks for the jacket and the box of European foods."

"You're welcome. Want to shoot hoops later? It stopped raining."

"Sure."

After dinner, Chet and Claire sat on the living room couch watching Jeff and Jeannie play one-on-one basketball in the driveway. Their faces were chapped from the cold November wind as they twisted and faked moves. Jeannie had on her game face, looking as mean as she could. Jeff tried to taunt her with his laughter. Chet and

Claire soaked in the scene, smiling at each other – content to have the opportunity to watch their children play once again. The McCormack family slept well that night in anticipation of their traditional Thanksgiving Day together.

Jeannie, Claire, and Anne prepared the remaining dishes for the Thanksgiving feast on Thursday morning, while the men watched football.

"Oh my gosh, Claire, the turkey smells wonderful. I love Thanksgiving."

"Thank you. It's almost done. I'm going to mash the potatoes here in a minute."

"I love Thanksgiving too, Mrs. Combs. Everything is centered around eating and relaxing. Christmas is great, but on turkey day there's no rushing to buy last minute gifts, decorations are minimal and best of all, we get to eat Mom's scalloped oysters."

"I can't wait. Haven't had them in years. Jack and Kev and I have gone to New York on Thanksgiving for the last five years."

Jeannie noticed that Anne didn't twist her hair and frown when she talked about Jack this time.

"Anne, would you put these salad bowls by the plates? See if we can do anything for 'the hard-working men' as you pass by them. Watching football is very strenuous."

"Sure, hand me the bowls, silly."

As Anne left the kitchen, Jeannie looked at her Mom in amazement. "What has happened to Mrs. Combs? She's actually laughing and genuinely enjoying herself. I was bracing for a downer holiday, but she's transformed. And she looks great. What's the deal?"

"The deal is she's found a way to move through the grief and actually experience joy. It's a day-by-day process, but she's reached out to me and the Bible Babes and Fr. Hernandez. Annie Combs is a changed woman. She does look good, doesn't she?"

"Miraculous change. I'm sure you had a lot to do with it."

"I helped, but God performed the miracle."

Chapter 36 : Thanksgiving

"Speaking of miracles, how are you feeling?"

Claire turned toward the stove to stir the potatoes. "Feeling absolutely wonderful."

Jeannie took the spoon from her Mother's hand and turned her around. "Okay, remember what I said on the phone last week. I want to see the reaction on your face. How are you feeling? Look me in the eye."

"Okay, I feel pretty good, but once in a while I have a memory from the coma. No big deal."

"What kind of memory?"

"Oh, I told you I had crazy dreams when I was unconscious and well, I remember them some times, but not very often."

"How often?"

"Not very often, darling," Claire lied. "Don't worry. I saw Dr. McDaniel last month and he says I'm fine. You know I meditate most afternoons and that relaxes me."

Jeannie stared into her Mother's eyes for several seconds. "Okay, but I'm going to ask Mrs. Combs to watch you like a hawk."

"Who's watching who like a hawk?"

"Annie, my overly protective daughter thinks I need someone to monitor my every move."

"Not just anyone. Mrs. Combs, I guess you know Mom has these dreams once in a while, remnants from the coma. It would give me peace of mind if you would once a week make her look you in the eye and tell you how she feels."

"I pretty much do that already, Jeannie, but I'll pay closer attention. Don't worry, honey, I've got your Mom's back. She's always had mine."

"Thanks, Mrs. Combs. I feel better already."

"Umm, I guess you two birds have me covered. At that, Anne and Jeannie started flapping their arms up and down like wings of a huge bird. They danced around the kitchen and then trapped Claire between them.

"Caw, caw, caw. We're watching you, lady. You can't escape."

"That's hilarious, Mrs. Combs. Hey, Mom, cocka-doodle-do, we are watching you."

"That's even better, Jeannie."

"You two are crazy. By the way the only bird that's important today is the one in the oven. Get out of my way, lady hawks, so I can get cousin gobble out of the oven."

In the kitchen of the McCormack household, three generations of women cooked and talked and danced around the room filling the house with laughter.

Claire loved to serve Thanksgiving dinner at sundown to create a warm holiday ambience. Jeannie dimmed the lights of the chandelier while Anne lit the candles. As the ladies paraded from the kitchen to the dining room, the smell of succulent turkey and butter-topped mashed potatoes enticed the men to the table.

Chet poured wine in each of the glasses. Jeff opened the lid of an old record player that had been around since the early seventies.

"Dad, it's Thanksgiving. We are officially allowed to play Christmas music, right?"

"Right, something pleasant, though. Let's hold hands and say grace."

The room was quiet, except for a soft violin version of Silent Night and the distant crackling of wood in the living room fireplace.

***Dear Lord, thank you for bringing the Combs and McCormack families together on this day of thanks. Everyone at this table experienced painful burdens this year. Please know that all who join hands now in prayer are thankful for the blessings that rose from our darkest moments. We are thankful, Lord. "Bless us, O Lord. And these, thy gifts, which we are about to receive. From thy bounty. Through Christ, our Lord. Amen.***

Anne lightly tapped a knife on her water glass and raised her wine goblet. "Thanks, Chet. I am very thankful for the blessings that have come to me out of the darkness. I'd like to make a toast of Thanksgiving to all of you. You have been a Godsend to Kevin and me. I know that if Jack were here, he'd raise his glass in highest admiration of the McCormack family."

Chapter 36 : Thanksgiving

Kevin smiled and tapped her glass with his. "Nice toast, Mom. Really nice."

After a round of clanking glasses and words of thanks, Chet said, "I better carve this Turkey. It's officially time to do what we've all being thinking about – gobble, gobble."

---

Thanksgiving 2010 was the culmination of a year filled with sorrows and joys.

Anne slowly but steadily was shaping a different way of life for Kevin and her. She would always love Jack and miss him. With the grace of God, she recovered her soul, allowing both of them to have true joy again.

Chet's soul mate had survived a life-threatening aneurysm. While the journal writings nagged at him, he could not deny the incredible joy and thanks he felt for having Claire back.

Jeff and Jeannie had experienced sixteen grueling days in July unsure of what the future held. When their Mom came home, they were infused with an almost childlike elation.

As these two families passed the mashed potatoes and turkey and cranberry sauce, it was apparent that their love and connection had endured the unexpected turmoil of 2010.

Chet smiled at Claire and tipped his glass lovingly to her. *Why won't she share with me what I've been reading?*

Claire mirrored the toast, acknowledging a cherished Thanksgiving moment. *How am I ever going to tell him what's been going on?*

Secrets could ignite at any moment.

# CHAPTER 37 : HIDING THE TRUTH

At 9 am on Friday, Claire, Anne, and Jeannie ventured to the mall for an all-day shopping spree.

Chet and Jeff slept in and were awakened by the doorbell.

"Oh, hi, Kev. Come in. I'll get Jeff up."

"Sorry, didn't mean to wake you, Mr. McC."

"No problem. It's 11 am. We need to get up. Well, there's Mr. Wonderful now. Good morning, son."

Jeff mumbled, "Man, I slept like a log. Hey, Kev, what's up? You look like you're going on a date."

"Well…?"

"Oh, don't mind me, fellas. I can't hear anything until I have coffee."

"Emily Peters texted me this morning. She wants to meet us at the tower at noon.' Tina and Pam are coming, too."

"What do they want to do uptown?"

She wrote 'H. Tower, 1p, the old gang hanging out.'"

"Okay, yeah, that might be fun. Haven't seen our high school ladies in a while. Dad, can I borrow the truck?"

"Sure. You guys want something to eat before you leave?" Chet started pulling leftovers from the refrigerator.

"No, thanks, Dad. I've gotta get a shower. Well, maybe a piece of turkey." Jeff and Kevin each grabbed a few slices of turkey and disappeared up the stairs. Within forty-five minutes, they were out the door, in the truck, and on the way to Hallowed Tower to reunite with the McNichols' ladies.

Aah, this is nice. Thanksgiving leftovers, today's paper, and hot coffee.

After savoring the dressing, turkey, scalloped oysters, and cranberry sauce, he cut a slice of both the pecan and pumpkin pies and poured another cup of coffee. He sat in the recliner in the sunroom, unable to take his eyes off the middle drawer of the small table. With each bite of the pie, he knew this would be his opportunity to read Claire's most recent entry. He would not have to wait until next week.

Chapter 37 : Hiding the Truth

*Okay, let's see what's going on. She wants to write something before she forgets it. Anne's saying the prayer to St. Michael the Archangel. She mentioned that to me.*

When Chet read the words from the journal, *'something evil with yellow eyes,'* he shook his head. The next paragraph intensified his worry.

*So, while everyone else is praying, she sees stories like she's in a movie theater. And she hears cries of pain. Oh, but of course, St. Michael the Archangel saves her. That's plain crazy.*

Chet kept reading, hoping there would be a logical conclusion, but with each sentence, he became more confused and scared.

*She's not really dreaming when she meditates. She thinks she's actually remembering these things that happened to her 'long ago and far away.' You mean, like in another galaxy, Claire? Why is it such a big deal for her to remember saying 'thy will be done.' We say it every time we pray the Our Father. And what does she mean by reveal and clarify? She's exhausted? I'm exhausted. No more reading today.*

Chet closed the journal, drumming his fingers on top of it, contemplating what to do.

*How in the world am I going to talk to her about the journal? Let's see – I could use the direct approach-- "Uh, Claire, I know about Michael." Or – fake disbelief-- "You left your journal out. I thought you wanted me to read it." Or righteous indignation—"Okay, Claire, yes I read your journal and I can't believe you haven't told me this stuff." I've got to do something, but not with the kids around. Put on your game face, Chet.*

On Sunday morning after Mass, Anne drove Kevin and Jeff back to college. Jeannie drove back to Chicago on Sunday afternoon. After everyone had gone, Chet considered approaching Claire about the journal, but talked himself out of it.

*She only has two more Bible Babes before Christmas. I'm going to wait until she puts those entries in her journal. Then, I'll tell her the truth. God help me. I hope I'm doing the right thing.*

All of the Bible Babes arrived on time for the eighth meeting of 2010. Having skipped one Wednesday insured at least fifteen minutes of non-stop chattering before the session would begin.

Dana placed a tray of homemade oatmeal cookies on the table next to Anne's salty snack of black olive canapés.

Bernie put two of each on her plate. "Thank the Lord; no leftover turkey. These look wonderful. We visited our son Peter and his wife Abigail for Thanksgiving."

"They live in New York, right?"

"Yes, and Abby is a New Yorker through and through. We must have trekked five miles a day around the city."

Roxanne laughed, "Well, that's a good thing, isn't it, after a Thanksgiving feast?"

"The walking was fine, but we ate turkey for breakfast, lunch, and dinner. We had a turkey and cheese omelet on Friday morning, turkey sandwiches for lunch and turkey tetrazzini for dinner. When we got up Saturday, I could smell turkey frying in the skillet."

"Let's see if I have this right. This would be your fifth turkey meal, counting Thanksgiving?"

"Yes, Tekla, and at breakfast on Saturday Abby talked about making turkey lasagna for dinner."

"I bet you were gobbling by then." At that, Tekla started clucking. Then she strutted around the room like a turkey with her behind sticking out and her head moving up and back. "Gobble, gobble, Bernie. Gobble, gobble, Roxanne."

Maureen and Anne joined in the turkey dance until the babes were in an uproar of laughter. Patti waved her hands up and down. "Come on ladies, let Bernie finish her story."

"Okay, okay, Patti."

The three turkey ladies sat down, but everyone still snickered.

"I'm sorry, Bernie," Tekla said, "I couldn't resist. I pictured you and Ralph saying 'gobble, gobble' so she'd get the message."

"It almost came to that, but Abby is sweet and I didn't want to hurt her feelings. We told them we wanted to take them out to dinner in appreciation of their hospitality. We ate meat lasagna at an Italian restaurant. We left on Sunday about 10 am."

"Finally, no more turkey, huh?"

"Well, Tek, yes and no. Abby handed us a little basket with our lunch in it."

"Gobble, gobble. Gobble, gobble. Let me guess…turkey salad sandwiches?"

"You win the prize, Tek. She packed turkey salad sandwiches, but we threw them away at McDonald's right after we ordered two Big Macs with fries."

The room filled with gobbles and laughter. Patti tapped the lamp with her pencil. "Bernie, that is too funny. I hope everyone had a wonderful Thanksgiving, but it's 7:50. Time for prayer-- Maureen."

> *Come Holy Spirit, fill the hearts of Your faithful and enkindle in them the fire of Your love. Send forth Your Spirit and they shall be created. And You shall renew the face of the Earth.*
> *O, God, Who by the light of the Holy Spirit, did instruct the hearts of the faithful, grant that by the same Holy Spirit we may be truly wise and ever enjoy His consolations, through Christ Our Lord, Amen.*

"Thanks, Maureen. I love the prayers I learned as a child. That one is perfect for this group. FYI, Claire was scheduled to present tonight, but she and I switched dates. She is planning a special session for next week. By the way, that's our last meeting before Christmas. We'll talk afterward about that. Tonight's reading is Revelation, 21:3-5.

> *Now the dwelling of God is with men, and He will live with them. They will be His people, and God Himself will be with them and be their God. He will wipe every tear from their eyes. There will be no more death or mourning or crying or pain, for the old order of things has passed away. He who was seated on the throne said, 'I am making everything new.'"*

Anne immediately responded to the reading. "What a beautiful piece of hope, especially for those of us who have lost loved ones. Won't it be wonderful when there is no more death or mourning or crying or pain? I especially like '*I am making everything new.*'"

"If only we didn't have to wait until the end of the world when God comes in glory," Dana responded. "Unfortunately, for now we have to live with death and sorrow."

"From the day Jack died until two weeks ago, I walked around in a dark haze. I even told God I hated Him. My days were filled with anger and regret. My nights were even worse. Well, you babes could see the pain on my face even with all that silly makeup."

"What happened two weeks ago, Anne, that changed you?" Roxanne softly urged.

"Something very simple, but remarkable. I saw Fr. Hernandez one evening. He has a quiet understanding way. After we talked a while, he asked me if I wanted to tell him something in confession."

"That's when I would've run out the door."

Maureen agreed. "Me, too, Tekla. I hate to go to confession. I guess I'm not a very good role model for my kids."

Anne smiled. "Maureen, before that night, I seldom received the sacrament of reconciliation. In fact, the last time I went to confession was two years ago. I was a chaperone at a retreat for parents and children. I only went then because Kevin was in line and I couldn't very well skip it. This time was different."

"How so?"

"Well, first of all, I was in such a low place that I had no where to go, but up."

"Annie, I'm sorry. We didn't know what to do to help you."

"You were praying for me. Believe me, that helped."

"Yes, we were praying for you."

"Anyway, I'll get back on track in regard to the reading. After confession that night, I felt that everything in me was made new. My soul was renewed through confession and then, I received Jesus in the Eucharist on Sunday. I have a new life because I was able to shed the old things that haunted me."

Chapter 38 : Bible Babies – Week Eight

Patti sat up straight. "Wow, I've never heard anyone be that joyful about telling their sins in confession."

"You know," Dana added, "maybe I should go to confession. I haven't been in ages."

"I go about once a month. Arthur goes every week," Roxanne said.

Bernie explained her confessional experience. "My German father insisted that we go to confession the first week of every month. The nuns took care of that schedule. I was always afraid when I was standing in line. Now, I only go to confession once a year to fulfill my Catholic obligation. Once a year. That's all."

"I guess many Catholics are afraid of confession," Claire said. "Once a priest called me a slut when I confessed that I had kissed a boy. Both Chet and I rejected everything Catholic when we first got married, but that's another story. I try to confess my sins about every six weeks. I still have anxiety standing in line, but afterwards, there is a sense of new life, new grace."

Anne raised her hand. "Oh, I have one more thing to add. Thank you, Claire for getting me to see Fr. Hernandez."

"You are very welcome, my friend."

"Hmm. Does anyone have something to add?"

"I'll pass and pray."

"Anne, very motivational. Anyone not want to pass and pray?"

Tekla blurted, "Pass and pray. All those in favor say aye. The ayes have it, madam chairbabe."

"Why did you choose that verse, Patti?" Maureen asked.

"You know, I'm not quite sure. Claire called last night and asked that we swap dates for presenting. Then, I opened the Bible at the end of the book and came upon this verse in Revelations. We always say that the Holy Spirit is the one who guides us in our scripture selections. Maybe this is a wakeup call for all of us to realize that we can breathe new life into our souls by going to confession. I guess my final thought on this is that I'm going to receive the sacrament of reconciliation this Saturday. Feel free to stand in line with me."

Bernie hesitated. "Certainly something to consider. Are we ready for final prayer?"

"Sure, Bernie." Everyone nodded in agreement.

"Maureen, we must have been on the same path when choosing prayers for tonight, because mine is also a Prayer for the Seven Gifts of the Holy Spirit."

With bowed heads and eyes closed, the ladies listened intently to Bernie's prayer.

> *O Lord Jesus Christ, Who, before ascending into heaven, didst promise to send the Holy Ghost to finish Thy work in the souls of Thy Apostles and Disciples, deign to grant the same Holy Spirit to me, that He may perfect in my soul the work of Thy grace and Thy love.*
>
> *Grant me the Spirit of Wisdom that I may despise the perishable things of this world and aspire only after the things that are eternal, the Spirit of Understanding to enlighten my mind with the light of Thy divine truth, the Spirit of Counsel that I may ever choose the surest way of pleasing God and gaining Heaven, the Spirit of Fortitude that I may bear my cross with Thee, and that I may overcome with courage all the obstacles that oppose my salvation, the Spirit of Knowledge that I may know God and know myself and grow perfect in the science of the Saints, the Spirit of Piety that I may find the service of God sweet and amiable, the Spirit of Fear that I may be filled with a loving reverence towards God, and may dread in any way to displease Him. Mark me, dear Lord, with the sign of Thy true disciples and animate me in all things with Thy Spirit.*
>
> *Amen. (Catholic Prayers Online)*

"As always, somehow, someway our group weaves together a beautifully connected meeting from Maureen's opening prayer to Anne's sharing and now to your prayer, Bernie . We are blessed to be Bible Babes."

"But tonight, we were Bible Turkeys," Tek blurted and then Anne and Maureen joined her in gobbling again.

Patti tapped the lamp with her pencil. "Okay, rowdy turkey ladies, wait one minute please. Next week, we're starting at 7 pm, so we can have a little more time for our Christmas party. Claire, Dana, Roxanne, and Bernie, can you please bring a sweet dish to share? Everyone else, bring a salty appetizer. See you next week. I can't believe this year is almost over."

Chapter 38 : Bible Babies – Week Eight

Dana blew out the candle.  Bernie and Roxanne gathered the trash.  Tekla, Anne, and Maureen – the three youngest of the group – made gobble sounds as they walked the turkey walk to their cars.

Claire laughed at the three women romping joyfully through the parking lot.

*I need to feel that kind of joy again.  We only have one more Bible Babes for the year.  After that, I have to show Chet what's in my journal.  God, give me the strength to tell him the truth.*

The next day, Claire reviewed Anne's words and tried to resist feeling too proud for helping her receive the Sacrament of Penance. After a warm cup of tea, she drifted off into a sense of contentment and joy. She could smell roses and baby's breath flowers. After meditation, she opened her eyes. The room had a soft pink glow as the winter sun made its slow dip to the ground. Claire pulled her journal from the drawer.

*The thoughts I had today were not memories from the coma, like the ones before. And yet, they seem to bring closure to some of what I experienced. A delicate figure placed a beautiful baby in my arms - a little girl wrapped in a pale pink blanket. I could feel her tiny arms and legs kicking with total delight. Then, this figure floated to an arch of white flowers and tucked one red rose lovingly inside the pure petals. The little baby girl in my arms yawned and I smelled the fragrant scent of true baby's breath.*

*I think this delicate figure was the guardian angel of the child I was holding. I gently placed the infant back into the angel's arms. A realization of why this baby was in this particular place stunned me. I literally couldn't breathe for a moment when I grasped the fact that this baby had been stripped from her mother's womb on Earth and then tossed into a sink, lifeless and nameless. And yet, as I gazed at her in her angel's arms, she was full of life as if resurrected. She was honored here with the name Mary Grace. Patti's verse from Revelation is fitting for this memory - "He who was seated on the throne said, 'I am making everything new.'*

*God, you are giving me much to consider and I know you won't give me any more than I can handle, but what about Chet? What will he think of all of this?*

By 6 pm on Wednesday, December 10, the snowstorm had subsided, leaving two inches of glistening crystals on the ground. Light flakes danced against the windows of the sunroom, creating a perfect atmosphere as Claire prepared for Bible Babes.

At 6:45 pm she gathered her special materials for the meeting, along with a tray of Christmas cookies. As she carefully steered her car to Angel of God, Claire's cell phone rang.

"Hi, hon. Are you almost home?" she asked Chet,

"No, I'm stuck in traffic. Probably won't be home until 8:30 or later. The roads don't look that bad, but traffic is crawling along at five miles an hour. What's the weather in Hallowed?"

"Looks like the snow has melted on the streets, but the yards have about two inches. I'm on my way to church right now."

"Hey, I thought Bible Babes starts at 7:30. Are you leaving early because of the snow?"

"No, it's our annual Christmas party. We're starting earlier to keep the meeting from running late."

"Sorry, Claire. You're breaking up. Did you say you'd be running late tonight?"

"Can't hear you, hon. Chet? Darn."

Both phones disconnected.

"Doggone cell towers." Guess she'll be late. Maybe that's a good thing. I'll have time to read the journal.

Neither rain nor snow nor sleet could keep Bible Babes from their weekly meetings, especially Christmas party night. Anne and Tekla arrived early to surprise the ladies with a festive room. They moved the cocktail table into the hall, replacing it with a larger foldup one. Anne pulled a tablecloth from a box.

"Tek, help me with this?" They held each of the ends fanning it into the air.

"Wow, Anne, this is beautiful. It looks like someone made it. The poinsettias are exquisite."

"Aren't they? Grandma Combs did all of the needlepoint. It was her wedding gift to us."

Anne slowly moved her hands over the stitching as if absorbing the threads of her life with Jack through the poinsettias.

"I've never been married, Anne. Gosh, I've never even had a date with a man, but I can imagine how much you must miss Jack."

"Thanks. I do miss him and I'm never going to forget him. I've decided to celebrate our life together by using the things that remind me of happy times. That's why I brought this tonight. Our family had Christmas dinner on Grandma's work of art every year."

"Happy memories?"

"Happy memories, Tek. Hey, we better get moving."

Tek strung white lights around the room and then turned off all of the other lighting.

"Oh, Tek, I love the white lights. They make the room glow."

"Yeah, they're my favorite. When I was a little girl, we had the traditional Christmas tree with different colored lights. I loved that, but when we went to Grandma's, I was mesmerized by the winter wonderland she created – white lights on a white tree, white lights on the fireplace mantel; she even had white lights strung in the bathroom. It felt magical."

"That must have been such fun at your Grandma's."

"Georgia and I loved being there with Grandma and Grandpa."

Anne flicked a lighter on the wicks of two white holy candles. The flames illuminated a small wooden manger in the center of the table. The ladies took a step back to take in the subtle elegance of the room. Although from two different worlds, both contributed their gifts of joy from a past Christmas. Anne put her arm around Tekla's shoulder. Tek bristled for a moment, not accustomed to being hugged much by anyone. Then, she relaxed, and was able to accept Anne's gesture as genuine. Both women not only shared joy, but they also shared the painful loss of love.

"Feels magical, Tek."  Tek nodded and turned away to hide a tear.

An onslaught of oohs and aahs flooded the room as the other six Babes trickled in.

Patti giggled.  "Tekla and Annie, this is wonderful.  The white lights look like little angels and where did you get that tablecloth?  It's unbelievable."

Before Anne could answer Tek explained.  "Grandma Combs made it.  She stitched the poinsettias for Jack and Anne when they got married.  This tablecloth has only happy memories – well not for me.  I mean for Anne.  And we're celebrating Jack's life by using it tonight.  Did I get that right, Annie?"

"Absolutely perfect, Tek."

Anne hugged Claire.  "We wanted to surprise everyone.  That's why I told you I had to leave home at 6 to pick-up my appetizer."

"You certainly fooled me.  Great surprise."

Anne clapped her hands.  "Hey, everyone, Tekla hung the lights.  Aren't they lovely?"

Dana, Roxanne, and Bernie walked around the room to give Tekla's contribution special admiration.  Tek beamed as they oohed and aahed even more.  "Her Grandma used to create a winter wonderland at her home during Christmas with a white Christmas tree and white lights everywhere even in the bathroom."

Anne winked at Tek.  Did I get that right, Tek?"

"You did, Miss Annie."

Patti noticed that Maureen was sitting quietly in her chair.  "Are you okay, hon?"

"I think so.  I'm a little uncomfortable and I didn't sleep very well last night.  Sorry, I need to sit, but Tek and Anne, thank you.  I'm feeling the Christmas spirit in here."

"Okay, Babes, let's get our plates filled with all of the goodies.  Maureen, you stay there.  I'll fix a plate for you."

Anne and Tekla carried a punch bowl from the refrigerator and carefully placed it in-between the sweet and salty food.

"Raspberry sherbet punch! You two have outdone yourselves."

Claire was excited about her presentation. The ladies chatted about Christmas shopping and food as they enjoyed their salty creations of shrimp, assorted sandwiches, barbecued meatballs, and Irish, German, and Italian cheeses with the obligatory carrot and celery sticks. Of course, the sweets included a variety of cookies, cream puffs, and Lebkuchen, traditional German cakes that Bernie and Roxanne had baked. Every year, the Babes looked forward to the small, butter-iced cakes that resembled soft gingerbread.

Patti tapped the lamp. Claire, why don't we get started?"

"Okay, here goes. Since this is our last meeting until after Christmas, I've done something a little different. Instead of one person reading the entire scripture, I've prepared an envelope for each of you with one or two verses inside to read." Claire passed around a basket with numbered envelopes. "Not only will this be the reading, but it's also a prayer. Don't open the envelopes yet, okay."

"Do we get a prize?"

"No prizes, Tek, but I think you'll enjoy it."

"Darn."

"When it's your turn, open your envelope, read the verse and then tell us your thoughts. Imagine that you are an observer of the entire event and you are hearing the words in your envelope for the first time."

Dana frowned. "But, Claire, we're not prepared. What if we don't have anything to say? I'm used to writing about the verse the night before I present, not right on the spot."

"Oh, come on, Dana," Roxanne coaxed, "it might be fun."

Bernie added, "And besides, Claire put a lot of effort into this."

Tek smiled at Dana. "Dana, sometimes spontaneous is interesting. If we're always prepared, are we really speaking from our hearts or is it from the logic of our heads? Give it a try, huh?"

Dana sighed, unable to counter Tekla's persuasive words. "Okay, but I have number one and I don't want to be first."

Maureen held her envelope out to Dana.

"I'll switch, Dana. I have number five. I may not make it that long."

"Really? Are you having contractions?"

"Slightly, but I'm fine. I just wanted to be first."

"Okay, then, let's begin with you, Maureen."

Maureen read Luke 1:26-28.

***In the sixth month, the angel Gabriel was sent from God to a town of Galilee called Nazareth, to a virgin betrothed to a man named Joseph, of the house of David, and the virgin's name was Mary. And coming to her, he said, 'Hail, favored one! The Lord is with you.'***

"Surely, Mary had to be confused by this statement from the Angel Gabriel, not to mention being terrified. She must have asked herself, 'why am I the favored one?' Her heart had to be beating very fast and she was probably frozen in place. When she asks Gabriel ***'and how is the Lord with me,'*** I imagine she's frightened knowing that there is no way she could possibly be pregnant. And the part that speaks to me is the fact that she is not married. I was scared when I got pregnant with our first son, Mikah, but I knew how I got pregnant and I certainly wasn't God's favored one. I hate to admit this, but I did consider abortion."

Claire noticed that Anne moved her head up and down gently. Her eyes teared up, but her expression was clearly one of compassion and understanding for Maureen.

"Then my wonderful boyfriend who became my incredible husband insisted that we marry. It was hard on our parents at first, but having Mikah was one of the most wonderful things that ever happened to our family. And now, three boys later and hopefully, a little girl on the way, we are blessed. I'm glad I accepted God's gift of life. Is that okay, Claire? That's what I envision at this point of the reading."

"That's exactly the kind of insight I hoped to hear. Next?"

Roxanne read Luke 1:29-30.

*But she was greatly troubled at what was said and pondered what sort of greeting this might be. Then the angel said to her, 'Do not be afraid, Mary, for you have found favor with God.'*

I've read Luke's entire narrative many times during advent, but I realized tonight that Gabriel has spoken a version of the word favor two times so far. There must be some significance. I like that he's slowing-down her heartbeat calming Mary's fear, but I'm drawn to the words favored and favor. Someone who is favored has been chosen or privileged. I think 'found favor with God' means that she is His preference. There are many choices we make that bear fruit years later, sometimes in mysterious ways. When Aunt CiCi brought Arthur to America, she had no way of knowing what the future held. She never married. Although the sorrow of losing her sister and brother-in-law remained with her till the day she died, Aunt CiCi was blessed with their child. I was blessed by marrying Arthur. Anyway, that's what I'm seeing. Number three?"

Patti read Luke 1:31-32.

*Behold, you will conceive in your womb and bear a son, and you shall name Him Jesus. He will be great and will be called Son of the Most High, and the Lord God will give Him the throne of David his father, and He will rule over the house of Jacob forever, and of His kingdom there will be no end.*

"Wow, this one is packed full of Old Testament promises being fulfilled. It's as though God told Gabriel, 'Gabe, make sure she's calmed down from the initial shock of seeing you and then without taking a breath, tell her she will bear Jesus, Son of the Most High.' This is one of the moments in the Bible when the new covenant is revealed. If we believe that the prophecies are true leading up to the birth of Jesus, then we must also believe the teachings of the New Testament, especially resurrection and the coming of Christ again. I love doing it this way, Claire. Number four?"

Bernie read Luke 1:33-35.

*But Mary said to the angel, 'How can this be, since I have no relations with a man?' And the angel said to her in reply, 'The Holy Spirit will come upon you, and the power of the Most High will overshadow you. Therefore the child to be born will be called holy, the Son of God.'*

Mary believes this is impossible since she has had no relations with a man. But Gabriel is ready for her reaction and says, 'The Holy Spirit will come upon you, and the power of the Most High will overshadow you. Therefore the child to be born will be called holy, the Son of God.' Now that probably got her heart beating very fast again. I think I would have started running away by then. Thank God that Mary did not run. How would we react if God asked us to do something that terrified us? I'm not sure I'd have Mary's courage. Number five?"

Dana read Luke: 1-36-38

*And behold, Elizabeth, your relative, has also conceived a son in her old age, and this is the sixth month for her who was called barren; for nothing will be impossible for God. Mary said, 'Behold, I am the handmaid of the Lord. May it be done to me according to your Word.' Then the angel departed from her.*

Claire held her breath waiting for Dana to speak, hoping she would not create another stir about tonight's method. Dana closed her eyes, sighed deeply in thought and finally shared her reflection.

"At this point, I think Mary started to understand the magnitude of Gabriel's message. She was very close to Elizabeth and surely had heard her talk with her own mother, Anne, about wanting a child. With Mary's acceptance that '…nothing will be impossible for God,' she humbly yields to God's word, to God's will. I wish I could have that kind of total surrender to the will of God. I should read this more often."

"See, Dana, I told you so. Don't you love the spontaneity?"

"I wouldn't go that far, Tekla, but it has its benefits. Number six?"

Tekla read Luke 1:39-42

*During those days Mary set out and traveled to the hill country in haste to a town of Judah, where she entered the house of Zechariah and greeted Elizabeth. When Elizabeth heard Mary's greeting, the infant leaped in her womb, and Elizabeth, filled with the Holy Spirit, cried out in a loud voice and said, 'Most blessed are you among women, and blessed is the fruit of your womb.'*

Now I get it, Claire. We have the first half of the Hail Mary Prayer. There are naysayers, who do not believe in honoring the Mother of Jesus, but here we have it right in the Bible, 'Most blessed are you among women, and blessed is the fruit of your womb.' I can picture Mary and Elizabeth laughing over a cup of tea. I think

Mary was still a wee bit worried about telling her parents she was pregnant, especially back in the day of stoning women. I can also picture her asking Elizabeth for advice. You know what I really like are the words 'the infant leaped in her womb.' What's it feel like, Maureen? You've got one leaping in your belly right now."

"Yes, I do, Tek. I like those words, too. It reminds me of being pregnant with each of my boys and now this one. It's incredible to feel that new life."

"Not any life, Maureen. Your babies and all babies are made in the image and likeness of God."

"Very true. Anyway, you're right, Tek. I love the idea of Elizabeth's baby leaping in her womb."

"I think everyone here except me has had a baby. It must be an awesome experience. A miracle. Something I'll never experience, but maybe I can visit and hold your baby one day, Maureen?"

"Definitely."

"Thanks. Oh, number seven."

Anne experienced that pang of guilt about the abortion, but she remembered Fr. Hernandez' words, 'Let it go because God now lets it go.'

Then, she read Luke 1:43-45

***'And how does this happen to me that the mother of my Lord should come to me? For at the moment the sound of your greeting reached my ears, the infant in my womb leaped for joy.' Blessed are you who believed that what was spoken to you by the Lord would be fulfilled.***

Anne avoided discussion of "the infant in my womb leaped for joy." She knew it would be too painful for her to say those words again. Instead, she emphasized "Blessed are you who believed that what was spoken to you by the Lord would be fulfilled."

"Many times scripture brings us to a new understanding of faith, as this one does. I'm in awe of the fact that it's been hundreds of years of Jewish history from Abraham to Moses to Jacob to Joseph, waiting for the Messiah. And here, in this one moment in time, in this Immaculate Conception, the world begins a new journey in faith. I sincerely feel that I have also begun a new journey in faith through the sacraments of reconciliation and the Eucharist."

Anne noticed that both Tekla and Bernie fidgeted when she mentioned reconciliation, as they had done when she talked about it a few weeks ago. Claire saw an impish smile on Anne's face as if she were channeling a message to her.

*It's my turn, my friend, to speak the truth about our Faith no matter how uncomfortable it makes others feel."*

*Keep it up, Annie. I may need your help in bolstering my own faith.*

"In this reading we are witnesses to the fulfillment of all of scripture up to this time. And yet it's only the beginning of the journey of faith, a new covenant with God for all of us. Even today God still wants us to believe that what he has spoken continues to be fulfilled. That's the last verse about the Angel Gabriel. Is there a number 8, Claire?"

"Yes, but it's not from the Bible, yet it is a comforting part of the Hail Mary Prayer.

**Holy Mary, Mother of God, pray for us sinners now and at the hour of our death.**

The first half of the Hail Mary comes from scripture, allowing us to know the extraordinary union that exists between Mary and God and the Holy Spirit to bring Jesus the Savior into the world. Of course, I want Mary to intercede for me with her son and believe me, I said this prayer over and over in my mind when I was in the coma because I could feel my body slipping away. I believed I was dying. Each time I said the Hail Mary, a serene awareness of life and hope flooded over me, even though I was unconscious."

"It's amazing to me, Claire, that in a comatose state, you still recited the Hail Mary, but I didn't realize the last sentence in the prayer is not in the Bible. Who wrote it?"

"Good question, Dana. I attended a retreat once where the priest explained the second half of the Hail Mary. I was in high school and we were questioning why it was a part of it, since it was not a Biblical reference. He enlightened us that sometime

317

around the Council of Trent in the 1500's, this sentence was added. I'm not sure why, but it was added."

Roxanne hesitated to tell yet another story about her life, but Bernie encouraged her with a wink. "When I converted from the Baptist religion, my first hurdle was the fact that I did not understand why Catholics prayed to the saints and to the Blessed Mother. At one of my classes on Catholicism, an old German priest, Father Gustavson, asked me, 'Roxanne, I've noticed that every time we meet, you have a questioning look on your face. What's bothering you?' I was shy, but I mustered the courage to ask, 'Why do Catholics pray to saints and to Mary? I was taught we only need to pray to Jesus, our Savior.' He paused for a moment and then asked me a question. 'Roxanne, every week when I walk you to the door to leave, you ask me to pray for you, don't you?' 'Yes, of course, Father. I'm struggling with pieces of the Catholic faith, but I believe you are a holy man and that your prayers will help.' 'Aah, am I Jesus? No, I'm not, but when you ask me to pray for you, you are not asking to pray to me, right?' 'That's true, Father.' 'It's the same when we pray to the saints and to the Blessed Mother. We know they are not God, but we ask them to intercede for us. If we are willing to ask people on Earth to pray for us, why would we not want to ask the angels and saints and Mary in heaven to pray for us?' Oh my goodness, that was the best explanation I had ever heard. From that moment on I couldn't wait to be saturated completely in the teachings of the Catholic Church. Sorry to take up your time, Claire."

"That was great, Roxanne. Your experience of converting to Catholicism has far more impact than anything I could say."

"I went twelve years to Catholic schools and the religion classes were good, but when I was young, I didn't absorb all of it."

"Same here, Dana. One of the best things I did was become a sponsor for a friend of mine. Our group met every Sunday for seven months. These sessions covered the history and teachings of Catholicism. Then, a priest or nun would talk to the group and we had rousing discussions. It gave me a deeper understanding of what I had learned in school. It's a huge time commitment, but well worth it."

"Who did you sponsor, Bernie?"

Roxanne laughed and patted Bernie on the knee. "Who do you think, Dana?"

"Oh, I should have guessed that."

As usual, the Babes started gathering their purses and Bibles in anticipation of the meeting's end.

"Good discussion tonight. Claire, is there anything else you want to add?"

"There is one thing I want to mention. No one is sure who wrote this last line of the prayer, but notice that we ask the Blessed Mother to 'pray for us sinners,' not 'those' sinners. We are all sinners. I take comfort in the blessing that we have others praying to God for us on earth and in Heaven. In any event, I chose to do it this way tonight because I believe that each line of Luke's story is rich with faith, and hope, and love. After all, that's what Advent is about. Everyone shared great insights. Thank you. That's it. Merry Christmas to all and to all a good night!"

"My goodness, we did that quickly. How did that happen?"

"Most of the food's gone, too. I guess the party's over."

Dana said the closing prayer of the final Bible Babes' meeting for 2010.

*Dear Father in Heaven, thank you for our voyage of faith this year. Guide us in our prayer journey to Christmas and help us to do your will as Mary did. Watch over Maureen and her baby. If it's Your will, please bring that little one before Christmas as she has requested. And Lord, keep all of these women and their families in the palm of Your hand through this season. We thank you for our many blessings and humbly ask that You bring us back together in January. Let's pray the Hail Mary together.*
*Hail Mary, full of grace*
*The Lord is with thee*
*Blessed art thou amongst women,*
*And Blessed is the Fruit of thy womb, Jesus,*
*Holy Mary, Mother of God, pray for us sinners*
*Now and at the hour of our death. Amen.*

After cleanup ritual, Patti concluded, "Okay, ladies, that's it until next year. Have a blessed Christmas!"

---

2010 had held moments of fear and anger and of joy and forgiveness for the Bible Babes. Newest member, Maureen, felt safe to reveal having an out-of-wedlock baby at the young age of seventeen. This opened the hearts of all the ladies with admiration of one so young who chose life. Roxanne's heart-wrenching story of Arthur's escape from Nazi Germany infused everyone with a new awareness and appreciation of freedom. As always, Patti and Dana were an inspiration by merely coming to the weekly meetings, bearing their loss of loved ones with dignity and yet willing to share their life-changing stories. Bernie's down-to-earth view of the world served as the group's common sense anchor. Her bond with Roxanne provided a model of love and loyalty of two friends. When Tekla admitted she was bi-polar, it was no surprise to the Babes. Yet, it seemed to free her to share more of her past with the group. Anne felt new joy after going to confession, gradually rising to genuine enjoyment of life once again. However, Claire held obscure memories close to her heart; not even Anne was aware of the mystery. Bible Babes would resume in January 2011. The Babes created an atmosphere that made their meetings a safe haven for sharing core beliefs and human frailty.

---

Claire attempted to call Chet on her way home, but gave up after three tries. *Either his phone died or it still isn't working. I hope he's home by now.* Chet had arrived home at 8:15, about the time Bible Babes was concluding. He grabbed a beer and made a ham sandwich for dinner in the sunroom. As he ate, he read Claire's latest entry.

*Finally, something that might bring closure to this.*

He read further, realizing that this was anything but closure.

*Now, she's imagining seeing angels and holding a newborn. Roses tucked in an arch of white flowers. What next? She seems to be in a place where angels hold aborted babies. This is different, though. This time she knows the baby's name – Mary Grace. I guess the angel told her. What am I going to do?*

Chet had only begun to read the last paragraph when he heard the garage door open. Within a few minutes, Claire turned the knob of the side door. "Hey, Chet, can you help me?"

"Sure, I'll be right there." Chet swallowed a bit of the ham sandwich and pushed the journal into the drawer.

"Can you take the cookie tray for me?"

"Sure.  Gee, three crumbled cookies left."

"You know I have more.  They're in the plastic container in the cupboard.  Did you have dinner?"

"Eating a ham sandwich now."

Claire tossed her coat on the kitchen chair and put her hands on Chet's cheeks.  "Cold out there."

"I thought you said you'd be late when we talked on the phone."

"No, I didn't say that.  Oh, I said we were starting Bible Babes early so we wouldn't run late tonight.  The cells were breaking up.  You probably only heard the words run late."

"Let's sit on the couch in the living room.  I'll bring a glass of wine to you."  Chet was nervous as he poured the chardonnay.

*Damn, did I close the drawer?  Stay in the living room, Claire, please.*

As Chet drew closer to the Monet, he could see Claire's reflection in a window of the sunroom.  She sat upright in a chair holding her journal.  "Hey, babe, here's the wine.  What's that book you have?"

Claire accepted the wine and then stared at Chet with cold eyes.  "You've been reading this, haven't you?"  Chet didn't answer.  "Don't deny it!"  Claire held up a string of ham fat.  "See this?"

"Yeah."

"Do you always use ham fat as a bookmark?"  Claire opened the journal to the entry that Chet had been reading.  She pointed to the grease stain on the page.

Chet started laughing.  "Okay, I'm smoked, Sherlock."  Then, he laughed some more.  Claire was not amused.

"Stop acting like it's not important.  You invaded my space.  Even in the front of the journal it has gold lettering that says 'For My Eyes Only.'  What gives you the right?"

"I'm sorry, Claire. I won't do it again."

"Have you read other parts of it?"

"What if I have, Claire?"

"I'll tell you what. It's none of your business."

Chet yelled, "What do you mean it's none of my business? It's not every day that your wife survives a coma and then starts remembering weird stories about hell and angels and aborted babies? Darn right I read it – from beginning to end."

"That's it, I'm going to bed. I'm furious at you. I don't want to talk to you anymore. I can't be around you tonight."

"Yeah, that really solves things. Always backing away, Claire. Maybe I wouldn't have to read your journal if you would tell me what's going on."

"When I've told you in the past what's going on, you do just what you did tonight. You either laugh to minimize my concerns or you get angry. I planned to share all of this with you, but when I wanted to share it. I can't – repeat – can't trust you. Good night. I'm sleeping in Jeannie's room." With journal in hand, Claire stomped up the stairs and slammed the door to Jeannie's room.

Chet sighed and whispered, "G'night." He tossed and turned alone in their bed. Claire sniffled as she lay on her left side of the bed in Jeannie's room. Both of them stared at the sky. The full winter moon's beams sparkled on the remaining snow in the yard. Dark clouds periodically drifted past, disappearing forever into that night. Claire and Chet knew the swirl of anger would also pass into that night. After a half hour Claire entered their bedroom and fell asleep next to Chet.

# CHAPTER 41 : AFTER THE CLOUDS DISAPPEAR

Claire awoke to the smell of coffee. She considered staying in bed so she would not have to confront Chet about the journal, but when she sat up, he was placing a cup of coffee on her side table.

"Good morning, my queen. Would you like a piece of toast?"

"No, thank you. Coffee's fine. To what do I owe this attention – guilt?"

Chet sat on the bed. "Guilt, remorse, conscience. Take your pick. You already sentenced me to sleeping alone."

"I was only in Jeannie's room a half hour. You were still awake when I came in."

"Okay, let's face it. You have a right to be angry with me for reading your personal journal. Now, let me ask you. Do I have a right to be worried about you? The last time you discussed any of this with me was weeks ago, right before you visited Dr. McDaniel. I intended to read a few sentences of the journal, but it only made me want to read more. Then, when I discover that these are not dreams, but memories, what am I suppose to think, Claire? My wife traveled to Oz and back and remembers things that are really strange."

Claire was silent. She placed the cup on the saucer and then held Chet's hand. "I see your point. I still wish you had asked me to read it."

"Would you have said yes?"

"No, but at least I would have been asked. Anyway, Pandora's box is open. Now what?"

"Well, I have to leave for work soon, but I didn't want to go if you're still mad at me."

"I'm not mad, Chet. There's a part of me that understands why you did it. There's even a part of me that's relieved. Any chance of coming home early tonight?"

"I have a 2 pm meeting, but after that I can leave. I could be home by 4. What's on your mind?"

"The journal. What else? You have to get to work. It's going to take time to wade through weeks of journaling and Bible Babes and the coma. I don't think we should rush."

"I agree.  Okay, 4 o'clock it is.  See you then, babe."

"See you.  Drive carefully.  Love you."

"Love you, too."

Claire felt a great weight had been lifted.  She was glad she could now discuss all of it with Chet.

Sometimes, meditation gave Claire comfort; sometimes she experienced only disturbing visions. Since the coma, or maybe because of the coma, she felt compelled to be especially attentive to her surroundings. The journaling helped her to sort through her thoughts in a way she had never done before. It allowed her to gain clarity about many things – the dreams, the questions, and especially the subtle insight she heard from Bible Babes.

*I may as well meditate and write an entry today to get it up-to-date for tonight. Chet looked really worried and I am, too.*

She went downstairs, poured another cup of coffee, and sat in the sunroom recliner.

Before she began her meditation, Claire wrote in her journal:

*I'm afraid of what I see and feel during meditation; yet I believe the Holy Spirit is guiding me.*

*Holy Spirit, please continue to reveal to me what I am to do with all of this. As we read the journal this evening, please give us guidance and insight. Amen*

The meditation session that day was unsettling. Claire began her deep breathing. Then, she said the Hail Mary, pondering what each of the women had shared on Wednesday. During this meditation she fell asleep and entered the world of the chambers once again. The horror of Hell slipped in and out of her dream. Claire was awakened by the sound of her own voice desperately reciting the Hail Mary.

*Stop. Stop. I can't take anymore. It's too much horror. She took a sip of her coffee, but it was cold. Yuck, I thought I just poured it. Claire stared at the clock. What time did Chet leave for work? 7:30. That was two and a half hours ago.*

Her neck was damp with sweat and tears streamed down her face, drained and unnerved by all that she had remembered. She knew she had to write about it, but multiple scenes flashed inside her head.

*I'll never be able to remember everything I saw today. It's too massive.*

After showering and dressing, Claire felt reasonably normal. Still the images haunted her. She fixed another pot of coffee and stared at the bare trees in the yard. Most of the snow had melted, leaving only deer tracks filled with muddy water.

Questions as murky as the puddles nagged at her. What she experienced in the coma was repeated week after week in Bible Babes. She simply could not explain how the Babes had chosen the same scripture readings she had seen and read in the coma. And, why did they choose them?

Claire knew she did not have the wherewithal to sort through today's meditation, but she had a crystal clear sense of the overall theme. She opened the journal to make an entry, hoping she could capture the chilling images circling round and round in her head. She tried several times to write a chronological description, but tore page after page from the journal. After forty-five minutes, calmness surrounded Claire and she wrote a poem that she called 'Chambers.' When she was finished, her angst had been partly swept away. She loaded the dishwasher and then prepared dinner.

Claire instinctively knew that what she experienced at Bible Babes and during meditation were linked to memories that happened in the coma. She no longer wanted to refer to any of this as a dream. These encounters were not fanciful imps floating inside her head, telling her bizarre stories. These occurrences were not portending predictions and they were not remnants of the medication.

*I can't deny it any longer. During the coma I went to Heaven and I went to Hell and back. I guess it really is time to discuss all of this with Chet.*

After dinner, Chet and Claire sat in the sunroom. Mid-December weather was unseasonably warm, so Chet opened a window halfway. As the bare limbs of trees swayed, a refreshing stream of air filled the room, a perfect setting for a much-needed discussion.

Claire pulled the journal from the drawer and sat next to Chet on the wicker love seat.

"Okay, are you ready for this?"

"I think so. What's the plan?"

"Let's read the journal together and maybe we can figure out what it all means."

"You started the journal after the fourth meeting, right?"

"Yes, but something you may not fully understand by reading the journal is that Bible Babes' scripture readings were the same verses that I read during the coma. Sometimes, even the prayers matched the prayers I said in the coma. And I haven't even written everything that happened."

"So, not all of it is in the journal?"

"Exactly and that's why I wanted to read the journal with you. I'll fill in the gaps. I can tell you this with certainty, though. Whether it was a prayer, or a reading, or a coma memory, everything intersected in the past five months. Remember, I did tell you about what happened the first three Wednesdays."

"I remember--the Angel of God prayer and someone chasing you through a tunnel. Jacob's ladder and you ride up an escalator. And, the third one. Hmmmm…oh, yeah…the woman who was bleeding and Jesus healed her. You said you didn't have that kind of faith and that you didn't want to be there."

"Very good. Now, let's go to the journal. If you have questions, that's fine, but please don't be condescending."

"Okay, let's get started."

Claire opened the journal for Bible Babes' week four. They read in silence. After reading a few sentences Chet asked, "You say you are not just observing; you're in the middle of all this.  Does that mean that the day you had this meditation, you were actually there?"

"No.  That's a good question.  Everything I told you about the first three weeks and everything I've written in the journal are memories, and they are very vivid.  The events happened in the past during the coma."

"But, when you meditate, you actually see things like angels holding babies?"

"Yes, I do. I can't explain how, but I do.  Let's read week five."

"Claire, I have to tell you.  I laughed when I read that you could march into Hell.  Really?  C'mon, Claire."

"We can end this right now, if you're going to be patronizing.  Make a decision."

"Sorry."

"Chet, you have a superior attitude about your Faith, as if you and only you really gets it about God.  With God, all things are possible.  I think He made it possible for me to see Heaven and Hell and I'm pretty sure He has a good reason."

"I said I'm sorry."  Chet changed the subject.  "What was Roxanne right about?"

"Roxanne told us about Nazi Germany.  Her husband's parents died at Auschwitz and his mother's sister brought Arthur to America when he was only eleven months old.  If there was ever a time when demons roamed the Earth, Nazi Germany is it."

"And you were willing to walk into Hell, Claire?"

Claire opened her eyes wide and frowned.  "Don't look at me that way.  I'm sincere.  I want to know if you were willing to walk into Hell, like you wrote?"

"I wasn't as willing as I wrote in my journal, but I knew that if I did I would be protected.  Week six."

Chet sat up straight.  "This one made the hair on my arms stand at attention."

Claire playfully punched Chet's arm.  "Serves you right for reading it without my permission."

"Now, who's being patronizing?"

Chapter 43 : Hindsight and Insight

"Touché. Anyway, I told you that each week in Bible Study the readings matched ones that were in the coma, but it didn't register with me right away. When I meditated the next day, it dawned on me that Maureen's reading from Wednesday was part of my meditation and was part of my coma. The telltale trickle of sweat rolled down my back."

Chet pointed to one of the sentences.

"What do you mean you were sitting in a movie theater? That seems odd."

"It was strange sitting in a movie theater of old. You know, like the old Elston movie theater with reel to reel film and the people I see on the screen are telling a story. An eerie part is that before they say something, I already know it."

"You knew Angela was pregnant and was going to get an abortion?"

"Yes, and I knew Jared was lying to her. The most awful scene was seeing Angela in Hell. Well, the rest is my commentary on the why of all of this."

"Claire, at the risk of making you angry, why you?"

"You mean, why not you?"

"No, I don't. Really, I mean why you? Even if this is all true, what did God tell you to do with what you saw?"

"What do you mean even if this is all true?"

"You realize all of this is a dream – whether you're in the coma, at the Bible Study group, or meditating? You may have ascended to a heavenly place, and even descended to a dark place, but you were and you are dreaming, Claire! Dr. McDaniel said sometimes there are permanent aberrations in memory. You might be confusing reality with fantasy."

"Then, how do you explain how the readings and the prayers in Bible Study are the same ones I dreamed in the coma?"

"I don't know, Claire. Maybe, none of this happened in the coma. And then, during Bible Babes, you sort of did a backward memory flip and inserted the prayers and the readings retroactively into the coma dream."

"Wow, that's a brilliant convoluted explanation. Retroactive dreaming? All I know is that I experienced everything in this journal and more. One moment I was reveling in a heavenly place and the next moment I was falling very fast to a dark place. And it wasn't a dream."

"Claire, when I read this stuff, my heart starts palpitating and my stomach churns. I'm trying to believe you, but it's bizarre. It's out of this world, hon."

"Wasn't your experience in Dallas, Texas thirty-five years ago out of this world, also? Did I make fun of you or tell you that what took place at the airport was all in your imagination? No. I stood by you. I expect you to have the moral courage to support me in this. Do you think I like remembering this stuff? Do you think I enjoyed my visit to Hell?" Claire walked to the wall by the fireplace straightening the Monet painting that Jeannie had given them.

Chet joined her. "'From Monet's Garden at Argenteuil to your Garden at Hallowed Haven.' We have great kids. Let's take a break."

"Aaaah! You are frustrating and inconsistent. Just never mind!" Claire walked briskly to the kitchen, then, a minute later peeked out the entryway. "Want a snack?"As she turned from the refrigerator she was face to face with Chet. "Wow, did you fly in here?"

"On Angels' wings."

"I mean it, mister. Don't start with the sarcasm."

Chet hugged Claire. "Hey, you know how I am. My fear gets the better of me sometimes. I'm working on it. Hang in there with me."

Claire laughed. "I'll hang in there, but a few minutes ago, I really wanted to hang you by your ears right next to the Monet." She poked Chet in the chest with her index finger five times, the same way she did to Jeff when he aggravated her. "Have faith the size of a mustard seed and nothing will be impossible. Nothing is impossible with God. Let's split a beer."

"I'm hungry. How about that snack?"

"You want cheddar or Swiss?"

"Both."

"Would you get the wheat thins please?  Has Jeannie called you recently to spy on me?"

"We talked this morning, but she's worrying less and less about you."

"Good, let's keep it that way.  What you and I discuss about the journal is for our ears only.  Got it?"

"Aye, aye, captain."

"Did she say when she'd be home for Christmas?"

"She said December 23$^{rd}$.  No, maybe it's December 22$^{nd}$.  I can't remember. You better call her."

"I'll give her a ring in the morning.  I'm calling Jeff, too.  His last day is Friday, the seventeenth."

"I'll mark my calendar.  When you talk to him, ask him what time for pickup."

"Okay.  Hey, why don't I meet you in town tomorrow night?  We can have our annual Brandy Alexander and do a little Christmas shopping for the kids.  What do you think?"

"Sounds good.  Let's meet at the Netherland at 6 pm."

"Aah, I like that.  Their decorations are the best.  I forgot to tell you, Anne and Kevin are going to Houston for Christmas.  They're staying with Anne's oldest brother, Fulton and his family.  I think he has a daughter about Kev's age and four older sons."

"Any of Anne's other brothers coming?"

"Not for Christmas.  Anne said they're having a family reunion on December 28, so I imagine the rest of them will be there.  With seven siblings in the Madison clan, they must have twenty or more nieces and nephews."

"That will be good for both of them.  And, honestly, I'm glad it's just going to be us on Christmas Eve.  I love Annie, but it's been a drain on all of us since Jack died."

"Tell me about it. On top of going through these unsettling memories, I've had to deal with Anne sliding down into her own special Hell. I was at my wits end trying to help her, but she's back to being herself, only a better version. She's more accepting. You should see her at Bible Babes. She used to complain about Tekla all the time, but last night she and Tek decorated the room for our Christmas party."

"I've seen her in church on Sundays lately. That's a change. Jack used to have to drag her on Sundays. You brought her out of her dangerous stupor. She looked tortured underneath all that makeup."

"The abortion tortured both Anne and her baby. It wasn't easy, but I did get her to meet with Father Hernandez. Then, he somehow encouraged her to confess her sins."

"Actually, it was God the Father, God the Son, and God the Holy Spirit who performed that miracle."

"That's the truth. Annie will still have ups and downs, but she's moving forward. What a relief."

"It's good she'll be with her family on Christmas."

"Well, speaking of torture, let's continue with the journal."

"Oh, hon, it's not torture. I'm burning off time in purgatory."

"Ha, ha. C'mon, sinner man."

Claire opened the journal to week six.

"Why is this one short?"

"That was the day Anne came to our home. She was a wreck physically and mentally. I could barely understand what she was saying through all her hysterical rant."

"Oh, yeah, I forgot it was that particular day. What was the funny story about you and Patti and Sister Veronica?"

"We talked about our second grade experience with Sister Veronica. Patti and I would trade candy back and forth while Sister was teaching Bible stories."

"Wow, you and Patti were soooo bad and wild."

Chapter 44 : Reveal and Clarify

"You were probably rolling houses with toilet paper by the time you were seven."

"We thought it was funny. You had to be there. Let's move on."

"Don't go to the next entry yet. There are only a few sentences in this one, but I think it's important that you are concerned about the dark verses. You wrote, 'Today was particularly frightening. All I could think about was the verse...***Depart from me, you accursed into the eternal fire prepared for the devil and his angels.'*** It does seem that Bible Babes have focused on gloomy scripture this year. Why?"

"The only explanation I can think of is that the Holy Spirit is guiding me through the coma and meditation and Bible Babes. Do you think that's possible?"

He caught her face out of the corner of his eye. He could see how anxious she was for him to give better support. Chet refrained from a cynical comment, softening his tone. "Claire, it must have been really scary for you in the coma. Who knows, maybe the drugs are the cause."

"Dr. McDaniel says no. Chet, I'm confused that the women in Bible Babes keep bringing the same lines of scripture to share that I read in the coma. Not only that, in the nine years that we have been meeting, we've rarely chosen verses about Hell or Satan. Why this year?"

"Don't know, Claire. You may not ever be able to wrap this in a neat package of understanding, but I could be more supportive. I'm going to stop being a naysayer at every turn. I will try to accept it for what you believe it to be."

"That helps. It's eight o'clock, but I want to finish this tonight. At least, let's read the remaining entries."

"I'm on board, hon. I promise, I won't be countering every line. Looks like you had time to really write on week seven."

Chet put his arm around Claire as they slowly read the journal entries for week number seven and eight. Periodically, he would point to certain parts of her journal and then cast an empathetic look her way. She leaned into him. Although tentative, Chet's acceptance of her secret fortified her.

After finishing week eight's entry, Chet closed the journal. He kissed her on her temple and tapped her arm. "Here's what I think, Claire. Somehow, you lived through very frightening experiences when you were in the coma, but you also were able to see beautiful events. You believe and now I promise to work on believing that these occurrences are real. I don't know how they're real, but I admit your account sounds authentic. God wants you to do something. You're not sure what that is, but you have a sense that the Holy Spirit will reveal and clarify. Am I right so far?"

"That's good. Keep going."

"You have many entities protecting you – your Guardian Angel, the Holy Spirit, St. Michael the Archangel, and the Blessed Mother. Whether it's a demon or an evil entity, you will be shielded from danger. On top of that you held a newborn infant, one who had been aborted and you know that her name is Mary Grace. I think that sums it up pretty well. The only piece missing is the why of it."

"I love when you use that incredible analytical mind of yours. And you are correct. The 'why of it' is missing. There's another part you need to know. I wrote it today."

"Let me read it, Claire?"

"In a minute. Let me explain something about the Hell I walked through. My Guardian Angel told me that I would see a very specific part of Hell."

Chet winched, bracing himself for the story. "Go on, hon. It's okay."

"The Hell that God wanted me to see is divided into three chambers. The first one is called Chamber Dark, the least punishing, but still a part of Hell. Angela, the young girl I wrote about in week five, is there. It was hard for me to accept that Angela had not asked God to forgive her during her entire life, even at the time of death. There were things I understood implicitly and this was one of them. God is a forgiving God, but he wants us to acknowledge our sins. We must ask to be forgiven. I can still see her beautiful face morphing into a gruesome distortion of a human being."

"Maybe you've already done what God wants you to do by getting Anne to confession. It's all about saving one soul at a time, isn't it?"

Chapter 44 : Reveal and Clarify

"You're right, but my gut tells me that it's something else, something beyond that. Maybe my pride is telling me I'm going to do this great thing for God. For Claire Dillon McCormack, it has to be bigger than saving one soul. I don't know. See how twisted and thorny this is? It's not a clear path."

"Hon, maybe it will become better defined as we talk about it together."

"Tonight has helped, especially now."

"Good, let's keep going. Things have been revealed to you, Claire. God is not going to desert you. Somehow, some way your mission will be clarified."

"By whom or what?"

"The Holy Spirit. Who else?"

"That's comforting. In fact, from now on, I'm going to refer to this journey as Holy Spirit Mission."

"Sounds more uplifting than dark chambers. By the way, are we finished with Chamber Dark?"

"Yes. Here's a distressing story. One thing that shocked me was seeing a priest in Hell."

"Really? In the same chamber as Angela?"

"No, not in Chamber Dark. Again, I'm looking at a reel to reel film of part of his life. I even knew his name – Father Mallory. My understanding of this place was that it held a larger number of lost souls than Chamber Dark. It was called Chamber Darker and the intensity of suffering multiplied. Father Mallory was there for one reason. It was true that he had been a kind person who championed the poor. In his view, he shepherded his flock of parishioners and taught them about God's love. However, in God's eyes, he had committed the grievous sin of omission by denying, avoiding, or omitting the truth about abortion. He failed to preach that a person involved in abortion in any capacity could lose his or her immortal soul. God judged Father Mallory to be derelict in his duties as a priestly descendent of the apostles. As a consequence of denying the truth about abortion, many souls were lost, including his."

"Another one of your implicit insights. Wow, a priest in Hell. It's hard to picture that. You can think you're a really good person and you'll get into Heaven. Then this priest ends up in Hell for what he didn't do."

"Isn't that what happened in Nazi Germany? The people who knew about the death camps and all the other atrocities. They did nothing to stop the Holocaust. They were as guilty as the prison guards. I literally felt sick to my stomach when I saw his life on the screen. However, there were all kinds of people in this darker room – lawmakers, rabbis, ministers, kings and queens, people rich and people poor. Actually, it was evident that not one of these residents had ever physically been involved in an abortion. They were condemned to Chamber Darker because they were abortion enablers on Earth. They ended up in Chamber Darker because they lied to themselves about their culpability."

"The third one must be Chamber Darkest."

"Oh, yes. In the coma, it was in the darkest, most evil place I have ever seen. All of the residents were abortionists."

"All of the residents, as you call them, were abortionists?"

"All of them! I discovered that anyone who had blood on his or her hands from an aborted baby would not be saved. They condemned themselves to Chamber Darkest, unless they asked to be forgiven."

"Of course, God forgives the worst of the worst. You and I both know that. Like the other chambers, I saw a sort of film version of one doctor's journey to Gehenna. His is a tale of greed leading to despair. He lost his wife and children and his soul. It was the darkest of chambers, but had the fewest members. The suffering was obviously more severe than the other chambers. Do you remember in high school Fr. Leonard said Hell could very well contain varying degrees of torment?"

"I kind of remember that. He always had an interesting way of presenting the truth. So, basically, this place was not Hell in its entirety?"

"That was my impression. There has to be a place for murderers and child molesters, but it wasn't in this part of Hell. And remember, no one would be in any of the chambers or in any part of Hell if they asked God to forgive them."

"Chamber Darkest was reserved for the worst of the worst?"

Chapter 44 : Reveal and Clarify

"Yes, it had a putrid odor, snakes everywhere, and demons with yellow eyes. I know it sounds like a science fiction movie, but it was more gruesome than any of those crazy films I've seen with Jeff. I was afraid, but amazingly felt safe."

"What strikes me, Claire, is the churning that was going on in your mind between babies and chambers. You tossed and turned during the coma, sometimes for hours. Then there were moments when you would rest peacefully. It seems to match what was happening to you."

"Back and forth I went from the breath of babies to the depths of the chambers. Then, the scripture verses were repeated to me in meditation and in Bible Babes. It became obvious that the chambers, the angels, the babies – all centered on new life and lost souls."

"Don't you see, Claire? This is part of the clarification. God only wanted you to see a very specific area of Hell. Each chamber only had stories of souls connected to the sin of abortion. And I agree with you about saving Anne. What you did was important, but I think there's something else here."

"I guess that's what I was trying to say before. If it was only about getting Anne to confession, Chamber Dark would have been enough to put a fire under me."

"Did you have to use that word?"

"You never miss a beat. Okay, it inspired me to help Anne. There's a strong possibility that I saw Chamber Dark to help me guide Anne. We still have to face the challenge of unraveling Chamber Darker and Chamber Darkest. Not an easy task."

"Back to the journal and Bible Babes. Did you ever get away from all the verses about Satan and Hell? Cheese and crackers, you ladies are meeting right before Christmas, and instead of reading about the coming of Jesus, you're talking about Hell?"

"That's what I said before, Chet. In nine years, we rarely talked about Hell until this year. To answer your question, we got away from the topic here and there. However, week after week verses led to discussions on abortion, child molesting, the Holocaust and all the other evils we see in the world. It has not been fun this year. And you can imagine how Annie reacted every week. Lots of tension."

"That must have been tough on you – putting up with Anne and not being able to share your story with me. I'm sorry, babe. What can I do to make things better?"

"I think you already have done a lot to make it better. I know you're working on believing and that's good enough for me."

Chet kissed Claire on the top of her head. "From now on, I want you to tell me everything. I'm on your side."

"I know you are, hon. Would you like to read the poem I wrote today?"

"I would love to read it."

Chet slowly and deliberately read Claire's poem.

---

*Chambers*

*I've been to Hell and back*
*And this is what I saw*
*Demon's probing hopeless souls*
*Buried in the burning coals of a dark chamber*
*A chamber filled with men and women - all condemned*
*They chose to bring an infant to a painful end*
*Without remorse before they died,*
*They became the unforgiven*
*Suctioned into Satan's world of rotted flesh and demons.*

*I've been to Hell and back*
*And this is what I saw*
*Another room, a darker chamber*
*Filled with souls, a higher number*
*Apathetic, sympathetic to all the pro-choice choices*
*They ignored the screams of tiny little voices*

*Inside the mother's womb*
*They washed their blood-stained hands in Pilate's bowl*
*Complacency and social justice replaced their very souls*
*Now, the demons spit on them*
*Inside the darker room.*

*I've been to Hell and back*
*And this is what I saw*
*The darkest of the darkest rooms*
*Filled with sullied butchers*
*Who tore a baby from the womb*
*Limb by limb, from tiny arm to tiny foot*
*Slayers of the young entrenched in Satan's evil soot*
*Smoldering forever in the womb of Hell.*

As much as he wished that all of this would go away, he was starting to comprehend there was more to it than dreams gone awry during her coma. He knew how passionate Claire was about stopping abortion and he criticized himself.

*Who am I to not believe her?*

When Chet finished reading the poem, he was visibly shaken and grabbed Claire's hand. "Claire, I'm sorry when I get judgmental and sarcastic. We'll figure this out together. I wish you had told me sooner. Please don't push this down inside of you anymore. I believe you and I want you to trust me."

"I feel relieved that my heavy secret is out. Honestly, Chet, I didn't grasp the magnitude of this until recently. Now it seems the coma events, the Bible Babes' visions, and the meditations have all blended together. There was a back and forth struggle in the coma from Heaven to chambers. The identical thing has happened here in the months since I came home."

"Are you afraid?"

"No, that's the strange part. When I remember the chambers, sure, I'm frightened of what I see, but when I'm awake and writing about it, there's a new sense of purpose for me. There is no doubt in my mind that I need to ramp up my involvement in stopping abortion. I'm not sure what that is, but I don't think that matters right now. The Holy Spirit will guide us."

"You're an amazing woman, Claire Dillon McCormack."

"Not that amazing. I have my doubts like you do. What if all of this is a dream? What would you say to that?"

"I'd say 'You – no we – could march into Hell if God wanted us to and be unscathed by the asp, the viper, the lion, the dragon – and any other of Satan's disguises.' How's that for faith the size of a mustard seed?"

"Did you memorize that?"

"I read it so many times the words are embedded in my brain like a metal plate."

"Thanks for tonight. It makes me love you even more. I feel really close to you now. Let's go to bed."

Bare limbs of winter trees continued to wave across the sky, sending crisp air into the room. They embraced and then Chet closed the window.

"Smells good in here, doesn't it?"

"Clean and fresh. Good sleeping weather."

Chet and Claire no longer had to hide their secrets in restless slumber.

Christmas was less than two weeks away. Chet and Claire spent the weekend toting down boxes of decorations. Claire put the small artificial tree on the dining room buffet table. From plastic boxes, she pulled ornaments that the kids had loved since they were babies.

In the last few years, Jeannie insisted on designing the large family tree in the popular motif of the day. Four years ago, she created the pink tree – pink ornaments, pink bows, pink lights.

When Chet and Jeff saw it, they laughed till they had tears.

"Dad, it looks like a tree from a shopping mall."

Jeannie was disappointed, but ignored their mockery. Claire had always enjoyed hanging their childhood ornaments on the official family tree, but acquiesced to Jeannie's well-intentioned though unwelcomed tree design.

"C'mon, guys. She spent a lot of time purchasing all of this."

"Thanks, Mom. Not to mention all the time I spent designing it. You boys have no class!"

"Hey, Jeff, maybe we can go shopping in the sunroom. There's a mall tree in there. We don't have to leave the house. We can shop at Jeannie's Mall." Chet and Jeff cackled even more. Hence, the McCormack Christmas tree was called the mall tree from that point on.

"Jeannie, I'll buy a small artificial tree and put the keepsake ornaments on it. It will look very nice in the dining room."

At first, they had hoped this was a passing fancy, but every year Jeannie devised a new theme for the mall tree. 2010 would be no exception. Claire placed her little tree on the buffet table in the dining room, carefully decorating it with keepsake ornaments. Each figurine or trinket awakened fond memories of past Christmases.

Then it was time for her favorite task. In 1988, Claire's Father had handcrafted a little stable for the McCormack family. She placed it in the middle of the wooden mantle and carefully arranged the crèche scene inside. Claire covered the floor of the stable with straw. She placed all the small fragile figures—the sheep and cows, the three wise men, the angel, and of course Mary, and Joseph. She kept the tiny baby Jesus aside until Christmas morning. This was Jeff's favorite job to lay the infant in his straw bed.

There was a fire burning that Chet had lit, and carols played in the background. They clinked their glasses filled with eggnog and walked around the inside and outside of the house admiring their holiday trimmings.

Both Chet and Claire agreed to delay further discussion of the journal until after the holidays. Since Jeff and Jeannie would be home soon, Claire hid the journal in her dresser drawer upstairs.

On the following Friday, Claire heard the garage door open. Within minutes, Jeff dropped his suitcase and laundry bag on the floor of the kitchen. "Smells like baked ham with brown sugar and pineapples."

Claire draped the dish towel over one shoulder. "Jeff, yeah, now we can officially begin the Christmas season." She put her hands on his shoulders and shook him back and forth performing the mother wave. "Oh, honey, you look great."

"Our son is doing great. Wait till you see his grades."

"What am I, chopped liver? Let me see. Let me see."

Jeff pulled a yellow piece of paper from his back pocket, holding it almost three feet above his mother's reach.

"Give that to me immediately, Jeffrey Michael McCormack."

"Or what?"

"Or, you will be eating oatmeal instead of ham for dinner tonight."

"Darn, you always get me with the food threat."

"A 3.8 GPA. That's terrific. Calculus, Introduction to Engineering, Engineering Graphics, First Year Written Composition, Government Ethics – all A's. Hmm, Theology of Human Marriage and Sexuality,--B."

"That professor hated me."

"Really?"

"Really, Mom."

Chapter 45 : Christmas

"Well, congratulations, Jeff.  Good grades in tough subjects."

"Thanks, Mom.  I'm starved.  Right now I want to pig out on the pig."

"Help yourself.  Before I forget, Anne and Kev are stopping by in the morning. I invited them for breakfast since we won't see them on Christmas day this year."

"Okay, cool. Yeah, Kev's excited about seeing his cousins.  It'll be a good break for him."

"Their flight leaves late in the afternoon tomorrow.  I hope the snow waits until they're off the ground."

"When's Jeannie getting home?"

"She's driving here on December 22$^{nd}$ and leaving on the 27th."

"Only five days?"

"She has parties and what not."

Chet laughed.  "That's our Jeannie.  She's independent, outgoing, travels all over the world, and loves her Chicago lifestyle."

"Dad?  Mom?  I have something to ask you."

"Okay, shoot, son."

"Well, remember Darlene Courtney?  You met her at orientation and I think you talked to her parents on Sunday at the orientation luncheon.  You know.  John and Cathy Courtney.  They lived in Hallowed, but moved to Toledo before Darlene started kindergarten."

"Yes, I remember meeting them.  Chet, we talked to them at the luncheon. John works in the automotive industry.   Darlene is a very pretty girl and nice."

Chet winked at Claire.  "Okay, what's the big question?"

"Well, Darly.  I mean Mr. and Mrs. Courtney invited me to go skiing with them in Michigan."

"Darly?"

"Yes, Mom, Darly.  That's her nickname."

"Michigan's pretty far to ski for one day."

"Very funny, Dad. They invited me to go with them from December 29th through New Year's Day. They rent rooms at a lodge every year and a bunch of aunts and uncles and cousins come. I figured I could fly to Toledo on December 28 and spend the night with the Courtneys. Then, we'll drive to Grand Rapids the next day. I checked the airlines and it's only $260 to fly one way from Cincinnati."

"Jeff, you're only nineteen and while the Courtneys seem to be nice people, I'm not sure about this."

Jeff was exasperated. "I knew it. I knew you guys would say no."

"Chill, grasshopper. We haven't said no. We'd like a little more information, like do you have the money?"

"Yes, I saved every paycheck last summer and Uncle Bud sends all of the nieces and nephews $100 for Christmas."

"I have a question. Where are you sleeping at the lodge?"

"Oh, Darly has an older brother. I'll be staying in the same room with him. I met him a couple of times. He's cool. A junior at St. Thomas More College in Indiana."

"Why the one way ticket? How are you getting back to Hallowed?"

"Well, I didn't plan on coming back to Hallowed. Darly has her own car. She's going to drive us to Cincinnati on January 2nd."

"I don't know, Jeff. It sounds complicated. And I was hoping we'd have a few days with you after New Year's."

"Mom, c'mon, please? I'm nineteen. I've never been skiing at a big resort."

"Dad and I need to talk about it."

"Jeff, I know you're nineteen and you want to experience new things, but your Mom's right. We need to discuss it."

Claire put on her parenting game face – no smile, raised left eyebrow. Chet nodded.

"What's on your mind, Claire?"

"I think I should talk to Darlene's mom tomorrow. Then we'll decide."

Chapter 45 : Christmas

"Why, Mom?  I don't know what you're going to find out in a ten minute conversation that you don't already know."

"Well, I think it's the right thing to do.  Don't worry, I'll be polite.  At the very least, we should offer to pay for part of this.  Skiing isn't free."

"Jeannie went on trips when she was in college.  She even stayed a semester in Rome.  And Mom, the night before I left for college, you specifically said 'live life to the fullest.'"

"Jeff, give it a rest.  We're not saying no, but we're not saying yes.  Your Mom wants to talk to Cathy Courtney tomorrow.  Now, let's have a ham sandwich."

"I know it's gonna work out."

"Don't be cocky.  We're not deciding until Mom talks with Darly's Mom."

"Bring on the ham.  Hey, Dad, where's the beer?"

"My Guiness is behind the Bud Light.  Go easy.'"

"As Jeff chatted on the phone with Darly, Claire looked at Chet and sighed, "And I thought changing diapers was difficult."

"Yeah, but eventually, they stop wearing diapers and then they start crawling, walking, talking, leaving home.  At some point, we have to trust that we've rooted them in good morals and ethics.  It's been this way since the beginning of time.  Children grow up, but parents don't grow out of them."

"That's a really good quote.  Did you make that up?"

"Straight from the noggin."

"And you're right.  We'll never grow out of Jeff and Jeannie."

Anne and Kevin arrived at the McCormacks the next morning.    Chet hugged Anne.  "Merry Christmas, ma'am.  I reckon you two are taking presents to the Madison herd down yonder in Texas.?"

"Chet, too funny.  Claire, this looks delicious."

"Have a seat.  I've got ham and scrambled eggs, hashed brown casserole, cranberry muffins and whatever you want to drink."

"Hey, Mrs. McC, I'm starved. Looks awesome. What do you think of Jeffer going skiing in Michigan?" Jeff cringed.

"I think it will be a great time for him, Kev. Darlene seems like a very nice girl."

"Jeff gave his Mom a quizzical stare. Chet winked at him.

"Yes, I talked with Darlene's mother early this morning. I like her. She has some of the same concerns I do, but we're saying yes."

"Whew, Mrs. McC, from the look on Jeffer's face, I thought you were going to say no. I'm extra glad because, this is my Christmas gift for you." Jeff pulled ski goggles from the bag.

"Nice, man. These are great. Thanks."

"Jeff, didn't Kev do a great job of wrapping your gift in the store bag?"

"Mom, guys don't wrap gifts."

"If you say so. I also have a present for each of you and Jeannie. They are wrapped. If you want to put them under the tree, that's fine. Nothing perishable."

"Thanks, Anne. The wrapping is beautiful."

"Amazing what they can do for you in department stores."

"I would like to put them under the tree. Poor bare tree is in the sunroom. At least I'll have these gifts to make it look festive. We're going to decorate when Jeannie comes home. And, we have gifts for you and Kevin. It's kind of sentimental. You can open it later if you want."

"No, I want to open it now." Anne carefully untied the ribbon and pulled a picture frame from the box."

"Hey, Kev, look. Last December at Hallowed Tower – you and me and Dad. This is special."

Kevin hugged his Mom. "My Mom is one of the strongest people I know."

"She is indeed, Kev. Anne, Chet picked out the frame from Exquisites."

"It's positively gorgeous with the engraving and etchings. Thanks, truly, from the bottom of my heart. I'm not going to cry. Jack wants us to be happy and I want to remember the happy times like last year at the tower."

# Chapter 45 : Christmas

Claire hugged Annie from the back of her chair.

"Hey, Kev, this is for you from all of us. It's wrapped because my Mom ordered it on line and did the feminine gift wrap thing. Hope you like it."

"Wow, thanks. A money clip. Whoa, a hundred bucks. Thanks."

"You can thank them for the money."

"Thanks Mr. and Mrs. McC. That's over the top."

"You're welcome. Enjoy your trip and spend it on you."

"Will do. Thanks again."

"I asked Mom to order the clip for you. You should see Kev's money when he pulls it out of his pocket. The ones and fives are folded in eight different ways like origami."

"That's why I kept asking you where you bought yours."

"And that's why I bought it for you, Kev."

"Thanks, man. Perfect gift."

Anne slipped her arms into her coat. "Well, time to head south, bud. It's a dirty job, but somebody's got to enjoy the warm Texas weather."

While Chet, Jeff, and Kevin stood outside in the cold December air, Anne and Claire talked in the doorway.

"Anne, have a wonderful trip. I'm glad it's not snowing."

Anne held Claire's hand. "Merry Christmas, big sister. I didn't think I'd be able to say those words to anyone ever again, but thanks to Father Hernandez and Chet and especially you, I've learned to trust again. Both of us almost died this year, but faith prevailed."

"That is the truth. Each of us had our very own brush with death, but God had other plans. 'Let not your heart be troubled. You have faith in God, have faith in me.' Enjoy the time with your brothers and their families, Annie. I'll be thinking of you. See you in January. Safe travel."

Claire, Chet, and Jeff stood on the porch waving as Anne and Kevin left for Christmas in Texas. It would be a respite away from a year marked with cold blows to hearts. Still, in all of the madness, Anne discovered that renewed faith and love of friends and family would sustain her.

---

On Monday afternoon, Jeannie arrived in a whirlwind of snow and presents.

"Deck the halls with bows of holly, fa la la la la la la la la. Ho ho ho, Santa Jeannie is here!"

"Hey baby girl, Merry Christmas. You look fabulous."

"Sister J, good to see you."

"Holy tomoli, Jeff, you've grown another three inches. Now, I only come up to your chin."

"You've got me beat, Jeannie. I only come up to his elbows."

"Mom, it's been like that for a long time."

"Yeah, you may be taller and bigger but I'm…"

Jeff and Jeannie yelled. "Tougher. We know. You're tougher."

"Groan."

"Watch out, Jeannie, she'll take you down."

"Things don't change much around here, do they Jeffy?"

"Hey, that's the way it should be. Your Mom and I are your anchor, your beacon of light, the wind beneath your wings."

"Okay, seriously, enough of the trite brouhaha. It is good to be home. Are we going to decorate the tree tonight?"

"It's up to you and Jeff."

"Fine with me as long there's food to give me strength. What's the motif this year, Jeannie? Are we having a pink mall tree?"

"No, but that was one of my favorite years for the tree. You liked it, didn't you, Mom?"

"It was pretty. It didn't look very Christmassy, though."

Chapter 45 : Christmas

"It's going to be beautiful, Mom, wait and see."

"You mean you don't want to hang those ornaments from years ago? The ones you made and the ones your grandparents and aunts and uncles gave you?"

"Mother, what picture is to the right of the fireplace?"

"The Monet you gave to us. I love it."

"Let's make the tree look elegant with angels and white lights, nothing else. Simple and deserving of sharing space with the Monet. I'll do all of the decorating."

"Well, when you put it that way, okay. I'll be back in a minute, hon."

Claire went into the kitchen where Chet and Jeff were eating shrimp cocktail.

"Well, guys, it worked again. We don't have to do anything to decorate the tree. How about a glass of wine, Chet. We can eat, drink, and be merry while Jeannie does all the work."

---

Although no words were spoken about Claire's walk to the precipice of death in July 2010, each of the McCormacks experienced a heightened awareness of family closeness. Bantering was merrier. Lobster on Christmas Eve tasted richer. Opening presents felt amazing. Singing Christmas carols out of key added to the celebration. Claire purposely absorbed the rhythm of the family rituals not wanting to miss one moment. Although she was not crazy about large and gaudy angels, she loved the look on Jeannie's face when she presented her creation to the family. Jeannie's face was a treasured Monet in Claire's mind.

Chet sipped his whiskey and gazed at the tree, squinting to get a glistening effect of the lights on the gold angels. The fact that Claire finally shared her journal with him, and only him, fostered a deeper intimacy in their marriage. Since childhood, his lack of trust in others and his disbelief that other's trusted him had been problematic. When Claire asked him to help her unravel the spiritual mystery, he was heartened by her gesture of trust.

Of course, Mass on Christmas Eve was the highlight of emotional relief for a family who had endured a spring and summer of death and fear. As the McCormacks entered Angel of God Church, the bell choir was playing 'What Child Is This.' The melodic ringing of the bells seemed to bounce from wall to wall, statue to statue, floating in and out of red poinsettias. Claire turned around slowly to take in the beauty and solemnity of the Church. On this blessed Christmas Eve, the sweet sounds of the choir, the blended smell of flowers and candles, even the feel of the wooden pew, imparted a kind of new holiness. It reminded Claire of the purity of her First Communion when she was seven. She held Chet's hand all through Mass thankful that he had realized the magnitude of what had happened in her coma and was willing to take a step toward belief.

During the singing of Stille Nagt, she noticed a tear on Jeannie's cheek and kissed it before it fell. Jeff put his arms around his Mom, gently moving her back and forth. "You really are corny, Mom." He did a quick turn-away and then back again. "I love corny."

On December 25, 2010, during midnight Mass, there was an affectionate familiarity that required no explanation. It may have been the physical closeness in the crowded pews or the smell of ancient incense or trumpets resounding 'Joy to the World.' Whatever the reason, the McCormacks cherished the blessing of being together at Angel of God Church. Gratitude for second chances rested quietly in their hearts.

The events of the past year had placed an indelible mark on each of them.

———————————

On December 27th, Chet and Claire watched as Jeff helped Jeannie carry her gifts and luggage to her SUV.

"That's it, Jeffy. Thanks. Come visit some time."

"Sure, that would be fun. Maybe in the spring or summer when school's out."

They did the brother sister hug, patting each other on the back and ending with a high five.

"Have a great time skiing. Send pictures."

"By sweetie. I think the weather is going to be okay. Call me from the road."

Jeannie put her arm around her Mother. "Will do. Mom, don't start crying."

"I'm not. It's only a sniffle, but the house is full of life and fun when you're around. Claire put her arm around Jeff and Jeannie. "When both of you are here."

Chapter 45 : Christmas

Chet put his arms around all three of them. "We miss you guys."

"Run for the hills, Jeff. They're about to lock us in our rooms forever."

Jeff squirmed underneath the circle of bodies. "Gosh, Mom and Dad, neither one of us lives that far away."

Jeannie whispered in Claire's ear. "Mom, I'll be back. I don't live in China."

Claire dabbed her eyes with a napkin. "I know, I know. You love your life in Chicago. Call us on New Year's Day. I want to hear about your New Year's Eve dance."

"You better get on the road, hon. This could go on all day."

"Bye, Dad. Love you. Bye, Mom. I'll call you in about two hours. Love you."

"Love you more."

Every time Jeannie left, a multitude of emotions flooded Claire's heart. She beamed with pure satisfaction seeing Jeannie's life unfold as an adult. Her daughter exuded beauty and independence with the added blessing of a caring heart. However, those sentiments were always coupled with pangs of disappointment that Jeannie had not returned to Hallowed to live after graduation. The constant coming and going tugged at her heart.

Both Chet and Claire knew it was time to let Jeff open his wings, however tenuous they might be. On December 28th they drove Jeff to Greater Cincinnati Airport. Chet parked his car at the curb and turned on the flashers. As they stood by the airport entrance, the winter air blew cold stripes of punishing wind across their faces.

"Son, here's a little extra cash in case you want to take Darly out to dinner or something."

"Thanks, Dad. Thanks a lot."

"Jeff, please call Dad or me when you get to the Courtney's."

"I will, Mom. Don't worry."

Chet patted his son on the back. "Jeff, have a good time and be good."

"Thanks again for everything, Mom and Dad. I better go. I don't know how long security is going to take."

Chet and Claire huddled together on the sidewalk shivering in the day's waning rays of sunset. They tracked Jeff as long as they could until he disappeared through the terminal.

While driving home to Hallowed, Claire and Chet talked about their wonderful Christmas and the joy of Jeff and Jeannie.

"When the kids were little, didn't things seem to last longer?"

"What do you mean?"

"Well, remember, we didn't have much money? We'd have to turn somersaults to get presents for them."

"I remember. When Jeff was four, he wanted a purple fire truck, which did not exist."

"Oh, gosh, we bought a plastic red one and then you took it into the garage to spray paint it purple on Christmas Eve."

"It seems that life goes really slow when you're a child. And then you get married and have children. For many years, every moment of the day and night is filled with obligations. And then one day it gains momentum and starts moving fast. Really fast."

"You mean, like this week with the kids visit? That went fast."

"That's exactly what I mean. It feels like I'm inside a snowball that's taking on speed and I can't make it stop. I want to roll it back up the hill. I want to unwrap the layers of snow and little by little relive the moments."

"Everything keeps changing, Claire, but we have to move with it."

"I guess. I'm being melancholic. You know how I am when the kids leave. I'll get over it."

Chet patted her knee. "I know, hon. Nothing stands still."

When they crossed the bridge, Claire gazed out the window at Hallowed Tower, jewel of the sky. It was a year ago that Jeff and Kevin climbed to the top to hang lights.  And yet, time since that night, the months since Jack's death, the days and hours and minutes of 2010 had vanished as swiftly as snow falling on warm ground.

*No, nothing stands still, not even in quaint Hallowed, Ohio.*

# CHAPTER 46 : HOLY SPIRIT MISSION

New Year's eve in Hallowed, Ohio had never been a big event. People celebrated with small intimate parties or went to a movie. The people who desired a gala event traveled to downtown Cincinnati.

Chet and Claire had no desire for New Year's parties. They sat on the couch in the living room with a view of the mall tree, which made them chuckle periodically. Outside, December's wind was still howling, so it was especially appealing to feel the warmth of the fireplace. The fire crackled and the smell of the burning wood created an atmosphere for a cozy, low-key evening.

At 10 o'clock, Chet opened a bottle of champagne. Hey, Mrs. McCormack, want to toast the New Year a little early?

"I do, Mr. McCormack."

Chet poured the bubbly and handed a glass to Claire. "Here's to the ending of a miracle year."

Claire tapped Chet's glass. "Cheers and here's to a new adventure in a new year. Chet, I've been thinking about Holy Spirit Mission."

"That's all you think about."

"I know we said we weren't going to talk about it until after the holidays, but the kids are gone and tonight seems like a good time."

"Okay what's on your mind?"

"The March for Life is coming up in January and I want to go."

"I knew that. You and Anne are going together, aren't you?"

"That was the original plan, but Anne's going on a retreat that weekend. She can't make the trip."

"She has really changed. What kind of retreat?"

"It's specifically for woman who have had abortions. Fr. Hernandez encouraged her to attend. I told her it was more important for her to be at the retreat than the March for Life."

"I know, but it seems that she can go on a retreat any time, but the March for Life is only scheduled once a year."

Chapter 46 : Holy Spirit Mission

"That's true, but she needs to attend this retreat as soon as possible. I don't want her to backslide."

"You know what you're doing when it comes to Annie. Are you still going?"

"That depends on you."

Chet flinched. "Oh, Claire. C'mon. No. I'm not the marching type, especially in D.C. in January. Hon, how about one of the Bible Babes?"

"I guess I could ask one of them, but I was hoping you would be my partner. You probably can't get away from work, anyway."

"It's not the work thing. The project I'm working on is in D.C., but I can't see myself marching. You're the activist in this family."

"Hmm. I remember two weeks ago a certain person telling me he'd be willing to march into Hell with me."

"That's different."

"You said and I quote, 'You – no we – could march into Hell if God wanted us to and be unscathed by the asp, the viper, the lion, the dragon – and any other of Satan's disguises.' How's that for faith the size of a mustard seed?' But you won't march into Washington?"

"Let me think about it. You start playing the guilt card and then I feel pressured. Give me a little time to digest all of this."

"Okay. I want you to read one more journal entry. It's something I added today."

Before he could say anything, Claire walked quickly to the steps. As she left the room, Chet grimaced.

*Oh, boy. Here we go. This is not going to be a fun New Year's Eve.*

She brought the journal from their bedroom, and sat close to Chet on the couch, pointing to the newest entry.

"This scared me more than any other event. Before this, what I saw was about people I didn't know. This one is very personal. I want to read it to you."

"Okay."

*During my coma, just when I thought I was finished with the horror of the chambers, I was told I had to return to the first chamber, Chamber Dark. I remember crying intensely. I couldn't understand why God wanted me to go back there and I resisted until I felt the serene sanctuary of God's love. As with all of my coma images, some things are clear and some are murky. This particular memory is vivid. I was in a train car. It was dark and oppressive with an evil mist hanging in the air. The insidious smell and taste of sulfur encircled me as though I were inside the very core of foul spillage. Then my mind was invaded by thoughts from the Evil One. He gloated about his abortion numbers and he said it was exquisite to have a reserve of condemned souls waiting to enter one of his chambers. What happened next tore at my heart. As I approached one of the seats in the train car, I noticed a figure with beautiful blonde hair. She was sitting next to a gruesome creature who was caressing her in a possessive way. I couldn't resist looking at her face. It was Anne. I touched what looked like her, but she was hard and brittle with deep circles under her eyes. Once I realized this was Satan's holding place for future residents of Hell, I scurried like a hunted animal. The evil fiend pursued me through the train car. He snarled obscenities and violently spewed pus from his dark wounds. I prayed to St. Michael and to my Guardian Angel and at last I sank into blessed safety.*"

"Yikes, that's about as personal as you can get, but we all know this story ended happily because you are sitting right next to me on the very last day of 2010. And, Annie is in Texas."

"There's more. Week after week during Bible Study, Anne bristled at the discussions. I could see fear and sadness in her face. Finally, she visited me one afternoon and through God's grace, I was able to convince her to talk with Fr. Hernandez."

"That was the evening you drove her to the church."

"Yes. You were at a St. Vincent de Paul meeting. It was fairly warm that night in November, so I waited in the car. Here's the entry that is baffling and logical all at the same time."

*While she talked with him that evening, I waited in my car, drifting in and out of sleep. Again, I found myself back in Chamber Dark in train car #522. Of course, 522 - May 22nd - the date of the abortion. The flood of fear returned and even more so because Anne was no longer in the train. I felt panicky. Was she dead? Did Satan own her soul now? And then, the pure comprehension hit me that this was a good thing. Anne was out of the demon's reach. Because she had asked God's forgiveness, Satan no longer imprisoned her living soul in the waiting car for the condemned. I heard someone pounding on my car window. I awoke. It was Anne and she was smiling.*

Telling Chet what she really wanted had been difficult for Claire in their marriage. Instead, she would rant and rave in a circle of resentment unable to ask for it directly, but not this time.

"You've heard it all, Chet. You told me you wanted us to figure this out together. You said you were open to believing me. You told me you want me to trust you and you don't want me to push it down anymore. Chet, I want you, not Anne, to march with me in Washington."

"You have a memory like an elephant. What the heck is the Holy Spirit mission for you? For us?"

The grandfather clock began its twelve chimes, signaling a new year. Claire and Chet kissed and then tapped their glasses together again.

"Happy New Year. To answer your question, your Holy Spirit mission, should you decide to accept, is to accompany me to Washington D.C. to March for Life."

"Sure, I'll go, even though I'm second choice."

"You are not second choice. You are the Holy Spirit's choice. That's why he made sure Anne is attending the retreat that weekend. Now, this spot is open for you."

"In that case, I accept Holy Spirit's mission to March for Life…with you! Happy New Year."

The Bible Babes commenced their meetings on the second Wednesday in January. Everyone gathered around Maureen and her baby girl, Mary Anne.

"I'm glad you could come tonight, Maureen. What a beautiful little girl."

"She is a blessing, even though she didn't cooperate about coming before Christmas. She was born at 7:13 am on December 25."

Anne moved closer. "Would it be okay if I hold her? Mary Anne is a sweet name."

"Of course."

Anne held Mary Anne lovingly in her arms. As she cuddled the tiny infant girl firmly against her chest, she could smell the clean, pure breath of Maureen's baby. No one but Claire comprehended the profound suffering Anne had endured with miscarriages early on in her marriage and then the abortion. Anne's eyes were watering, but her face looked serene.

"She's beautiful, Maureen."

"Thanks, Anne. We plan to call her by both names. I've always loved the name Anne and after our Christmas meeting, I thought what better way to honor the Blessed Mother than to give our child the first name of Mary in honor of her, and the middle name of Anne in honor of Mary's mother."

A newborn could make a room full of Babes reduce their conversations to baby talk and talk about babies. Finally, Maureen settled into her comfortable chair nursing Mary Anne. The ladies munched on the sweet and the salty snacks, sharing with each other the ups and downs of the Christmas season until Patti tapped her pen on the lamp.

"Tek, you ready?"

*Dear Father in Heaven, Thank you for bringing all the Babes together this year. We are amazed and humbled by the birth of your Son in a stable. We recognize that the birth of all infants is precious in your eyes. Please bless and watch over our newest Bible Babe, Mary Anne. Amen.*

"Did you make that up, Tekla?"

"Right on the spot, Patti."

"That is cute calling Mary Anne our newest Bible Babe. Tek, you keep us laughing. Thanks for a very lovely prayer. Bernie, it's your turn for scripture tonight."

"Turn to Mark, Chapter 10, verses 13-16. I think you all will like this one.

***People were bringing little children to Him, for Him to touch them. The disciples scolded them, but when Jesus saw this He was indignant and said to them, 'Let the little children come to Me; do not stop them; for it is to such as these that the kingdom of God belongs. In truth I tell you, anyone who does not welcome the kingdom of God like a little child will never enter it.' Then He embraced them, laid His hands on them and gave them His blessing. (Mark, Ch. 10, V13-16)***

Okay, who wants to be the first to share?"

Claire volunteered. "This reading fits right in with what's happening in Washington this week. Chet and I are going to participate in the March for Life. In fact, we've been acting like children, checking the itinerary, looking online at pictures of last year's march, reading up on the issues. We even get to visit pro-life Congresswoman Jackie Smyth. Okay, back to the reading. To me, Jesus is of course telling us to be as open and accepting as a child in our pursuit of Heaven. What stands out is His reaffirmation of the pure value of innocent life, one that has not been influenced yet by evil in the world. Short, but that's all I have."

She didn't want to share too much about the March for Life. Anne had really made great strides since her confession, but Claire still chose her words carefully when referring to babies.

However, Anne surprised her. "I think you're exactly right about reaffirming innocent life… especially innocent life of the unborn. I admire you and Chet for marching in Washington even if you are acting like children. Just kidding, my friend."

Claire was encouraged to hear what Anne said. Her words resonated another step toward healing. "Thanks, Anne. You know how Chet is, but I finally talked him into it. I actually think it will be fun."

"Who wants to talk?"

"I'd like to say that I am ecstatic that we have returned to uplifting verses."

"Amen to that, Roxanne."

"This reminds me of how excited little Arthur, Jr. was when people came to visit. He loved his great Aunt CiCi. She was the only person who could tell him about his Grandma Katrina. I can picture him jumping up and down in the yard when she got off the bus. He knew he was not allowed to enter the street. As soon as she stepped onto the driveway, she would drop everything and open her arms. I'd watch from the doorway as he jumped up to hug her. There was no hesitation, no question, no doubt he wanted to fly into her arms. If Jesus stepped onto my driveway and opened His arms, I think He would want me to jump into them and be as welcoming as my little Arthur."

"Roxanne, that is a great analogy. Thank you. Next?"

Anne's eyes sparkled. "I'd like to be next because a light bulb went off in my head as soon as I heard Roxanne's story. A few meetings back, I mentioned that I had gone to confession and communion. I felt I had been renewed. Now, I receive the sacrament of reconciliation every two weeks. What popped into my head tonight is the image of Jesus with open arms, like you said, Roxanne. I see Him beckoning me with His left arm, placing His hand on my head, and saying 'Your sins are forgiven.' That's Jesus' arm of confession. Then, He pulls me up with His right arm and says, 'This is my body and this is my blood poured out for many for the forgiveness of sins.' That's Jesus's right arm of receiving the Eucharist. I remember going to confession and then making my first communion when we lived in Texas. There was no question in my little innocent mind that Jesus had forgiven my sins and that I had received His body and blood in communion. This is a roundabout way of saying that when I receive these sacraments in the present, I experience a childlike renewal and joy jumping into Jesus' powerful arms."

After Anne's heartfelt sharing, the room fell silent. Claire was confident that Anne would continue to heal. Maureen, Dana, and Patti stated the Bible Babes' pass and pray.

Tekla wiggled nervously in her chair at the mention of confession.

"Gosh, this is the second time you promoted the sacrament of reconciliation. It still scares me. I only have bad memories of going to confession, especially right before I was diagnosed. I need to ponder this for a few days. Annie, I've got to say you are certainly convincing. That's it for me."

"Let's have lunch next week, Tek. It's taken a very long time for me to want to go to confession. I'll call you on Tuesday, okay?"

"Yeah, sure. I'd like that." Tek's life had mostly been devoid of friends until she joined Bible Babes two years ago. Even a small gesture of meeting for lunch moved her in a tender way.

"I guess it's time to find out why you brought this scripture, Bernie."

"When I chose this verse, I was thinking of my grandchildren. When I visit, their moms or dads will say, 'Stop pestering Grandma.' And, unless I'm taking my afternoon nap, I always tell them 'They're not pestering me. I want to hold my sweeties,' or 'I want to play a game with them.' Children hunger for love and affection. Right or wrong, their parents can't always be there for them. They have jobs, bills to pay, meals to cook, homework to check, all kinds of interruptions. When I'm with my grandchildren, I try to focus on them as much as possible. Of course, this verse radiates what Roxanne and Anne echoed about being childlike. There's another element here. When we open our arms to our children or grandchildren or friends, we are emulating Jesus who never turns away from us. In a sense, He wants us to pester Him in the same way that I want my grandchildren to pester me. As a bonus, I learn a great deal from my sweet little darlings."

Bible Babes was off to a good start in 2011. After final prayer and cleanup, Maureen bundled Mary Ann in a lamb skin bunting, said a quick goodbye, and rushed to get her baby out of the January wind. Most of the Babes followed suit; there had been little snow, but temperatures dipped into the twenties with wind chills in the teens.

Anne and Claire talked in the parking lot for a few minutes, even though the January wind and flurries beat against their faces.

"Wow, it's cold tonight and I heard the temperatures are going to be subzero this weekend. Fortunately, I will be in a warm, cozy room at the Convent Retreat House."

"The retreat is Friday through Sunday, right?"

"Yeah, it starts Friday night at seven and ends Sunday at six p.m. You'll still be in Washington, won't you?"

"We leave Sunday morning and return on Tuesday evening. If it's going to be subzero in Hallowed, it's going to be worse in Washington. I guess I'll be freezing my tushee off."

"Claire, I think I'm heading in the right direction, but I'm a little anxious about the retreat."

"You are moving exactly in the right direction. Your talk blew me away tonight. You had them captivated with Jesus' left arm of confession and right arm of the Eucharist. Seriously, they were really listening. You have a gift."

"Thanks. The words came from my heart."

"Obviously, you impacted Tek."

"Life is still sad for me, but it comforts me to put my worries in Jesus' care. I know I have to forge ahead. I wonder who will be at the retreat."

"Holy women like you – taking one step at a time to heal the wound."

"I don't think of myself as a holy woman."

"Well, you are and the other women on your retreat will be holy, too. Otherwise, they wouldn't be there. Call me Monday morning. I want to hear about the retreat. Now, let's forge ahead home, eh?"

"Anne chattered her reply. "Sssssounds good. The cold is unbearable tonight."

Claire hugged Anne. "Okay, my friend. Let not your heart be troubled. Good night."

# CHAPTER 48 : THE MARCH

On Sunday Chet and Claire met the March for Life group in the parking lot of St. Elizabeth Church. Although they did not know any of the parishioners, they felt very welcomed. Mary Jo Sutton, the trip planner, had talked with Claire and Chet several times on the phone and genuinely encouraged them to be a part of their parish group for the March.

The motor coach was surprisingly comfortable. Mary Jo and Dan Sutton along with the planning group provided drinks, donuts, and sandwiches to the forty passengers. After an hour into the trip, Mary Jo led the group in the rosary.

"Hail Mary, full of grace. The Lord is with you."

Claire was in awe of Mary Jo's soft melodic voice.

*I have never heard anyone say the Hail Mary with such reverence. She sounds like an angel.*

The trip was long, but the bus was full of laughter, prayer, and moments of true holiness. Claire appreciated that she and Chet were on this journey together. Sharing the journal had been a difficult marathon of questions, anger and fear for both of them. They loved each other and believed their marriage was solid. Yet, there were times when sharp edges of hurts jutted out, opening past wounds.

In sharing the journal, Chet and Claire unearthed valuable truths. There were no defined indicators of Holy Spirit Mission, but a spiritual calling pointed in the direction of saving babies. In the course of this discovery, the shape of their marriage changed. Chet's cynicism and disapproving tone softened. In turn, both trusted more and disputed less.

After ten hours, the bus pulled into a parking lot across the street from the Basilica of the Immaculate Conception. By the time the group arrived at the Basilica, the pews were occupied with many young and old soldiers of Christ. Mary Jo had told the group to find a seat wherever they could and to meet at the bus after Mass.

The sun descended into the earth, spraying final rays of light through the stained glass windows of the Basilica. Ushers dashed here and there giving directions, herding most of the remaining people downstairs to watch the Mass on a large screen.

Chapter 48 : The March

"Chet, let's walk up the aisle. We're probably not going to get a seat, but I want to see the altar."

"I'll follow you."

Chet and Claire walked with confidence as if meeting someone in a front pew. In silence, they stared at the four marble columns surrounding the altar. Behind it was a mural of majestic Jesus clothed in red, His hands outstretched, His eyes penetrating. A mural of the Blessed Mother mesmerized both of them, especially the snake that lay beneath the lady's feet.

"Sir, ma'am, has someone saved a seat for you up here?"

"No, we only wanted to see the altar. Where do you want us to go?"

"There's plenty of seating downstairs with a widescreen TV. I think you can see everything better down there. The steps are through that door to your right."

Chet and Claire walked in front of the first pew where several nuns were seated. When they reached the end of the pew, one of the sisters tapped Claire on her arm.

"We can fit you in our pew. They can scoot over."

"No, Sister, that's okay. We can sit downstairs."

"I insist." With the wave of Mother Superior's hand, each of the sisters moved a few inches to the left. She motioned for Chet and Claire to enter. Then Mother Superior sat on the end.

"It's a tight squeeze, but it will be worth it. I'm Sister Monica. Is this your first time at the march?"

"Our very first, Sister Monica. I'm Claire and this is my husband, Chet."

"Nice to meet both of you. What city?"

"We live in Hallowed, Ohio on the outskirts of Cincinnati."

"Aah, you are from a hallowed, holy place. What a wonderful name for a little town."

"What city are you from, Sister?"

"Our convent is right here in Washington, across from the Holocaust Museum."

"Thanks, Sister, for allowing us to be in prime seats."

"My pleasure. I have to sit on the end because I'm doing the second reading."

Ushers dimmed the lights allowing hundreds of candles to illuminate the church. Once in a while someone opened a door causing a draft. The candles flickered, creating a prism of colors from the soft beige walls to subtle specks of gold on the columns. Even the crown on Jesus' head seemed to glow with the fire of life and love. This was a solemn Mass to prepare and emblazon the participants to fight the good fight against abortion in the March on Washington.

Feeling uncomfortable as the only man sitting in the Dominican nuns' pew, Chet rolled his eyes at Claire. She smiled and patted his knee.

"The Holy Spirit is in charge. Go with the flow."

Sister Monica looked at Claire, holding her index finger to her mouth.

Claire held Chet's hand tightly, trying to control her laughter as she remembered grade school days with Patti Waring.

The beauty of the women's choir singing 'The Magnificat' brought solemnity back into focus. A procession of bishops, priests, altar boys and girls completed the ambience of sacredness in this Mass offered for all aspects of life. The Holy Sacrifice of the Mass commenced. After both the men's and women's choir sang the Gloria in Latin, a young priest stepped to the podium.

"First Reading: Genesis 3:1-5, 14

*Now the serpent was more cunning than any beast of the field which the Lord God had made. He said to the woman, 'Did God say, You shall not eat of any tree of the garden?' The woman answered the serpent, 'Of the fruit of all the trees in the garden we may eat; but of the fruit of the tree in the middle of the garden,' God said, 'You shall not eat, neither shall you touch it, lest you die.' But the serpent said to the woman, 'No, you shall not die; for God knows that when you eat of it, your eyes will be opened and you will be like God, knowing good and evil.'*

Claire nudged Chet. He nodded towards Sister Monica and said nothing for fear of being admonished. He pushed his shoulder gently against Claire, moving his head ever so slightly up and down in acknowledgement that he knew what Claire was thinking. People shifted in their seats preparing to sing the Responsorial Psalm. A lovely young woman explained the response for the participants. Then, the haunting melody of a lone flute echoed down the aisle as she sang.

> Responsorial Psalm 91
>
> *R. Be with me, Lord, when I am in trouble.*
> *You who dwell in the shelter of the Most High,*
> *who abide in the shadow of the Almighty,*
> *say to the LORD, "My refuge and fortress,*
> *my God in whom I trust."*
> *R. Be with me, Lord, when I am in trouble.*
> *No evil shall befall you,*
> *nor shall affliction come near your tent,*
> *For to his angels he has given command,*
> *that they guard you in all your ways.*
> *R. Be with me, Lord, when I am in trouble.*
> *Upon their hands they shall bear you up,*
> *lest you dash your foot against a stone.*
> *You shall tread upon the asp and the viper;*
> *you shall trample down the lion and the dragon.*

Chet held Claire's hand tighter knowing this must be uncomfortable for her.

*Is this what she's been trying to tell me? Is this what happens to her over and over – scripture from coma events bombarding her at every turn? Please, God, make it be a coincidence.*

The church was quiet except for the distant sound of a baby crying and the rustle of the Bishop, priests, and deacons taking their seats.

As Sister Monica approached the podium, the glow of the cathedral created an atmosphere of holy reflection, especially for the women in the pews. Before speaking, Sister Monica glanced back at the portrait of majestic Jesus. Then, her resonant voice and dramatic inflections persuaded even the clergy to listen intently.

"Second Reading: Revelations 12:7-9

*And there was a great battle in Heaven, Michael and his angels fought with the dragon, and the dragon back with his angels; and they prevailed not, neither was their place found any more in Heaven, and that great dragon was cast out, that old serpent, who is called the devil and Satan, who seduceth the whole world; and he was cast unto the earth, and his angels were thrown down with him."*

Claire felt a familiar trickle of sweat down her back, but at least Chet was with her. Sister Monica returned to the pew sitting up straight with hands folded in her lap. Again, everyone in the church stood as the choir sang 'Alleluia.' The Bishop rose to the dais.

"The Gospel of the Lord.

Gospel Luke, Ch. 1 V. 26-38

*In the sixth month, the angel Gabriel was sent from God to a town of Galilee called Nazareth, to a virgin betrothed to a man named Joseph, of the house of David, and the virgin's name was Mary. And coming to her, he said, 'Hail, favored one! The Lord is with you.' But she was greatly troubled at what was said and pondered what sort of greeting this might be. Then the angel said to her, 'Do not be afraid, Mary, for you have found favor with God. Behold, you will conceive in your womb and bear a son, and you shall name him Jesus. He will be great and will be called Son of the Most High, and the Lord God will give him the throne of David his father, and he will rule over the house of Jacob forever, and of his kingdom there will be no end' But Mary said to the angel, 'How can this be, since I have no relations with a man?' And the angel said to her in reply, The Holy Spirit will come upon you, and the power of the Most High will overshadow you. Therefore the child to be born will be called holy, the Son of God. And behold, Elizabeth, your relative, has also conceived a son in her old age, and this is the sixth month for her who was called barren; for nothing will be impossible for God.' Mary said, 'Behold, I am the handmaid of the Lord. May it be done to me according to your word." Then the angel departed from her. The Gospel of the Lord.'*

Bishop Francis motioned for people to sit. Claire fanned herself feeling the flush of warmth on her face. Chet held her hand tighter.

"Welcome to the Basilica of the Immaculate Conception. I see waves of faces – all ages from many different cities and countries. I sincerely thank you for coming here to battle the ravages of abortion. The readings for tonight were not randomly chosen. There is a specific reason for each of them. We'll start with the Gospel of

Luke. Luke tells us that the Angel Gabriel visits this humble maiden. The angel says, *'Do not be afraid, Mary, for you have found favor with God. Behold, you will conceive in your womb and bear a son, and you shall name him Jesus. He will be great and will be called Son of the Most High.'* You might say what a wonderful message to be told that you have found favor with God, that you will conceive a son. But was it a wonderful message to a young woman, who knew she could be stoned if pregnant and unmarried? And what would Joseph, her betrothed, think of her? Mary was very afraid and confused. That's why she said to the angel, *'How can this be, since I have no relations with a man?'*

We are here to end abortion, but we must not forget the women who have had abortions and are in despair. Their fear is similar to our Blessed Mother's when Gabriel appeared. Don't misunderstand; it is fundamental that we end this scourge of killing innocent babies. Remember, though, many women and men live tortured lives because of a choice they made. We are also here to give loving aid to them. It is essential that we lead these souls to Christ's salvation.

We know how this beautiful story proceeds. Mary accepts that she is to be the Mother of Jesus, Son of God. Her humble prayer *'Behold, I am the handmaid of the Lord. May it be done to me according to your word'* is the inspiration for 'The Magnificat,' the amazing opening song tonight. Okay, I said that all of the readings were chosen for a specific reason. First, I talked about the joyful verses of Luke, but now I want us to examine the first reading from Genesis. The purpose of this reading is to help us understand that evil has existed on the face of the Earth since Adam and Eve listened to the serpent. Satan does have a great deal of evil power, but God is infinitely more powerful. The serpent lies to the first residents of Earth. He tells them *'No, you shall not die; for God knows that when you eat of it, your eyes will be opened and you will be like God, knowing good and evil.'* He continues to lie to us. Some people don't believe in Hell or Satan, but he's real all right or else you – we -- wouldn't have to be here in the dead of winter.

Let's talk about our responsorial psalm and the scripture that Sister Monica dramatized eloquently. They're kin to each other. Psalm 91 gives us strength to battle evil. God has our back, as you young people might say. When evil comes near you,

God has commanded His angels to guard you. That's the truth. With their guidance, *'you shall tread upon the asp and the viper; you shall trample down the lion and the dragon.'* When you march tomorrow, remember these words. Do not be afraid because God does have your back when we do His work. Finally, yes finally. I see a few heads nodding awake once in a while. Who is one of the most powerful angels in Heaven? Michael the Archangel. He fought the great dragon and his rebellious angels. You may not know this, but Michael was sent to guard Jesus on Earth. And Michael the Archangel still guards the Catholic Church today.

My sermon began with Mary's story and her acceptance of God's will. Our will may not coincide with God's, but if we say yes to Him, He will provide guidance and protection. He sends us help in our time of need through Jesus, the Holy Spirit, and all the saints and angels. With the power of God surrounding you, go forward tomorrow and '*let not your hearts be troubled*.'" May God bless you in the name of the Father, the Son, and Holy Spirit."

From that point on, memories of the coma, Bible Babes, meditation, the journal, conversations with Chet, and Holy Spirit Mission orbited around Claire's brain like planets around the sun. The sermon pushed Chet over the threshold and into the axis of believing Claire. After Mass, they quickly thanked Sister Monica and rushed to the bus.

When they arrived at the hotel, they escaped to their room to avoid talking with the group.

"This was quite an evening, Claire."

"I feel bad skipping dinner with the people from St. Elizabeth's, but I don't think my nerves could handle chit chat tonight. I'll apologize to Mary Jo and Dan in the morning. I'll say we were too tired from the trip."

"At this point, hon, that's the least of our worries. Tonight opened my eyes about what's been going on with you. Now I know what you mean when you say the coma events, the Bible Babes' visions, and the meditations have all blended together."

"I didn't expect what happened tonight. And it wasn't one scripture. I heard every one of the same readings in the coma, Bible Babes, and meditation. Tonight we hear them at Mass before the March for Life. As much as I want to know what Holy Spirit Mission is, I don't enjoy the eerie feeling."

Chapter 48 : The March

"Same here. We've been through a lot, Claire, but this is unnerving. Do you think there's any chance at all that tonight was a coincidence?"

"Do you, Chet?"

"No. There are too many pieces to the puzzle that fit perfectly. You told me to go with the flow. No angels have appeared to us, at least not on Earth. I know God won't ask us to do more than we can handle."

"Bishop Francis' talk could have been taken right out of one of the Bible Babes' meetings. He even ended it with 'let not your hearts be troubled.'"

"We should sleep. Tomorrow's going to be cold and busy."

At 8 am, St. Elizabeth's group boarded the bus to the National Mall. Although the actual march would not begin until later, there was an exciting program of music and speakers. Photographers and journalists wandered through the crowd taking pictures and asking questions. The diverse multitude of people from all walks of life filled the cold winter air with exhilarating enthusiasm. Then, the atmosphere turned somber as eight women and two men approached the front of the stage.

Out of the corner of her eye, Claire noticed a very beautiful woman standing next to Mary Jo. She looked familiar and yet, Claire knew she was not a passenger on their bus.

*Where have I seen her?*

At that moment, Mary Jo motioned for Claire to come over.

"Claire, I want you to meet my sister, Coni. She came all the way from California for the March. She and I have participated in the March for ten years. Coni, Claire is new to the March – first timer."

Coni smiled, "Thanks for coming, Claire. You will be fired up after this. It's a 'happening.'"

"That's awesome you traveled this far for the March. You must really be passionate about the cause."

"Well, it's my husband who is the passionate one. He started coming about twenty years ago, before we met. His passion for rights of the unborn inspired me.

It's hard not to be pro-life when you have four children. This year is special. Jared is one of the speakers on the stage."

Mary Jo cautioned, "Shhhh. It's starting."

Fr. Perone, a representative of Priests for Life, opened the event with a prayer.

*Father, we beg Your blessing for the Right to Life, the unborn, the weak, the sick and the old; all who are finding themselves being targets of the vicious culture of death; that our Lord Jesus bless and protect all who stand up for the Christian dignity of persons. That God enlighten those who are traveling down death's highway by their involvement, in any way, with either the contemporary death culture, selfism, relativism, or any of the new age errors of our times, that God envelop our culture with His Divine protection and help us both individually and as a nation to true enlightenment, conversion and repentance of our selves and our culture. Help us to turn from our national sin of abortion, and return to, and once again become a Christian nation, on the narrow road, that is, the path to becoming a nation and culture, under God. Amen. (A Prayer for America, Catholic Online)*

Then, one by one, each of the ten people on stage took a small step forward and began their litany of regret.

"My name is Carla and I regret that I had an abortion."

"My name is Nancy and I regret my three abortions."

"My name is Greg and I am sorry I drove my girlfriend to the abortion clinic to kill our baby."

Claire was listening and watching intently, but was especially drawn to the last person in the group. He fidgeted with a piece of paper.

*He must be Coni's husband.*

The vague familiarity of his face was disquieting. Claire again felt an uncomfortable trickle of sweat roll down her back even though it was a chilling 18°. Coni's husband approached the podium. He had been chosen to give a more in-depth speech about the regret of abortion. He nervously cleared his throat and began.

"Good morning. My name is Jared and I regret that I had an abortion. Yes, 'I' had an abortion. As the father of an unborn child, I am as culpable as the baby's mother. For years, I told myself that I had done everything I could to keep her from aborting our baby. My college sweetheart, Angela, thought that a seven-week unborn was no different than a tumor. I told Angela I loved her and was willing to marry her and raise our baby. She would have nothing of it. She wanted a career. She had fallen prey to the propaganda of 'my body, my choice.'

Again, I'm as culpable as the mother of my baby. I really didn't do enough. When I was gathering my thoughts for this speech, I looked up the word culpable in the thesaurus and found the following interchangeable words: Guilty—yes, I am guilty of murder. Blameworthy-yes, I find myself to be worthy of blame for killing my baby. Liable – I am liable for the loss of my innocent baby and the impact of that loss on society.

What could my baby have done for the world? Maybe my baby would have found a cure for cancer or AIDS or multiple sclerosis, or starvation. My baby could have brought more souls to God. My baby could have provided a simple, gentle touch to heal the suffering of a lone individual. What could have been? I asked myself that question for many years until one day I was sitting alone in a church in San Diego. As I knelt, I put my head down and began to cry. A priest tapped me on the shoulder. I looked up. You see, by then Angela had changed her name to something flashy. She was a successful actress and I was wallowing in self-pity. I thought God could never forgive me for what I had done and not done. And I selfishly thought I could never forgive Angela's choice of career over me.

The priest told me he had to lock the church. I stood-up to leave. He took one look at my face and gently said, 'Come with me.' He walked me to the front of the church, put his arm around my shoulder, pointed to the crucifix and said, 'You don't have to beat yourself up anymore. He's already died for whatever awful thing you did.' And then I confessed the greatest sin and regret of my life.

Eventually, my life did get better. A few years after my Confession, I met my beautiful wife, Coni, who is God's messenger of love and understanding. Now, we are blessed with four children. Do I still feel the pain of my baby's loss? Absolutely. I love my wife; I love my children. I am blessed, but I am forever changed. I made a horrible decision. That is why I wanted to speak with you today. Thank you especially to the other nine brave people who publicly admit their regretful choice of abortion. We do not expect you to applaud us. We only ask that you pray for us.

We are here for a reason on the National Mall. And we are here on Earth for a reason. As I told you, I am culpable of my baby's abortion through my half-hearted marriage proposal many years ago. It is the greatest sin and regret of my life. But I have been forgiven because Jesus died on the cross. Last year Angela died. I pray that she is reunited with our angel in Heaven. Forgive me, Angela. May you rest in peace."

The audience remained silent as Jared had requested. Claire was trembling as she walked through the crowd. She was thrown into the memories of Chamber Dark and her stomach churned with sadness and fear. Sadness for this young father who painfully poured out his sorrow. Fearful for Angela, who was not in Heaven with her angel as Jared hoped. Seeing Jared and Coni in the flesh confirmed that everyone and everything Claire saw in the coma was real. That discovery cinched a growing apprehension of what might follow.

The color drained from Claire's face. "Are you okay, hon? Let's find a place for you to sit."

"No, I'll be okay."

"Did you see a memory of something?"

Claire pulled Chet away from their group. "I don't want to say too much here, but when Jared talked about his girlfriend, Angela, didn't that ring a bell? And, when Mary Jo introduced me to her sister, I remembered seeing her in one of the films in the coma."

"What do you want me to do, Claire?"

"There's nothing we can do at this point? My cell is ringing."

"Claire, hi."

"Oh, hi Anne."

"Is this a bad time to talk?"

"I'm really cold, but go ahead." Claire pulled Chet closer and mouthed Anne's name to him.

"Well, you sound strange."

"It's freezing here. What's up? How was the retreat?"

Chapter 48 : The March

"It was the most wonderful experience I've had in a long time. They had speakers who were incredible. Women who talked about their abortions and how they recovered and forgave themselves. Oh, and Fr. Hernandez was there for confessions. I'm feeling good, Claire. I think I've finally turned the corner."

"Oh, Anne, I'm thrilled to hear that. Let's get together later this week. I want to hear all the details. Hey, we're starting to line up for the March." Chet put his arm through Claire's, guiding her toward the throngs of attendees.

"I want to tell you one more thing and then I'll let you go. On the last day of the retreat during Mass, Father talked about the verse from Revelation, *'He who was seated on the throne said, I am making everything new.'* Then, each of us was given the opportunity to name our baby and offer this new gift of life to God. Out of the blue or out of the spirit, the name came to me – Mary Grace!"

Claire's knees buckled and she dropped the phone. Chet steadied her. "What's wrong, Claire? What's wrong, hon?"

"I'm okay. Can you get my phone? I'll tell you about it as soon as I hang up. I'm fine."

"Claire, Claire, are you there?"

"I'm here, Annie. Sorry, I dropped the phone. Tell me again."

"Mary Grace, Claire. I want you to be Mary Grace's spiritual Godmother." Claire could hear the joy in Anne's voice.

"Sure, I'd be honored."

"I hear the noise of the crowd. Enjoy the March. See you soon. Have a safe trip home."

"Bye, Annie. Happy for you."

"What's going on, Claire? You look pale again. Annie must have given you bad news."

"No, it's not bad news. She's fine."

"Then, what is it?"

"During the retreat she gave her baby girl a name and asked me to be the Godmother."

"And that makes you almost faint?"

"No. There's more. Remember, the newborn of Heaven I held and somehow I knew her name?"

"I remember. Mary Grace?"

"Yes, Mary Grace, Chet. That's what Anne named her baby. Mary Grace was a newborn of Heaven when I was there. Don't you see? I held Anne's baby, Mary Grace."

"Listen, don't worry. I promised you we'll get this figured out together. Do you want to go back to the hotel?

"No. I want to march. Let's catch up with the group."

They ran toward St. Elizabeth's flag.

Mary Jo waved her hands. "Hey Claire, we're over here, ten feet to your right."

Claire saw Mary Jo, but Coni and Jared were gone.

"Hi, Mary Jo, sorry we lagged behind. A friend phoned me. Where's your sister and her husband?"

"Oh, they're marching with their church from San Diego."

"Jared's speech was mesmerizing. I was hoping to meet him again. I mean I was hoping to meet him."

"Darn, they aren't staying in D.C. tonight. After the March, they're rushing to the airport to catch a four p.m. flight."

The March for Life was calm and captivating and cold. As Claire stared at the Supreme Court Building, she thought about how politically appointed judges made a decision to legalize abortion in the United States of America thirty-nine years ago. She along with others had done nothing to stop it. A nation under God of supposedly good people accepted the decision--some even embraced it. She thought about Jared's speech when he said, 'I didn't do enough.' She thought about her experience with Anne and her regret of not doing enough.

Chapter 48 : The March

The wind had died down.  Claire watched the sky.  White doves flew in a circle above the National Mall.  In that moment Claire found the quiet spot inside that reassured her.  She tapped Chet on the shoulder.  "I want to tell you something.  I'm feeling much better.  We're getting closer to Holy Spirit Mission.  I'm glad we came."

"I'm glad we came, too.  What else?"

'The March for Life is important, but you and I have to do more.  This is not enough.  And we're going to discover what that is here in the capital of the United States."

Late in the day, St. Elizabeth group visited the office of Congresswoman Jackie Smyth, a solid pro-life representative.  She served refreshments, answered questions, and was genuinely interested in their concerns.  After dinner, the group returned to the hotel.  Chet and Claire said polite good nights to everyone and went to their room.

After showers, they sat side by side in the bed.  Claire grabbed her journal, writing as much as she could remember about the Basilica, Sister Monica, the readings, Bishop Francis' sermon, the March, Jared, Coni, and Anne's phone call about Mary Grace.  Chet contributed aspects that Claire had forgotten or not seen.

"Wow, you've written seven pages.  That's a lot."

"Thanks for helping me with details I forgot.  I can't believe how many coincidences happened today."

"I'm exhausted.  How about lights out?  Want to snuggle?"

"Sure, I'm tired, too."

Chet pulled Claire closer.  "Good night, babe.  Let not your heart be troubled."

"My heart is not troubled when I'm with you."

Claire said her nightly prayers, concluding with a plea, "God, please reveal and clarify what you want us to do."  Then she fell asleep in Chet's arms.

# CHAPTER 49 : GOING HOME TO HALLOWED

On Tuesday morning, Claire and Chet packed the suitcases in silence. Chet, bewildered with the truth that he could no longer escape, surfed channels of the TV. Claire hoped that she and Chet could review the journal on the ride home to sort through the facets of their stay in D.C. Maybe the mission was shrouded in a small sentence or line of scripture. Both were perplexed at the complexity of Holy Spirit Mission, yet fully grasped that they owned the mystery.

They ate a small breakfast in their room and then went to the lobby to gather with the group before boarding the bus home. It was cloudy with the threat of snow on the horizon. As the bus pulled away from the hotel, Mary Jo began morning prayers with the group. Claire closed her eyes listening to her lyrical prayers. Mary Jo prefaced a reading from the Bible.

"Hey everyone, we have a long trip ahead of us, but I want to thank each of you for Marching for Life. The following reading is from Ephesians and it tells us to 'put on the armor of God.' And that's what we have done here these past few days. This is Ephesians, Ch. 6, Verses 10-20.

> ***Finally, draw your strength from the Lord and from his mighty power. Put on the armor of God so that you may be able to stand firm against the tactics of the devil. For our struggle is not with flesh and blood, but with principalities, with the powers, with the world rulers of this present darkness, with the evil spirits in the Heavens. Therefore, put on the armor of God that you may be able to resist on the evil day and, having done everything, to hold your ground. So stand fast with your loins girded in truth, clothed with righteousness as a breastplate and your feet shod in readiness for the gospel of peace. In all circumstances hold faith as a shield, to quench all flaming arrows of the evil one. And take the helmet of salvation and the sword of the Spirit, which is the Word of God.***

As the driver twisted the bus through the D.C. streets in the early morning traffic, Claire glanced down one street in particular, Raoul Wallenberg Place. She was drawn to a single word on a building. That word was 'destruction.' She soon realized why the word 'destruction' was on this building. It was the Holocaust Memorial Museum. As a little girl, she was fascinated with stories of the Holocaust, especially *The Diary of Anne Frank*. Claire remembered at thirteen finding it horrifying that a girl close to her age would be sent to a Nazi death camp to die. She had cried herself to sleep that night. Images of Anne Frank and her family pierced her heart with sadness.

The bus was at a stop light in front of the museum. As Claire stared out the window, she remembered studying about the Holocaust in high school history class. She recalled Mr. Bell's poignant lesson on the 1948 United Nations' Convention on the Prevention and Punishment of the Crime of Genocide. She remembered his passionate discussion of man's inhumanity to man. He taught them that genocide is the specific intent to destroy particular groups. Claire had heard the comparison many times of abortion to genocide. Now she knew, she really knew what she had to do.

She poked Chet. "Chet, go tell Mary Jo that we have to get our luggage."

Chet jumped in surprise. "Why?"

"We're staying one more night in Washington. Let's get off the bus now."

"What! Are you crazy, Claire? We can't get off the bus in the middle of D.C."

"Yes, we can. Do it, please. Hurry. We are getting off the bus."

"Okay, okay, Claire. I'm not going to argue with you, but can you give me a clue why you want to do this?"

"Here's the clue. Holy Spirit Mission. I know what we have to do now. C'mon, let's go. We're going to spend one more night in Washington. We'll make an appointment tomorrow with Congresswoman Smyth and tell her the plan."

Chet repeated, "You solved the mystery this very moment on the bus? Holy Spirit Mission?"

"Exactly. Now, let's go before the traffic starts moving again." Claire pushed Chet toward the front of the bus. The St. Elizabeth's group chattered as Chet and Claire hurriedly ran up the aisle to talk with Dan and Mary Jo.

Claire said excitedly, "Mary Jo, Dan, we want to get off the bus. Can you ask the driver if that's possible?"

Mary Jo raised her eyebrows. "Is there an emergency? What's going on?"

"Well, it's not an emergency in the usual sense, but I feel a powerful urgency. The Holy Spirit is calling us to follow His mission. I know it sounds crazy, but when we get back to Hallowed, I'll explain everything."

Chet shrugged his shoulders and rolled his eyes at Dan. The bus driver had heard everything and opened the door even before pulling over to the curb. Then he ran to the undercarriage of the bus and opened the bay doors. Chet and Claire waved goodbye to a busload of baffled passengers and stepped down into the cold slush on the sidewalk. Chet grabbed their two bags. He turned to tip the bus driver, but he had already closed the bay doors and hurriedly jumped back in the bus. Chet could see him shaking his head in disbelief.

"Okay, now what, Claire?"

"Well, first, let's go into that little diner and get a cup of coffee. I'll give you a full report of what we need to do." They sat in a back booth of the coffee shop. Claire took a sip of coffee and presented the plan to Chet. "Okay, here goes. Did you notice the Holocaust Museum when the bus was stuck in traffic?"

"Yeah, I guess. I was kinda dozing off, though."

"On that building is the word destruction. During the Holocaust, the Nazis wanted to destroy Jews and other people they considered to be marginal."

"I know all that, Claire. And I also know that some Jewish people do not like the comparison of abortion to the Holocaust."

"That's not the point. When I looked at the museum, I started to remember Mr. Bell's history lesson in high school. We learned that shortly after World War II, after the Holocaust, genocide became an international crime because genocide is the specific intent to destroy particular groups."

"Claire, where are you going with this? We heard all this at the March. What does that have to do with Holy Spirit Mission?"

"Okay, okay. Here's what I believe the Holy Spirit wants us to do."

After Claire spelled out the details of the plan, Chet was grinning from ear to ear. He paid the bill and outside whistled loudly for a taxi. "Claire, you call Jackie Smyth's office and get the appointment. I'll get us a hotel room for tonight. We've got work to do."

At the hotel, Claire and Chet stayed up late working on the rough outline of her plans. Claire explained what she envisioned. Chet drew the mockup. At 1:30 am,

Claire pleaded, "Let's go to bed, Chet. C'mon, lights out. This is good enough for our first attempt."

"In a minute. I want to redraw one of the displays."

The next thing Claire heard was the hotel alarm clock buzzing at 7 a.m. Chet was still sitting at the desk asleep.

"Chet, hey, you crazy architect. It's 7 a.m. We need to get ready to see Congresswoman Smyth in two hours."

"Oh, wow. I didn't even make it to the bed, did I? But, I did finish the initial plan. I hope you like it."

"I'm sure I will, Mr. Perfectionist. I'll get my shower and then take a look at it." Claire handed Chet a cup of coffee.

While Chet was getting ready, Claire reviewed the plans. She was excited and motivated as she looked at the preliminary proposal. Now, it was only a matter of getting the plan implemented. That made her nervous and apprehensive. Chet and Claire packed, skipped breakfast, and took a taxi to Congresswoman Smyth's office.

On entering the office, they placed their luggage by the door. Jackie Smyth's assistant, Heather, greeted them at the reception desk. She was twentyish and pretty. She reminded Claire of Jeannie, not so much in looks but in her confident and friendly manner. After a few minutes, she led them to Congresswoman Smyth's office.

"Thanks, Heather, now go. I don't want you to be late."

"Thanks Mrs. Smyth."

The Congresswoman smiled warmly at Claire and Chet. She shook their hands and then motioned toward Heather as she was leaving the office.

"She has been a gem of an intern. I'm fortunate to have her working with our office this semester. Today is the monthly Intern Club luncheon and she's in charge of setup. I think it's important for her to attend the social events with her peers."

"Our daughter did an internship in one of the large law firms and they had events like that. It helps them in many ways."

"There's more to a job than doing office work. They all get together once a month to talk about college, D.C. social life, and of course the representatives and senators they work for. Okay, Claire, you told Heather yesterday that you have an idea for a project to promote the rights of the unborn."

Claire was a little nervous. "Yes, Chet and I stayed over from the March. We worked on the plan for several hours last night, but of course it's still in a preliminary stage."

"I'm a staunch advocate of the rights of the unborn and I'm always interested in ways to stop abortion."

Claire responded passionately. "That's the reason we wanted to talk with you. Honestly, this concept popped into my head only yesterday. However, for several months the Holy Spirit has guided us in this direction. I've never in my life taken on a project like this."

"Claire, tell me what you are proposing. Give me a brief summary of your idea."

Claire gulped. "I would like to get funding to build a museum in Washington D.C. that chronicles the history of abortion in our country. There, I said it. I know it's an expensive and outlandish idea. We were on the bus to go home yesterday. When we passed the Holocaust Museum, I realized that we needed to have this whole horror of abortion out in the open. People need to know, really know that we are committing genocide against the unborn."

"Couldn't agree more, Claire, about the genocide comment. But you're right – it is outlandish and expensive. This is a huge undertaking. With all that's going on with the economy and with the liberal view of women's rights, it would be a hard sell."

"I know. It's almost impossible."

"Well, I didn't say that. All things are possible with God."

Chet interjected. "We know it would take a lot of money to get this built. We don't know anyone with that kind of money. Would you like to see our first draft of what we envision the museum to be?"

"Absolutely. And don't be discouraged. I love the idea. There are plenty of good people who would want to be a part of something like this."

Chapter 49 : Going Home to Hallowed

Chet showed her the drawings and descriptions of the museum exhibits. Jackie Smyth studied them intently, wincing at the stark presentation of the history of abortion. Then, she sighed and sat back in her chair.

"Look, Claire and Chet. I love this concept, but you're going to need a boat load of money, which means you'll need fund raisers and builders and a whole array of professionals. The first step is to talk with someone who can point you in the right direction of a good fundraiser. My fundraisers are the political types. I think you need someone who deals in buildings, construction, etc." At that, Congresswoman Smyth turned to her computer to look at her list of contacts.

"Aha, this man might be able to help you. I met him about three weeks ago at a dinner at the White House. His name is Darren Adams and he owns several companies. Wheels and deals with architects, builders, etc. Let's see, his investment firm is called The One. Of course, what else would he call it? He thinks he is the one. I don't have a lot of information about him, but several of the members of the Housing Sub-Committee work with him on projects. He might be able to lead you down the right path. Okay, his info is sent to my printer."

Claire felt a surge of confidence. "I know this is a lot to expect, but do you think you could ask him to meet with us today?"

"Well, I can give him a call. He owes me since I moved to another seat at that dinner. He wanted to sit next to Senator Cahalan to lobby her for more construction funding."

"Chet added, "Our flight leaves Dulles around 5 p.m. If there's any chance he could meet before 2 p.m. that would be great. But if not, we'll stay another night."

The congresswoman handed them the printed contact info while she called Darren Adams. "Darren, Jackie Smyth here. How are you? Did you get anywhere with Senator Cahalan?" She laughed. "You are the sly one, Mr. Adams. Hey, the reason I'm calling. I have a couple here from my district. They have an interesting concept for a museum and I was wondering if you could talk with them. They're from Hallowed, Ohio. Yes, it is a quaint town, but how would you know? Anyway, what's on your schedule in the early afternoon? They're going back home today and need to get to Dulles for a 5 p.m. flight. You know how awful that is." Congresswoman

Smyth looked at Claire and Chet. "1:30 p.m.?" Both nodded an enthusiastic yes. "Okay, Darren, thanks. I guess the ball is in my court now. I owe you one. Bye, now."

Claire shook Jackie Smyth's hand. "Thank you. This is awesome!"

"My pleasure. Please let me know how it goes. I'm on your side for this one. Call me or send an e-mail."

She led them to the office exit. They grabbed their bags and entered the elevator. Both looked at each other in disbelief.

Claire giggled, "Can you believe it? We're actually going to meet with a big shot Washington D.C. investor."

"Well, let's not get too excited. This is a huge undertaking, Claire."

"Don't burst my bubble yet, hon. It's such a relief to have a clear picture of our Holy Spirit mission. I know we can do this. I'm starved. Let's get lunch."

# CHAPTER 50 : HE LIKES IT

After lunch, Claire and Chet took a taxi to the Olympia Building. Darren Adams' office was on the twenty-sixth floor overlooking the Potomac River. The double office doors were made of beautiful glass framed by dark walnut wood. His company name, 'The One,' was emblazoned in gold letters on the left door. On the right door an etched logo displayed a handsome man standing atop a large building holding the number one above his head.

Nancy greeted them in a professional manner. Although polite, she looked down when speaking as if embarrassed. She was a large boned woman, maybe five foot six with curly red hair pixie-style. There was sparse makeup on her freckled face. Nancy wore a white blouse, navy blue blazer, and a matching skirt that fit snugly around her hips.

"Good afternoon, Mr. and Mrs. McCormack. Mr. Adams is on a call, but he'll be with you shortly. May I get you bottled water, a cup of coffee?"

"No thanks, we're fine. We're catching a flight right after our meeting with Mr. Adams. Is it okay if we leave our bags here in the corner?"

"Sure, that's fine."

*Gosh, she seems to be shy and backward to be working here.*

During her senior year of college, Nancy Lawson was selected to be Darren Adams' intern for one semester. Many of the young female interns were savvy, charming, and good-looking. None of the members of congress or senate had an interest in hiring Nancy. Her college counselor knew someone who knew Darren Adams. He agreed to make her an assistant.

Nancy led them to Mr. Adams' office.

"Thanks, Miss Lawson. And thanks for skipping that intern luncheon. We've got very important work to do this afternoon."

Claire watched Nancy's demeanor. She lowered her eyes and her face flushed with shy discomfort. "That's okay, Mr. Adams. I know you do important work. I enjoy learning from you."

As Nancy left the room, Darren motioned to her. "She's not exactly intern material. The senators and congressman all have dynamite interns, gorgeous young women and of course good looking guys. A friend of mine asked me to give her a job. She's competent, but I'm trying to teach her the way Washington works. You've got to be tough to survive in D.C. Anyway, I'm all for helping out young adults, especially someone as bashful as Nancy. I'm trying to get her over that."

Claire smiled. "I was very shy when I was her age. She'll rise above it one day."

"She's only here for three more weeks. Hopefully, I can help her in that short time."

Then, Darren turned his attention to Chet and Claire. "By the way, I apologize for being late. Now, what can I do for you? Jackie tells me you two have an interesting idea for a museum."

Nancy tapped on the door.

"What is it, Nancy?"

"I'm sorry to disturb you, Mr. Adams. Mrs. Adams is on the phone."

Darren took a deep breath. "Tell her I'll call her back, Nancy. Would you hold my calls, please?"

"Yes, Mr. Adams."

"Always something going on at the home front with three kids, a wife, and a dog. We won't be interrupted again. Nancy does a great job of following orders. Where were we?"

Claire took the lead. "First of all, thank you for seeing us on such short notice. We came to Washington for the March for Life. The March and a few other things prompted us with an idea for a museum, similar to the Holocaust Museum."

"There's really nothing like the Holocaust. The Museum, I mean."

"I agree. I'm not saying it's about the Holocaust or even the Holocaust Museum, but it seems it might help in our fight against abortion to have a central place where people can learn about all aspects of abortion. Instead of the propaganda thrown around by Planned Parenthood."

Chapter 50 : He Likes It

"Hmmm. That's an interesting concept. Yes, the fight against abortion is definitely one of my areas of interest. How did you come up with this idea?"

Claire gave Darren Adams a brief description of what had happened on the bus.

"When I saw the word destruction on the side of the Holocaust Museum building, it made me think about what horrible destruction we have inflicted on the unborn in this country. And so many people have bought into the abortion lie."

***Enter by the narrow gate, since the road that leads to destruction is wide and spacious, and many take it; but it is a narrow gate.***

"Don't do much with organized religion now, but those old Bible verses stuck with me. I studied the Bible in Sunday school. Every once in a while, I can't resist the urge to fling a quote from scripture out there. Anyway, how can I help you?"

Chet explained further. "Congresswoman Smyth suggested we talk with you since you're in the construction business. She thought you might be able to point us in the right direction to get this venture off the ground."

"Okay, let's see what you have."

Claire handed him the plans for the museum and like Jackie Smyth, Darren studied them closely.

"So, you already have a name selected   Museum of the Innocents. That's a good one. ***'Then was fulfilled what had been said through Jeremiah the prophet: A voice was heard in Ramah, sobbing and loud lamentation; Rachel weeping for her children, and she would not be consoled, since they were no more.'*** Let me be honest with you. This kind of thing is a hard sell. What did Jackie say about getting something in the educational budget for this?"

Chet pushed on. "Not much chance of that. Look, we know it's a huge task, but we're willing to put in the time to make it happen. What would you suggest we do?"

Darren hesitated for a moment. Claire studied Darren as he talked. His hair was thick, wavy black with a slight strip of grey. He was taller than six feet, dressed in an Armani suit with a monogrammed, crisply-starched blue shirt. He exuded confidence and finesse.

*He certainly looks successful and Congresswoman Smyth recommended him, but she hasn't really known him that long. Still, I like that he took on Nancy when others wouldn't.*

"I have several contacts in D.C. I'd be willing to pitch the idea to a few of them. Who knows? There are plenty of people who might want to invest. I mean they may not even be pro-lifers. They might look at it as a good investment. It's a solid plan considering you put it together in one evening. You two are a good team and the bottom line is... I like it."

Chet and Claire traded optimistic grins.

"What firm are you with, Chet?"

"Bartholomew Incorporated, a small architectural firm in Cincinnati. Actually, we're renovating the old Archer Building over on Madison Avenue."

"I'm familiar with the site. We don't usually bid on ones that small, but I started my career in that building. When I was thirteen years old, I helped my Dad pour concrete for Archer. When I was sixteen..."

Claire half-listened to their conversation. She glanced through the window into the young intern's office. Nancy stood in front of a twelve-foot tall, antique mirror that was framed with golden angels. It was captivating to watch as Nancy admired herself in the mirror. She was giggling and seemed to be miming an imaginary conversation, reminding Claire of Jeannie at twelve years old.

Winter sun glistened on the cherubs, swirling golden dots around the room, creating a surreal, hypnotic effect. Claire became lightheaded. When the dizziness subsided, she turned abruptly toward Darren to rejoin the conversation. An uncomfortable bead of sweat rolled down her back. She heard Chet talking.

"Sure, we'll leave the plans here. That way you can show them to your associates."

"What did you say, Chet?"

"I was telling Darren that we can leave the plans here. He's going to show them to potential investors. A picture's worth a thousand words."

Claire did not want to embarrass Chet, but she felt uneasy about leaving the plans with a man they had just met, even if he was recommended by Jackie Smyth.

## Chapter 50 : He Likes It

"Well, I really want to clean them up a bit, especially my part. Working on them at the hotel was not optimal. I'd like to have something more professional looking."

"That's fine. You can e-mail them to me." He opened the door to Nancy's office indicating the meeting was over. "Well, folks it's been charming meeting with you, but my assistant and I are scheduled for another appointment across town."

Chet tried not to show his irritation that Claire refused to give the plans to Darren, but he was exasperated with her behavior. He laughed nervously. "Hey, Darren, thanks for your time and expertise. We'll get those drawings to you this week. I guess Claire wants to make them more presentable."

Darren shook Chet's hand and then looked at Claire.

"Claire, I don't blame you for not leaving the plans. It's an impressive idea. I understand you need to have a certain level of trust."

Claire's cheeks flushed in embarrassment. "Oh, no, no. It's not that I don't trust you. I want to make the plan more professional looking."

Darren turned his back to Chet so he could face Claire. "Well, you are wise to protect the plan. There are wolves in sheep's clothing, especially in D.C. *'Beware of false prophets who come to you disguised as sheep but underneath are ravenous wolves.'* Sorry, that old-time religion keeps coming out."

Claire felt obligated to compliment Darren. "I wish I could quote the Bible like that. I'm in a Bible study group, but Catholics didn't memorize the Bible in grade school or high school. I'm impressed."

"Thank you, Claire." Darren stared directly into Claire's eyes and held both of her hands, moving them back and forth. "Mrs. McCormack, you make your changes to the presentation and then get back with me, okay? I hope I can be of assistance." Darren turned around.

"Chet, good talking to you. Have a safe trip back to Ohio. Give me a call when you're at Archer the next time. I'd love to see it again."

Claire picked up the plans holding them possessively against her chest, arms folded.

Darren opened the door to Nancy's office. "Hey, Nance, would you show them out?"

She stood up leading them to the outer office door. Nancy lowered her eyes. "Have a pleasant trip back, Mr. and Mrs. McCormack. Good-bye."

Chet picked-up their bags. As the elevator doors closed, Claire could feel his anger, seething from heavy sighs, arms crossed, head down, eyebrows furled.

"Okay, get it over with. You're mad because I didn't leave the plans with him."

"Claire, in the middle of Washington D.C., you drag me off the bus which is our ride home. You get a Congresswoman to set an appointment with an important investor and then when he offers to help, you won't give him the plans. He even acknowledged he likes it. Claire, what in the name of Heaven, do you want?"

They exited the elevator and started down the long, dimly lit tunnel that led to the street.

"I don't know. For some reason, I didn't feel comfortable. He was kind of quirky, quoting the Bible. I felt a little strange around him. Didn't you?"

"No, not really. He may be dressed like a million bucks, but he told me how he got started by pouring concrete when he was sixteen after his Dad died. He's a self-made success, Claire. He's bound to be a little quirky. You should have stayed in the conversation. The personal stuff seals the deal, hon. I'm not mad at you. Just disappointed."

"So, you think I'm over-reacting?"

Chet smiled. "Only a tad. We're in this together. We can send them later this week."

"Thanks, honey. Gosh, maybe I should have given him the plans."

"Not if you really feel uncomfortable, Claire. But, think about it, you finally have clarification in your mind about this and then, you turn your back on his help."

"You're right. I have trouble trusting people. You know that. What time is it?"

"2:45. Why?"

Chapter 50 : He Likes It

"I'm thinking of running back up there to give him the plan."

"Wow, we'll be cutting it short. Are you sure?"

"Yes, I'm sure, Chet."

"Okay. I'll get a taxi. I'll be waiting for you in front of the building. Hurry, you want to catch them before they leave for their appointment." Chet grabbed both bags and walked briskly through the tunnel.

Claire hurried to the elevators. She was shaking and felt embarrassed about not giving Darren Adams the museum plans. She thought about what she might say to him.

*Hi, Darren. I want to apologize. I was in a coma for sixteen days last year. I wasn't thinking clearly. No, that's too personal. I'll say, Mr. Adams, I've reconsidered and would really appreciate it if you would pitch the museum plans to your business contacts. Oh, what the heck, I'll figure it out when I get there.*

Chet walked into the cold D.C. air and hailed a taxi.

The driver took the luggage and placed it in the trunk. With a thick foreign accent, he asked, "Where you going, sir?"

"Dulles Airport, but I'm waiting on my wife. She'll be here in about ten minutes. Go ahead, start the meter."

"Very good. Women! Always waiting on them, huh? Where you from?"

"Hallowed, Ohio."

"Never heard of it."

"It's near Cincinnati."

"Oh, sure, Cincinnati."

"What brings you to D.C.?"

"The March. We came for the March for Life. Got here last Sunday."

"Yeah, the March. I hope they keep marching every year. Good daily fares for the cabbies. I guess you're a religious guy, huh?"

"You could say that. How about you?"

"Not much. You know, I've been in the states twenty-five years. Over time got away from going to church and all that. I mean I don't think you need a church to be a good person. We should treat people with respect and mind our own business."

The driver looked at Chet through the rearview mirror and noticed that he was nervously looking at his watch. He turned on the FM radio tapping the beat with his fingers on the steering wheel.

The elevator doors opened on the twenty-sixth floor. Claire carefully pulled the large glass doors to The One Office. She could hear voices.

*Great, they're still here.*

With the museum plans in hand, Claire approached the door to Nancy's office and then stopped cold. She could hear their conversation.

"Mr. Adams, you promised your wife you would call her. I didn't know we had an appointment across town."

"I can call her later, Nancy. By the way, we do not have an appointment across town. I wanted to get the McCormacks from Hallowed, Ohio out of my office. Lesson for you, my dear, that's what happens when you stay in a podunk town all your life. They don't have a clue about my world."

"Is that why you told them we have an appointment?"

"Partially, but I've been thinking about you lately. You've come a long way in the last two months. I'd hate to see you return to that podunk farm town in Indiana after you graduate."

"Well, I'm smart, but it seems you have to be one of the beautiful people to make it in D.C."

Darren walked Nancy to the mirror and stood behind her. "You sell yourself short, Nance. You're very pretty in a down home kind of way."

"I am?"

"Nancy, I think it's time for you to come of age."

Claire was frozen, not knowing if she should stay or go. She could see Darren in the mirror with Nancy in front of him. He pulled her against his body and slipped his right hand down the front of her skirt. Claire heard the zipper snap. Then she could see the outline of Darren's hand thrusting up and down underneath Nancy's navy blue skirt.

Nancy struggled as she tried to pull away from Darren.

"This is not a good idea, Mr. Adams. I don't think we should be doing this."

"Nancy, you've been reading too much of the Bible. *'But of the fruit of the tree in the middle of the garden God said, You must not eat it, nor touch it, under pain of death.'* What a crock!'"

He pulled Nancy closer, plunging his hand into her again and again. She moaned in pleasure and seemed almost spellbound by him.

Claire wanted to vomit. She wanted to do something, but what happened next immobilized her. Darren continued his violence, the muscular strength of his arm almost lifting her into the air. In a millisecond while Nancy's eyes were closed, Claire saw Darren admiring his reflection in the mirror. Claire heard Darren's heavy breathing. The room reeked of his telltale cologne and sweat reminiscent of the smell of urine in the horrific compartments of Hell.

She saw his eyes turn mustard yellow, his gaze unnatural and unholy. Claire backed away cautiously, filled with the kind of dread she experienced in the chambers. She opened the office doors carefully and slid out. Somehow, she made it to the elevator pushing the down button several times. Finally, it arrived. She leaned against the back wall, thankful she was the only occupant. It seemed an eternity to get to the ground floor. When it stopped, she ran out the elevator doors and continued running through the dimly-lit tunnel.

Her anxiety expanded like a hot air balloon, almost to the bursting stage. Claire imagined that Darren had seen her and was coming after her. She moved in and out of the shadows, twisted around people and almost fell on top of a baby stroller. She was sobbing. The memory of running through a tunnel like this before muddled her thinking.

It was a dream, wasn't it?

She dredged up the appearance of a sinister entity chasing her in the dream. Now she felt that same terror. Everywhere she saw the demon's eyes, Darren's eyes, eyes filled with yellow pools of evil. The tunnel seemed longer and darker than before. She kept looking back to check if Darren was following. At one point Claire dropped the folder holding the plans and had to turn around to get it. Some people glared at her, some stared but walked on by. An older gentleman asked her if she needed help. She couldn't talk but shook her head, picked up the folder, and kept charging toward the exit.

At last, she burst through the door to the street, running, heart pounding like a fist against a wall, sobbing and gasping for air. Chet was in the taxi waiting for her. Her body shuddered in icy fear. There was a sensation of cold blood coursing through her veins dumping fear into the opening of her soul. She would never forget Darren's yellow eyes. Would they follow her forever? Claire grabbed the door and leaped into the taxi like a frightened animal screaming.

"I saw him again. I saw him again. I know he's real."

The driver glanced into the back seat. "You okay, lady?"

"She's okay. Head for Dulles." Chet tried to talk quietly. "Claire, tell me what you saw. What do you mean you saw him again?"

"He had yellow eyes and I started running. I had to get away."

"Who had yellow eyes?"

Claire spit out his name. "Darren Adams."

Chet pulled her to his side attempting to comfort her. "You're safe now. Tell me what happened. You look awful, babe. I've never seen you like this."

Claire gasped an incoherent rambling, "I went to his office. I saw him in the mirror with Nancy. He had his hand up her. She whimpered. The room smelled putrid, like rotten eggs. I thought I was going to throw-up. I tried to scream but nothing came out. His eyes – oh, his eyes turned yellow and he looked as evil as the ones I saw in the coma. Chet, he's a demon or worse, he's Satan. I had to get out of there. That poor girl. I didn't know what to do."

Chet held Claire tightly, "It'll be all right, Claire. We'll be home soon, honey. I've got you."

Chapter 50 : He Likes It

The driver asked again, "You okay back there, lady?"

Chet reassured, "She's okay."

"Lady, don't worry. No such things as demons or devils. Don't believe in that stuff. Nobody does anymore. Sounds like a plain, old lousy guy. Lots of rats in D.C."

Chet could see the cabbie looking at them through the rearview mirror. The driver continued what he thought were comforting words for his passengers.

"There are strange people in D.C., that's for sure, but there are no demons from Hell. That's old black magic. Whaddya call it – myths, yeah myths – made-up stories to scare people. That's why I stay away from religion."

Claire closed her eyes and rested on Chet's shoulder all the way to the airport. When they arrived, the driver stepped out to get their luggage for them. Chet took both suitcases and paid him. As they walked toward the entrance to Delta Airlines, the cabbie gave one last bit of advice. "Hey, lady."

Claire was weak, but slowly turned around.

"Listen, you take care. No such things as Hell or demons. I don't believe in them. And I don't believe in Satan."

Before Claire or Chet could say anything, the driver jumped into the cab and was gone.

They entered the airport and walked toward the kiosks to get boarding passes. Claire pulled Chet by his arm to stop him for a moment."

"And that's the way he likes it."

"Who likes what? Claire, you're scaring me."

"It's exactly what the cab driver said. It's exactly what a lot of people say. 'I don't believe in Satan.'"

Claire cautiously looked around the airport and stood on tiptoe to whisper in Chet's ear, "And that's the way he likes it."

## *THE END FOR NOW...TO BE CONTINUED*